"Did you watch the speech?" Nate asked.

"Yes. It was really effective. We're getting up a mob in our neighborhood right now to tear all global warming believers from their homes and burn them at the stake."

"Oh, I see what your daughter meant about Zombie Mom."

"That speech was beneath him. Or if it wasn't, it should have been. The nictovirus is the villain, not environmentalists."

"Identifying and neutralizing the opposition is sound political strategy," said Nate. "Now all the controversy will be about whether the President should have been nicer or whether the environmentalists deserve—"

"I understand the theory, Nate," said Cecily. "I just don't agree that it justifies slandering a legitimate political movement."

"Meaning that you're a global warming alarmist?" asked Nate. "Your ox is being gored, is that it?"

"I'm an environmentalist. I knew the facts about global warming but I always thought it was a convenient way to get the world to take actions that are necessary whether humans are causing global warming or not."

"So I should put you down as pro-plague, then?" asked Nate.

BY ORSON SCOTT CARD FROM
TOM DOHERTY ASSOCIATES

Empire
The Folk of the Fringe
Future on Fire (editor)
Future on Ice (editor)
Hidden Empire
Invasive Procedures
    (with Aaron Johnston)
Keepers of Dreams
Lovelock
    (with Kathryn Kidd)
*Maps in a Mirror: The Short
    Fiction of Orson Scott Card*
    (hardcover)
*Pastwatch: The Redemption
    of Christopher Columbus*
Saints
Songmaster
Treason
The Worthing Saga
Wyrms

THE TALES OF
ALVIN MAKER
Seventh Son
Red Prophet
Prentice Alvin
Alvin Journeyman
Heartfire
The Crystal City

WOMEN OF GENESIS
Sarah
Rebekah
Rachel & Leah

ENDER
Ender's Game
Ender's Shadow
Shadow of the Hegemon
Shadow Puppets
Shadow of the Giant
Speaker for the Dead
Xenocide
Children of the Mind
First Meetings
Ender in Exile

HOMECOMING
The Memory of Earth
The Call of Earth
The Ships of Earth
Earthfall
Earthborn

FROM OTHER
PUBLISHERS

Enchantment
Homebody
Lost Boys
Magic Street
Stonefather
Stonetables
Treasure Box
*How to Write Science
    Fiction and Fantasy*
Characters and Viewpoint

HIDDEN EMPIRE

ORSON SCOTT CARD

TOR®

A TOM DOHERTY ASSOCIATES BOOK
NEW YORK

This is a work of fiction. All of the characters, organizations, and events portrayed in this novel are either products of the author's imagination or are used fictitiously.

HIDDEN EMPIRE

A Tor Book
Published by Tom Doherty Associates, LLC
175 Fifth Avenue
New York, NY 10010

www.tor-forge.com

Tor® is a registered trademark of Tom Doherty Associates, LLC.

ISBN 978-0-7653-5971-1

First Edition: December 2009
First Mass Market Edition: January 2011

Printed in the United States of America

0   9   8   7   6   5   4   3   2   1

To Beth Meacham

Back in '83 you believed in my version of King Horn.
*You still believe. And help. And bear with me
in spite of all the woes.
Editor? Yes, one of the best.
Friend? You do it from the heart.
This book is, in so many ways, for you.*

HIDDEN EMPIRE

ONE

SICK MONKEYS

This is a dangerous planet. Only a politician would try to tell you otherwise. And I'm not talking about wars—we're America, we win our wars. There are earthquakes, storms, volcanoes. Plagues can appear out of nowhere and slaughter millions of people. Blights can wipe out our crops. A meteor the size of a bus could hit the earth and send us back to the Stone Age. An extraordinary solar flare could destroy our electronics or heat our atmosphere so much our crops all die and we starve.

And whom do we put in charge of helping us prepare to cope with such disasters? People whose only talent is for getting elected, and whose entire future consists of the run-up to the next election. It's not their fault—anybody who *doesn't* think and act that way won't win. It's the fundamental problem with democracy. No long-range thinking. So we're just sitting ducks, waiting for the next disaster.

If you want to know what destroyed the Roman Empire, it was two plagues, a century apart, that killed about thirty percent of the population each time. That's why there weren't enough soldiers to keep the legions at full strength. That's why the emperors had to invite in the barbarian tribes to farm the abandoned land and fill the abandoned cities.

Only now we're talking about the whole world. Whom do we invite in to settle the empty land when it's the whole world that's been depopulated?

CHINMA WAS the fourth son of the third wife of the aging chief of his small tribe in the Kwara state of Nigeria. There was no shortage of other sons, most of them adult, and nothing much was expected of Chinma. People constantly told him to shut up, even his mother, even when he wasn't saying anything.

He got the idea at quite a young age that his very presence was annoying to everyone.

The easiest way to avoid getting cuffed or shoved or slapped or yelled at was to disappear. And the easiest way to disappear was to go up. People didn't look up very much. He could go up into the trees and keep company with the monkeys. They yelled at him, too, and threw things at him, but they were more afraid of him than he was of them, so it was actually fun.

That's why by the time he was twelve years old Chinma could climb any tree to the smallest branches that could bear his weight, and catch monkeys by enticing them with fruit while holding very, very still and looking in another direction until they were close enough for Chinma to make his grab.

All of this was useless to everyone until the happy day when Ire, the second son of the first wife, came back to the village from the big city, Ilorin, with news. "They're paying money for white-face monkeys, especially if you can get the whole family."

Ire sat there in the yard in front of the big house, telling Father and the important brothers how much money, and who was paying, and how he found out about it, and then they started arguing about how they could go about catching the monkeys.

Meanwhile, Chinma ran to a good white-face monkey tree, climbed it, caught the papa monkey, scampered back down, and brought the monkey to Ire.

All the men fell silent.

"What's your name?" asked Father.

"Monkey-catcher," said Ire. And that became Chinma's new name.

Father was against paying Chinma anything for the monkeys he caught. "We've been feeding him for all these years, it's about time he started earning his way." But Ire said it was business, and in business you pay everybody something, so they'll work harder.

So now Chinma was important and had money, a hundred naira for every monkey, five hundred for the papa monkeys, two thousand if he brought in a whole family. He almost always got the families—once he got the papa monkey, it was pretty easy to get the babies, and once he had the babies, he could use them as bait to get the mamas.

Ire bought cages for the monkeys and it didn't take many weeks before all the white-face monkeys in their neighborhood were gone or hiding.

So they got in the family truck and began to range far out into the country. Father and Ire had bribed all the right people, so there was no trouble with police—or the roaming gangs of thugs and brigands who, as often as not, were the police out of uniform, or their brothers-in-law. It seemed like a safe way to make money—and it all depended on Chinma's knack for climbing trees, winning the trust of monkeys, and bringing them down in good condition, every member of the family.

Ire said that somewhere far away—South Africa or Great Britain or America—scientists were studying the white-face monkey because its cries seemed to be like language. "Not *our* language," said Father, and everyone laughed. Only it wasn't really all that funny, since only about three thousand people spoke their language, Ayere, and all of them lived right there in Kwara state.

They knew that other tribes had lost their language, for to survive in Nigeria you had to know at least one of the major languages—Ibo, Yoruba, Hausa—and if you had any hope of becoming educated, you had to learn English as well. How many languages could one head hold?

"They ought to take *us* to America and study *our* language," said Ire.

"With our luck," said Father, "they'd take us to Liberia."

But the truth was they were very lucky. This white-face monkey trade was bringing in cash, which there had never been very much of in their village of Oyi. "Our oil well," Father called it. But he meant the monkeys—not Chinma, even though Chinma caught every single monkey they sold.

When he mentioned this thought to Mother, she slapped his shoulder, twice, and very sternly told him, "And who drives the truck? And who found out that these monkeys were worth something? And who fed you all your life till now? You think you're so important."

He apologized. But he *was* important, and he knew it. Nobody told him to shut up now, nobody in the family forgot his name. He was Monkey-catcher, and when the family was making money, he was right there, up a tree, catching it and bringing it down to them.

Until one day, in a remote stand of trees, not even large enough to call it a woods, surrounded by grassland on all sides, Chinma climbed a tree and found a troop of white-face monkeys that had no timidity at all. They did not scamper away from him. He did not have to coax them. They just sat there, waiting for him. The papa monkey hissed and showed his teeth. He snapped at Chinma, too. But he did not run away.

Chinma avoided the teeth and carried him down the tree. "He's a biter," said Chinma to Ire.

"So am I," said Ire, and laughed. Whereupon the papa monkey twisted around in Ire's hand and bit him savagely on the thumb. Ire shouted and dropped the monkey, but Chinma immediately caught it again—it was easy, because the monkey ran away so slowly.

"Are you all right?" Chinma asked Ire.

"Just put it in the cage," said Ire testily, and he resumed sucking on the wound. "Get the rest of the family."

As Chinma brought down each of the babies, it was one of the other brothers, not Ire, who put them in the cages. Ire sat in the cab of the truck sucking on his wound and keeping up a low murmur of cursing.

There were only two females—it was not a large troop, because it shared the stand of trees with an aggressive troop of red-bellied guenon monkeys. Chinma only recognized them because his family had brought him books about monkeys after he became valuable to them. These guenons were very rare, especially such a large group, and most people thought the only ones still alive were in the West Africa Biodiversity Hot Spot. It was very important that these monkeys were here.

Chinma decided not to tell the brothers about them. They would want to catch them and sell them, too, and Chinma knew it would take a lot more bribes because these monkeys were so endangered.

Instead, Chinma would tell a scientist about them, so they could get protected. Of course, that would mean going in to Ilorin, where they turned in the white-faces, which they had never let him do. But he had never asked, either. Maybe he was valuable enough now that they would let him.

Up a tree, he went for the largest female. Like the papa monkey, she didn't try to move away. As Chinma inched closer, she seemed to snarl and he expected her to try to bite. But she didn't. Instead, just as he got hold of her by the back and neck, she sneezed in his face.

Sneezed or gave him a raspberry—he wasn't sure which—but it amounted to the same thing. Monkey spit and snot all over his face. And he couldn't even wipe it off, because he needed one hand to hold her and the other hand to help him climb. And by the time he got down the tree, the stuff had dried on his face.

"This one spits," he said. "Or sneezes."

And this time he was listened to—they held the she-monkey away from them as they took her to the cages in the back of the truck.

When all the white-face monkeys were in the back of the truck, Ire slid over on the front seat. "I'm not driving," he said.

"I will!" said Ade, who was the firstborn son of Chinma's mother.

"I don't care," said Ire.

Ade was stunned. Ire never let a son of one of the other mothers drive the truck. But when Ade climbed into the cab and turned the key to start the truck, Ire just looked out the window.

"Don't go home," said Ire. "We're going straight to Ilorin."

"Why?" asked Ade.

"Shut up," said Ire. But then Ire looked at Chinma, who stood outside the window of the driver's side. "How do you like this? I need a doctor. Your stupid monkey poisoned me."

"I told you he bites," said Chinma.

"You didn't tell me it was poisoned!" said Ire fiercely. "You're not getting paid for any of these monkeys."

Ade shook his head at Chinma, as if to say, Don't argue with him.

And Chinma realized that if they were going straight to Ilorin, they couldn't drop him off at home and so he wouldn't even have to argue in order to get taken there. He swung himself up into the back of the truck with the monkeys, and cooed and talked to them all the way there.

They were the unhappiest, least excited, most tired monkeys Chinma had ever seen. Ire was right. There *was* something wrong with them.

In Ilorin, Ire insisted they go to the clinic first, even before taking the monkeys to the scientists. He got out of the truck and staggered toward the clinic and Ade drove the truck off, as Ire had ordered. But Chinma was worried. What if the clinic didn't have the right medicines? Most of the medicine that got into Nigeria was intercepted by high officials and sold on the black market, so clinics rarely had a good supply of anything.

They drove on down Highway A123 from the clinic and turned at a big traffic circle. They crossed the railroad tracks and then turned right again on a narrow paved road with warehouses and small factories. It was one of the warehouses where Ade brought them and stopped the truck.

To Chinma's disappointment, there were no scientists here, just a couple of Nigerian men without shirts. Scientists always wore shirts. Chinma's brothers off-loaded the cages—they were still too big and heavy for Chinma to carry them—and took them inside the warehouse. Chinma stopped and looked around. There were lots of animal cages here, though most of them were empty.

The brothers started to carry empty cages back out to the truck.

"What are you looking at?" one of the warehouse men asked Chinma in Yoruba.

"I wanted to see a scientist," said Chinma, in English because he didn't know the Yoruba word for "scientist."

The man laughed at him. "You think they come here? It's stinky here."

Chinma was disappointed, but then he thought: I can tell one of the doctors at the clinic.

That was why he was the first one off the back of the truck when they got to the clinic again—he didn't want to give anybody a chance to tell him to wait out in the parking lot. He ran inside and went right up to the lady in a white dress who sat behind a table in the waiting room.

"I want to talk to a doctor," he said in English.

"What's your problem?" she asked.

"No problem, I have to tell something."

She pointed to the other people in the waiting room. "These people all have problems. They need the doctor. If you don't have a problem, then go away, little boy."

That was all right. People were always saying no,

and if you waited long enough sometimes you got a chance to do it anyway. Meanwhile, he had other business.

"How is my brother Ire?" asked Chinma.

"Your brother?" asked the lady.

"We leave him here. An hour ago," said Chinma. "Then we take the monkeys and come back."

"Did your brother have a bite on his hand?" asked the lady.

"Monkey bite," said Chinma.

She stood right up and grabbed him by the wrist. "Come with me!"

One of the men waiting in a chair against the wall started to protest that he had been waiting much longer.

"Sit down or go home," said the lady. And then they were through the door into the treatment room.

Chinma could see five beds, and all of them had somebody lying or sitting on them. Ire was not any of them. Then he realized that a curtained-off area must have another bed in it. The lady went there and pulled him inside the curtain.

Ire was on the bed. His eyes were wide open and he was breathing very thickly and heavily, his chest heaving. The doctor was on a cellphone, talking to somebody. He waved the lady away.

"This is his brother," said the lady, ignoring the doctor's wave. "It's a monkey bite."

"Monkey bite," said the doctor into the phone.

"Wait. Listen while I question the brother." Then the doctor turned to Chinma. "What is this man's name?"

"My brother Ire. He works here. In Ilorin. At the factory, an accountant."

"Where did he get this bite?"

"Long way down the highway," said Chinma. "Long dirt road. Trees . . . alone . . ." He didn't have enough English to describe the large but isolated stand of trees where the monkeys had been.

"We need to get someone out there to find the monkey that bit him," said the doctor. "Can you lead us there?"

Chinma shrugged. "My brother Ade lead you. Why?"

"It's a scientific matter that you wouldn't understand," said the doctor.

"Why go to the trees? The monkeys—"

"Quiet, little boy, I'm on the telephone," said the doctor. Then he went back to talking medical language that Chinma mostly didn't understand. After a while he flipped the phone shut.

He told the lady in white to give Ire an injection. "We've got to get his blood pressure down or . . ."

Then the lady pointed to the corner of Ire's eye. Blood was seeping out between the eyeball and the place where the eyelids joined, and dripping down his cheekbone toward his ear.

"Oh Lord in heaven," said the doctor. "Give him the injection."

"Not me," she said, backing away.

"It's not—what you think," said the doctor.

"It's close enough that you're thinking the same thing," said the lady in white.

The doctor took back the syringe and jammed it into Ire's upper arm and pushed the plunger. Then he handed it to the nurse. "We can't use this again," he said.

"Of course not," she said.

The doctor went outside the curtain and Chinma followed. "All of you!" the doctor said. The other patients looked at him. "You must get up and leave this building right now."

"But I need . . ." an old lady began to say.

"Leave this building," he said. His voice carried a lot of authority. But Chinma could also hear that he was afraid. Maybe the others could tell that, too, because they didn't argue. He made them go out the back way, so they wouldn't pass near to the curtained bed where Ire lay.

That was when Chinma knew that Ire was dying.

"So the monkey *was* poison like Ire said," Chinma said.

"What?" asked the doctor. "Listen, boy. Some other doctors are going to be here very soon, and I need you to take them out to where you found the monkey. Do you know what kind?"

"White-face monkey. The papa monkey bit—"

"Just answer my questions, boy, there's no time for nonsense! You mean a putty-face monkey?"

"Yes," said Chinma.

"And you say your other brother can drive them there?"

"Yes, but—"

"Then let's go get that brother."

Chinma headed for the back door, but the doctor grabbed him. "The front way," he said. "I need to clear the waiting room."

As they walked toward the door to the waiting room, Chinma saw the nurse lady finish rinsing out the syringe and put it with a stack of other syringes to dry. She must have forgotten that they weren't supposed to use it again. Or maybe it was a different syringe and she had thrown Ire's away.

"Ire will die?" asked Chinma.

"Shut up," said the doctor. "Do you want to start a panic?"

I think sending all the patients out of the clinic through the back door is more likely to start a panic than anything I might say.

But Chinma kept his mouth shut and the doctor opened the door to the waiting room. "We're closed now," he said. "Go home."

"But I'm very sick," said the man who had complained before.

A mother with a three-year-old pointed to the whimpering child's broken arm.

"Do your best, do your best," said the doctor. "It's for your own good. This clinic is not a safe place for anyone right now."

As they left, the smell of medicines finally got to

Chinma and he sneezed on the sick man, who glared at him. "Sorry," said Chinma, and he ducked to avoid the inevitable cuffing.

When the people were gone, Chinma led the doctor out into the parking lot. Ade strode up to them. "Where were you?" he demanded in Ayere. "I went in but there was nobody at the table and a sick man told me to get out or he'd infect me."

The doctor gripped Ade by the upper arm. "I need you to take me and a couple of other doctors out to where your brother got bitten."

"Why?" asked Ade.

"If you want your brother to live, you'll do it," said the doctor.

"I'll do it," said Ade, "but it's stupid. What does the *place* have to do with it?"

"Because we have to find the monkey that bit him, that's why," said the doctor.

Ade looked at Chinma, and Chinma rolled his eyes. "I tried to tell him but he told me to shut up," said Chinma in Ayere.

"What is he saying?" demanded the doctor. "Speak a language somebody understands."

Ade answered him. "We take all the monkeys."

"All the putty-face monkeys," said Chinma, trying to be accurate.

"Took them? Where?"

"A warehouse, other side of the tracks," said Ade.

The doctor glared at Chinma. "Why didn't you *make* me—" But then he caught himself and grimaced. "Yes,

I should have listened. I've turned into one of *those* adults."

Five minutes later they were at the warehouse. The men were already loading the monkey cages into a panel truck but they hadn't left yet.

The doctor told them to stop. "These monkeys cannot leave Ilorin," he said in Yoruba.

The foreman laughed at him, hooking his fingers through the wires of the cage. "We have the permits and unless you have an order from a judge and a policeman to back it up—"

Then he screeched and snatched his hand back from the cage and brought one finger into his mouth to suck on it. "Damn monkey."

Chinma looked into the cage. It wasn't the papa monkey, it was one of the mamas. Not the one that sneezed on him.

The doctor leaned in close to the man. "You are now a dead man," he said, "unless those monkeys stay right here."

The warehouse man looked puzzled but he had stopped laughing. "What do you mean?"

"I have a man in my clinic with blood coming out of his eyes because that monkey bit him."

Chinma thought of telling him it wasn't really the same monkey, but he decided not to.

The warehouse man sat down on the ground and began to cry. "Ebola," he said. "Ebola."

"It's not ebola," said the doctor. "It's something else. That's why the scientists have to look at these monkeys.

Do you understand me? Maybe they'll find out things that will let them save your life."

The warehouse man shouted at his coworker. "Get those cages out of the truck!"

Chinma's brothers helped the man take the cages back into the warehouse.

Now the doctor could squat down beside Chinma and talk to him. "In the cab of the truck your brother Ade told me that you do the monkey-catching. He said that you warned your brother that the monkey was a biter."

Chinma nodded.

"Did it bite you?"

"No," said Chinma. "I was quick."

"And the man in my clinic—"

"Ire," said Chinma.

"He did the same thing I did, yes? He wouldn't listen to your warning."

"A monkey . . . spit on me," said Chinma. He couldn't think of the English word for *sneeze*. "Will I die?"

"Are you feeling sick?"

"No," said Chinma.

"You saw how sick your brother was. If you had the same thing, you'd be even sicker, because your body is so much smaller."

The scientists came, not as soon as Chinma hoped, but perhaps soon enough. Nor were they in a truck. They were in a helicopter, and the doctor waved them down into the parking lot. The chopper belonged to the World Health Organization and the scientists came out of it wearing suits that covered every inch of their bodies. They breathed through filtration masks and peered out through goggles. They looked like huge white insects.

The monkey cages were loaded on the chopper and one of the scientists left with them. Then they all went back to the clinic.

Ire was dead when they got there. And the nurse was lying on the floor, crying. "I'm sick," she said. "I caught it from him."

Chinma and his brothers and the truck and the unbitten warehouse man were held in quarantine for twenty-four hours, but none of them showed any sign of illness. By the time they were pronounced healthy and turned loose, the warehouse man and the nurse and the doctor were all dead.

Their bodies were flown out in helicopters and then the army came in and used flamethrowers to burn out the clinic. Then bulldozers knocked down the walls and gravel and earth were brought in to cover the ruins.

Before he left, Chinma did have one chance to tell one of the scientists about the red-bellied guenons. He was one of the Nigerians; Chinma was too scared of the white scientists to talk to them.

"Will you take me out to where they live?" the Nigerian scientist asked in Yoruba.

"Are you sure?" said Chinma. "They were living right where the sick white-face monkeys were."

"I won't let any of them bite me," said the scientist.

So instead of going home with his brothers, Chinma went back out to the stand of trees. He only got lost once when he missed the turn from the highway; once they were on dirt roads his memory of the route was perfect.

The scientist looked up into the trees and swore softly. "They never live in populations this size," he said. "The largest troop we ever found was thirty."

"I don't think they're sick."

"Oh, these guenons might have the same thing that killed your brother, Chinma," said the scientist. "Only to them it's like a cold, they just cough and sneeze and then they're fine. When the putty-faces caught it, though, it affected them worse. Made them really sick and lethargic and weak. But they'll probably live, too."

"And when Ire got bit . . ."

"It got past all the body's natural defenses. Straight into the blood. Fatal in six hours."

"I wish I'd never caught a monkey in my life," said Chinma.

"It's not your fault," said the scientist.

"I never thought it was my *fault*," said Chinma. "But if I hadn't been such a good monkey-catcher, Ire wouldn't be dead now. And that would have been better. The money we made wasn't worth Ire being dead. I'm going to bury all my money with him."

"You can bury it if you want," said the scientist. "But you can't bury it with him. His body will never be returned to you. You understand? You saw them knocking down the clinic, didn't you?"

"Are they going to come out and knock down these trees and kill these monkeys?"

"I hope not," said the scientist. "But they do have to come out here and determine whether the disease originated with the red-bellied guenons. It would be a shame to have to destroy the largest free troop ever found of an endangered species."

"Will they wear those suits?"

"Of course," said the scientist. "We're extremely careful when we know there's a new disease involved. No one knows what it might do."

Chinma refused to let the scientist take him all the way to the village—he knew that if he arrived in the scientist's truck, all his brothers and sisters would hate him and the big ones might beat him because he thought he was better than everyone else. They would say he thought he was a scientist now and taunt him, or say he let the scientist do bad things to him so he was filthy now.

So the scientist dropped him off on the highway a half-mile from the dirt road leading to the village. Before he drove away, the scientist gave him a notebook and a pencil and told him to take notes, because that's what scientists did. And after he had copied all the pictures from his cheap little digital camera to his laptop, the scientist gave Chinma the cheap little digital camera he had been using. "It runs on batteries and you have to have a computer to get the pictures out of it," said the scientist. "Do you have a computer?"

Chinma didn't know anyone with a computer, but

he wanted the camera, so he nodded and the scientist smiled and gave it to him. Then he drove away.

Chinma hid the notebook in a bush before he got to the village, and he kept the camera in the deepest pocket of his pants. He would never show it to anyone or they would take it away from him.

Back at the village, Father made the obvious decision. "No more monkeys," he said. He glared at Chinma.

For once, somebody spoke up for him. "Chinma warned Ire," said Ade. "It wasn't his fault the monkey was sick."

"I know," said Father.

Chinma took the box where he kept all his money and handed it to Father. "To make up for the monkeys we'll never catch now."

"No," said Father. "You earned this."

Several times over the next few days, Chinma smelled something that triggered a sneezing fit. Not just one sneeze, but many in a row. "Get out of the kitchen," said Father's second wife. "Nobody wants you sneezing on the food."

"I think it was the pepper that made me sneeze," said Chinma.

"Well, I have pepper in the kitchen, so get out," she said again.

But Chinma had what he wanted—one of the plastic bags that the women washed and reused again and again in the kitchen. Chinma went back to the notebook and pencil and put them in the plastic bag and left them hidden because if he started writing in a notebook they would say he thought he was a scientist now and they'd beat him and steal the notebook. Later I'll come back and get it. Later I'll take notes and be a scientist.

It wasn't until the fifth day that Chinma began to get really sick, with a fever and vomiting. And by that time, three of the other children were having occasional sneezing fits, too. So was Father.

And off in Lagos, where the Nigerian scientist lived and worked, he also had sneezing fits, and so did his closest colleagues.

"Flu," said the scientist.

"Flu," said his colleagues.

But when the scientist ran a fever so hot that it made the nurse who discovered it run screaming for a doctor, they stopped saying "flu" and the men in suits from the World Health Organization came back. If the scientist had not been so sick, he would have told them about Chinma and even where his village was, because Chinma had told all about his home as they rode together in the car to see the red-bellied guenons.

Instead, like Ire before him, the scientist lay on his bed, racked with fever, blood seeping out of his eyes and then from his ears and nose and finally from random breaks in the skin all over his body. His brain was bleeding, too, so even if he could have talked, he would have had nothing to say; he didn't remember anything except the pain and the fear. And then he felt nothing at all.

Here is the amazing thing: Chinma did not die.

Father died. Many of the other children died. The two wives ahead of Mother died. But Mother and Chinma and Ade lived, and so did a scattering of others in the village.

But when it was over, instead of 3,000 speakers of Ayere in the world, there were only 1,500.

And the neighboring villages were full of people having sneezing fits. So were the streets of Ilorin and Lagos. And because it took days before people infected through their lungs had any symptom worse than the sneezing fits, there was plenty of time for such people to get on buses and ride to other cities, or get on planes and fly to other countries.

It was a lucky thing that at first it was a disease of poor and uneducated villagers, and of the shopkeepers in Lagos where the Nigerian scientist had sneezed before he died. None of them were the kind of rich and educated people who flew across the Atlantic or north across the Sahara. So far, at least, the airborne epidemic was confined to West Africa.

But it was consistently killing between thirty and fifty percent of the people who caught the infection. And all you had to do to catch the thing was be within ten feet of someone who sneezed the virus into the air.

TWO

FAVORITISM

In the past, "stimulating the economy" has meant pork. Meaningless projects that did no more than pump money out of Washington and burden future generations with debt—and for what? There's nothing to show for it.

We're not doing it that way this time. We're going to do work that matters. The stimulus money will go only to projects that will pay for themselves many times over. Future generations will forget that we were stimulating the economy—but they'll remember what we built.

COLONEL BARTHOLOMEW Coleman liked the city of Kiev. He liked it so much that he walked everywhere he could, so he could enjoy walking among the people, and seeing the shops and houses and parks at street level, and taking odd routes through buildings so he couldn't easily be followed by car.

If he were a spy, he thought, this was just how he would move through the city. Instead, he was the opposite of a spy. He was going to a meeting with his counterpart in the Ukrainian military, which was precisely what he was supposed to be doing, only they had to meet like spies because otherwise they were sure to be overheard by the Russians, who could be assumed to have listening and watching systems or paid informants in every government office in the city.

They would have met at the post office at Independence Square, or at the Khreschatyk Metro station, but everyone met there and the crowds were too big to make it possible to spot observers.

So instead Cole walked along Volodymyrska Street, took a winding, pointless route along Zolotovoritska, Reytarska, and Strilestska, only to cut back down Yaroslaviv Val to the Golden Gate, right by the Metro station that had brought him here. As far as he could tell, no one was following him. Of course, they wouldn't need to if they had followed Colonel Bohdanovich.

Bohdanovich was a good man, one of the best thinkers and strategists in the Ukrainian army, but he was far too young to have had any combat experience. He'd done observer duty here and there, so he had *seen* combat, but he hadn't actually fought. To Cole, that meant Bohdanovich didn't have the edginess that made a man truly watchful. Not until you'd had people shooting at you and lived through it did you acquire the habit of looking around you as if your life depended on it.

Then again, Bohdanovich knew the city and, unlike Cole, he could usually tell Russian operatives from

Ukrainian civilians. Again, a matter of experience. Cole's training and experience had been in Middle Eastern theaters of war, unless you counted some serious combat in the District of Columbia and field operations in the mountains of Washington State during the brief Progressive Rebellion three years before. None of that prepared him to know anything about how Russian spies handled themselves in a country that they believed ought still to be part of the Russian Empire.

A sad empire it was these days. He had walked the streets of Moscow only the week before, and was constantly struck by the glumness of it all. Grim-faced shopkeepers gave perfunctory service to despairing customers, or so it seemed. Pedestrians all seemed to dread whatever destination they were heading for.

In Kiev, by contrast, there was a sense of eagerness. Though Russia itself began here, and Ukraine had been the breadbasket of the Russian Empire long before the Communists took over, this was a new country and it felt like it.

Was there such a thing as a national character? Cole believed there was, and Cessy Malich encouraged him. "When people band together in communities," she said, "they can't help but influence each other. In a happy community, individual sadnesses are soothed by the surrounding élan; in a sad one, individual triumph or relief is quickly dragged down to match the surrounding despair."

Nowhere was this clearer than here on the streets of

Kiev. The city's buildings were generally as shoddy-built and decayed and polluted and ugly as in the rest of the former Communist countries, and it's not as if there were any great wealth to create architectural showplaces. But the people were bright-spirited. Flowers bloomed wherever they could be planted. Bright signs and displays demanded attention to shop windows. People nodded to one another, greeted one another, smiled.

It was contagious. Cole found himself smiling back at them. Initiating smiles of his own.

He spotted Bohdanovich standing on the corner of Lysenka and Prorizna, and to Cole's disgust the man was in uniform. Why not wear a nice flag while he was at it?

Cole walked up to him and started to greet him in Russian—there was no way Cole could learn all the distinctions between the Ukrainian and Russian languages just for this brief assignment—but Bohdanovich smiled in a vague way and cocked his head and then interrupted Cole.

"Ah, yes, the coffee shop on the corner of Franka and Yaroslav. Notice that I'm pointing the wrong way, so please start out in the direction I'm pointing and then take your time about meeting me there." Then Bohdanovich smiled again and turned away.

Okay, so the guy wasn't an idiot after all. He was just a friendly officer that a stupid American tourist asked for directions. Only if there happened to be a Russian observer who recognized Cole and knew that he and Bohdanovich already knew each other would there be a problem, and if the Russians were already *that* on top of things, they might as well just invite them to the meeting.

In the coffee shop, Bohdanovich had already ordered borscht and coffee, and he waved Cole over to his table. They sat cornerwise against the wall, so they both had a view of the big window facing the street and so nobody could come up behind them.

"You're paying," said Bohdanovich in English.

"Happy to," said Cole.

"But you notice I still ordered cheap."

"The American taxpayer thanks you."

Then they got down to business, speaking softly in English. Bohdanovich spilled salt across a small area of the table and drew a rough map of Ukraine on it, and they shared whatever information they had about Russian army bases and how quickly they could mobilize and get into Ukraine and after about twenty minutes of this they were both chuckling ruefully.

"So you're saying," said Bohdanovich, "that the best place for us to defend Ukraine from a Russian invasion is in Slovakia."

"Unless you want to try to blow all the bridges on the Dnieper, and how long would that hold them up? A day?"

Bohdanovich sighed. "At last I understand the hopeless bravery of the Polish army, defending against the Germans when there was no barrier to stop the blitzkrieg."

"All you have to do is hold on to the west, in the more mountainous country. Keep the army intact. Let the Russians occupy everything without resistance, bombing nothing, leaving the whole infrastructure intact. Then use small special ops groups you left behind to make their supply lines impossible while you counterattack in a place of your choosing."

"So many tanks."

"Tanks need gas. Make sure they can't find any between the Dnieper and the Russian border. Blow up every tanker truck that tries to make it through. Learn the lessons of Iraq."

"Ukrainians are not suicide bombers," said Bohdanovich.

"Of course not—it won't be terrorism, it'll be sabotage, and the Russians will never know where you're going to hit them."

"Our special ops don't have enough experience."

Cole grinned. "We can take your kids along on some of our operations. It won't be hard to learn."

"Oh, yes, the legendary Bartholomew Coleman can say that, the man who single-handedly stopped a civil war in America by pinpoint operations against enemy supply depots."

"I was defending my country against people who wanted to take away our democracy. That's what you'll be doing, too. Believe me, your men will do whatever it takes to learn what we have to teach them."

Bohdanovich nodded, but he still wore the sad, fatalistic expression that almost everyone in the Ukrainian military always had.

"And you'll have secure supply lines through Poland and Romania," Cole added.

"Will we?"

"They're allies," said Cole. "And I can assure you that President Torrent *will* keep his word."

"President Torrent will keep his word, I believe you," said Bohdanovich. "But will the Poles and Romanians? Once Russian tanks start to roll across borders, they'll all be terrified of offending the giant."

Cole leaned back. "Well, that's what this is all about, isn't it?" he said. "Everybody's so afraid of Russia. You and the Estonians and Lithuanians are talking tough but Russia is hoping that everybody will panic and back down and they can take back the whole empire without firing a shot."

"It worked in Georgia."

"It sort of worked," said Cole. "And it sort of didn't."

"The Georgian government does what they're told."

"But Ukraine and the Baltic states and all the Muslim republics are still independent. Georgia made you warier."

"The first time Russian troops cross a border, everybody's a coward."

"Do you mean that?" asked Cole. "Is that a serious assessment of your own government's likely response if, say, Estonia gets attacked?"

Bohdanovich thought about it for a while. "I don't know," he said. "They all talk about springing to the attack if Russia is the aggressor against one of the little countries—that's our plan, our policy—but the Russians know that. They probably won't roll the tanks, they'll just cut off the oil to Estonia, and then as long as the oil is still flowing to Ukraine we'll be frozen in place, we'll do nothing, and Estonia will cave in, and then *we'll* cave in, one by one."

"Like dominoes," said Cole.

"I'd like to think that at some point my country will stand and fight. Even if it's only in the western hills of Ukraine, and even if it's a hopeless war and we stand all alone. But I don't know."

The waiter came up to the table. "Anything else?" he asked in Ukrainian.

"Vodka," said Bohdanovich.

"Not for me," said Cole in Russian.

The waiter looked at him coldly.

"He's American," said Bohdanovich. "He never learned Ukrainian."

"Do you have Coca-Cola?" asked Cole in English.

The waiter smiled and left.

"Colonel Bohdanovich, you have to look at this rationally. Why is Russia pushing things with all their neighbors?"

"To restore the empire," said Bohdanovich. "The democracies are prospering and Russia is the sick man of Europe, even with all their oil. The Russian people are angry, population is shrinking, life expectancy is going down, Russia is a mess. So their fearless leader bullies the little countries, the ones that used to be part of the empire, and the Russian people feel proud again, they remember the big soviet empire. Nobody riots or goes on strike, nobody kills the fearless leader and takes over the government."

"And if they can get Ukraine and the Baltic states back into the empire," said Cole, "they think it might jump-start their economy."

"No, they're not stupid," said Bohdanovich. "They know that it's our freedom and independence that make us prosperous, and when they get us back into the empire it will all go away. The Russians don't want to steal our prosperity, they want us to be as poor and miserable and drunk and sad as they are."

The waiter set down a glass of vodka in front of Bohdanovich and a glass of Coke in front of Cole. Cole slid his Coke over in front of Bohdanovich. "Don't give them a head start," he said.

Bohdanovich smiled. "One vodka doesn't make me drunk, it makes me Ukrainian."

"So the best strategy," said Cole, "is to persuade them to back off."

"Which is why we must have nuclear weapons." Which was Bohdanovich's mission, of course, to try to find a way to get Cole to get President Torrent to allow some American nukes into Ukraine so that the Russians would be deterred.

"Not a prayer," said Cole, "and you know why." Nukes would be a provocation and would absolutely guarantee an invasion—and in the end, the American nukes would end up in Russian hands. Not an acceptable risk.

"Then how would *you* keep Russia from walking all over us?"

Cole smiled. "It's all about appearances," he said. "The Russians don't want to appear to be imperialists. It's like Hitler pretending to be looking out for Germans living in Austria and Czechoslovakia and Poland. The Russians are pretending that it's all about Russian nationals living in the Baltic states. If they send troops in—or cut off the oil—it will be to protect the interests of Russians who are an oppressed minority."

"Exactly," said Bohdanovich. "But if we try to expel them—"

"No, no," said Cole. "You do the opposite. Well, not *you*. Make it Estonia, where the national language is nothing like Russian. The Estonian government declares that they understand the plight of the 'visitors,' the Russian nationals, and they are going to make sure that they don't suffer any disadvantage. In fact, the 'visitors' are going to have the very best that Estonia has to offer."

Bohdanovich belched softly. "They already do."

"No, no, you're missing the point. They need to make it extravagant. Exaggerated. From now on, any Russian national who wants to get into the best schools and universities will be admitted, no questions asked. They declare that they are Russian nationals, and they go straight to the head of the line. Native Estonians will go to the lesser schools. Therefore the lesser schools will all be taught *in Estonian*."

"So it's segregated," said Bohdanovich.

"But the Russian nationals get the *best*. And in order to get that 'best' they have to *declare* themselves to be Russian nationals . . . and *not* Estonians. They're still citizens, but they have a strong incentive to make a decision, a clear dividing line. Russian nationals on this side, as 'visitors,' and real Estonians on the other side. And it's not just schools. Everywhere—movie theaters, butcher shops, the post office—Russian nationals can always go straight to the head of the line. Just show their papers or even speak Russian and zip—they get waited on ahead of everyone else."

Bohdanovich shook his head vehemently. "So the Estonians do it to themselves instead of waiting for the Russians to come in and take over? They'll never."

"The point is, Russia will have no pretext. Russian nationals in Estonia are getting the best of everything. Instead of a persecuted minority, they're being treated like lords, like conquerors. How could Russia justify cutting off the oil or attacking? It would be naked imperialism instead of looking out for Russians. In fact, Russian citizens will be *envious* of the advantages Russians are getting in Estonia—they're sure not getting any of that at home!"

"So the Estonian people become second-class citizens in their own country?"

"No," said Cole. "That's the beauty of it. They become the only *real* citizens. Any Estonian of Russian descent who claims 'visitor' status is confessing that he's not a real Estonian. It's social death. They know they don't deserve this special treatment. They know it's resented. They know they're only getting it because of the big Russian army across the border. So if they march to the head of the line or put their kids in the Russian-language schools and universities, they're saying to everybody, I'm not Estonian."

"You think they won't? They'll be happy to! You don't know how arrogant Russians are."

"*Some* Russians," said Cole. "*Some* Russians will accept all the perks. But others won't. They'll see what's happening. That this is a division, a way to mark who is really Estonian and who is really just a Russian visitor. They don't want to go back to Russia—are you kidding? Who would want to, when they're prospering so well in Estonia? I give you ten years and there won't be more than a few thousand 'visitors' left in Estonia. Everybody else will have declared themselves to be Estonians, *not* Russians, and now what does Russia do? The Baltic states aren't one-quarter Russian anymore, there are almost no Russians there at all."

"It will never work. Baltic Russians think they *deserve* special treatment. They'll just take advantage of it."

"It's worth a try," said Cole.

"The Baltic nations have too much pride. *We* have too much pride."

"Too much pride to survive? Look, it's all about keeping the Russian army behind their own borders and keeping the oil flowing until the Russian economy destroys itself. Already the Russian army is underequipped and undertrained and underpaid. Already corruption is sucking the life out of the Russian economy. Already the population of Russia is falling. And if you deprive the fearless leader of his big bold conquests, things only get worse inside Russia."

"So after a while the Russian threat goes away, and then—"

"And the worse it gets in Russia, the less the Baltic Russians want to be Russian and the more they want to be Estonians and Latvians and Lithuanians."

"So maybe it works," said Bohdanovich. "How does that help Ukraine?"

"In the short run, you can't stop the Russian army from crossing the border. In the long run, the Russian economy and the Russian army can't keep it going against a determined resistance. You *will* win, if they invade. You think the Russian generals don't know that? So they don't want to invade Ukraine. They only want to invade one of the Baltic states, because it would be over immediately and then everybody else falls in line. If the Baltic states make it politically impossible for the fearless leader to invade them, what does he do? He's dictator of a failing country, he's getting less and less popular, he has to invade *somebody* because he can't actually fix any of the problems."

"So he invades *us*, thank you very much!"

"No," said Cole. "He orders his generals to invade Ukraine, and they know it's a losing proposition, so they arrest him and take over the government and use the military to root out the corruption and try to fix the economy."

Bohdanovich laughed. "Oh, you're better than vodka. You're better than an American movie. The world doesn't work that way."

"No," said Cole, "the world works *exactly* that way, if only somebody had the vision to see past their fears and take bold, surprising action."

"Go to Estonia, then, and sell this idea to them."

"No," said Cole. "I can't."

"Because your president won't let you be a crazy man," said Bohdanovich.

"Because *you're* going to do it."

"My government won't—"

"Not your government," said Cole. "You."

"Me? I'm just a colonel."

"Your reputation is known. You're going to talk to your counterpart in Estonia, and you're going to tell him the same story I just told you. Only you won't tell him you got it from me. It's *your* idea. And then you'll tell him to take the idea to his own government. Again, not *your* idea, *his*. No American fingerprints on it. No Ukrainian fingerprints on it. Estonia's own plan for dealing with the Russian minority. They do it, it keeps the Russians from taking action, things get worse and worse in Russia, and there's finally a coup that gets rid of the fearless leader."

"Or else he invades Ukraine."

"And you win. You and your very well-supplied

army with special forces disrupting their supplies *win* in an extended campaign against their impoverished, badly trained, underequipped, depressed, and vodka-swilling army."

"Does your president know the nonsense you tell people in other countries?"

Cole laughed. "Oh, I'd never tell him an idea as crazy as this."

"There you are," said Bohdanovich triumphantly.

Cole leaned in close to him and whispered, "But he might just tell it to *me*."

Cole put down enough money to pay for lunch—and a few more drinks if Bohdanovich decided to stay and think about it. Then he got up and walked out of the coffee shop.

THREE

POLITICS AS USUAL

It's hard for governments to spend resources on projects that won't have any immediate return. For instance, it is a scientific fact that someday a large object from space will collide with Earth. If the object is large enough, it could destroy all life on our planet. If it is smaller, it might simply destroy human civilization.

A meteor large enough to cause us terrible damage might still be so small that with existing technology, we would not detect it until only a few weeks before impact. Wouldn't it be nice if, when such an object appears, a technological civilization from Earth had had the foresight to set up distant observation stations to detect such an object years before any possible collision?

Wouldn't it be nice if that technological civilization had even installed an automatic system that would obliterate or turn away most such objects without any conscious human intervention? And what if this system were built with such high tolerances that it could last for a hundred thousand years without any further maintenance? That way it could go on protecting the human race even if we stupidly allow ourselves to lose our high technology.

There has been only one civilization, one nation in the history of the human race that could realistically aspire to achieve such early-warning and protection systems to benefit the whole world. And that is the United States of America.

But we're a democracy. That means that it is extremely hard for our government to take expensive actions whose benefits do not come before the next election.

And since we can't predict when we will actually *need* this system to warn us of or deflect a dangerous meteor, how can the American government justify taxing our people *now* to pay for a system that may not save the world for a hundred years? Or a thousand?

Yet if we, with our present level of prosperity and technology, do *not* create such a system, then when an Earth-wrecking object approaches and there is nothing that can be done in time, they will spend the last days of their lives cursing our names, remembering what we could have done, and chose not to.

I will certainly not be president long enough to see such a project to its conclusion. But neither was John F. Kennedy still president, or even alive, when his moon-landing project came to fruition. Yet if he had not begun it, it would not have been achieved. And it was that achievement that laid the groundwork for what we in turn must do.

Oh, and yes—spending money on developing this system will certainly stimulate our present sagging economy, and the benefits of the new technologies will once again spread through the world.

Already, all the people who are smarter than me are readying their criticisms. They will say, "Don't we have enough problems right here on Earth, right now, that we shouldn't waste money on space?"

All I can do is ask those of you who are as dumb as me to

remember that this is a project that will someday save the human race. Our children may well bless our names because we just weren't smart enough to know we couldn't or shouldn't do the job.

CECILY MALICH stood at the kitchen sink, scrubbing the mixing bowl and watching through the window as her firstborn son, Mark, mowed the back lawn. His man-height was beginning to come on him—at age thirteen, it was right on time, or maybe a little early. He was wearing shorts, not because the spring weather in northern Virginia was really warm enough yet, but because all his long pants were too short.

She'd take Mark shopping later in the afternoon. She hated to do it, because there were only another couple of months of school, but she couldn't send him to school any longer in pants that showed so much ankle. Not to mention the fact that the crotch was too high, which forced him to wear his pants way too low on his hips.

Other boys might welcome the excuse to look cool, but not Mark. When she asked him, "Is this really a problem? Isn't this more stylish anyway?" Mark looked at her rather coldly and said, "Dad would never have wanted me to wear my pants like this."

Mark never pulled the "dad" card except when it was true. Reuben *would* have disapproved. "Pull your pants up, son," he would have said. And Mark would have said, "I will, sir, but it really hurts when I do."

And then Reuben would have said something like, "What, you think you've got such big balls now that you need to have more room for them? You running out of ball space?"

And Cecily would have said, "Reuben, please don't teach him to be crude."

And now she wished he would say "balls" or whatever he felt like saying, just so he was here to say it.

How can you wipe your eyes when your hands are covered with citrus-scented Dawn?

People had been right, after Reuben was killed—when enough years passed, you don't cry every single day. You can think of him without crying at all. But then sometimes it hits you, all the things he's missing, all the things that their children needed him to do and say, and he would have said it, he would have done it, he was a great father, and he was cheated out of all of it because some ideological maniac who served as his secretary for years suddenly pulled out a pistol and shot him in the eye.

Their little civil war ended up amounting to almost nothing, though it certainly didn't look that way at the time. It was a terrible danger—states and cities were seriously trying to join the revolt. It could have destroyed the country. And Reuben had somehow become a pawn in their game. He was sacrificed like a chess token.

Well, he had never been a chess piece in *this* house. He was a *father*. In the outside world, Reuben had been—what, a knight? What *would* a brilliant special ops officer be if they were inventing chess today? He was certainly not a king—that was Averell Torrent. But the game of chess was set in that outside world. Inside their home, there were no games. That's what so many people didn't understand about life. The real world is the one within the walls of home; the outside world, of careers and politics and money and fame, that was the fake world, where nothing lasted, and things were real only to the extent they harmed or helped people inside their homes.

And there Cecily stood with the suds drying on the mixing bowl, and with tears drying on her cheeks because she was no longer thinking about Reuben, she was thinking about what was wrong with the world.

With *other people*'s worlds. There was only one thing wrong with *her* world, and that was Reuben's absence.

Mark was no longer mowing—the back lawn was done.

In fact, he was standing in the kitchen, by the door to the laundry room. "You zoned out again, didn't you, Mom?"

"I was having philosophical moments."

He came up and, with the damp hand towel, wiped her cheek.

She took the towel from his hand and wiped the other cheek. "Well, you caught me," she said. "Somewhere in there I thought of your father and the absolutely stupid reason why he isn't here with us now and I think I was conducting my side of an argument and the sad thing is the people I'm arguing with would never, ever listen to someone like me or ideas like the ones I believe in so it's a complete waste of time."

"Dad *is* here, Mom," said Mark.

"Well, in our memories, of course," said Cecily. "Except J.P., he was too young when your father died."

"We tell him stories," said Mark.

"I was watching you out the window," said Cecily, "and I was thinking that I'm just not going to be able to teach you how to be a man."

To her surprise, Mark slammed his fist down on the thin part of the counter in front of the sink. Some water splashed. "I don't need you to teach me to be a man."

"Oh, you already know it all?" she asked, more surprised than snippy.

"Dad already taught us how to be a man before he died," said Mark.

"Not everything."

"You wouldn't know," said Mark.

"Because I'm not a man?"

"Because you weren't his child," said Mark. "So you didn't watch him the way we did."

"Maybe you're right," said Cecily.

"I'm right," said Mark.

"So why are you angry with me?"

"Because you think we weren't paying attention."

"I don't think that, I think you were too young to learn the things you need to know now."

"Well, you're wrong. I was too young to *understand* what it all meant, but it was like holography, Mom. Every day with Dad taught us everything about what a man's supposed to be, and all we have to do is remember and think and it's all clear. He taught us how to *learn* to be men. And what a man's supposed to learn to be."

"So what does that mean? That you're going to be a soldier?" Because she feared that more than anything, and yet knew she should expect it, too.

"I'm going to do my duty, whatever that turns out to be," said Mark.

"Just your duty? You have no more ambition than that?"

"See?" said Mark. "That's what I'm talking about. One of the things we learned from Dad. I don't care if I'm ever important or famous or even in charge. I'm just going to do what is necessary and right. That's a *man's* ambition."

"Yes," said Cecily, realizing he was right. That he had truly understood at least that aspect of his father.

"I don't want to be your *boss,*" Mark added.

"I don't want you to be," said Cecily. "And the President isn't my boss. It's not like I go in to the office every day."

"Right, you're an independent contractor, but you only have one client, and you jump whenever he calls."

"Not *whenever,*" she said.

"Right," said Mark. "Sometimes you make him wait until the cookies are out of the oven."

"Speaking of which, the snickerdoodle dough is cold enough now, so get it out of the fridge and help me ball it and roll it in the cinnamon sugar."

"I have to wash my hands."

"I have to finish washing up the cooking dishes, so let's both get back to work."

At that moment Lettie spoke up from the dining room doorway. "How come Mark gets to mow the lawn *and* roll the snickerdoodles?"

"Because I don't snitch half the batter," said Mark on his way out of the room.

"Well, I don't eat any grass clippings, but that doesn't mean I get to mow the lawn!" Lettie called after him.

"You're ten, Lettie."

"You let Mark mow the lawn when he was ten."

"I did not."

"I'll find the old calendar and show you."

"Maybe I did, but because he's doing it I don't *need* you to do it, I need you to do other things."

"You just think it's boys' work and all you want me to do is girls' work."

"Whatever work you do becomes girls' work while you're doing it," said Cecily. "I consult with the President *and* I bake cookies. Both women's work, when I'm doing them."

"You know what I mean."

"And you know what *I* mean. Full communication has happened. We are both so amazingly smart."

Cecily made her big-eyed face at Lettie, and it worked—as it always did. That face had made Lettie laugh since she was a toddler, and even now at the ripe old age of ten it still had the same effect.

"If you ever do that face in front of my friends, Mother—"

Cecily made the face again. "Then they'll all pity you and think you're *so* brave to have survived being raised by a crazy mother."

"They already do," said Lettie.

"Then they can't have any of the snickerdoodles when they come over."

"It's Saturday and none of my friends are coming over today."

"See? My punishment of your rude friends will be complete. They will get *nothing* from me, speaking coo-kimentarily."

Mark came back in. "Why do you bother arguing with her?" he asked. "She just does it to keep you talking."

"I argue with her because I'm right and she's wrong," said Lettie.

"She's right," said Cecily. "My children are all so much smarter than me."

"Are you even *watching*, Mother?" asked Mark. "Look at her fingers—they're covered with cookie dough. She's been snitching right in front of you."

"I was not snitching," said Lettie. She launched into her adult-intellectual imitation. "I was preemptively rescinding Mom's decision to deprive my friends of their share of the snickerdoodles."

"So what are you going to do?" said Mark. "Wait till you pass the cookie dough out your butt, form it into little balls, cover them with cinnamon sugar, bake them, and take them to share at school?"

"Mark," said Cecily. "That is a nauseating idea."

"I was just interested in how snitching cookie dough *now* will somehow get her friends the cookies they were being denied."

"I never said I was getting the cookies for them," said Lettie in her snootiest fake-professor voice. "I was merely removing from the common stock of cookie dough that portion which *would* have gone to my friends, so that the community does not profit from my friends' deprivation."

"I wish you kids would occasionally speak at grade level."

"We always do," said Mark. "Just not necessarily the grade we're in."

They settled down to forming and rolling the snickerdoodle balls and laying them out on the cookie sheets. The phone rang.

Mark said, with mock impatience, "It's probably the President again."

It was. Or rather, the chief of staff, Nate Ogzewalla. "Can you come in?" he asked.

"I'm baking cookies," said Cecily, sticking out her tongue at Mark and Lettie.

"Go out to Langley," said Nate, "and we'll get you in by chopper. No reason for you to fight the traffic."

"It's Saturday, and the traffic won't be that bad, and I want my car with me so I can leave whenever I want."

"Have we ever held you prisoner in the White House?" asked Nate.

"It's a waste of taxpayer money to send me in and out by chopper."

"It saves the President an hour of waiting for you," said Nate. "That's what that particular budget is for. Just pretend that all the money paying for the trip comes from some corporation that you particularly hate."

"I keep thinking it comes from the taxes paid by some small businessman who can't hire two employees he needs because he's so grossly overtaxed."

"That's stinkin' thinkin'," said Nate. "You need to get back in your twelve-step program."

"But I already 'let go and let Nate.' "

"That's blasphemous," said Nate. "Better make restitution. Now if you don't mind, I have six ambassadors waiting here in my office while I talk to a cookie-bakin' mama."

"Such a lie," she said. "You never let ambassadors talk to you *personally*."

"Bring me a cookie. I want proof that you baked them."

"I'll burn one just for you." She hung up.

"So who's tending us tonight?" asked Lettie.

"I'm thinking maybe I'll put Mark in charge."

"No!" said Mark. "Don't do that to me! When I'm in charge, they take off all their clothes and run around the neighborhood naked and then I have to lie to you and pretend that they were good so you don't feel guilty about leaving them with me."

"It's not true," said Lettie. "He just sits and plays computer games and orders us to do stuff."

"She's confusing me with Nick."

"I know the difference between you and Nick," said Lettie. "He *wins* his videogames. You just sit there swearing at the screen."

Mark pressed a cinnamon-covered dough ball onto the base of her nose.

"Gross!" said Lettie. "You got some of my snot on the cookie dough!"

"The germs will all be killed in the baking," said Mark.

"I'm not allowing that cookie into my oven," said Cecily.

"Not even to become the cookie you make for Nate?" asked Mark.

"*Mister* Ogzewalla to you, buster," said Cecily.

"Sorry," said Mark. Then he reached over, took the slightly snotty dough out of Lettie's fingers and stuck it into his mouth, licking the residue off his fingers.

"I'm going to throw up," said Lettie.

"No, *I'm* going to throw up," said Mark. "But I couldn't bear to see any of Mom's precious, hard-earned cookie dough going to waste."

"It was bad enough being nauseated the entire time I was pregnant with the two of you," said Cecily. "Nobody told me the nausea would continue as long as you lived in my house."

"How did *I* get included in the morning sickness?" said Lettie.

"It was your snot," said Mark.

"It's not like I put it up my nose myself," said Lettie.

"I'm going upstairs to change clothes. Put the first batch in the oven and set the time."

"How long?" asked Mark.

"Oh, can't you read a recipe?" asked Cecily.

"Oh, it's a research project!" cried Mark joyfully. "Lettie, Mom has decided to homeschool us!"

Cecily smiled all the way up the stairs. She looked into the room Nick shared with Mark and saw her second son actually doing homework—though there was a save screen for a game on the computer, so he had probably been playing until he heard her footsteps on the stairs. But Cecily didn't mind—Nick's grades were excellent and he had played games obsessively before his father died, so she didn't have to worry about it as a concealed grief response. Unless it was after all, in which case she could think of a lot of worse things he could do in order to help him deal with his father's death.

She changed into her serious clothes. She had developed her policy-wonk wardrobe years before and, because policy-wonk clothing never, never changed styles, and because she hadn't gained any weight since then— a God-given gift for which she did penance to all her thickening friends ("Five children and you haven't gained an *ounce*?")—it all still fit.

Midway through changing she picked up her cellphone and called Stevie Popadopolos, a friend from church who had no kids and was usually glad to come sit with the kids at the drop of a hat. The kids liked her fine—perhaps because she spent all her time playing with Annie and John Paul, the eight- and six-year-olds, and left the older kids alone.

"Should I bring Ticket to Ride or have you finally bought the game?" asked Stevie.

"Europe, America, Germany, Switzerland, Nordic countries, I think we have them all," said Cecily.

"And nobody's lost any train cars or destination cards or anything?"

"Lettie removed every destination card that leads to Duluth," said Cecily. "But if you bring your own set, she'll just remove them from yours during the game."

"Thanks for the warning. And . . . do I smell cookies in the oven?"

"Am I that predictable?" asked Cecily.

"Saturday is cookie-baking day at the Malich house," said Stevie. "Who doesn't know *that*?"

"The President," sighed Cecily.

"Oh, he knows, he just doesn't think cookies are important."

"And his political maneuverings *are*? I don't think so."

"I'll be there in half an hour," said Stevie. "Tell the President that he should send a chopper for the baby-sitter, too."

"He only sent the chopper for me the one time," said Cecily.

"And you're saying he's not sending one *this* time?"

"Well, no, he actually is, but this is only the second time."

"Seeya!" sang Stevie triumphantly, in her church-soprano voice.

Cecily sighed and finished dressing in time to limit the kids to one hot cookie each as they slid the first batch off the sheets.

THE CHOPPER had taken her above the traffic and the bridges and the river, Nate had his little bag of cookies, and of course Cecily spent an hour and a half in a conference room waiting for the President. Nobody even bothered to apologize for things like this—it was part of the President's life.

Some politicians would make her wait as part of some power game. Lyndon Johnson used to put people in their place by holding their meeting in the bathroom while he took a noisy, smelly dump. But Torrent didn't play games like that—though Cecily suspected it was only because he was so absolutely convinced of his own superiority that he didn't need to put other people down in order to prove it to himself.

When her wait ended, though, Torrent didn't send a flunky to get her. He came striding into the room himself and said, "Come on into the Oval, Cecily, we've got us a top-secret situation."

"Meaning the conservative wing of the Republican Party has discovered you're a socialist? Or the dove wing of the Democratic Party has discovered you're an imperialist?"

"For once it isn't politics," he said.

"Well, since that's the only thing I know anything about, I don't know why I'm here."

"So Nate could get your cookies, of course."

"Did he save any for you?"

"No, but I saw the cinnamon on his face."

Which was his way of making sure she knew that *he* knew what kind of cookies they were. Torrent was good at having enough details to fake sincerity really well. Everyone had assumed when he first took office that since he had been a Princeton history prof and then National Security Adviser, he'd be good at foreign policy and a babe in the woods when it came to politics.

Instead, he turned out to be a superb politician. Partly because he didn't have the stupid idea that his political instincts were enough. He did nothing, politically, without getting advice and learning all he could from the people who knew. Which is what he usually called Cecily in for—her outside-the-beltway perspective. Not that she lived in Arkansas or anything, but she had never lost touch with people who were outside politics. She had a good sense of what people were thinking in every region of the country. Of course she worked hard to stay current, analyzing all the polls and staying in touch with correspondents all over the country. That was what kept her valuable to the President— valuable enough that she was paid six figures a year for a few consultations a month.

And her consulting fees came equally from the

budgets of both parties—no way was her salary going to come out of tax money. For her it was an ethical issue. For Torrent, it was a matter of not wanting to have to appoint her to a position that would make their conversations part of the public record.

"Political consultants don't have any kind of privilege," she had reminded him once.

"They do in *my* White House," he said. And so far she had remained out of the media gossip and invisible to the blogs, so maybe he was right. Or maybe nobody was going to say anything remotely critical of a war hero's widow. Maybe Reuben was still protecting her.

When they were inside the Oval Office with the door closed, he said, "Just so you know, Cole got the idea planted with Bohdanovich and he's already talked to his Estonian counterpart, so who knows, maybe something will come of it."

"Just remember that I'm not an expert on Russian and Baltic politics," said Cecily.

"Hey, your ancestors came from Serbia."

"Croatia. And that has absolutely nothing to do with the Baltic states. Or Russia, for that matter. Croatians are *Catholic*."

"It's still eastern Europe," said Torrent. "And it's a good idea, if they really do it."

"It might be politically impossible in Estonia."

"I don't know. The Estonians have a very ironic sense of humor. I think they'll get the joke without anybody having to do anything so inflammatory as explain it publicly."

"Why did you call me in?" asked Cecily.

"Oh, was I off topic?" Torrent said, with only a little snideness.

"I have a babysitter with the meter running," said Cecily.

"Are you hinting we should pick up her tab?"

"No," said Cecily. "But she did ask for a chopper ride."

Torrent looked at her for a moment to see if she was joking.

"Yes, she *did* ask, but no, of course I don't want you to do it."

"What I brought you in for," said Torrent, "was because of an outbreak of a new disease in Nigeria."

"Ebola doesn't happen in Nigeria."

"Then it's a good thing it isn't ebola," said Torrent. "I don't think they've even named it yet, though it'll probably be called Ilorin, after the city where it first showed up."

"How cute," said Cecily. "The name even starts with 'ill.' "

"Right, you're not a medical expert. What I need you for is to vet our response to it."

"Is it an epidemic?"

"No, not at all. Just a couple of cases. It kills too quickly for it to be an epidemic. I mean, nobody who was infected lived as long as twenty-four hours. And it takes blood contact to spread it."

"Like HIV?"

"No, more like ebola—bodily fluids getting passed."

"So then it's not a problem."

"It's a problem," said Torrent. "Even ebola has survivors. Not many, but some. This one is a hundred percent."

"How many total?"

"Three."

"Civilians?"

"One civilian, two health workers—a nurse and a doctor who treated the first patient. The doctor was sharp enough to call in guys in hazmat suits to deal with everything from then on, so nobody else got infected. They burned his clinic to the ground, they isolated every monkey that had the pathogen, everything was burned or frozen and removed for further study."

"And so this is a problem how?"

"We had a couple of scary hours there. And it occurred to us that with all our planning, we don't really know how to respond to something like this. Not medically, but politically. So we've come up with a plan and we want to run it past you."

"I'm listening."

"Quarantine," he said.

"The traditional method."

"And it has the great advantage that if you can really make it stick, it works."

"But that's the job of the government of whatever country has the first outbreak," said Cecily. "It's not under American control."

"That's not the kind of quarantine I'm talking

about. There's not a government in Africa that can be trusted to enforce an effective local quarantine."

Cecily thought for a moment. "You're talking about quarantining an entire continent?"

"We could do it," said Torrent. "We can't stop it from spreading inside Africa, but we can prevent any plane or boat from leaving Africa."

Cecily laughed. "Seriously?"

"I'm serious we can do it, but you're not referring to that, are you?"

"Let's see how this will play. 'Dear American people, we're going to let everybody in Africa catch this terrible disease and die, but that's okay, because they're only black people, and the rest of the world won't catch it."

"Come on, you know me better than that."

"That's how it'll play, and you know it."

"Not if I give a speech in which I explain, There's nothing we can do that will stop it from spreading within Africa. But maybe we have a chance to save the rest of the world by sealing off the continent. Let the disease run its course there, let the governments in Africa handle quarantining between countries as best they can. And when it's under control, we can resume communications and the rest of the world will be safe."

"Okay," said Cecily. "But you say it like this: It's too late to put this monster back in its cage. We have only two choices. Either it rages through the entire world, devastating every nation, killing billions of people. Or we confine it to one continent and prevent it from spreading even further. It will still do terrible damage in the continent where it first appeared. We can't do anything about that and we never could. But as President of the United States, I have no choice but to take the actions that will protect the people of this country. These actions will also protect the rest of the world, outside the continent of origin."

"They'll just say I'm avoiding saying 'Africa.' "

"You say it once at the beginning, then you avoid repeating it. Then when people ask you—and if the reporters don't, black leaders will—you refuse to answer any hypotheticals. 'What if this disease had first emerged in Europe? Would you quarantine Europe?' Or Britain, or Australia—whatever you say will be hopelessly wrong. So you look them in the eye and say, 'This disease originated in Africa. I have no choice about that.' And refuse to discuss it further."

"Political results?"

"It all depends on what happens in Africa."

"But which way works best for us?"

"Does it matter? Can you affect it?"

"Assuming there's no cure, and no vaccine. If we have a cure or a vaccine, of course we'll make sure that it gets delivered everywhere we can."

"I assumed that," said Cecily. "Politically, for you, the worst outcome is that the governments of Africa respond vigorously and the disease is confined to a few countries at most and then it dies out because they quarantined themselves and one another effectively. Then you'll look like an idiot because you consigned an entire continent to this plague, and it was never that big a threat. Torrent the mass murderer."

"Oh, please," said Torrent.

"Come on, you're the historian," said Cecily. She was never sure whether he was playing devil's advocate or really needed her input.

"So how do I manage that?"

"You promise to support African countries in taking effective measures on their own. But you'll only support those countries that respect the international quarantine. You keep making reports about who the good guys are. You make it so that African countries behaving responsibly is *your* program, and your international quarantine is only for the losers."

"Okay. But are you really saying that my *best* political outcome is for the plague to spread disastrously through all of Africa?"

"Sadly, that's the ugly political truth. The worse it is in Africa, the smarter you look for having confined it to that one place. And you can't keep it there forever."

"I don't have to," said Torrent. "I only have to keep it there until the CDC comes up with a vaccine that isn't as bad as the disease."

"Which could take decades," said Cecily.

"Or six months," said Torrent. "Hold it in Africa till we find a vaccine, and then we'll share it with the whole world."

Torrent always had an answer. Torrent always had a plan. The trouble was, Torrent always had more plans than he had answers, and no one could ever hope to see all of them.

"If I find out that your administration has done a single thing to encourage the spread of the plague through Africa," said Cecily.

"You know me better than that," said Torrent. "Besides, if I were that kind of president, then I'd just have you killed."

"If anyone would obey such an order."

"If I were that kind of president, then I'd surround myself with men who would welcome orders like that. But I'm not that kind of president, and I don't have that kind of executive branch under me, so you have nothing to worry about."

But Cecily was thinking again of her old suspicions— that Torrent, with his huge network of connections, had somehow been behind the whole civil war from the start. That both Aldo Verus, who ran the Progressive Restoration that took over New York City, and General Alton, who threatened the supposed military coup that provided the Progressives with their pretext, were really set into motion by Torrent himself, one way or another.

After all, that was the idea that first brought Torrent to her attention. Reuben had studied with Torrent in graduate school, and came home to her with the ideas from Torrent's classes.

Torrent had the theory that people who compared America with the Roman Empire always missed the point—we weren't an empire yet, we were still a republic. By this view, America was not going to fall, it was going to *change,* from republic to empire. And then it would be in a position to last, as Rome had lasted, for four centuries of world domination and another thousand as a successful power among powers.

After the civil war ended, Cecily and young Captain Bartholomew Coleman had gone over Reuben's old class notes, which were written in Farsi as a way of keeping them from prying eyes. And it became clear that Torrent regarded a civil war in America as a necessary prelude to Americans being willing to endure the rule of a benign emperor like Augustus, who kept the republican forms but ruled with an iron hand.

She and Cole had decided that all they could do was watch and wait, to see if Torrent really thought of himself as the new Octavian, the nephew and adopted son of Julius Caesar who emerged from the civil wars to become the emperor Augustus.

It was convenient, for their purposes, that because of their vital roles in helping to bring the little civil war to an end, they remained in Torrent's confidence. Cole was still Torrent's go-to man for small clandestine military operations, while in the open he was an NSC staffer and in that capacity went all over the world gathering and sharing information for the National Security Adviser. And Cecily, of course, was a political consultant. Both of them had plenty of opportunities to watch what Torrent did and to see the way he thought.

And as far as they could tell, this man had no imperial ambitions. He was working the system to make sure he got reelected—but nothing in his actions suggested that he intended to violate the Constitution at any point. Or at least, no more than any of his predecessors had done.

But it was disturbing to know, from his semilighthearted remark about *not* being the kind of president who would have her killed, that he still had a clear idea of what a dictator would look like and how he would operate. In fact, if she were just a little more paranoid, she would interpret his remark as a serious threat to her: Whatever I do, don't turn against me, or you'll just be killed.

And yet there was no history of Torrent's opponents disappearing, except politically. As far as anyone could tell—and Torrent did have enemies who would certainly have noticed and spoken up if there were any pattern of convenient suicides or fatal illnesses—Torrent was a politician, not an emperor in the making.

That might just mean that Torrent was such a good historian that he had learned the lessons of such vicious dictators as Adolf Hitler, Josef Stalin, Pol Pot, Kim Il Sung, and Mao Zedong. They were all hated and feared, and their iron fists were covered with blood that all the world could see.

If Torrent was determined to be Octavian, he would maneuver so that his dictatorship came as the fulfilment of the dreams of the people. Save us! they would cry, and he would modestly and reluctantly accept the laurel leaves they forced upon his head. "Just call me 'first citizen,' Octavian had said, as he carefully preserved the Senate of Rome. But only after making sure that all its members were obedient to him.

Cole and Cecily had agreed that there were certain markers they'd watch for. One was if Torrent tried to get the Constitution amended to allow him to serve more than two terms. Another was if Torrent seemed to be laying the groundwork for the presidency to become a puppet show, as Putin had done in Russia back in the first decade of the century. Elect somebody else, but Torrent still pulls the strings.

Either way, it would probably be the beginning of the end for the American republic. Like most of the dictatorships in the world, America would still have a lovely constitution, and there would be an active show of preserving it. But it would mean nothing, because the real power would flow through different channels. Torrent had long been a man with wide networks of influence. Could he turn it into the real government behind the façade? Of course he could.

But *was* he doing it?

The man who threatened that he could have her killed might very well be doing it.

"I see the wheels turning," said Torrent. "What are you thinking?"

"That I hope you never have occasion to use this quarantine plan. Because it really would apply only to Africa. There's no way to quarantine Asia, if we get a really ugly new flu out of Hong Kong or Singapore or India."

"But we could quarantine Australia or South America—"

"Neither of *them* has a history of originating world-wide epidemics."

"So what if it's a policy that can only apply to Africa? That's the continent where the most frightening and repulsive and untreatable diseases seem to originate."

"I know," said Cecily. "And I've told you all that first occurs to me about the political fallout from a decision to quarantine. But I'm still not sure that's the best course."

"What, you seriously think I should let a world-killing plague loose on the world? Whom does *that* help?"

"I'm thinking that it's not nice to mess with Mother Nature," she said. "I'm no expert on epidemiology, but I know the basic history. Don't historians now think that one of the great epidemics that depopulated the Roman Empire was measles? Once it spread through the world and killed a third of the population, it settled down to be a childhood disease that was usually not fatal."

"Because the only people who lived to have children were the ones with natural resistance to the disease," said Torrent.

"Exactly," said Cecily. "If a disease is incurable, untreatable, and unpreventable, then isn't the human race better off to endure the onslaught and eventually emerge at the other end of the disaster with a natural resistance to the disease?"

"How would I write *that* speech? 'My fellow citizens, I have decided that a third of you should die so that a generation from now, this disease will be no more serious than measles.'"

"I'm not talking about politics and speeches now," said Cecily. "I'm talking about right and wrong."

"Well, you think about that," said Torrent, "and let me know what you come up with. But presidents don't have the luxury of ignoring politics."

"Of course you do," said Cecily. "The only time you don't is when you care about getting reelected. And how many elections can a sitting president lose? Just one. The only price you pay for doing the right but unpopular thing is to lose that one election, and then you're done."

"Unless they lynch me," said Torrent.

"My, but we're sounding like Stalin's government in World War II, when they were sure that because Hitler had broken the back of their army, the people would have Stalin and his cronies all hanging from the lampposts of Moscow."

"If I let death come into this country, when I could have kept it out, a plague so terrible that every household lost a third of its members, they'd be *right* to lynch me. As long as we're talking about right and wrong."

"Let's not fight," said Cecily. "This is all hypothetical, right? The disease was stopped in its tracks, wasn't it?"

"This time, yes."

"And by the time such a terrible thing actually

happens—a disease that *doesn't* wipe itself out by being too quick a killer and too hard to spread—you probably won't be president anymore, so you can relax about it."

"I don't relax about anything," said Torrent. "I always assume that all the worst things will happen in my administration, and I plan how to deal with them."

"Politically."

"In every way. I didn't just ask you about the politics of it. And I meant it when I asked you to tell me what you come up with on the moral front."

"You can be sure that I will."

"Then you've been a great help to me. Thank you for coming in."

"You pay me far more than my contribution is worth. Advice is supposed to be cheap."

"*Good* advice is a scarce commodity. It drives up the price."

"Averell," said Cecily, "tell me the truth. Is this Ilorin thing really under control?"

"Yes," he said instantly. "It's already just a footnote in history—an epidemic that didn't happen. But it was so quick and devastating that it put the fear of God into our hearts, at least here in the White House. What if, what if, what if. I had to have a plan."

"Of course you did," said Cecily. "You wouldn't be a great president if you didn't think that way."

She headed for the door, but stopped before she reached it. "Are they preparing a vaccine for this disease? In case it breaks out again?"

"They are," said Torrent.

"As a high priority?"

Torrent shrugged. "They say yes, and I make sure they're funded, but these medical researchers, their idea of hurrying is more likely to involve decades than years."

"Speaking as a mother now, I want that vaccine to exist."

"I'll light a fire under them," said Torrent. "I want the vaccine to exist, too. I'm too young to die."

"If history has taught us anything, it's that diseases are smarter than we are."

"Not smarter," said Torrent. "They just don't give up."

FOUR

MINGO'S BRIDGE

It's not about ending our dependence on "foreign" oil. It's about having some oil left in the world to do the things that only oil can do.

We can turn anything into electricity—sunlight, tides, rivers, coal, shale, corn, wind, garbage, the heat of the Earth. We will never run out of electricity. So every vehicle that *can* run on electricity, *must*.

Because there will never be a battery-powered airplane, so far as we can foresee. Nor will we have electric rockets any time soon. Even after all the oil that we've burned in the past century, we still have enough oil left to keep all our planes in the air and put new satellites in the sky for thousands and thousands of years.

When President Eisenhower started the interstate freeway system, it was one of the great works of civilization. Now it's time to put our money into something else, to bet our future on something else.

I'm asking Congress to abolish, by the year 2015, the transport across state lines of vehicles powered by the internal combustion engine, except hybrids, which will have until 2020.

We are funding the development of lighter, longer-lasting, and faster-charging batteries.

We are providing tax incentives for service stations to provide quick-charge outlets in addition to, and eventually instead of, gas pumps.

Above all, we are embarking on a new national electric railway system. Passenger and freight service will once again reach into every city of more than twenty-five thousand people, and electric streetcars will be built for urban transport in all those cities.

On a corporate level, we are separating the trains from the track. Just as airlines share the air routes, so also the train companies will share the new double and quadruple tracks, express and local, urban and intercity. They will compete to offer you better and better service. Comfortable seating, plenty of luggage room, continuous cellphone and broadband internet service. Onboard food and shops from popular franchises.

The federal government will do for trains what it has done for airlines—we will maintain a Rail Traffic Administration that, using computers and highly trained operatives, will control the safe flow of rail traffic throughout America, without collisions or delays.

These trains will go where you need them to go, they will operate on schedules that suit your needs, and within a few years you will wonder why you ever wasted time driving yourself, hour after hour, across the country or around town, then searching for a parking place.

I will not be president when the whole system is complete—neither was Eisenhower when the interstate highway system finally reached every important destination. But within the next six months, you will be reading and watching videos about Railway One, the presidential train, the rolling White House, which I will use instead of an airplane for all my travel within the lower forty-eight states.

I will still fly to Alaska and Hawaii.

COLE LIVED in a boardinghouse behind the Library of Congress. It wasn't a particularly secure location, but he made up for the easy-pick lock on his room by never bringing anything home that contained any secrets. Even his telephone was discardable, and instead of saving numbers in the phone, he kept the ones he needed in his head.

He also didn't own a car. He kept a narrow-tired street bicycle and used it to get around D.C.—it helped keep him fit. Even though he hadn't run as many operations as the rest of Reuben's old jeesh in the years since they fought their way into Aldo Verus's subterranean stronghold in the mountains of Washington, he had worked hard to stay fit. At thirty-one, he wasn't going to give his superiors any excuse to shift him away from combat assignments.

Most days, the bike was as fast as any car—it was mostly downhill from where he lived to the White House and the Pentagon, and he could scoot through blocked-up traffic. Going home was when he got the exercise, uphill all the way. But he took pride in never leaving top gear all the way home.

Cessy Malich asked him once, when he rode the Metro out to see her and the kids, why he didn't buy a house. "You make enough money, I know you do," she said.

"Spying on me?" he asked.

"I've spent my whole life living on officers' pay, and I know what a colonel makes."

"I don't need a house," he told her.

"If you *have* a house, though, you're more likely to be attractive to women."

"I have buns of steel, Mrs. Malich. I don't need a house."

What he couldn't tell her was: He knew what a home was, because he had been so often in hers. It was a fatherless house, just like the one Cole had grown up in. He had been nine when his father died of cancer, only a year younger than Mark Malich was when Reuben was assassinated. Reuben's kids knew he had loved them and was proud of them, so in a way he was still in their lives, but that wasn't enough. Cole wasn't going to marry and then leave his children fatherless. Only when he knew combat was over forever would he start thinking about a home with wife and children. And if he was fifty and couldn't find a good woman who wasn't a widow or divorcée and well past child-bearing, that would still be better than having children of his own and leaving them fatherless.

If he had children, it would make him timid.

Not that it had slowed Reuben down—but that was just the point, Reuben *should* have slowed down, should have gotten out of the military and taken a job as a consultant somewhere, so he wouldn't die.

Then again, he might have gotten cancer, like Cole's father did. Or been run over by a bus. You never knew what was going to happen in this life. Which was why it was better to own nothing, to have no one waiting for him to come home, to live without any extraneous responsibilities, not a dog, not a goldfish, not even a houseplant that needed him to come home.

I could die and nobody's life would change, thought Cole fairly often, and with satisfaction. He was doing this right.

So when he got home after eleven at night, running up the three flights of stairs with his bike on his shoulder, he didn't have to walk softly inside his room, or be careful not to turn on the wrong light. He just grabbed his toothbrush and face towel and trotted down the half-flight of stairs to the shared bathroom on the landing.

All the bathrooms in this ancient D.C. townhouse were afterthoughts. No doubt when the place was first built, toilets were chamber pots under the bed and you had to pay the maid extra to fill a tub with hot water for you. Once a month, probably, and you used cologne and pomade the rest of the time and reeked and scratched your lice and fleas like everybody else.

With that perspective, having a full modern bathroom only half a flight down from his room was the height of luxury.

His cellphone rang while he was washing his face, but he toweled off at once, enough to flip the phone open and hold it to his face without shorting it out. Hardly anybody had his number, and they only used it when it mattered.

"Mingo here," said the faint, tinny voice on the other end. Domingo Camacho was a civil engineer who specialized in bridges. He was also part of Reuben's old special ops team, which Cole had sort of inherited after Rube was killed. These guys had followed Rube into combat again and again in several theaters of war. Even though they had also fought with and under Cole on plenty of missions since then, nobody had any illusions—they were still Rube's jeesh. They liked Cole. He even imagined that he had earned their respect. But they were not friends, not deep-core friends, not like they had been with Rube.

The only person in Cole's life that he thought of as a true friend, a friend of *his,* was Cessy Malich, and he made damn sure she had no idea how important she was in his life, for fear she might get the wrong idea and think he wanted to take somebody else's place.

"So what's up?" asked Cole.

"Got a bridge I want you to look at, Cole."

"Highway bridge? Railroad? Dental? I won't even know what I'm looking at, Mingo, I'm not the engineering type."

"You'll like this bridge," said Mingo.

"It's like flights that end with a landing you walk away from—if it gets me to the other side without falling down under or on me, it's a good bridge."

"Ride your little Schwinn down to the railroad station and I'll pick you up in my big, ugly, outdated, soon-to-be-illegal internal-combustion nonhybrid gas-guzzling SUV."

"To see a bridge," said Cole.

"Okay, not the whole bridge, just a particularly fine truss."

"If this is some ploy to get me to come to a surprise party, it won't be my birthday for eight months."

"That's why it's a surprise, bonehead. Do you have a headlamp on your Schwinn? Or will you be carrying a flashlight?"

"Aw, Mingo, you want me to be *safe*."

"I want you to see my bridge. Wear your bike helmet. All the smart kids do."

Of course it wouldn't be a bridge. It would be some damn thing Mingo had thought up for special ops and he wanted Cole to see it because he had the President's ear, and any military procurement process that began with an inquiry from the President was put on the fast track. Usually the fast track to rejection, but that was true of practically everything. You just hoped you could make a little money during the prototyping and testing phase before Congress stepped in and made some political hay out of refusing to fund such a ridiculous item in the military budget. Hey, they had to put *something* in those budgets for Congress to eliminate.

Cole thought of his bed with momentary longing; he knew he wouldn't get back to it until way late tonight—if not tomorrow morning. And he had a nine o'clock meeting. There was once a time when he could skip a night's sleep and be no worse off, mentally, than a staffer who'd had a martini at lunch. Now, though, in his debilitating postthirty condition, he would spend the day in a fog.

Better be worth it, Mingo.

Back down the stairs with the bike over his shoulder. At least he had had the chance to empty himself into his fine, modern toilet. Bicycling with a full bladder over rutty D.C. roads was almost as bad as doing crunches with dysentery.

Naturally, Mingo would not pick him up where he had said over the phone. After all that had happened during the Progressive War, they didn't trust any phone to be secure. Cole assumed that Mingo would be watching his alleyway, and he came out of it in the opposite direction from the railroad station, then began riding east on Independence Avenue, heading toward the hospital.

To his surprise, Mingo didn't pick him up on Independence. Maybe it was too busy a thoroughfare for him, even at night. So Cole swung south on Eighth Street toward the Eastern Market, which was deserted, except for whatever criminals might have chosen this spot for their rendezvous. Cole didn't expect to reach the market, and he was right. A black SUV turned right directly in front of him, forcing him to swerve west on a nub of C Street. Mingo had the back of the SUV open and waiting for his bike by the time he caught up.

"We bike riders think drivers like you are evil," said Cole.

"We SUV drivers think you Lycra-wearing bike riders are sissy boys."

"I'm not wearing Lycra," Cole pointed out, as he walked around to the passenger door.

"That's the only reason you're making it out of this neighborhood alive," said Mingo.

It took half an hour, and Cole dozed a little during the drive. He woke when the road changed—rougher, sharper turns. When Mingo pulled up next to three other cars in a makeshift parking lot, there was a bridge looming over them. But it was an old bridge, a narrow one, and not very high.

"Wow," said Cole. "This bridge is one step up from a culvert."

"There are lots of reasons why a bridge might be special. For instance, this bridge is part of a country lane called—are you ready?—'Lonesome Road.'"

"Is there a girl in a prom dress who hitchhikes near here?"

"Just watch," said Mingo. "It's even better than that."

Cole was already watching. He had spotted the three guys on top of the bridge before they even came to a stop. In the light of a thin moon, he couldn't see much, but he knew they were carrying weapons, and he recognized Load Arnsbrach and Arty Wu from their posture and movement. He assumed the third guy must also be a member of Rube's jeesh. So this was definitely not about the bridge. It was about war.

It was for these guys—and Cole—that President

Torrent had persuaded Congress to give him the power to override the time-in-grade laws, and promote Cole to colonel and the other guys to captain in recognition of their expertise and accomplishments during the Progressive Restoration rebellion. Each one of them now commanded forces of varying size on special missions, but between missions they continued to train together. It was gratifying to Cole that they were still including him in whatever it was they were doing out here in the middle of nowhere—even if they brought him in last.

The three men on the bridge hopped up onto the rail and then jumped.

They weren't rappelling—no ropes, and they came down way too fast. But when they hit bottom, they didn't fall and roll like parachuters, either. They just . . . landed. And stood there.

Now they were close enough that even in the weak light, he could see they were wearing something over their shoulders. And down along the outsides of their legs. Cole recognized the general lines of the HULC combat exoskeleton developed by Lockheed-Martin to help soldiers carry heavier burdens for greater distances.

"What have you done, added shock absorbers to a HULC so you can jump off bridges?"

Mingo answered gleefully. "By the time Lockheed announced the HULC to the general public, they were two generations beyond that."

"Let me guess—this is the great-great-grandchild."

"More like a nephew," said Mingo.

The third guy was Cat Black, the man who had

come with Cole in the first penetration of Aldo Verus's fortress. "You ain't seen nothin' yet," said Cat. Then he squatted and jumped straight up. No run-up, nothing. Just a single bound, and he landed on top of the bridge.

It was only about a twelve-foot jump, but since no living person could jump that high and land on his feet without a pole or one hell of a pogo stick, Cole was impressed. "Leaps small bridges with a single bound."

"And not vulnerable to kryptonite," said Mingo.

"So it's not just for load-bearing anymore," said Cole.

"When they run cross-country with these things, it looks like they're running on the moon. Feels like that, too—lower gravity. Like bounding down a shale slope. Practically flying."

"And then you run out of batteries and fall flat."

Arty and Load were standing close by, ready to demonstrate. "Run out of juice or something breaks down, you do this," said Arty. He pushed the chest bar forward and said, in a sharp whisper, "De-vest."

Immediately the whole exoskeleton collapsed, as if it suddenly discovered it had half a dozen knees and elbows built into it. There it was on the ground, in two neat piles, and Arty was completely free of it.

"But it doesn't run out very soon," said Load. "When Young Potus announced that we were going to research a fast-charging, lightweight, high-capacity battery, he knew perfectly well that we already had *this*." Load was now showing Cole the hip assembly of the exoskeleton. Cole flipped up the lid that Load had unlatched for him, and saw a power supply amounting to the bulk of four lantern batteries.

"That's all?" asked Cole. "What is it good for, ten minutes? Fifteen?"

"Two hours," said Mingo triumphantly.

Cat was back down from the bridge now. "I've field-tested it, Cole," he said. "Two hours of running, jumping—cross-country, urban, all around a stadium in the middle of the night. Two solid hours. And if I only walk with it, then it's good for four."

"Plus," said Load, "it recharges itself in direct sunlight."

"If you pee your pants, does it absorb it and turn it back into drinkable water?" asked Cole.

"Wrong sci-fi story," said Mingo. "This one turns it into beer."

"What if you step wrong?" asked Cole. "Does it keep you from breaking a leg?"

"It offers some protection when you walk at normal speeds," said Mingo. "When you run and jump and leap, then you have to be as careful as you normally would doing that stuff. Only you're leaping four times as far, mile after mile. So yeah, it's protecting you some."

Cole looked around from one to another. "So whose baby is this?"

Mingo grinned.

"You invented it yourself?"

"I'm on the team. Combat consultant. I got them to make these three prototypes and let me field-test them with the best soldiers that I knew."

"I'm hurt that I wasn't in the A-team," said Cole.

"Well, see, you *are*—for the new stuff," said Mingo. "What you just saw, we've been doing that for a year now. It takes a long time to get through the learning curve—when you first start out doing anything other than trudging along, you tend to fall over a lot. Now we've added something new that makes it even harder to learn. Only now it's brains, not skills, so we thought of you."

"I'm flattered," said Cole. "I think."

"There's your problem," said Mingo. "Second-guessing everything." He led Cole over to one of the other cars—a Honda Accord, which was probably Arty's, since he always talked about how you couldn't kill one with a tornado. The trunk popped open and there were a bunch of helmets.

"I get it," said Cole. "You do all the same stuff, only now you do it on your head."

Mingo handed out helmets to all of them.

"One size fits all?" asked Cole.

"It sizes itself. If you feel a slight tingle as it adjusts, don't mind it. It's synching to your brain waves."

Cole laughed.

"He laughs, but it's no joke," said Arty. "It's calibrating your eye movements and then finding what part of your brain is controlling them. It learns to recognize your eye movements from the brain waves alone."

"So train it," said Mingo. "When you've got it on. Like this." Mingo stood close to Cole, so he could see, in the darkness, everything Mingo did.

"Mode. Adapt," he said. "Command. Go." And then he clicked his tongue. "Okay, what I just did was put it into the mode to learn a new soldier's pattern. Then I told it that the 'go' command—like pressing ENTER on a keyboard—was that click. So watch my eyes now."

Mingo clicked his tongue twice, then a pause, then twice again. He looked up and to the right, then down to the right, then up to the left, down to the right, down to the left, down to the right.

"See, you don't use straight up or straight down for commands, or straight left or right," said Arty, "because you've got to do that all the time in combat. And if you *do* look up to the right, for instance, but you do it slowly, with your head following the movement, it knows not to obey it as a command, because you're just looking up and to the right. See?"

"No," said Cole, "but I have a feeling that I will."

With his own helmet on, Cole got the training pattern right the first try. Then, with the helmet active, he began to see what these commands did.

Up right brought up a display in front of his eyes showing vital statistics on eight different soldiers. "The first one is yourself," Mingo explained.

"I'm happy to report that I have full health. If it ever falls too low, can I replenish it by inserting another couple of quarters?"

"In combat," said Mingo, "it also monitors the number of shots you've fired and tells you when you're going to need to reload soon."

"Does it tell me when I need to pee?" asked Cole.

"Only if you're wearing a catheter," said Mingo.

"Or a condom," said Load.

Cole tried the up-left command. This one was really disconcerting—it put a circular picture in the middle of his vision. After a moment, he realized that what he was seeing was himself—from Load's point of view.

"You can cycle through the field of vision of all seven members of your team," said Mingo. "But we don't use the click command. It's jaw movement—sharp downward movement, but without opening the mouth. So as commander, at any time you can see exactly what each man on your team is seeing."

"Meanwhile, I get shot because I'm not watching out for myself."

"Like I said, there's a learning curve," said Mingo. "But it doesn't take long before your brain lets you watch both things at once. Like focused vision and peripheral vision."

Cole passed his hand through the air in front of his face. The other guys laughed. "Come on," Cole said, "where's the display I'm seeing?"

Mingo reached up and touched the two flexible rods that extended forward from the helmet at cheekbone level. Instantly the display disappeared. When Mingo removed his fingers, the display returned.

"I figured those were the projectors," said Cole, "but what are they projecting onto?"

"Your corneas," said Mingo. "It even adjusts for contact lenses, if you wear them. For a while they tried to project directly onto the retina, but then the projectors really did interfere with your normal range of vision. Plus they were worried about side effects from projecting directly into the eye. So they project from the sides onto the cornea directly over the lens of each eye. It does both eyes at once so you'll have depth perception. But also if one of them is damaged, the other can do it alone. It only projects onto the one eye, so it's not as clear, but it'll do."

Down left and down right didn't do anything at all. Mingo explained. "The down-left command puts you in contact with home base. Whatever they want to make available to you, it comes in on that display command. And the down-right command puts you in sync with your DCGS, so they can feed you information from any UASs you have, up to four drones—Pred or Reaper, view of ground or air, live camera or a data display. Only we aren't synced with any DCGS right now, and besides, it takes about a week of wearing the helmet before the drone display stops making you throw up."

Not being connected to any station of the DCGS— the distributed common ground system that relayed data from Unmanned Aerial Systems, or drones— meant that what they were doing here was definitely off the books. But that was par for the course with Rube's jeesh.

Cole took the helmet off. "This is a field commander's best dream. To know all the time what your guys are doing. *How* they're doing. But it scares me."

"Come on," said Mingo. "Afraid it'll fry your brains?"

"I'm afraid I'll get too dependent on it, and then it'll cut out on me in combat."

"It could happen," said Mingo, "but the only things that could do it would probably also blow up your head."

"What if there's a heavy concrete wall between us?"

"That's the beautiful thing," said Mingo. "It has two redundant transmission systems for you and your team. There's radio, but there's also an ultra-low-frequency digital sound system. If you get far enough apart and you're using the sound transmission system, the display gets a little blocky."

"Pixelated," said Arty helpfully.

"Twitterpated," said Load.

"Pixelated," insisted Arty.

"I do believe in pixies, I do, I do," said Load.

"This helmet is smarter than I am," said Cole.

"And the exoskeleton is stronger," said Mingo. "But you're the one telling them both what to do."

"So what's the mission?" asked Cole.

The men glanced at each other. "No mission," said Mingo. "I mean, you're the guy who has the President's ear. What if he had something special for you to do? You could say, 'I've been practicing with the boys and we've got some good tricks.'"

"So you can take these prototypes out of the country?" asked Cole.

"If we need to," said Mingo. "The helmets aren't a prototype, they're in production. And within two weeks, we'll have enough exos for the whole jeesh."

"I'm going to need to take the time to learn how to use all this. Get fluent with it."

"Well," said Mingo, "this *is* my day job."

"And one thing I'm not clear on," said Cole. "You want me to learn how to do this *with* you guys? With me as commander? Those days are over, guys."

"Not for us," said Cat. "Look, man, we followed Rube, and all of us got used to our own niche. You came in, you learned our niches fast, you used us right. None of us were trained to do Rube's job—and so you did it. That's your niche. You don't choose the target, you just lead us in acquiring it. Like point guard on a basketball team."

"Meaning I'm not as tall and can't shoot as well, but I see the big picture and can tell you where to pass."

"No, that's basketball," said Cat.

"But you compared this to basketball. Point guard, right?"

"It was an *analogy*, Cole," said Cat. "We're not in the army anymore. We're all free agents. But when we play together, the team needs a leader just the same, and you're it."

"And you bring me in last."

Cat grinned. "Need to know, man."

"And you're not last," said Mingo. "These are all we've got in the loop right now. Babe, Drew, Benny, they've been out of town a lot, no time to learn it. We haven't even told Babe about it—he's all over India, trying to learn how to improve their advertising methods."

Cat imitated Babe's voice. "Just put a naked woman in the ad. Not your mother! A *young* woman. A *beautiful* woman."

"It's worth working on, don't you think?"

"Just one problem," said Cole. "What does an EMP do to this stuff?"

"What?" asked Mingo.

"An electromagnetic pulse," said Cole. "Like the thing Aldo Verus used to bring down two planes when his people took over New York City."

"I know what an EMP *is*," said Mingo. "But it took a howitzer-size piece of equipment. You think you're going to face an enemy that has one of *those* tucked under his arm?"

"I don't know what we're going to face. I'm just saying."

"EMP devices are like poison gas," said Mingo. "Anybody who uses it has to figure it'll get used against *him*."

"But what if we face an enemy that doesn't have any high-tech stuff for an EMP to affect?" asked Cole.

"Well, the EMP device would be a high-tech device, right?" asked Load. "If they've got no electronics, the EMP would be one of the electronics they ain't got none of."

Cole grinned. "Worst-case scenario?"

Cat gave an Elvis sneer. "Worst case, man, is me putting this foot deep inside your proctological zone."

"Do these exos come off so easy if their electronics

are fried? Or do you have to fight your way out of them while somebody's shooting at you?"

Load gave a command to shut down the exo he was wearing. Then he flipped the shoulder bar forward and gave it a sharp twist one way, then the other. His exoskeleton collapsed like a rag doll. "It's got a mechanical solution, too," said Mingo.

"By the way," said Cat, "we been calling them 'Bones' and 'Noodles,' on account of it taking longer to say 'exoskeleton' and 'electronically enhanced command helmet.'"

"I'm sold," said Cole. "I'll order a hundred thousand of them."

"Fully operational by 2015, at that number," said Mingo.

"But eight, for now," said Cole. "Unless you're adding somebody else to the team."

"Eight was good enough for Rube," said Cat. "And it was good enough for you, too, during the civil war. Don't see any reason to change."

"If Jesus could have trained his apostles better," said Mingo, "he wouldn't have needed twelve."

"Eight is enough," said Arty. "Who knew?"

"Unlike you lazy retired guys," said Cole, "I have to go to work in the morning. I also have to arrange the time off to train with you. Can I get back to you about all that?"

"Of course," said Mingo. "You'd better start biking home about now. I suggest cutting over to Highway 28 and taking that north to Dulles. Unless your buddy

Little POTUS is willing to send you air transport. Or, I guess, your own special train."

"Hey, I grew up with electric trains," said Cole. "Mine were just smaller. And Mingo, you promised to give me a ride back."

Mingo grinned. "I could give you your own set of Bones. It's way faster than the bike."

"But it attracts more attention. And I'd be likely to trip crossing the Potomac."

"Naw," said Cat, "you can leap the Potomac. At the falls, anyway."

"Now wouldn't *that* have been useful a few years ago."

Of course they all knew he was referring to the day Rube got murdered—they had to rescue Cole from the middle of the river, where Aldo Verus's walking tanks had him pinned down after a crazy chase through D.C.

"Just remember," said Arty. "This isn't an *Iron Man* comic. There's no shielding. Unless you wear Kevlar."

"So I'm not bulletproof."

"But you *can* leap short buildings in a—"

"In a single bound," said Cole. "I'm getting it."

"And . . . don't tell the President yet, okay?" asked Load.

"Tell him what?" asked Cole. "You mean he doesn't know about it?"

"He doesn't know that this technology is in our hands," said Mingo. "And he probably doesn't know how effective it is. But hey, we could jump the White

House gates in front of the Secret Service and be inside before they started shooting at us."

"Let's not put that to a test just yet," said Cole.

The others laughed. A little nervously, or so it seemed to Cole.

After Mingo dropped him off in front of his rooming house, as he carried his bike upstairs Cole thought back on the conversation and wondered why they had used breaking into the White House as their example. Just because it was so well defended that it symbolized a tough target? Or was there something else on their minds?

FIUE

SURUIUOR

We keep gathering together in ever-larger communities. Towns. City-states. Kingdoms. Empires. The art of living together in large numbers is called "civilization," and people who can get along well in such an intense social setting are called "civilized."

But we must never forget that the only reason humans keep banding together in ever-larger numbers is because it enhances our ability to survive as a species. If it did not do so, those human traits we call "civilized" would have been extinguished generations ago, and the traits we call "barbaric" would have predominated.

The job of families is to create children and rear them to carry out all the behaviors that promote the survival of the civilization. Families use the civilization to enhance their children's ability to reproduce successfully by expanding the gene pool and ensuring the general prosperity; a civilization uses families to perpetuate the successful values and behaviors of that civilization so it can persist across time and continue giving its members superior ability to reproduce.

The laws of evolution apply to civilizations as surely as to species and individuals: Only the fittest survive.

So it is a foolish civilization that ever acts in such a way as to interfere with the successful reproduction of its own citizens. Whether consciously or not, the citizens of such a civilization will abandon it, either by moving away or by reducing their allegiance to it until they are willing to see it be conquered, overthrown, or culturally transformed back into a reproduction-enhancing entity.

Civilizations fall either when they stop working, or when they are confronted by a civilization that is better at its job.

CHINMA WAS up a tree, checking on his money, when the thugs arrived. Chinma knew it was wrong to care about his stash when the family was in such desperate straits. But Father had refused to take his money when Chinma offered it. And now Father was dead and the family was poorer than ever. Nor was there any help to be had from the rest of the tribe. Half of them were dead, the survivors struggling just to keep their poor farms productive.

Chinma knew he should offer the money to his mother. But he didn't trust her to use the money wisely. This was a terrible thing to think about his own mother, he knew. But she was too smart for her own good sometimes. And too good at other times to be very smart. She might turn the money over to the new chief—whoever that would be, now that Father was dead, and all of his most promising sons. Or she might take the money and flee alone back to Yoruba lands, where she had been born and raised; and whether she would take Chinma or not, he could not be sure.

But what could he, a twelve-year-old boy still

emaciated from the ravages of the monkey sickness, do with this much money? There was nothing to buy in the village, and no way to get from the village to Ilorin, and there was no city closer. Besides, they had heard that everyone in Ilorin was sick or dying or dead now.

Chinma was not stupid. He knew that it was *his* illness, which he caught from the monkey sneeze, that was spreading now, not Ire's sickness, for the people got sick the way Chinma had, very slowly, with sneezing first and then headache and mucus in the lungs and then coughing so violent that you could tear muscles or break ribs, and then the constipation and the diarrhea and the unbearable thirst. And, if you were going to die, bleeding from the eyes and nose and ears, which spurted a little with every sneeze or cough.

But Chinma had not bled, nor had his mother, nor his brother Ade.

Could he ask Ade what to do? No. Once Ade would have been wise, but now he stayed always near to Mother, doing only what she asked. It made a kind of sense—Mother had nursed Ade carefully through his long illness, and then he had nursed her in turn when he was better and Mother had caught the disease from him. Ade now belonged to Mother, body and soul.

Chinma felt no such loyalty. Mother had *not* tended him. Only her eldest son was worth the risk. When the illness was at its worst, Chinma had had to crawl to the river and drink. They wouldn't even share the filtered water that they drank in the house. And then when *they* were so sick they couldn't get up to fill their cups from the filtered water, and the filter jug was empty anyway, he brought them water from the river, a little at a time because he was so weak he couldn't carry a full pail. He tried his best to help them, but he gave up when Mother screamed at him because his baby sister died and said it was because he brought dirty river water to them.

Chinma had lived without anybody's help. What did he owe to any of them now? He had earned this monkey money. *He* wasn't the one who made the monkeys sick. And what if he had come down the tree and said to Ire, "I don't think we should take these monkeys, they sneeze and bite"? Ire would have laughed at him and called him a baby, and then if he still wouldn't bring them down, Ire would have beaten him until he *did* go up and get them. Chinma had not been given any choices, except one—to be careful not to let the papa monkey bite him. He would be dead now like Ire if he had. So all that was in Chinma's power, all that had ever been in his power, was to save his own life as best he could.

He was about to come down from the tree when three trucks came roaring into the village. This never happened—who did they know who was rich enough to own three trucks? Men leaped out of the trucks with automatic weapons and started firing. These were not warnings—they aimed at people and shot them down. They fired into the houses and huts at hip level.

Chinma's family and fellow villagers ran screaming toward the forest, but the bullets followed them. They spared no one—not the babies, and not the women, not even to rape them as Chinma had heard such raiders always did.

There was nothing Chinma could do to help. He could only cling to his branch and hope that they didn't look up. A glance would not reveal him if he held very still, but there were not so many leaves between Chinma and the ground that if they actually searched the treetops they would fail to see him.

But they did not look up. Why would they? There were only birds and monkeys in the trees, not boys— why would there be a boy in the trees?

Only when the shooting stopped did Chinma remember the little camera in his pocket, the one the scientist had given him. When he was sick no one had found it because no one took care of him or even came near him.

Chinma knew that the camera ran on batteries. That's why he had never taken a picture with it—for fear that the batteries would run down before he could get to a computer. But now he would take pictures so people could see what these robbers had done to his village.

So from the tree he took three pictures, of three bodies he could see lying on the ground. Two of the pictures also had robbers in them. And then one of them came to the others dangling one of Chinma's baby nephews by the ankles. Chinma couldn't see which one it was, but it had to either be Ire's youngest or little Iko, Ire's sister's son, because they were the only babies that had lived through the plague. The baby was crying.

The ruffians laughed, except for one who seemed to be in charge, because he started yelling at them in Hausa. Chinma only knew a little Hausa, and only because it was the language of the northern Muslims who ruled Nigeria. But he understood enough to know that some of what he said was: "Do you want to get sick? Do you want to die? I told you not to touch anybody! This is the place where the sneezing sickness started!"

So all of this death had come to the village because of Chinma, after all. Everything began with his catching those sick monkeys. But he hadn't chosen them, had he? He couldn't help that he got sneezed on—how could he know the monkey would do that? He didn't make it happen, he was the second victim, after Ire.

And why would these men come here to kill everybody when the disease had already swept through the whole tribe? Everyone knew that once you caught a sickness from another person, if you lived through it you couldn't catch it again. This was the one place in all of Nigeria where it was certain you could *not* catch the monkey sickness. Yet they had come here and killed them all. Ignorant, stupid robbers. Why was it their business anyway?

The man in charge was still yelling, and the other men were still gathered around the baby, when more trucks arrived. Only this time it wasn't robbers. This time it was the army.

For a moment Chinma expected the soldiers to start shooting, to kill these robbers and punish them for having wiped out the village. But instead, the soldiers walked through the village checking to make sure everyone was dead. Now and then there was a gunshot.

The boss of the soldiers walked to about ten paces away from the boss of the robbers and demanded, "Did any get away?"

The thieves all shook their heads vehemently.

The soldier boss pointed with his weapon at the baby, which was now lying on the ground, still crying softly. "Why is that alive? Who touched it?"

The robber who had carried the baby tentatively raised his hand.

"Pick it up!" shouted the soldier boss.

The robber picked up the baby. Nobody was laughing now.

"Toss it up, high in the air!" shouted the soldier boss.

It was as if the robber was trying to toss the baby to Chinma, it came straight toward him.

The soldier boss raised his weapon and fired a long burst. Because of the angle from where the soldier boss was, the bullets cut through the leaves about twenty feet from Chinma, but still he flinched. He didn't know if he got a picture or not, but he had pushed the button as soon as the firing started, and maybe he pushed it more than once. He was so scared his hands trembled, and because of that he almost lost his hold on the branch, and then he almost dropped the camera, and then he made a noise, a loud gasp.

But they didn't hear him, because the robbers were laughing and saying, "Good shot! Good shooting!"

some in English and some in Yoruba, but none of them in Hausa.

When he was done with firing, the soldier boss yelled again, but in English now, to be sure they all understood him. "Did you find anybody else and keep them alive? Did anybody get away? Tell the truth!"

The robbers all swore that they had killed everybody, the villagers were all dead, nobody got away. Chinma got the insane idea of screaming at them that they were not as smart as they thought, *he* had gotten away. But he held his tongue.

The soldier chief walked away, and as he did, he replaced the clip on his weapon. The robbers started heading back toward their trucks. Then the soldier boss turned around again and started firing, but this time at the robbers. Since the robbers were all armed, some of them tried to defend themselves. But there were other soldiers already in place to cut them down from the sides.

Many of the bullets hit the trunk of the tree Chinma was clinging to, and he felt the sharp vibrations all the way up to his high branches.

When all the robbers were dead, the soldier boss called one of his men—in Hausa that Chinma could not understand at all—but the order he gave became clear when the man fired a flamethrower at the corpses of the robbers. The flames kept coming out and coming out, and the burning bodies stank and the smoke came right up to where Chinma was and it was all he could do not to cough at the smoke and the stink.

He was also afraid that the tree would catch on fire, forcing him to climb down and die, but there had been plenty of rain and the wood did not burn. The flame-thrower soldier moved away and then set fire to every building in the village and every body lying on the ground.

Then two more trucks came, not army trucks but flatbeds that each carried a bulldozer. The drivers of the bulldozers wore masks on their faces like the doctor and the nurse had worn. They drove their bulldozers through the village, knocking everything down and pushing all the bodies into the flames of the ruined houses. They worked for another half hour, piling dirt on top of the fires so everything was covered. They also knocked down three trees, but not the one Chinma was in.

When the bulldozers were back on the flatbed trucks, the soldier boss held up a thick wad of naira and the bulldozer drivers came toward him. The soldier boss also waved to the drivers of the flatbed trucks and they got out of the cabs and came to him. When they were all in place, the soldier boss drew his pistol and shot them all.

Chinma got pictures of them. And of the flame-thrower soldier burning their bodies, too. Then soldiers got into the flatbed trucks and drove them away. Soldiers also drove away the army trucks and the robber trucks, but they left the family's truck burning.

Chinma stayed in the tree all the rest of the day, and

all that night, even though mosquitoes found him and for all he knew were infecting him with sleeping sickness and malaria and every other disease. Better to die of a disease than for the soldiers to realize he was still alive and come back for him.

But they did not come back.

Chinma didn't know how many pictures the camera could hold, but the next morning when he came down, carrying the camera and his money, parched with thirst and soaked with urine, he did not let himself go to the river and drink until he had taken pictures of the burned wreckage of the houses and the charred bodies that were still visible, especially the bodies of the bulldozer and flatbed truck drivers.

Then he went to the hiding place of the notebook the scientist gave him, watching all the time for soldiers or robbers or anyone at all, but there was no one. He went back into the underbrush until he was not visible from any road, and sat for three hours, writing down everything that happened. He couldn't stop himself from writing, I'm sorry, I'm sorry, over and over, even though he knew it was not really his fault. He wasn't even sure what he was sorry for. Sometimes he was sorry for having brought the sickness to the village instead of dying quickly the way Ire had. Other times he was sorry that he had been up a tree instead of dying with the rest of his family.

He knew that he was bad at writing. Everyone said he made the letters wrong and wrote them on top of one another or even went backward on the line, but he tried very hard to keep the words in order and leave spaces between them.

When he was through writing, he put the notebook back in the plastic bag and tucked it inside the waist of his pants and pulled his shirt down over it. Then he began to walk.

He walked first to the nearest Ayere-speaking village, but exactly the same thing had happened there. He took a few more pictures and wrote a little more in the notebook. He did not bother going to any of the other Ayere villages. He knew now what the government had done. They were all Muslims and Hausas and stupid—even if they figured out that the safest villages in all of Nigeria were the Ayere villages, since the disease had passed through them first and was gone, they didn't care. They wanted to kill the Ayere, whether to stop the plague or punish them for starting it, and because they had never cared about the non-Muslims and non-Hausas, except to make sure they did their jobs, paid their taxes, and kept their mouths shut, they did not hesitate—they killed every Ayere.

Except one.

He made his way through the brush beside the highway, only coming out onto the road in order to use its bridges to cross streams or go over deep gullies. It took him till well after dark before he got to Ilorin, but that was fine with him, he did not want to come there in daylight.

Chinma did not know where to go or whom to talk to. Anybody might be working for the government. And he had no idea where to find the scientists from the World Health Organization.

So he curled up behind rusty oil barrels near the railway station and slept the rest of the night. Maybe the oil fumes kept the mosquitoes away, because he wasn't bitten any more that night, but he did wake up with a slight headache.

By daylight, he could see that Ilorin was like a ghost town. He did not know that there was a complete curfew; there was no one on the streets to tell him. Every now and then he heard a vehicle, but he always hid himself, and that was the right thing to do, because the only cars and trucks belonged to the army. The soldiers were all wearing doctors' masks.

I hope a monkey sneezes on you, thought Chinma. I hope a monkey *bites* you, every one of you.

Finally, he came to a huge tent that covered a parking lot, and saw people in white hazard suits going in and out. Scientists. He could trust the scientists.

But there might also be soldiers, so he found a route that kept him mostly out of sight until he could make a short dash to the tent and then slide under the edge of it instead of going through the big door.

He came up behind a stack of metal boxes that were marked with strange words in English. They might be medicines. They might be food. Chinma was very hungry, and thirsty again, too, and he knew that he smelled very bad. But he had his camera and his notebook and he had to give it to someone who wouldn't just destroy it.

So he crept out from behind the boxes and looked around. People were bustling all over, and inside the tent many of them were not wearing hazard suits, though everyone had doctors' masks on. Chinma saw that most of the faces were black, which meant they were probably Nigerians and might or might not be in the pay of the government. But there were white faces, too, and when he saw a white man sitting at a computer, typing, he made his way toward him, pulling out the bag containing the camera and the notebook and the pencil.

The man looked at him and then jumped a little, startled.

Chinma held out the plastic bag. "I have pictures for the computer," he said in his best English.

"How the hell did you get in here?" demanded the man.

"Pictures for the computer," said Chinma.

"Are you out of your mind?" the man said. "Are you trying to infect everybody?"

"I was already sick and I'm better now," said Chinma.

"A survivor?" asked the man.

Chinma didn't know that English word. "I have pictures for the computer."

The man reached for the bag, then jerked his hand

away. He got up, walked a few paces away, and came back pulling rubber gloves onto his hands. Then he took the bag, which by now Chinma had opened.

The man took out the camera, looked at it, and then rummaged in a box on the floor under the table until he came up with a cord, which he attached to the computer and to the camera.

Chinma was shaking as he watched the man type and move the computer mouse and type again.

And then the pictures came up onto the screen, tiny pictures, lots of them.

"They are very small," said Chinma.

"These are just thumbnails," said the white man. He moved the mouse and clicked it and one picture filled the screen. It was a picture of two of Chinma's sisters, lying dead on the ground.

"Aw, kid, don't you know? We've got a hundred thousand dead people, we don't need pictures of more."

Chinma was puzzled for a moment. Had the soldiers killed so many?

Then he realized—the man hadn't seen the bullet wounds. He thought they were dead of the monkey sickness.

"Guns," said Chinma. He pantomimed holding an automatic weapon. "Huh-huh-huh-huh-huh-huh," he said, like the sound of the gun.

A passing black woman saw him and immediately rushed toward him. "What are you doing!" she shouted. "Trying to infect Dr. Wangerin?" And then she turned to Dr. Wangerin. "This tent has been contaminated and your president's quarantine now makes it impossible for you to leave!"

"The boy's all right," said the white man—Dr. Wangerin. "He already had the nictovirus and he hasn't contaminated anything. What I'm looking at now is something very different. Acute lead poisoning."

He clicked again and a new picture came up. This time it was a picture of the soldier with the flame-thrower setting fire to the bodies of the robbers.

The Nigerian woman's eyes got big and she began to move away.

"Stop right there," said Dr. Wangerin. "Where do you think you're going?"

"She tells the government about the pictures," said Chinma.

The woman shook her head and put out her hands as if to ward off Chinma's words.

"The government pay her to tell on you," said Chinma. Any Nigerian would know this, from the way she was acting. But of course the white people would have no idea.

"Sit down!" said Dr. Wangerin to the Nigerian woman. Looking terrified, she obeyed. "Security!" he shouted.

Within a few moments she was in handcuffs and in the custody of two white men with pistols. Meanwhile, the light-haired security man noticed Chinma, and despite Dr. Wangerin's assurances, he seemed very angry with the dark-haired one.

"Never mind the boy," said Dr. Wangerin.

"Complete mission failure," said the light-haired gunman to his companion.

"Your mission now is Dr. Bekaba," said Wangerin. "She doesn't leave this place until I say so."

"We have to turn her over to the authorities," said the dark-haired security man. "Those are the conditions of our work here."

"Yes," said Dr. Wangerin. "But not for one hour. Got it? She talks to no one, and no Nigerian comes anywhere near me for one hour. Then you can turn her over to the police—which is probably who she's working for anyway."

"The police shoot her," said Chinma.

"What?" asked Dr. Wangerin. "She's their spy."

Chinma shrugged. A spy who got caught by Americans would simply be shot, and then they'd pretend she was working for some rebel group instead of the government. Why didn't these white people understand how things worked in Nigeria?

Dr. Wangerin turned back to the pictures, showing them now to the men with guns.

"It's mass murder," whispered the light-haired gunman.

Dr. Wangerin did something and the computer did something and then he detached a little square thing from his computer and handed it to one of the men with guns. "Get out of this country immediately and take this with you."

"The next plane leaves in—"

"The next plane leaves when I say it does. It has to leave before we turn this woman loose. Do you understand?"

"Of course," said the light-haired gunman. "But can't you just email it?"

"I'm going to try that as soon as you're in the air and gone," said Dr. Wangerin. "We don't know how closely they monitor what we send on the internet, though. So as soon as I start transmitting, they might arrest us all and take our computers."

The woman spoke up. "They will shoot the boy immediately."

The three white men looked at her.

"Please take him and me out of the country with you or we are both dead."

Dr. Wangerin started to explain to her. "We can't take Nigerians to America without visas, it would be—"

The light-haired gunman interrupted him. "I think these pictures will make a clear case that this boy needs immediate political asylum. It's within my authority to bring him in to a military base. Dr. Bekaba is another matter. As a Nigerian government spy, we can't take her. But if we consider her this boy's guardian, we can't leave without her."

"She was going to turn him in," said Dr. Wangerin acidly.

"The boy is right," she said. "If I stay here, I'm dead. I will not harm the boy."

Dr. Wangerin rolled his eyes. "Do you think I'm stupid? If you had a way to do it, you'd kill him right now."

"I would not," she said. "I'm a scientist!"

"You're a spy working for a bunch of thugs."

"We're all spies, if they tell us to be spies," Dr. Bekaba said. "Or else they kill our families. I'm not a *spy* by choice."

Chinma could understand English much better than he spoke it, and he had gotten the idea that they were going to take him out of Nigeria.

"Can I have my notebook?" he asked.

"Is this evidence?" asked Dr. Wangerin, holding it up.

"I write everything."

Dr. Wangerin turned to the dark-haired gunman. "Then get this scanned and I'll send it as a PDF first, before the pictures."

"I write in my language," said Chinma.

Dr. Wangerin looked at him for a long moment. "What language is that?"

"Ayere," said Chinma.

Dr. Wangerin turned to the woman. "Do you speak Ayere?"

She shook her head. "Nobody speaks Ayere. Just a few thousand people in a half-dozen villages north of here."

"All dead," said Chinma.

Dr. Wangerin looked at him, then glanced back at the pictures. "The Ayere-speakers—that's where the nictovirus first appeared, wasn't it?"

Chinma had figured out that *nictovirus* was the

English word for monkey sickness. "I get sick first," said Chinma. "Monkey spit on me." But he knew *spit* wasn't the right word. So he pretended to sneeze.

Immediately the others recoiled from him as if he had just set off a flamethrower.

"No, no, not sick!" said Chinma. "I show you monkey! Monkey do this." And he faked another sneeze, but not so realistically this time.

"You mean 'sneeze,'" said the light-haired gunman.

Dr. Wangerin looked at him now with a kind of awe. "You were—you were the first person infected?"

"Monkey bite my brother Ire," said Chinma. "Monkey . . . *sneeze* me."

"'Ire' was the name of the first victim of the aggressive form of the disease," said Dr. Wangerin. "I think the disease nexus just walked into our tent."

"That is why they kill my village," said Chinma. "I writed it in my notebook."

"I believe him," said Dr. Bekaba. "Of course they'd kill all the Ayere-speaking people. To punish them for starting this plague."

"So nobody can read his language except the boy himself?" asked the light-haired gunman.

Dr. Bekaba shook her head. "There are language experts in some of the universities here."

"Are there any in the United States?"

"I wouldn't know," she said. "Probably. Specialists in obscure African languages. And the boy doesn't speak English well enough to translate it himself. But he speaks Yoruba, don't you, boy?"

Chinma nodded.

"I speak Yoruba, like everybody around here," she said. "He can translate it into Yoruba and I'll render it in English. On the plane."

"Under close supervision and wearing the handcuffs every moment," said Dr. Wangerin.

Chinma thought Dr. Wangerin was very smart.

So did Dr. Bekaba. "As soon as I'm gone, they'll kill my family."

"We know your address. Will all your family be at home?" asked Dr. Wangerin.

"Yes, everybody's at home, because of the curfew," she said.

"I'll send an ambulance for them," said Dr. Wangerin. "We'll tell the authorities that we have reason to believe your family has been infected but we need to study them while still alive to observe the course of the disease. So they'll let us bring them here."

Dr. Bekaba nodded.

"We'll have to lie to your family, too," said Dr. Wangerin. "Until you're all in the air and out of here."

She nodded again.

Dr. Wangerin turned to Chinma. "You did the right thing, young man. These pictures—I think they'll bring down the Nigerian government."

"I think they'll start a civil war," said the light-haired gunman.

"How did you get a camera?" asked Dr. Wangerin.

Chinma turned to Dr. Bekaba and explained to her in Yoruba about the Nigerian scientist who rode with him out to see the trees where he had caught the monkeys. "I never knew his name," he said.

Dr. Bekaba translated for Dr. Wangerin, who nodded. "The other nexus," he said. "Now we know he didn't get a second, new infection from the monkeys out in the bush, he got it from this boy."

It took a moment, and then Chinma understood. The Nigerian scientist who gave him the notebook was dead.

He burst into tears. The scientist had been good to him. And Chinma had infected him, just like Father and all the others who died. In a way, even the villagers killed by the robbers and the army had died from Chinma's infection, too.

Since Dr. Bekaba had translated only what Chinma had told her, nobody knew why he was suddenly crying.

"Poor kid," said Dr. Wangerin. "He's lost his whole family." But Chinma's family had already abandoned him to die when he got sick. He had no more tears for them.

"He's lost his *country*," said Dr. Bekaba, though she was the one who would feel that loss, not Chinma. He had no country now.

"He's crying because he knows he's safe now," said the light-haired gunman.

"He's not safe," said Dr. Wangerin, "until he's out of Nigerian airspace. See to it that it happens, Captain Austin."

"Yes, sir," said the light-haired gunman. "And I can

promise you, President Torrent will know this boy's whole story within three hours."

"Oh, you have the President's private number?" asked Dr. Wangerin, amused.

"No," said Austin. "But I know someone who does." Then he turned to Chinma. "It's going to take a few minutes to get this set up. No offense, kid, but you stink. I'm going to strip you and hose you down and give you clean clothes. All right?"

Chinma stopped crying and nodded. "Thank you very much, sir," he said.

"The kid's polite," said Austin. "Maybe I'll get him in to meet the President."

"First get him and his notes to somebody who can speak Ayere, and get that SD chip to the proper authorities."

"Bullshit," said Austin. "I'll get these pictures *and* the photocopies of the kid's notes up on YouTube and Facebook and everywhere else I can post them. *Then* the authorities can have them."

Dr. Wangerin nodded. "You're right. We don't want this to get buried."

"Our government may not be run by thugs," said Austin, "but all governments think that the people shouldn't be told anything. So we'll tell the people first. The genocide of an entire tribe is *not* going to be kept secret in order to preserve our good relations with Nigeria."

Dr. Wangerin frowned. "That means they might shut us down here."

"And how much more were you going to accomplish?" asked Austin. "The nictovirus is out of the bag. There's no boundary in Africa that's going to keep it in now."

Dr. Wangerin looked at Austin with new interest. "You've had that opinion for a long time, but you haven't said a thing till now."

"Not my mission," said Austin.

Dr. Wangerin stood up. "Well, you're right. Hose down the boy. Keep Dr. Bekaba in custody and do not trust her to be alone with the boy or even close to him. Maybe she hates the government as much as she says, but maybe she'd also do whatever it took to bring down the plane with him on it—and you and those notes and that chip. And me. Because I'm going with you."

"You are?" asked Austin.

"Once this goes public," said Dr. Wangerin, "my work here will be finished. So I'm leaving now instead of waiting for the embassy to work out a deal to get me out."

All Chinma understood was that he was going to America and he was getting a bath.

"Food?" he asked. "Water?"

"You got your priorities straight, kid," said Austin. "Water, food, a bath, clean clothes, and then an airplane."

"My name is Chinma."

"Chinma," Austin repeated.

"I am the last Ayere," said Chinma proudly. Because Ayeres were always proud to be Ayere.

SIX

THE REAL WORLD

In a world with real menaces, it always struck me as a kind of wishful thinking, this notion that global warming was our most urgent danger, one so dire that it was worth the risk of wrecking the world economy in order to take steps that everyone admitted would be futile—even if human activities *were* causing global warming, a fact nowhere in evidence.

Throughout the entire time that the global warming alarmists were savagely attacking anyone who dared to raise a voice of reason, this fact remained clear to anyone who cared to notice: The world was markedly warmer in 1000 a.d. than it is today, without anything like present human carbon emissions. The sea level was higher, and the human race coped with it. The weather was more clement, we had fewer terrible storms, our harvests were bigger than normal, we suffered fewer losses from disease, and yet somehow the human race managed to muddle through the crisis.

Our global warming bubble thrived on ignorance—of science and of history. Then we were faced with a real danger: the nictovirus, the "sneezing flu." Isn't it astonishing how quickly any mention of global warming simply disappeared? It was hard to get very exercised about warm weather when a rampant new disease was killing between thirty and fifty percent of those who caught it.

Yet there are those who heard the news of this devastating epidemic with, I'm sad to say, feelings of relief. If this became a pandemic, it would accomplish what they had long desired: the decimation or, if I may coin a word, the dimidiation of the human race. Fifty percent kill-off? Just what they were hoping for, to get the world population closer to sustainable levels.

They'll deny it, of course. They'll pretend to be shocked that the President of the United States would say something so terrible. But I have read what they wrote over the past ten, twenty, thirty years, and I have done something unforgivable: I remembered it.

Sane people will do all they can to preserve every human life that *can* be preserved. Only the utterly uncompassionate will take satisfaction in the thought that the nictovirus will "reduce the surplus population."

Yet even now, these very voices pretend to be compassionate. They claim there is something unfair or even racist about forcing Africa to suffer this epidemic alone, and demand that the quarantine of Africa be lifted. What is their purpose? To allow the nictovirus to spread outside the confines of Africa and kill off a third to a half of the human race.

Here is the truth about these people: They want us dead. They have always wanted us dead—along with five and a half billion of our fellow human beings. But you and I and every other decent, compassionate person on this planet take the opposite view: We are determined to save every life we can by preventing the spread of this disease until we have developed a vaccine or an effective treatment.

"TOO INTELLECTUAL," said Cecily.

Mark, Nick, Lettie, and Annie were all in the living room with her, watching the President's speech on Fox News. Mark insisted on Fox because that was the news channel Dad always watched when there was any kind of important story.

"I understood him," said Mark.

"You're an intellectual," said Cecily. "I rest my case."

"*I* understood him," said Nick. "And I'm a video-game addict."

"It's about time we had a politician with a brain who thinks we have brains too," said Mark.

"Well excuse me for not having a brain," said Lettie, "but what does global warming have to do with the sneezing flu?"

"Didn't you know that global warming causes everything?" said Mark.

"Don't be sarcastic," said Cecily. "Lettie is like most of America—she has no idea what the President was saying."

"Maybe it was his strategy," said Mark. "Sound really smart so that the people believe you, imply that the global warming people are trying to spread the plague, and voilà: You've just demonized all your opposition."

Cecily recognized the echo of her own skepticism in her oldest son, and nodded glumly. "I hate it when Torrent plays raw politics like that."

"Is he right?" asked Nick. "Are there people who really want to cut the human race in half?"

"There is a segment of the environmental movement that believes the human race should never rise above a population of about half a billion," said Cecily. "They don't advocate doing it by means of an epidemic, but presumably they will think that cutting the human race in half is, to put it crudely, a step in the right direction."

"So he's right," said Nick.

"He's right-*ish*," said Cecily.

"Hey, you're the one who advises him," said Mark.

"I didn't advise him to demonize the environmental movement."

"Bet it works, though," said Nick. "I mean, they have to *deny* what he said, right? So they have to come out in favor of the quarantine, right?"

The phone rang. Cecily ignored it.

"Um, Mom," said Lettie.

"Um, Lettie," said Cecily, "there's nobody I want to talk to. If you're so worried, answer it yourself. But I'm not talking to anybody. Tell them I'm dead."

Lettie got up and walked into the kitchen, where the cordless phone hung on the wall. "Hello?"

"She's going to say you're dead," said Nick.

"Maybe it's not for me," said Cecily. "Did you think of that?"

Lettie walked into the room, talking into the phone. "I'm sorry, she's dead."

Cecily pantomimed screaming as Mark and Nick and Annie all laughed. "Give me the phone," she said.

"Oops," said Lettie into the phone. "She has risen

from her earthen grave and is reaching for the phone with mud and roots and a tattered apron hanging from her half-rotted arms. Do you wish to speak with Zombie Mom?"

"Give me that," said Cecily, getting steadily less amused as the other kids laughed even harder.

"Here she is," said Lettie, then handed it to Cecily, who snatched it with a half-serious glare at her oldest daughter. "Ow. The eyes of Satan," she said. "I've been zapped."

Cecily left the living room and leaned back against the kitchen counter. The edge of it cut into her butt. Which was fine with her—she was in the mood to feel a little pain. And to inflict some.

Of course it was Nate Ogzewalla on the phone, as she had known it would be. "Did you watch the speech?" he asked.

"Yes. It was really effective. We're getting up a mob in our neighborhood right now to tear all global warming believers from their homes and burn them at the stake."

"Oh, I see what your daughter meant about Zombie Mom."

"That speech was beneath him. Or if it wasn't, it should have been. The nictovirus is the villain, not environmentalists."

"Identifying and neutralizing the opposition is sound political strategy," said Nate. "Now all the controversy will be about whether the President should have been nicer or whether the environmentalists deserve—"

"I understand the theory, Nate," said Cecily. "I just don't agree that it justifies slandering a legitimate political movement."

"Meaning that you're a global warming alarmist?" asked Nate. "Your ox is being gored, is that it?"

"I'm an environmentalist. I knew the facts about global warming but I always thought it was a convenient way to get the world to take actions that are necessary whether humans are causing global warming or not."

"So I should put you down as pro-plague, then?" asked Nate.

"Am I on the radio, Mr. Limbaugh?" asked Cecily.

"Relax, I'm just teasing you," said Nate. "The President knew you'd hate this and he wanted me to call you just to reassure you that he is going to 'clarify' his statement later today to calm people down."

"He shouldn't have—"

"Shouldn't have riled them up in the first place, I hear you, Mrs. Malich. But he had to make a decision. He's got to rally support behind a ruthless policy of quarantine. He had to make it seem like somebody else was ruthlesser so that people would see the quarantine as an act of protection."

"'Ruthlesser' is a very ugly word," said Cecily.

"The official purpose of this call, Mrs. Malich, is to ask you one question."

"Ask it and then get off the phone," said Cecily.

"This is from the President himself, you understand."

"I understand. What's the question?"

"The question is: 'Are you still speaking to me?'"

Cecily sighed. "Tell him that he'll find out the answer to that when he speaks to me himself, instead of hiding behind his chief of staff."

"I'll tell him that it's a yes," said Nate.

"Of course I'm still speaking to him. I'm not thirteen, I don't give people the silent treatment. The question is whether there's any *point* in speaking to him, considering how often he decides against me."

"That's not fair, Mrs. Malich. He goes along with your views more than any other adviser he has."

"Ten percent of the time?"

"More like fifty, and nobody else is close. And he's going to need your advice more and more in the days to come, so please overlook this little act of evil on his part, and stay on the team? Please?"

"Yes," said Cecily, and then hung up.

"Wow," said Mark. "You really are angry about this."

Cecily looked toward the doorway to the living room and saw all four of the older children there, watching her. "None of you has the right security clearance to be listening to a conversation between the White House chief of staff and the 'President's most-trusted adviser.'"

"This quarantine," said Mark. "If refugees get on boats, like the boat people after the Vietnam War or the Cubans who fled to Florida, is he really going to have the Navy blow them up?"

"Yes," said Cecily. "But they'll give warnings and

humanitarian aid first, and if they turn back toward Africa our ships will escort them safely home."

"It doesn't sound very Christian," said Mark. Then he went upstairs.

Nick shrugged. "I guess Mark doesn't get it. This is the real world, not Mass." Then Nick headed upstairs.

Lettie and Annie stayed in the doorway, looking at her. "I know what Jesus would do," said Annie.

"No you don't," said Lettie.

"Absolutely I do too," said Annie. "He always healed the sick."

"Because he *could*," said Lettie. "He could do miracles."

"Our scientists are working as fast as they can on a vaccine and a cure," said Cecily.

"And meanwhile we're telling Africans to take a couple of Advils and call us in the morning?" said Lettie, in her snottiest voice.

Cecily sat down at the kitchen table. "It must be terrible over there. In Africa."

"It's always terrible," said Lettie. "Malaria. Sleeping sickness. And they don't even have clothes."

"They have clothes, Lettie," said Cecily.

"I've seen the pictures. They run around naked and their jugs hang down to here."

"Most Africans wear clothing like ours, only cooler," said Cecily. "Don't confuse Annie."

"I'm not confused," said Annie. "Remember, Lettie's been my big sister my whole life."

"While I had a couple of blissful years without Annie," said Lettie.

"Go away, children," said Cecily. "Mommy's thinking."

"Does that mean dinner's going to be late?" asked Lettie.

"Yes," said Cecily. "Either late or pizza."

"I vote Donato's," said Annie.

"Papa John's," said Lettie.

"Go away or I'll whip up a batch of oatmeal Jell-O."

"They don't have that flavor," said Lettie.

"I'll use orange Jell-O and put raw oats in it. Lots of fiber *and* horse hooves," said Cecily. "And since you refuse to go away, I'm going upstairs to my room so I can lock the door and get some thinking done."

They followed her up the stairs naming even-more-disgusting Jell-O flavors; Cecily didn't have the heart to tell them that some of them were real, at least according to stories about church suppers from her Protestant friends. Like carrots in orange Jell-O. And minimarshmallows in lime. But Lettie topped them all with her suggestion of "athlete's foot in licorice Jell-O." Cecily was laughing in spite of herself as she closed the door and locked it.

She wasn't thinking about the President's speech anymore. She was thinking about what Nick had said. "This is the real world, not Mass."

Somehow Nick had gotten the idea that being Christian was something you did at Mass, and the rest of the time you lived in the "real world." That was not what she and Reuben believed, not what they wanted their kids to learn.

And yet the President's quarantine policy was not very Christian. Or was it? Jesus healed lepers, but he didn't say that *un*healed lepers should be allowed to roam freely through society. He ate with the publicans, but not with the lepers. He healed the sick, he didn't let them run around infecting people.

Still, though, she felt there was something deeply wrong with blowing up boats full of people desperate to escape from a plague-ridden land. And it would certainly come to that. Maybe the President would find a way to keep footage of it from ending up on YouTube, but it would certainly happen. Or some refugees would rig their boat with explosives, and if the U.S. Navy refused to let them pass, they'd blow themselves up—as close to the American ship as they could. And they'd make sure there was another boat nearby, shooting video so everybody could see.

A public relations nightmare, but if she were African, especially if she were in a country where the nicto-virus hadn't come yet—which was most of Africa so far—she'd be plotting provocative acts to get America to change policy.

Or would she? Quarantine was sound practice in a deadly epidemic, and Africa had a long tradition of it. She remembered reading about it when ebola first surfaced and somebody wrote about it in *The New Yorker*. African villagers would seal up your house and leave food at the door. When you got so sick you couldn't get up to take the food anymore, they'd figure you were dead and burn the house down. It's how a village survived in an epidemic. How was President Torrent's policy any more ruthless? Was it just a matter of scale?

I have to think about this, she told herself. I haven't found the right answer yet. There has to be a middle way.

SEVEN

GENERAL COLEMAN

The right of a government to rule over the citizens of a nation is not absolute. It's like the right of parents over their children. As long as the parents take reasonable care of their children, they rule supreme in their home. But when they neglect them or beat them or misuse them to a degree that outrages the sensibilities of their neighbors, the children are taken away and given to someone who will protect and provide for them.

The standards for governments are much lower. They may arouse the disgust of their neighbors, but some truly vile governments have been able to abuse their citizens for many years without interference from outside. Nevertheless, there is a time when a government can go too far. When a government wages open war and conducts genocide against a portion of their populace, then any nation that has the power to intervene to protect the people from their government has a moral responsibility and a legal right to do so.

At this time in history, America is the nation most likely to have the means to intervene, if any nation does. This does not make us the policeman of the world. It's not our *job* to save people from every bad government. The question really is: Can we live with ourselves, as a people, if we have the power to prevent unspeakable evil, and yet we choose to do nothing?

We answered that question when we failed to intervene to save the lives of countless thousands in Bosnia and Rwanda; we answered it a different way when we intervened in Kosovo and Iraq. To intervene will almost certainly cost American lives; but to refuse to intervene deeply injures the American soul. Who are we as a people? When we decide that we're the good guys, the world will see that America does not lack for soldiers willing to risk their lives to help— no, to save—people in faraway lands.

COLE ASSUMED that he was called in to the White House because of something to do with the epidemic. Estonia and Latvia had both passed "honored visitors" legislation but they, like everyone else in the world, were watching the plague in Africa and following the news stories about reactions to President Torrent's declaration of a blockade of Africa.

It felt to Cole as if history were on hold. As if history were a game and he had been a professional player on one of the teams, but now the game had been called on account of plague. He had no expertise in any African language south of the Sahara, had no idea about the culture, and had even less of an idea about how to deal with an epidemic.

At the same time, the whole continent was in an uproar. Cameroon and Benin had both tried to stop the flood of Nigerian refugees, knowing perfectly well that many of those fleeing the nictovirus were already infected and would spread it wherever they went. But what good was it to guard the roads? People could take to the bush at any point and there was no stopping them. Nor was there time to build an Israeli-style fence. There were now reports that refugees had gone beyond Benin and were creating a refugee problem—and spreading the disease—in Togo, Ghana, and Burkina Faso.

With all this going on, why had Cole's name even crossed President Torrent's mind?

No use speculating when he was going to find out in a few minutes. Cole submitted to being scanned and searched—he understood the need for security, but couldn't help remembering that the last man elected to this office before Torrent had had all the same security in place, and somebody punched a rocket through a window where he was having a meeting with the Joint Chiefs, SecDef, and the National Security Adviser, killing all of them.

But just because the last successful assassination could not have been stopped by these security methods did not mean that they weren't still stopping other potential assassinations. Political murders could come from foreign powers, domestic revolutionaries, and nut jobs. White House security was primarily for stopping the nut jobs.

Of course, if I wanted to kill the President, I could do it with my bare hands before anyone in the room could stop me—unless there was another guy with special ops training, and even then, he'd have to be markedly better than me, if I had a head start.

Not that I would kill the President, thought Cole. But there's no guarantee that you won't get a nut job someday with genuine security clearances and superb military training.

If this president dies, thought Cole, it will probably be from this sneezing flu epidemic. Wasn't it an epidemic that struck down the Roman emperor Marcus Aurelius and his co-emperor Lucius Verus? Political and military power did not immunize you against viruses.

Thinking of Lucius Verus made Cole think of another Verus—Aldo Verus, who was still in prison for having led the conspiracy that seized New York City and tried to launch a civil war. Wouldn't it be ironic if this sneezing flu killed President Torrent, but left Aldo Verus unscathed? American prisons were probably as safe a place as any in the world right now. Certainly safer than shopping malls, movie theaters, or hospitals.

Cole found himself cooling his heels in a waiting room. He expected to wait a long time, since he had glimpsed the Joint Chiefs standing together in a much nicer waiting room. No way would Torrent keep *them* waiting in order to take a meeting with Cole!

So Cole's first surprise of the day was when he was called almost at once to a conference room and shown to a seat at the large conference table. Only a moment later, the Joint Chiefs were brought in—and seated at the same table. They looked even more surprised to see him than he was to see them. They were thinking, What are we doing at a meeting with *him*?

It was almost anticlimactic when the Secretary of Defense, Secretary of State, NSA, and Surgeon General came in. This was an African epidemic meeting, all right, and this group must have had many such meetings during the month since the sneezeborne version of the nictovirus first appeared. So what was Cole doing at this one?

President Torrent came in and didn't introduce anybody to anybody. He picked up as if they were in the middle of an unfinished meeting—which, in all likelihood, they were.

They began with reports from the Navy and Air Force about the blockade of Africa. SecDef pointed out that American forces in the rest of the world were stretched too thin—this would be the logical time for China to invade Taiwan, for instance. But now that the Chinese had pulled all their people out of Africa, they would watch what happened with the epidemic there just like everybody else. They'd hardly commit to a major war if they could expect to be savaged by an epidemic in mid-campaign.

"What worries me," said the President, "is North Africa. We made the decision to treat the Sahara as a better barrier than the Mediterranean, and Morocco, Algeria, and Libya insisted they'd take responsibility for blocking any traffic coming north. Which makes sense, since they don't want to have the epidemic reach their population, and they have no problem being ruthless with refugees. But how *capable* are they? How much can they detect at night or out in the desert?"

"The Horn of Africa concerns us more than the Sahara," said one of the Air Force generals. "Can Egypt and Sudan really keep their border sealed?"

"My concern is small boats in the Red Sea," said Torrent. "It's such a short distance to cross over into Arabia."

The brass went over what they had on that topic, and Cole thought, maybe I'm here because of the Horn of Africa problem. I speak Arabic fairly well. But then, the Arab countries of North Africa were making it a point to protect their own desert borders—and none of them had a history of welcoming American advisers.

The meeting went on for more than half an hour, talking about the UN and the NGOs, which had withdrawn all their people but were now clamoring about how to deliver aid on the continent. There was no mention of Cole's presence and certainly no one talked to him.

Finally, it began to sound as if they were wrapping up. Concluding remarks from everybody.

Until President Torrent said, "One more thing, and it's not small."

And without any other cue than that, everyone took a moment to glance at Cole and then away again.

"I think you remember and recognize Colonel Coleman's achievements during the civil war. Working with a team assembled by my late friend Reuben Malich, Colonel Coleman—then a captain, of course—handled a great deal of ultrasensitive work, assaulting and taking out multiple rebel caches throughout the country, without ever sustaining a single casualty of his own and without any human collateral damage. And you are all familiar with his taking of the enemy's nerve center in Washington State."

Murmurs. Glances. Mostly, though, steady downward looks. The Joint Chiefs were not happy about whatever it was that was about to happen—and it was clear they had no more idea than Cole did about what the President had in mind.

"Colonel Coleman has no experience whatsoever in any part of Africa, and it is certain that he cannot pass for native, so we can't expect him to blend in there. What we can expect is that with the proper breathing apparatus and reasonable care, he and various highly trained special operations teams can do much to shape events there—without coming home with the nictovirus. But if, in the course of their work, one or more of them contracts the virus, we will extract them like any other wounded soldiers, and then provide every possible care until they either do or do not survive the disease. I wish I could say their high level of fitness works in their favor, but we have heard reports of this disease sparing feeble old people and children, while taking men and women in the prime of life. So there are no guarantees."

Cole almost spoke up, but the President, apparently sensing what he was about to say, preempted him.

"I do not expect that this will interfere with Colonel

Coleman's team in any way—the virus is simply one more enemy they must be wary of and treat with the same caution and respect they already use in confrontations with human enemies."

The Army chief spoke up, rather like the wise-ass kid in a high school classroom. "I hope you won't be expecting him to disguise himself as one of *that* enemy."

Everyone chuckled, and Torrent showed no impatience, though Cole knew he was irritated. Torrent was often irritated when people interrupted him, but he tried never to show it. This guaranteed that he was interrupted even more—but it also kept people from thinking of him as arrogant or jealous or power hungry.

"We have recently received absolutely firm intelligence that the government of Nigeria is following a genocidal policy. Since the nictovirus only kills between twenty and fifty percent of its victims, we regard their one-hundred-percent fatality rate as something that must be stopped. Furthermore, it must be *seen* to be stopped so that in these trying times other governments do not resort to the same methods.

"We believe that the Nigerian government, which as you know is absolutely controlled by the northern Muslim Hausa-speaking minority, is creating a firewall of dead and burned-out villages between the Muslim areas of Nigeria and the non-Muslim south, where the vast majority of the people in the most populous nation in Africa live."

"We're supposed to protect the southern majority with a few special ops teams?" asked the Army chief.

"If you mean, are we going to protect them by building our own defended wall, then of course not. We don't have a large enough army to accomplish that if we sent them all to Nigeria, which we most certainly will not do, since the chance of controlling infection with such a large and differentially trained number would be impossible.

"No, Colonel Coleman's mission will be to destroy any and every team the Hausas are sending out to murder non-Muslim villagers. They may believe that with so much death already happening in Nigeria, a few thousand more will not be noticed. But they *have* been noticed. This is one genocide that will not go on.

"And in case anyone thinks I have turned altruistic, think again. We are accused of ruthlessness in our dealings with Africa. But we will show, through Colonel Coleman's work, that we care very much about the people of Africa. To survive the disease and be murdered by your own government seems to me to be precisely the kind of irony that our special ops troops exist to eliminate."

The Secretary of State raised his hand slightly from the table. "Sir, this will be a clear violation of national sovereignty—acts of war against a nation with which we are not at war."

Torrent nodded. "I believe that when a government starts carrying out a policy of genocide against large segments of their own population, they cease to be the legitimate government of that portion of their people. In this case, they are essentially abandoning the south while not allowing anyone else to come in and take their place. I expect we'll soon hear about a complete breakdown in social order in the south. The government will speak of thugs and rebel elements causing trouble, and will deny that they have withdrawn all loyal Muslims, including the loyal portions of their military, north of the firewall they are creating. They will say that the chaos in Nigeria is caused by the American quarantine."

"So Colonel Coleman is your answer," said the Secretary of Defense.

"No," said President Torrent, "*General* Coleman is my answer."

The military men in the room stiffened with displeasure. Torrent must have seen it, too, because he added, "Relax, this is a brevet appointment only—his permanent rank remains colonel. But for the duration of this assignment, he will be, and will be treated as, a major general. He will request troops, materiel, supply, transportation, and communications resources, and he will be given them instantly. Affected officers are free to offer alternatives, *once*. But anyone who obstructs General Coleman's missions will answer to me, and I can promise you that careers can end over this."

Torrent clearly understood what motivated bureaucratic officers, though Cole doubted any president had ever spoken so plainly before.

To raise a mere colonel to such a lofty rank, however colorful his reputation and however close to the President he might be, would make Cole one of the most hated men in the U.S. military. What Cole was seeing in the stony expressions of the Joint Chiefs was a wordless but immediate decision that Cole's career was over as soon as this president was out of office.

Torrent must know exactly what he was doing—he was a historian, wasn't he? He had just transformed Cole into a "creature," a courtier who was important only while the ruler who "made" him was in office. That was one way of assuring the loyalty of your subordinates. But it was not the best way, especially with someone like Cole.

But it would certainly *seem* to work, because Cole would fulfill his assignments faithfully. And since this set of missions would almost certainly kill him, between bullets and viruses, the issue of Cole's future was moot.

Well, Cole told himself, I always served at the pleasure of my commanders, and this is the commander in chief. If he wants to use up my career on this assignment, so be it. I can't do special ops forever—no matter how much you train and how hard you work out, your body gets older and stops doing what it used to be able to do.

As final assignments went, this wasn't a bad one.

Cole assumed that the meeting was now over, but at least he had the sense not to stand up to leave until he was dismissed. Because President Torrent wasn't done yet. He nodded to the aide standing at the door he had come through, and the door opened again.

In walked, of all people, Jared Austin—"Babe"— the North Carolina boy who had declared himself the token white southerner in Rube's jeesh. And with him was a young African boy—clearly African, not African-American, from the respectful way he carried himself and the way his face betrayed no emotion at all.

"Folks, I'd like you to meet Chinma. As far as we know, he is the last living member of the Ayere tribe."

"You mean those pictures were real?" asked the Navy chief.

Cole had not doubted the pictures going around the internet were real, he was simply unsurprised by atrocity stories from Africa.

"Former special ops captain Jared Austin took it upon himself to make sure the pictures of the massacre of the Ayere tribe were released online before notifying anyone above him of their existence. Without a context, however, and without any official word, nobody knows what to make of them. I think you know how many pundits have declared the pictures to be fakes."

Cole caught a flicker of emotion from young Chinma. An expression of contempt.

"So I am going on the air at ten P.M. tonight to introduce Chinma to the American people. You see, Chinma is the monkey-catcher who first caught the sneezing flu and unknowingly passed it to other humans.

"I want it understood that Chinma was not doing anything illegal by catching putty-nosed monkeys. *Cercophithecus nictitans,* from whose species name we derived the name of the nictovirus, are neither rare nor protected, and there was quite a demand for the capture of intact troops of the monkeys in order to study their reputed language ability. He was aiding science and harming no one.

"Chinma is continuing to cooperate fully with medical researchers who have stuck him so full of needles I'm surprised you can't see through him." Several men laughed, but Cole noticed that the most response Chinma showed was a flicker of a smile. "But he is not here because he was the original vector for transmission from monkeys to humans.

"No, I brought him to you because he happened to be high in a tree the day that robbers came into his village."

And Cole realized: This kid took the pictures of his own village, his own family, being slaughtered. There was no chance he could have fought the armed men who came to destroy his people. But he could record their faces. And Cole bet that while Westerners might suppose the pictures to be fakes, or ignorable, as Cole had, those pictures must be playing very differently in Nigeria and throughout Africa.

The government thugs had killed everyone they saw—this despite the fact that everyone still alive in Chinma's village had already had and recovered from the nictovirus. Chinma's village was the least likely place in Nigeria for someone to catch the disease. But helpless, angry oligarchies carry out stupid, pointless cruelties. It's how they reassure themselves that they are still in power.

"This, my friends," Torrent was saying, "is the legal

basis for our intervention in Nigeria. Chinma's pictures include three slightly blurry but identifiable shots of a general in the Nigerian army personally shooting a baby—Chinma's nephew—that had been tossed into the air for target practice. We have a great deal of other evidence that the Nigerian government's solution to the epidemic is to slaughter any southern Nigerians who live near the Muslim sections of the north, creating, in effect, a firewall to block infection.

"In the long run, this policy will not work—the World Health Organization reports that the nictovirus is already in the north among the Hausas. Meanwhile, Chinma's pictures are the incontrovertible documentary evidence of this policy of genocide and of the commission of war crimes. By international law, Nigeria now has no federal government, and we will intervene to prevent any further attacks by the Hausa military against southerners. Even in the midst of a devastating epidemic, the natural laws of humanity still apply, and we will act to protect those southerners who survive the disease from the criminal acts of their former government."

The Chief of Naval Operations asked the obvious question. "Is young Mr. Chinma able to answer questions from the media? Because the European media are going to claim that he's part of an American scam."

"Like the moon landing," murmured the NSA.

"We all know how America is constantly searching for opportunities to expend American lives and money in pursuit of high-handed imperialism," said Torrent. "Naturally, it is to be assumed that we are really seizing Nigerian oil."

Everyone chuckled, but Cole thought that it wasn't really wise to say such things. Even if Torrent was quoted accurately, irony disappears in print and these words would be taken at face value, as a rare moment of candor from an American president.

Torrent had not forgotten the original question. "Chinma speaks English quite well," said the President. "Though it's his fourth language."

"English is my favorite language," said Chinma.

His voice—high, not yet changed, but clear and firm—brought surprised laughter, and the boy looked confused.

"No problem, son," said Torrent. "They're laughing because they're happy and relieved you speak English better than the average American college freshman."

The President went on telling the story of how Chinma happened to have a camera and notebook, and how he and half his tribe had survived the nictovirus, only to be massacred. It was a sad story, but Cole could see the gleam in the President's eye. This boy's heroism was accomplishing more than making public the crime committed against his people.

He was a survivor, first of the terrifying disease, and then of an equally terrifying act of genocide. Then, grimly determined to get justice for his murdered family, he brought his story to Americans, and Americans got him out of Nigeria and brought him here to safety.

Americans loved stories in which Americans are the good guys.

President Torrent had obviously used this meeting as a dry run for the press conference, and it looked like a slam dunk. Suddenly this disease was not about masses of people in far-off Africa—it was about this sad but engaging boy, his suffering, his terrible losses, and his heroism. It helped that the bad guys in this story were Muslims, though Torrent was careful not to make a big point of it. The American people were used to hearing of Muslims doing unspeakable things, but now they had unforgettable pictures.

There would certainly be international protests when Cole started taking special ops teams into Nigeria to bring the fear of God into the hearts of these heartless murderers, but American support for the actions would be almost unanimous.

Cole tuned out the continuing questions and comments, most of which boiled down to praise for Chinma, which, since there were no cameras in the meeting, meant that they were sucking up to the President and not to the public.

Left to his own thoughts, Cole could not help but remind himself: I'm a general. Not permanently, and it won't count when I retire, but right now I have the President behind me and everybody has to salute me or at least answer my emails. If only Dad could have fought off the cancer long enough to see me get *here*.

Cole was immediately ashamed of his momentary glee. His "battlefield promotion" had only happened because hundreds of thousands of people, probably *millions,* were dying, and the Nigerian government was killing the survivors.

I'm going to have to take men into combat and lay our lives on the line again and again—in danger from both enemy action and a deadly epidemic. And I'm *thrilled* about it?

But such conflicted feelings were common. Everyone knew that it was in wartime that military careers were made. In peacetime, the climbers always rise to the top of the military bureaucracy, and then when war broke out, you had the devil's own time trying to get rid of them and put good field generals in their place.

Bureaucratic generals always hated successful field commanders because they were pretty much opposite personality types, and the ascendancy of one meant the total eclipse of the other. Torrent hadn't put Cole in the Joint Chiefs, but they all by damn knew his face and his name, and he had enormous clout because of the President's obvious trust in him.

Let's not screw this up, Cole told himself. You never thought you'd get anywhere near this kind of position. Being assigned to Reuben Malich looked like the death of your career, and now, three years later, you're in a place other soldiers only dream of.

The meeting ended and everyone left—except the President, Chinma, Babe, and Cole.

Torrent's private words to them were brief. "This boy has spent his first days in America getting stuck with needles and constantly watched, waking and sleeping, while adults forced him to figure out what he wrote with a pencil in the jungle on the day his family was murdered. I want your advice on something. I'm thinking that Chinma needs a good American home. One where they understand something about the pain of having a family member murdered."

Cole's first reaction was: You can't do that to Cecily Malich. And his second reaction was: If Cecily was the first person I thought of, she's probably the right choice.

"Do you think she'll do it?" asked the President.

"If you ask her, sir," said Babe.

"Well, no," said President Torrent. "At the moment I'm not sure she's speaking to me. She didn't like my speech last night."

"Sir," said Cole, "she won't do it for you, and she won't do it for me, and she won't do it for Babe. But she'll do it for Chinma."

"No," said Torrent with a smile, "she'll do it for God."

It was good to know that Torrent was aware that Cecily took her faith seriously. But it was not so reassuring that Torrent thought it was amusing.

"So the two of you will take him to Cessy?" asked Torrent.

"Maybe," said Cole, "we ought to ask Chinma."

Torrent's eyebrows rose in a my-bad expression. "It *is* a free country, isn't it," said Torrent. "Go ahead and ask."

Babe looked at Cole with amusement, as if to say, You opened your mouth, you do the asking.

"We know a family," Cole said to Chinma. "A good

American family. Their father, Reuben Malich, was a great soldier. Mr. Austin and I both served under him. Reuben tried to save the life of the President who was killed a few years ago. But then he was murdered by someone he trusted. His wife and children miss him every day. They're good people. They're Christians—Catholics—I don't know what that means to you."

"My family was Christian," said Chinma. "Not Catholic, though."

"It won't matter, I promise you. They might have a place for you while you're living here in America. Do you want to come stay with them? Because if you'd rather go back to where you've been sleeping the past few days, you can do that instead."

"Soldier family, please, sir," said Chinma.

"Good choice," said Babe. "The woman can cook."

Chinma's face lit up. "Really? Food in America is very bad. No fire!"

Ah, thought Cole, Chinma isn't saying American food is raw, he's saying it's bland. I'll have to warn Cecily. Use pepper!

The boy was too old to hold anybody's hand, but Cole would have expected him to stay close to Babe; after all, it was Babe who got him out of Nigeria and put his pictures on the web. But no. Chinma walked by himself. As if he didn't quite trust anybody—which would be understandable.

But maybe he knew how alone he was in the world, and he was determined to act like a man.

EIGHT

BRAVE BOYS

People know many things, and half of them are wrong. If only we knew which half, we'd have reason to be proud of our intelligence.

What is knowledge? A belief that is shared by all the respectable people in a community, whether there is any real evidence for it or not.

What is faith? A belief we hold so strongly that we act as if it is true, even though we know there are many who do not believe it.

What is opinion? A belief that we expect other people to argue with.

What is scientific fact? An oxymoron. Science does not deal in facts. It deals in hypotheses, which are never fully and finally correct.

CECILY WAS in the kitchen, fixing dinner. Nick was upstairs, playing videogames. Lettie and Annie were out on bicycles, probably going on busier roads than Cecily officially permitted them to use, but they would at least be wearing their helmets. John Paul was alternating between coming into the kitchen and complaining that he was bored, and going into Nick's room to offer unwelcome advice on whatever game Nick was playing.

Mark was in the back yard, looking up into the tallest oak in the neighborhood. And the Nigerian boy, Chinma, was somewhere up in that tree. Judging from the angle of Mark's neck as he looked up, Chinma was very high in the tree.

Chinma had asked for permission before climbing the tree. He was such a polite boy. But so quiet, so inscrutable. Babe had taken her aside to warn her that Chinma showed almost nothing in his face. "It's an African thing. Particularly a Nigerian thing. You don't want to let anyone see any emotion, except, when you feel threatened, a cheerful smile."

"So a smile isn't a good thing?" asked Cecily.

"A real smile is. Believe me, you'll know the difference."

Of course she had taken in the boy, but Cecily couldn't help resenting the fact that somehow the President and Cole and Babe had decided her life wasn't complicated enough, so *she* of all the people in the D.C. area needed to take this boy into her care.

At the same time, it was flattering, too. When they wanted the boy to have a good, safe home, they thought of her.

Unless they somehow thought they were doing her and her kids a favor, giving them a wonderful new brother, someone to take their minds off their troubles. Men sometimes thought that way, because few of them had any calendar sense. Her husband had been dead for three years. Any comfort she might have derived from having a pet child added to her family in the aftermath of Reuben's death, the need for it had long since passed.

None of them would have guessed the real reason she felt comfort at Chinma's presence in her home. To Cecily, it was a sign that God still knew where she lived.

She would never say this to anyone outside of church, because it was such an unintellectual idea. To think that God bent events to bring certain people together would simply be scoffed at by hard-minded men like Torrent or Cole or any of the people who knew her only as a policy wonk. But Cecily lived in a world where, when someone had suffered enough, God would assign some person or family to be angels in their life, to bless them. Clearly Chinma was on the suffered-enough list, and it felt good to Cecily that she and her family had been chosen as the angels of comfort.

Even if Torrent or one of Reuben's soldiers believed *they* had thought of it, Cecily knew that God could make anybody think of anything, and make it seem like a good idea. It didn't take away any of their freedom, for God to use them as an instrument of his will. To them, it was something they did in passing. To Chinma and Cecily, it was a potentially transformative connection.

And if Chinma's coming to their home was only temporary, and it accomplished nothing more than this, Chinma had finally arrived in America. Until now he had been in institutional custody, surrounded by walls, breathing air-conditioned air, and dealing only with soldiers and doctors and scholars and politicians.

Now, though, Chinma was high up in an American tree, looking out over an American landscape, with an American boy at the bottom of the tree looking up at him with . . . what, awe? Consternation? Hard to read Mark's expression in profile.

And now she wouldn't have to. He was trudging toward the house.

Cecily had taken Cole's and Babe's warnings about the food seriously. She had never thought of American food as bland and flavorless, but as Babe said, "They have to do something with a diet consisting mostly of flavorless yams, so they spice everything to the limits of human endurance. The more subtle flavors we appreciate are indistinguishable to them."

"What are you saying, they can't tell a tuna sandwich from peanut butter?"

"They could probably tell the difference, they just wouldn't care," said Babe. "Like the difference between Sprite, Seven-Up, and Sierra Mist."

"I can tell the difference," said Cecily.

"But compared to the difference between them and champagne . . ."

"I'll spice things up a little," said Cecily.

"No, you don't get it," said Babe. "Chinma won't notice you spiced it unless it's so hot it makes your children cry. So get him some pepper sauces and let him add it to his own food."

So Cecily had made a run to Wegmans and come back with a dozen tall narrow bottles of sauces that bragged about how impossibly hot they were. She had also bought a dozen jalapeños and a few habaneros, and handling them both with rubber gloves, and leaving all the seeds intact, she had made two different sauces that had *not* been attuned to American tastes at the factory.

Tonight would be angel-hair pasta with a choice of tomato and alfredo sauces. The tomato sauce was Newman's Own Sockarooni, which was too spicy for Mark and Annie, though Lettie and Nick were fine with it.

Mark came into the kitchen. "I can't believe how high he climbs," he said.

"Well, he can't climb higher than the tree."

"Close, though," said Mark. "He's on branches so tiny they swayed five feet when he put his weight on them. Every breeze swings him around like a tetherball. And he doesn't even look nervous."

"If he weren't a climber," said Cecily, "he'd be dead now."

"If he weren't a climber," said Mark, "he wouldn't have been sneezed on by a sick monkey."

"Are you brave enough to try one of these hot sauces for me?" asked Cecily.

He looked at her like she was insane. "No," he said. "Are you trying to poison me by burning through my mouth? I saw those peppers you bought."

"I'm afraid he'll think I'm playing a really cruel prank on him," said Cecily.

"Tell him you think it's too hot for human consumption, but he's free to try it if he wants. He's my age, he can decide what he wants."

"I keep forgetting he's your age, he's so much smaller."

"I had the benefit of American nutrition, Mom. All those nitrates and monosodium glutamate and high-fructose corn syrup make a boy grow tall and namby-pamby."

"Nobody called you namby—"

"I like alfredo sauce on my noodles, Mom. And when you dare me to eat death-by-pepper sauce, I don't take it as a challenge, I take it as attempted murder."

"That doesn't make you a wimp."

"I take pride in my wimphood, Mom. I'm not a man like Dad was—I'm not a soldier in the making."

"Your father never expected or even wanted his sons to be soldiers."

"I know that, Mom. You think he didn't tell me? But I knew that he wished I were a different kind of boy. Worse grammar and more bugs in my hair."

"Your father was so proud of you, Mark, that it made him cry sometimes. For heaven's sake, don't invent a version of your father that you can't live up to!"

"If I had lived in Chinma's village, I wouldn't have been up in a tree, taking pictures of the slaughter of my family so I could testify against the murderers later. I would have been one of the people running around screaming till they shot me."

"So Chinma was the right kind of hero for the job God chose him to do," said Cecily.

"Yep," said Mark. "Didn't you ever wonder if Elijah or Peter had an older brother who just didn't amount to much?"

"Didn't *you* ever wonder if any of those prophets had sisters?"

"Nobody expected girls to do great things in those days—and they still had Deborah and Esther and Ruth."

"Yeah," said Cecily, "like lying down at a cousin's feet was anything like challenging the priests of Baal."

"It took courage all the same," said Mark.

"Ha! I got you to say it! Bravery doesn't take the same form every time."

"*You* don't get it. I'm not brave, but I also don't *want* to be brave. I don't want to climb a tall tree. Or a short one. I don't want to eat that death-by-pepper sauce, or even Newman's Own Sockarooni stuff. And I'm *happy* that way. I just recognize that God isn't going to have any particular use for me because I'm not the kind of kid who does anything spectacular."

"You don't know what you can do until it's time to do it," said Cecily.

"If men with guns came into my village, I'd think, Oh, I guess this is how I die. I wonder if it will hurt. I hope not. I don't like to hurt. And I'd still be thinking that when they came in and shot me and everybody else."

"I can see that you've played through this whole script in your mind."

"Several times," said Mark. "And the only difference

between the versions is whether I die screaming and begging for my life, or just sitting there waiting patiently for the end to come."

"All these years I've known you," said Cecily, "and I had no idea you were suffering from chronic clinical depression."

"Mom, I'm happy being who and what I am. I imagine all kinds of lives I might lead, and the only ones that look good to me are the quiet, safe, boring ones. Finding a wife and never looking at another woman. Raising my kids and being happy as long as they don't actually become drug addicts or criminals. Going to a job every workday and taking two weeks of vacation every year. All the things that everybody says are boring, that's what would make me happy. I never ever wanted to be like Dad. I never wanted to do his job."

"He certainly never knew that."

"Why would I tell him?" asked Mark. "Besides, I couldn't have put it into words then. When he was still alive. I just knew."

A thought occurred to Cecily. "Are you trying to tell me something?"

Mark thought for a moment, then laughed. "I'm trying to tell you what I told you," he said. "And no, I'm not gay. It's girls I have disturbing dreams about."

"Disturbing?"

"Wow, you're in a creepy mood," said Mark. "I'm not doing anything *weird* in my dreams. It's just *disturbing* to be committing the sin of fornication every night. Father Thaddeus tries to convince me that it's perfectly normal and he won't even assign me penance for it beyond the prayers I already say, but I can't help but think that I'm awfully *eager* to commit mortal sins with any bimbo who happens to show up in a dream."

Cecily couldn't help laughing. "You say you're not brave, but do you know how many boys would die of embarrassment before saying anything like this to their mother?"

"Yes, but they don't have you as a mom, so it *would* take courage to say it to *them*. Give it up, Mom, this is the kind of argument I can't lose."

"I didn't know it was an argument."

"Oh, come on," said Mark. "You try to convince me I'm a perfect son, and that gets me to tell you all the bad things about myself, and then you reassure me I'm not bad, so I tell you worse things. I swear, you ought to be training priests how to take confessions. Or interrogating captured terrorists. You're like a waterboard without all the gasping and gagging and crying."

Cecily hugged him and laughed so hard she cried. "I'll tell you something, Mark. God *does* have a mission for you, and that's to make me happy while you're growing up in my home."

"Well, then, things are working out nicely for both of us," he said. "But then I think of Chinma and I remember that it can all be taken away. Men show up with guns, or a disease strikes and kills half the family, and . . ." Then he shrugged.

"And that wouldn't take away anything from the happiness we already had," said Cecily. "When your father died, it hurt me worse than childbirth, worse than a broken bone. But a broken bone doesn't erase all the running you did before, and Reuben dying didn't take away a single happy moment of our lives, and childbirth—wow, that left me with *prizes*."

Chinma was standing in the doorway to the back yard. "There are many, many cars," he said.

"Cars?" asked Cecily.

"On all the roads. Going every way. How do they know where to go?"

Cecily was confused by the question. Chinma had ridden in cars and trucks—he knew that they didn't steer themselves. So the question wasn't about cars, it was about people. "They're all busy, doing their jobs, taking care of their lives. So one car is headed to the store to buy food, another one is taking someone to his job, and all those people get up in the morning and decide what they need to do and then they do it."

"In cars," said Chinma.

"Not if our president can help it," said Cecily. "Cars are burning up all the oil in the world. We need to get rid of as many cars as we can, and change the rest to electricity."

Chinma nodded wisely. "Then you can walk and be strong," he said.

"Yes," said Cecily, laughing. "That would be good."

"Are you afraid?" asked Chinma.

"Of what? I'm afraid of a lot of things."

Chinma nodded wisely. "Your boy Mark, he's afraid."

Mark's jaw dropped. Cecily certainly understood why. It was such a rude thing to say right in front of him. But then, wasn't that better than saying it behind his back?

Before Mark could recover himself enough to reply as angrily as he would obviously want to, Cecily chuckled and spoke. "Afraid to climb trees? I would hope so! What you do is very dangerous," she said.

Chinma flashed a brief smile. "Trees never hurt me."

"Well of course not," said Cecily. "It's the *ground* that hurts you, when you fall out of the tree."

Chinma laughed. "Ground never hurt me, either!"

It took a monkey's sneeze to destroy your world, thought Cecily. "You have the climbing experience to be safe in the trees. Mark doesn't. It's sensible for him to be afraid of climbing trees—especially climbing as high as you do, where the branches are so small. But he's brave about other things, you'll see."

Chinma looked at Mark coolly, as if sizing him up. Mark turned to his mother, keeping his expression calm, but obviously saying to her, Can you please get him off the subject of *me*?

"Is he a soldier?" asked Chinma.

"He's only thirteen years old!" said Cecily.

"In Liberia and Sierra Leone, they made them soldiers. Ten years old. Eight years old."

"And that was a monstrous crime," said Cecily. "Those men who forced little children to fight and kill, God has seen what they did and condemns the evil in their hearts."

"God sees but he does nothing," said Chinma.

"He forgives those soldier children for doing things they didn't understand." But Cecily knew as she said it that she wasn't answering what he was really saying.

"God is weak," said Chinma. "God is afraid."

He sounded so angry and contemptuous that at first Cecily wanted to cry out an affirmation of her faith: No, God is good! But how could she say that to this boy, after all he had suffered through?

Mark *did* cry out, "God is *not* afraid!" When he himself had felt under attack, Mark had said nothing; but when it was God being attacked, he could not keep his silence. Both responses said good things about Mark.

"Sometimes," said Cecily, "I hear my children quarreling, but I don't stop them, I keep doing my work, and after a while I hear them make peace with each other. If I stepped in every time they quarreled, then they would never learn how to make peace by themselves."

Chinma nodded—which Babe had warned Cecily did not mean agreement, but rather comprehension; or not even that: Nodding could simply mean, "I understand that you are through talking and I will pretend that I understood so you don't go to the trouble of saying it again."

"God lets us do terrible things to one another," said Cecily. "And he lets nature do terrible things, like this sneezing flu."

"The doctors said it isn't flu," said Chinma.

"The nictovirus. Monkey sickness. Does the name matter?" asked Cecily.

Chinma kept his face solemn when he said, "It mattered to the doctors. They made everybody stop saying 'sneezing flu.'"

Had she caught a twinkle in his eye? Was Chinma mocking the doctors?

Mark spoke up. "They can't cure it, so all they can do is make everybody call it by the name they chose." God, apparently, Mark would defend; the doctors were on their own.

"Let me tell you something," said Cecily. "Back in the days of the Roman Empire, Christians were still a small minority when a plague struck. Very much like the sneezing monkey flu." Which won a brief smile from Chinma—and an eye-roll from Mark, as if to say, What are you doing, joking about this disease that he brought back from the jungle and that killed half his family?

"The plague was very bad," Cecily went on. "About a third of the people who caught it died. It terrified everybody. The rich fled the cities and went to their country estates. Even the doctors ran away, because they couldn't cure it. If a family member got sick, the family would lock them in a room, or throw them out of the house, or run away from the house so they wouldn't all catch the disease."

"Come on," said Mark.

"Families in the Roman Empire weren't as close as ours are," said Cecily. "Husbands were often twenty years older than their wives. They practiced infanticide, they treated daughters as if they had no value, husbands could order their wives to have an abortion even though they knew it might well kill her. They didn't value the kind of family loyalty we have."

Mark still looked skeptical. Cecily figured that was a good thing, that he had a hard time believing families could be as uncaring as they were in the days of the Roman Empire.

Chinma, for his part, had no trouble believing this. He was nodding, more to himself than to her.

"But among the Christians," said Cecily, "things were different. Women were valued. Infanticide and abortion were forbidden. And when a family member got sick, the rest of the family took care of him, even though they knew they might easily catch the disease themselves and die from it."

Now it was Chinma's turn to look skeptical, while Mark was reassured.

"They really did—the Roman writers of the time, even the ones who hated Christians, commented on the fact that not only did Christians nurse one another through the plague, they even went and took care of sick pagans, not just their pagan friends, but total strangers."

"And God protected them, right?" said Mark.

"No," said Cecily. "God did not protect them. Christians got sick at exactly the same rate as anybody else. But they didn't die at the same rate."

"So they were healed," said Mark, demanding confirmation of his faith.

"In a way," said Cecily, "but it wasn't miraculous.

Not like you're thinking. When people are sick, their bodies are doing all they can to fight the infection. But they need food and water to keep up the fight. When everybody runs away, there's no one to provide that food and water. No one to wash them or bathe them to try to keep the fever down. No one to put blankets on them when they're cold. No one to take away their bodily wastes. So even if their body *might* have fought off the infection, they died because they got too weak to keep fighting, or they caught a secondary disease from the filth around them, or they were weakened by exposure to the cold. You see?"

"So the Christians' nursing people helped them live?" asked Mark.

"Exactly. It seems that with good nursing, only about ten percent of the people who were afflicted died. So a perfectly understandable kind of miracle happened. Because Christian love triumphed over their fear of this terrible disease, only one out of ten Christians who got sick died of the disease, instead of three out of ten. And even though the Christians doing the nursing usually got sick, they knew someone else would nurse *them*, and so they, too, had a much better chance of survival."

"And the pagans they helped," said Mark, "I bet they became Christians."

"I don't know if you can become a true believer out of gratitude, but maybe you listen to the gospel more receptively if the people teaching you about Jesus had already proven to you that they had a Christlike love for you. Maybe, out of gratitude, you give God a chance to touch your heart."

Mark was already leaping ahead of the discussion to the conclusion that mattered to him. "So that's why Christianity took over the Roman Empire," he said. "More of the pagans died because nobody nursed them. More of the Christians lived, and the pagans they helped *became* Christian—"

"And after two such terrible plagues, a century or so apart, Christians were no longer a tiny minority, they were a very large minority, and they had a powerful reputation for sincerely living up to their beliefs."

Chinma turned away and walked angrily to the kitchen door, as if he were leaving. Then he turned back, and his face bore a terrible expression of grief and rage, and tears were flowing down his cheeks. He had shown almost no emotion till now, and now he was showing more emotion than Cecily had ever seen one face contain.

"Where were the Christians!" he shouted. "My mother and brothers were Christian but they blamed me and shut me out the door. I was all alone to be sick! Where were the Christians!"

Then Chinma shoved open the glass storm door and ran out into the back yard and scampered back up the tree.

"Wow," said Mark.

"That poor boy," said Cecily. "Nobody told me that his own family didn't nurse him when he was sick."

"Aren't there any Christians in Nigeria?" asked Mark.

"Millions of them," said Cecily. "And for all we know, they're mostly doing what they should, caring for one another. It's just a tragedy that his own family didn't live up to the standard of faith set by the Christians in the early Church."

"I would never leave you or any of the family," said Mark fervently. "I'd take care of you until I caught the sickness myself, and I'd keep taking care of you until I died."

"I know you would," said Cecily. "And I would do the same for you."

"You can't tell me that people in the Roman Empire didn't love one another!" said Mark. "I don't believe it."

"There are people *today* who don't love one another, Mark. And in a society where no value is placed on family loyalty of that kind, there would be a lot more people who would feel no obligation to put their own lives at risk for the sake of their family. And besides, what if the whole family was sick all at once? Who takes care of one another then? The Christians sought one another out, took care of people who *weren't* in their family. But the pagan religion didn't have that kind of loyalty. I'm not making this up, Mark. Even the emperor Julian, when he made a last-ditch effort to stamp out Christianity and restore paganism, demanded that pagan priests do what Christians were doing— take care of other people. The pagan writers of the time all affirmed that the Christians acted just the way I'm describing."

"Yeah, well, this is proof then," said Mark.

"Proof of what?"

"That America is definitely *not* a Christian nation, or we wouldn't be blockading Africa, we'd be helping."

"The President is trying to keep the disease from spreading throughout the world. He's trying to save lives."

"And all those people who ran away from the plague in Rome, they were just trying to save lives, too, right? Their own!"

"Mark," Cecily began.

"Where did you get all this stuff?" asked Mark.

"A book," said Cecily. "I read it several years ago." She got up from the kitchen table and went to the shelves in the living room. It was hard to remember where it was—it's not as if the house was on the Dewey decimal system, so books often got put wherever there was an empty space on the shelves.

But there it was, Rodney Stark's *The Rise of Christianity*. She slid it off the shelf and handed it to Mark, who had followed her into the room. He looked at the cover. "How do I know this isn't just crap?" asked Mark.

"You read it, you see what you think of the evidence he assembles, and you make up your own mind."

"It's not like he was there at the time."

"Often being there at the time," said Cecily, "means you don't see things clearly at all."

Mark looked up at her with his most sarcastic expression. "So you mean just because you have meetings with the President, that doesn't mean you're always right?"

"No, it doesn't," said Cecily, more than a little outraged. "I never said it did!"

Mark didn't even hint at an apology. In fact, he could barely hide his delight at having offended her. This was so *not* like him—he usually couldn't stand offending anybody and was all over himself with apologies.

He held up the book and backed toward the stairs up to the bedrooms. "I'm going to read this," he said. "I'm going to find out whether Christians are any different from other people."

"No matter what you find out," said Cecily, "you know me and you know our family and you know that you would never have to face a plague like this alone the way Chinma did."

"That's because we're a good family," said Mark. "Not because we're *Christians*."

"So you agree with Chinma," said Cecily.

"He's the only one around here who's actually lived through a plague," said Mark. And then he was gone.

NINE

DEFENDING THE DEAD

Human beings are not designed to keep secrets. Every aspect of our being is shaped for the sharing of information—through speech, gesture, facial expression, posture, and every other deliberate or inadvertent sign of emotion and intent.

Thus it should not surprise us that every would-be dictator, tyrant, conqueror, prophet, colonizer, politician, artist, and dogcatcher in history clearly signaled his intentions long before he acted, and in plenty of time for others to prevent them. Neither Hitler nor Churchill, neither Pol Pot nor Abraham Lincoln, ever did anything they hadn't told us and shown us they would do.

That they are rarely prevented has more to do with our inattention, cowardice, or ambition to ride his coattails than with his particular skill. Dogs might run from the dogcatcher as soon as they see the net, but they rarely tear out his throat and kill him, which is, of course, the only rational course of action for the dog that values its life, liberty, or happiness.

JUNGLES WERE not the ideal environment for using exo-skeletons. The foliage didn't know it was supposed to get out of the way, and it had a nasty habit of hiding awkward geographical features. So there were no leaping moonwalks in the woods. That was for open country and urban combat. Instead, wearing the Bones allowed them to walk at a brisk, near-running pace without any fatigue.

With UASs patrolling the entire boundary zone between the Muslim north and the epidemic-plagued south of Nigeria—heavily armed drones like Predators and Reapers, or a few old unarmed Shadows and Hunters—Cole had a pretty good idea of where the enemy was, and which towns were their targets.

Not that any targets made sense for the Nigerian army—or, more properly now, the Nigerian Muslim army, the northern army, the Hausa-speaking army. Did they really think they could keep the epidemic at bay by creating a no-man's-land between the nicto-ridden south and the Muslim north? This epidemic was going around the edges of any wall you could put up. Eventually, it would get into northern Nigeria through Niger or Burkina Faso or Chad or Cameroon. They didn't have the money or manpower to seal *their* borders, and someone would get through, sneezing.

But for now, their scorched-earth policy was working—there were no cases of nictovirus reported in the Muslim north. And the Muslim nations of North Africa, beyond the Sahara, were perfectly happy for their brothers in Nigeria to do the bloody work of keeping the plague as far away from them as possible.

Cole's special-ops mission, on the other hand, was to stop the Nigerians from enforcing their quarantine—even as other U.S. forces, now helped by British, Brazilian, Australian, and Indian ships, worked to enforce President Torrent's quarantine. Cole was quite aware of the irony, and if he hadn't been, Cecily made sure his eyes were opened before he left. She was all smiles as she went straight for the jugular.

"So what you're saying, Cole, is that it's wrong for the Nigerian Muslims to use their army to protect themselves from the epidemic, but it's right for America to impose a quarantine on the entire continent of Africa."

"It's not a double standard," said Cole.

"Pray explain the difference," she said, handing him a plate of cookies. "Your bullets are made in heaven?"

"First of all, the government of Nigeria is supposed to be protecting the whole country. Instead, they're savagely attacking their own citizens to protect, not the uninfected, but the *Muslim* unaffected."

"So they're a bad government," said Cecily. "Name a good one."

"They're an evil government," said Cole, "and I don't have to name a *good* one, I only have to count the *better* ones, and that list is in the high double digits."

"So they deserve whatever you guys in your Iron Man suits do to them."

Actually, yes, but Cole understood she believed otherwise. "They're funding this genocidal treatment of the southern Nigerians by stockpiling the money from the sales of oil, all of which is found under the ground in southern Nigeria. So the north is stealing from the south the very means by which they're destroying them."

"The ironies of geography," said Cecily. "Again, is this grounds for your going in and killing?"

"Cecily, you know the business your husband was in. You know that this would have been his assignment if he were alive."

"Or he would have turned it down and ended his career over it."

"The southern Nigerians are an oppressed, unarmed people in the midst of one of the worst plagues in history. The northern Nigerians are slaughtering those who survived, people who already faced death once, and lived. They're making war against the people they are supposed to protect, and they're using their victims' own money to pay for it."

"And what is *your* goal?" asked Cecily. "To stop the northerners from keeping the plague away from their families. You won't really have succeeded until babies are dying of the nictovirus in the north as well as the south. You are actually aiding and abetting the nictovirus."

"Why are you doing this?" said Cole. "You know that what we're doing is right. The Nigerian government is like the crew of a submarine shooting at the lifeboats of survivors of a ship the sub just sank. It's an atrocity."

"Why is it the other guy is the only one who commits atrocities?"

"Never mind, Cecily," said Cole. "I can see by your face that I'll never persuade you. And that's surprising, because usually you at least try to see my side."

"I can see your side," said Cecily. "I've got a much clearer view of it than you do, from over here on my side."

"Let's talk again when somebody's trying to commit genocide against someone you care about," said Cole—which he knew was unfair, but unfairness in this argument was *her* choice, not his.

Cole had left feeling hurt and angry. He couldn't understand why she was being so deliberately obtuse. There must be something else going on in her mind that he was not privy to, some missing argument that would make her position sensible.

Philosophy was for professors and, apparently, presidential advisers and war widows. Cole was in the business of war.

There were six other special-ops teams at work on the Nigerian operation, all of which reported to Cole, but most of them were involved in supporting the police forces in the cities of the south by seeking out and destroying the bands of robbers that had inevitably grown up in the countryside. Nigeria could not survive as a society if safe transportation were not maintained.

So far only Cole's team had the Bones and Noodles—they were still prototypes. And Cole worried because they weren't well trained with them, especially not himself. He could walk along just fine, of course, but leaping and running and throwing in combat conditions made him deeply uneasy. He couldn't yet trust his reflexes to respond properly, and he'd overleap and hit his head on something, or throw too far or, second-guessing himself, not far enough. Which is why he barely trusted himself with grenades.

Babe, Drew, and Benny were as undertrained as Cole, so when they encountered enemy forces, the four of them served as the baseline force, while Mingo, Cat, Load, and Arty did all the scampering around the enemy's periphery, so they seemed to be everywhere at once.

The whole jeesh, of course, did all its yelling in Arabic. It wasn't the native language of the Hausas they were facing, but the Hausas would have heard Arabic in their mosques from childhood on up, since good Muslims wouldn't dream of translating the Quran into an inferior language. Cole hoped that it would sound to the hostile forces as if their own scriptures were screaming at them. And since English was the colonial language of Nigeria and most people spoke and understood it to some degree, Cole's jeesh used Farsi for the communications they didn't want the enemy to understand.

Having a lot of high-tech sources of information didn't make you infallible—no serious soldier would ever think it did. Today they had guessed wrong about the target of a foray by a group of nearly a thousand Nigerian Army regulars. Cole had assumed that a group that size, riding in trucks on main highways, would be making a major assault on a fairly urban area—a real counterstrike.

Instead, they pulled down a group of side roads and struck at a series of Ibo villages. They had apparently known something that none of Cole's intelligence sources had told him—that in the absence of Nigerian government authority, a number of Ibo regions had taken to calling themselves Biafrans.

Old memories died hard, and the Nigerian Civil War was still fresh in many minds. The reason the Hausas of the north had sent such a large force was to strike many villages at once, so that the message would be clear: The Hausas would be back, and no Biafran nation would rise from the ashes of the epidemic.

"Having drones that watch from the sky don't make us local," said Cat, when they realized what was happening. They could see only where the enemy was, never where they intended to go or what they intended to do when they got there.

All they could do was move as quickly as possible to where the UAS operators spotted Nigerian squads striking. They got on their chopper and dropped down into a yam field a few miles from the enemy. They wore masks that filtered out or killed any microbes in the air, so they could avoid getting infected themselves—the nictovirus still raged through the villages of Nigeria.

It was in the first village that Arty, never very squeamish, pulled the scarf from around the neck of what seemed to be the village headman, who had apparently been strangled in front of the whole village before the rest were massacred. The scarf turned out to be a Biafran flag.

"They had to do this up close and personal," said Babe. "And you can see from the bodies, a lot of these villagers had the nicto."

"So I guess there are higher priorities than avoiding the epidemic," said Cole.

"Or lower ones," said Drew, from a few paces away. He beckoned them to follow him toward a semiconcealed location away from the main village, and Cole, Mingo, and Cat came over.

They never allowed the whole team to assemble in one spot—too easy for an enemy to wipe them all out at once with a well-placed grenade, or surround them and cut them off from escape. So Load, Arty, Babe, and Benny stayed spread out to watch the perimeter.

The corpses of three women hidden behind some brush showed clear signs of having been raped before they died.

"Somebody broke discipline," said Mingo. "The whole point of the Hausa quarantine is to avoid physical contact with people who might be carrying the nicto."

"Well, strangling doesn't do that job, either," said Drew.

"Bet the guy who did the strangling wore a gas mask and a protective suit," said Cat.

"Bet the guys who did the raping unzipped their protective pants," said Mingo.

Drew gestured toward the women's slit throats. "Everybody calls it sneezing flu, so people think they can only catch it from a sneeze. I bet they killed these women first, so—no sneezing, but the bodies were still warm. Dead wouldn't bother some men, if they thought it meant they were safe."

"So I have a question," said Cole. "And Babe is the one most likely to know the answer." He started to move away from the others. Behind him, he heard the others still talking.

"Burn the bodies?" asked Drew.

"And notify the hostiles that we're on their trail?" asked Cat. "What are you thinking?"

"Cole's wearing the big Noodle, not me," said Drew.

Meanwhile, Cole had made his way over to where Babe was on watch. Without any need for orders, Mingo had run ahead to take Babe's place, and Babe jogged back toward Cole.

"You've been with the doctors," said Cole. "So you know stuff about how this disease spreads."

"I was doing security. They didn't exactly discuss the science with me."

"Well, you're likely to know more than the rest of us. What I need to know is—first, there are two forms of the disease, right? The one spread by blood contact, and the other by sneezing."

"That's just a working hypothesis," said Babe. "There were only four who died from the quick bloody disease. Everybody else has the slow-to-show sneezing version, because that's the one people live long enough to spread."

"That's the thing," said Cole. "Are they the same virus?"

"Maybe somebody knows now, but they'd be in Atlanta or Reston, where the monkeys and the corpses of the first victims were taken. When I was with the doctors they didn't have a clue."

"Damn," said Cole. "I have to know—the guys who did this rape, are they going to catch the sneezing flu and show no symptoms for a week, or are they going to drop dead with blood coming out of their eyes six hours after they did this?"

"Who cares?" asked Babe. "Just a few more guys we don't have to kill."

"If they only catch the sneezing flu," said Cole, "then the most important thing we can do is make sure these guys live to get back to Hausa country."

Babe got it at once. "Oh, man. A bunch of Typhoid Marys."

"As soon as the epidemic reaches the north, then this whole operation goes away. It's going to happen eventually, because there's no way, not even genocide, to hold this back. The only real boundaries are the Sahara and the ocean, the way Torrent planned it."

Babe grinned savagely. "Sounds like you think Torrent planned this epidemic."

"I meant the way he planned the African quarantine," said Cole, irritated.

"I know what you meant," said Babe.

"I don't know what *you* mean," said Cole. "Torrent isn't some evil scientist who created a virus and cleverly implanted it in a troop of monkeys that someone might or might not have found."

"Unless Chinma was a plant," said Babe.

"Paranoia check," said Cole. "You spent hours with the boy. Was he some stooge, or did his whole family really die?"

It was obvious Babe knew that Chinma was no fake. "Why can't it be both?" said Babe defiantly.

"Keep it real, Babe," said Cole. "You're scaring me, and not about President Torrent."

"Just speculating," said Babe. "Things occur to me, I talk them out."

Not if you didn't think they had *some* merit, thought Cole. And he remembered the guys talking about how the Bones would get them over the White House fences before the Secret Service could even react. "Back to my question," said Cole. "This village was still in the grip of the nicto. Could these rapists catch sneezing flu from the corpses?"

"Why are you asking me?" asked Babe.

"Because I hoped you knew."

"You're wearing your Noodle, aren't you?" asked Babe. "Ask the experts. Phone a friend."

Cole felt like an idiot. He had gotten used to using the helmet to monitor the location and condition of the other guys, and was beginning to get used to watching the UASs, though he had to sit down and shut out his peripheral vision with his hands in order not to throw up when a drone's-eye view of Africa was zipping and jagging around in his field of vision. But he was too used to operating cut off from home base. The helmet's ability to talk by satellite relay to AFRICOM in Stuttgart—or to the Pentagon, or the President—was simply not reflex to him yet. He flicked to that channel and asked his question.

They continued reconnoitering the area, knowing that some Army film editor back in the States would be cutting together footage from their Noodles that would be watched on the evening news. Cole wondered if they'd show the raped women, and if anyone would get the implications. Probably not. But just in case, he opened the channel again. Only this time he clicked his way to the channel that got him straight to Torrent. A feature that had been installed at the President's insistence.

Torrent was probably the first president to carry a bunch of cellphones in his pockets, each a secure line to a different person or group. No waiting to talk their way through layers of bureaucracy—it was like a dozen pocket hotlines. Cole had never used it till now, but if he stated his concern to his counterparts in the States, they'd obey him only if they felt like it.

"In a meeting," said Torrent as he answered the phone.

"Footage of raped women is in today's feed," said

Cole. "Can't be shown or discussed in the news for at least a week."

"I'll take your word for that," said Torrent. Cole broke the connection.

Cole realized that he was trusting Torrent completely, with no more conversation than that, to make sure the information was not aired. And Torrent hadn't even asked to know Cole's reasons.

I'm fully on his team, Cole realized.

Then he remembered Babe's paranoid speculation and realized: Maybe I'm the only one here who is. Were these guys testing me when they joked about attacking the White House? About Torrent as a tyrant? And what were they testing *for*? Are they probing to see what I think about Torrent before . . . what, inviting me to enter a conspiracy?

No, no, it was the assassination of a president that brought Cole into this jeesh. An assassination that was going to be blamed on Reuben Malich, and probably would have been if Cecily had not had the ear of LaMonte Nielson, the Speaker of the House, when he was advanced to the presidency to fill out the interrupted term. These guys had fought beside him to protect the Constitution and keep the country together. They'd never . . .

Or *had* they fought for the Constitution? Soldiers rarely discussed their motives, and for all Cole knew, these guys had fought the Progressive Restoration with him because it was a leftist movement, not because it threatened the union. But surely he would have known, during those months of fighting together, if these were a bunch of right-wing nut jobs.

Reuben Malich would never have assembled them into his jeesh if they had been. Because Reuben most definitely was *not* a right-wing nut job, or even, really, all that conservative. Traditional conservative, maybe, the way Cecily was a traditional liberal, neither one so extreme as to block them from having a happy marriage and seeing eye to eye on most things.

Don't start distrusting your own guys, Cole.

It was only a few minutes before he got a response from the disease experts, though because he didn't need to know, he had no idea whether the answer was coming from Reston or Atlanta or some other unknown location. The epidemiologist couldn't very well announce to the general public that they had brought these devastating disease agents into the United States in order to study them, though anybody with an ounce of sense would realize that they'd had no choice.

"They're *almost* the identical virus," said the voice in his ear, "but not quite. The blood-only virus has a slight difference that makes it so much more virulent. You know what 'virulent' means?"

"I'm Googling it on my BlackBerry," said Cole. "Go ahead and assume I know."

"I'm not sure what you're hoping to hear," said the voice.

"I'm hoping to hear accurate information on which I can base field decisions," said Cole.

"Is one of your men infected?" asked the voice.

"Negative. We need to know whether raping fresh but infected corpses could transmit the sneezing form of the disease."

"My God," said the voice. "Oh my God." Maybe he was retching, or maybe not.

"I'm in a war zone here, I need an answer so I can decide what to do about the enemy force that did it."

"They've got to be quarantined. The nictovirus in *either* form can be transmitted by blood-to-blood contact. If the victims were sick, the . . . rapists probably have the virus now, too."

"All I needed to know," said Cole.

"Can you even do that? Quarantine the enemy?"

"We call it 'killing them,' and yes, we can," said Cole. Then he clicked off the connection and said, more to himself than to Babe, "But we won't."

"We really won't kill these bastards?" asked Babe.

"They've probably already killed themselves," said Cole. "The nicto was still rampant in this village. The odds are that at least one of those women they raped was sick."

Babe laughed nervously. "Man, isn't this, like, an atrocity? Like when they sent smallpox-infected blankets to freezing Indians to make sure they got sick and died?"

"Bit different, here," said Cole. "We didn't infect the blankets. These guys were volunteers."

They gathered in thicker brush outside the village and Cole explained the plan. "We can track these guys," he said, "but only to make sure they rejoin the main force. We don't want to kill them."

"Come on," said Mingo. "Are we going to let them get away with this?"

"We're not here to punish," said Cole, "we're here to protect the main population from attacks. Killing Hausa soldiers ourselves is only one means of doing that. The north is going to get this disease sooner or later. But sooner will stop them from slaughtering a lot of southerners."

"I don't know, man," said Drew. "That's women and children now."

"Did you see who was dead in that village? We're letting their own kind of war flow back at them— we're not even doing it, we're just letting *them* do it, as if we hadn't been here."

Mingo laughed sharply. "Drew's just shittin' you, Cole," he said. "He likes making you go off on a rant about why us killing people is okay and them killing people isn't."

Cole took a deep breath. "I knew that," he said, knowing that they would know that he knew that they knew that he didn't know any such thing, which made it a joke. And, pleasantly enough, they laughed.

"So what do we do, let them continue this rampage?" asked Cat.

"No," said Cole. "But we go intercept other squads and leave the one that did *this* alone. I think once we start shooting up one of the raiding parties they'll all be called back—these guys know what we can do, and they don't want to die. So they'll all link up with the main body as fast as they can—and get infected on the way back to base."

Cole assigned one drone—or, rather, assigned the human operator of the drone in his workstation in some town in California—to follow the perpetrators of this attack, while Cole used the other drones to locate the nearest squad. They took off at a jog along a dirt track that seemed to lead in that direction.

And indeed it did. They reached another village that had already been destroyed. The bodies were still warm, the blood undried. "Right behind them, dammit," said Cat.

"Think we can outrun their trucks?" asked Cole.

They laughed and began to run. Great bounds, rather like kangaroos, only one foot at a time, each step like flight, as if they were nearly weightless.

Cole lagged behind. It was where he was supposed to be, as the wearer of the main Noodle, so he could monitor everything that was happening. It was also where he naturally ended up, since he was less experienced than some of them at running in Bones, and he was also distracted by a much larger and more complicated heads-up display than the others were seeing.

Besides the electronics, though, he could see them with his real eyes as they bounded along ahead of him. It reminded him of the *Terminator* movies, with a relentless robot chasing a speeding truck on foot—and gaining on it. Not that the trucks were speeding—on these roads? Tracks, really.

When they got within range, the jeesh started shooting, and then the trucks *did* speed up. Which worked rather nicely, since two of them ended up crashing off the road and into the trees.

The lead team—the experienced guys, Mingo, Cat, Load, and Arty—kept right on running past the wrecked trucks—nobody fired at them. By the time the slower guys got there—five seconds later—there were Nigerian soldiers crawling out of the wrecked trucks and some of them were ambitious to bring their weapons to bear.

In Farsi, Cole gave the order not to wipe them out. Just bloody them enough to get their heads down. It didn't take much—nothing like a car wreck to take the fighting spirit out of a guy. In moments they were scurrying or limping or crawling away in the brush. Those that could. When you sprayed out bullets, you couldn't help killing *somebody*, even if you weren't trying to eradicate the enemy force.

The voice of the drone operator came back into Cole's ear. "That team you set me to follow?" he said. "They got the distress call from this team, and they're closest, so they're coming."

"That is sweet," said Cole. "How close?"

"About five minutes away at current speeds."

Cole immediately gave the order to the whole jeesh: In about three minutes, at my order, stop firing and disengage. Rendezvous just north of the first village.

When the others reached the rendezvous site, Cole was already there, sitting on a low tree limb with his feet on the ground, watching what the drone was showing him. "They're a bunch of regular good Samaritans, these rapist bastards," said Cole. "They're picking their injured buddies up, binding their wounds, loading them on trucks."

"Sneezing on them?"

"Hope so," said Cole. "My Noodle focus isn't sharp enough to see."

They moved out again, to more remote enemy squads, and they were able to stop two of them before they could wipe out the villages they were assigned to, though in one of them, the village leader had already died with the Biafran flag around his throat. After that, a general retreat must have been ordered, because the whole Nigerian Army force got onto the main roads and headed back north to safety.

Cole could have ordered in a strike and wiped the whole group out. That was the nice thing about Torrent's having announced this campaign to stop the genocide in Nigeria—they could bring in air strikes in full view of civilians in the most populous country in Africa. But this was one time when they wanted the enemy to escape. Though he did have his guys intercept them once and fire at them just after they passed, to give the illusion of hot pursuit. Cole didn't want to have it occur to the enemy that the Americans had deliberately allowed this regiment to return home mostly alive.

When Cole's team returned to base—which was not much of a base, just a location on high ground far from any villages, where they stashed supplies—they were grim but exhilarated, a combination of emotions that Cole had seen with such intensity only in the aftermath of victory.

"I love these Bones!" shouted Arty. "I'm Superman!"

"Really?" asked Mingo. "Because you *look* like Elmer Fudd."

"Oh, right, a Chinese-American Elmer Fudd," said Arty.

Cole let them banter. All but Cole had their Bones and Noodles off, letting their chips download a software update from satellite. Meanwhile, Cole was monitoring the drones, which were staying high and out of sight and earshot, so the enemy would not know how easily they could have been destroyed at any time. They were halfway through dinner when he was able to announce, "Typhoid Mary is safely home with the babies."

"Too bad it'll spread to Niger," said Babe. "And Burkina Faso. *They* weren't off killing Ibos and Yorubas."

"There was never any hope of containing it within southern Nigeria," said Mingo. "Epidemics have their way."

"So what do you think? Will President Torrent's quarantine of Africa fail, too?" asked Cole.

"Don't know," said Mingo.

"You say it like you also don't care," said Cole.

"Do you really think *Torrent* wants to confine this epidemic to Africa?" asked Babe.

How deep was their hatred of Torrent? "Why else would he take the heat he's getting from everywhere?" said Cole. "'Heartless Americans,' 'the Butcher of Africa.'"

"Now everyone will believe that he *tried* to prevent it," said Babe, "even though he really wants it to spread."

"Why would anybody want that?" asked Cole.

"Oh, no," said Load Arnsbrach. "We've said bad things about his papa and he's getting mad."

Cole looked around at them, puzzled and angry. What was *this* about?

Then they broke out in laughter. It was all a joke.

Yet it had not been a joke at all, Cole knew that. But he laughed with them as if he didn't.

"Did they really think they could withdraw into the north, enforce a quarantine, and still rule the whole country?" asked Benny. "I mean, all the oil's in the south. These clowns move north, they got no source of new money."

"The epidemic shut down the oil wells anyway," said Drew, ever the professor. "And they have enough money stockpiled to run the government for years—if the fat cats are willing to dip into their Swiss-bank savings accounts. The epidemic dies down, dies out, they come back, take over the wells again. Who's in any condition to stop them?"

"They can still do that," said Mingo.

"Not really," said Drew. "By delaying the epidemic, it's hitting them later. It'll be peaking in the north after it's run its course in the south. If the southerners can get the oil wells running by themselves, get organized as a government, they could buy the weapons—or some helpful nation could give them some—and take their country back."

"Biafra," said Mingo. "So those villagers didn't die for nothing."

"War's an indiscriminate vampire," said Drew. "It sucks blood, it doesn't care whose."

"So is the epidemic in the south nearly over?" asked Cole.

"How long has it been going?" asked Drew.

Babe answered. "Six weeks since it broke out of the first villages," he said.

"Well, it took six months for the worst of the Great Influenza Epidemic of 1918 to run through its main killing force," said Drew.

"Isn't everybody already sick who's going to get it?" asked Arty.

"As soon as the news got out, most people went into hiding. It's not like they all went to the movies or kept showing up at work. But they have to eat. So they'll start going out into the countryside, scavenging. The only people who are safe are the ones who already had it and recovered. Everybody else is virgin territory."

"Including us," said Cat.

They all nodded or looked away. That was the thing

they all knew. Somehow, no matter how careful they were, they'd end up in hand-to-hand combat with a guy who tore off their mask and sneezed in their face. This wasn't a safe time to be in Africa, even if you were authorized to kill anybody you saw.

And the worst thing was, even if they didn't catch the disease they still couldn't go home. The end of this assignment meant going into quarantine themselves, until it was fully demonstrated that they did not have the disease. Only where would the quarantine be? Gitmo? The Cubans would draw the line at that. It would have to be on board a ship at sea, which wouldn't be allowed to dock until everybody on board had been clean for a month or two—or until everybody on board had either died of the disease or caught it and survived.

But as soldiers, their survival depended on *not* thinking too far ahead. If they had wanted a safe life, they wouldn't have joined up with Reuben when he formed this jeesh, and they wouldn't have brought Cole into their Bones and Noodles training so that President Torrent would know about their capabilities when he needed them.

They also knew that the chance of the quarantine of a continent actually working was slight. Somebody would get out. Some small boat or plane would sneak through from Sudan into Egypt, or from Mali to Algeria, and it would erupt from there to the whole world.

But maybe not. Maybe this would work. Maybe by fighting here, they were saving the lives of billions of people all over the world. That was a job worth doing.

And even if they failed, it was better to die trying than just to sit back and let it happen.

Cole wondered. Does President Torrent really expect the quarantine to fail? How could it possibly benefit him if it did? How would cutting the world's population in half accomplish any goal that he could possibly have?

If the guys really believed this—if it wasn't just Babe—then did it mean they were crazy? Or that Cole was crazy not to see what they were seeing?

They weren't crazy. They might be wrong, but whatever had them thinking ugly thoughts about Torrent wasn't a hallucination.

What did they know that they hadn't told him?

TEN

CHRISTIAN CLARITY

I took an oath to preserve and protect the Constitution of the United States. If the nictovirus reaches our shores before we develop a vaccine, it is highly unlikely that our present form of government would survive such a devastating crisis. The worldwide economy certainly would not, and since our national prosperity and safety depends on that network of trade, we would suffer a collapse as well. A slow, shortsighted, soft-handed government could not stand against the waves of fear and violence that would come.

Slow, shortsighted, and soft-handed are the hallmarks of democratic republics like ours. That's the kind of government we Americans like, because it doesn't bother us much. And that's why I'm determined to do everything I can to prevent the plague from spreading through the world and causing a collapse that could, in the long run, kill as many people as, and be more destructive of civilization than, the nictovirus.

When there is nothing we can do to save a drowning man, our responsibility becomes to save ourselves.

IT WASN'T the largest news story, but it was there on every network. Three hundred Baptists and a scattering of members of other churches, demonstrating as near to the White House as the security forces allowed. They carried signs:

> Matthew 25:40: Let Us Help Them!
> Mr. President, We Are Not Afraid!
> Christians help the sick
> God has not forgotten Africa! Neither will we!
> Matt. 9:35: Let Us Follow Him!

Some of the signs were hand-lettered, but most were machine-printed so they could be read easily on television sets.

The commentaries were predictable. Fox News gave a sympathetic interview to one of the leaders of Christians Going to Africa. Every other network interviewed the craziest-looking individual protesters. But the message got out either way.

"We're not afraid to die," said the leader of CGA. "We all die eventually. We're afraid of facing God without having done all we could to help his children."

Cecily got home to find Mark sitting in front of the television set, and it was obvious he had been crying. He didn't look up when she walked in the house, so after she set down her purse and the mail on the kitchen table, she came back into the living room and sat down beside him, saying nothing at all.

He was watching the MSNBC coverage, which was almost fawningly supportive of President Torrent's position. Two commentators were talking to each other. "It's like President Torrent is the parent of teenagers, and he has to say, 'If everybody else was jumping off a bridge, would you want to do it, too?'"

"President Torrent is trying to keep the rest of the world safe from this terrible epidemic, and these people want to run the risk of spreading it, just so they can feel better about themselves."

"So you're saying that they aren't actually being generous, they're—"

"It's a very selfish thing to do."

"Of course, they *would* be risking their own lives, if they were allowed to go to Africa."

"What do they think three hundred untrained caregivers could do in a continent of a billion sick and dying people?"

Mark whispered his answer from the couch. "They could try."

"Mark," said Cecily. "There's nothing you can do."

He glanced at her, then turned back to the screen. "That's what Chinma said when he saw this news story. He said, 'They don't know anything, they don't want to go there, they don't want to die like that.'"

"He's one of the few people in America who actually knows what he's talking about when it comes to the nictovirus."

"But he lived through it," said Mark. "Most people do."

"Mark, there's ninety-nine percent 'most' and there's fifty-one percent 'most.' The one's almost a sure thing, the other's like a coin flip. Chinma knows better than these people."

"Remember when he said, 'Where were the Christians?'"

"Yes," said Cecily. "In my nightmares."

"I can carry a sign," said Mark.

On the television, the male MSNBC commentator was saying, "Aren't there plenty of needs for charity in America? Why are they so eager to go to Africa? Because it's against the law for them to go, that's why. They're *not* going—so they get all the credit for being charitable, without actually having to do anything!"

Cecily took the remote out of his hand and pushed the numbers for Fox News. They were rerunning clips of the latest U.S. Army special operations in Africa. Atrocity footage, mostly—bodies of villagers who had been shot, and U.S. soldiers, faces covered with breathing masks, holding up a Biafran flag. Since it was cut together from electronically enhanced helmet footage, the camera was jerky and no view was held for more than a moment or two. But that almost nauseating quickness and jerkiness of movement made it feel all the more immediate and real.

"*They* get to help," said Mark.

"Help what?" asked Cecily. "They're working to spread the plague further."

"You know that's not true," said Mark.

"What did you say to me?" asked Cecily. "Are you accusing me of lying?"

"Are you trying to pick a fight with everybody?" asked Mark.

"Not even with you," said Cecily. "But it's very bad form to call your mother a liar."

"Not a liar," said Mark. "A *hider*."

"Oh, really? What am I hiding from?"

"The truth," said Mark.

"And when did you ascend this pinnacle of wisdom, from which you can see truth that nobody else can see?"

Mark turned to her for the first time, making no effort to wipe the tear-streaks from his cheeks, as if he had forgotten they were there. "You only get nasty and sarcastic like this when you know you're wrong."

Cecily was flabbergasted. "I'm not being nasty *or* sarcastic—"

"Both," said Mark. "Dad said so."

Cecily flumped backward onto the couch and stared out the sheer-draped front window. "Oh, did he, now?"

"It was after the two of you had a fight."

"We never fought in front of you children—"

"Pardon me, a 'difference of opinion with raised voices,'" said Mark. "And I said to him, 'Why is Mom so mean when she argues?' And he said, 'That's a good sign. She only gets nasty and sarcastic when she knows she's wrong, and that means that pretty soon she'll realize it and change her mind, so it's a sign that everything's going to be fine.'"

Cecily was furious at the idea that Reuben had told

their oldest boy such an absurd blanket interpretation of her arguing style. She was also grief-stricken all over again, hearing this repetition of something Reuben had said to *her* more than once. "It's just the way you fight, babe," he said. "It's your 'tell.'"

Mark interpreted her silence as a willingness to compromise. "I want to go demonstrate with them tomorrow."

"Mark, you're thirteen."

"It's summer, I can walk to the Metro station, I can make my own sign, I just need a ride to Office Depot tonight so I can buy the tagboard and stuff."

"I'm not letting you go into the District by yourself tomorrow, and that's final."

"Come *with* me, then," said Mark.

"No," she said.

"You know you agree with these people. That's why you were so nasty with Colonel Coleman—"

"*General* Coleman, now that he's working to spread the plague into the north of Nigeria," said Cecily.

"You know he's not working to spread the plague, he's stopping the government from killing their own citizens."

"You aren't supposed to eavesdrop on other people's conversations."

"I was in my room with my door closed. Talk softer next time. Meanwhile you're just mad because you can't do anything about the sneezing flu. But you can."

"Those people on TV are not helping, they're just bringing ridicule down on Christians."

"They can't help what the TV people say about them. You know what those scriptures say? The ones on the signs? One of them is where Jesus says, I was hungry, and you fed me, I was sick and you cared for me. And the other is where it says that Jesus went around preaching and teaching and healing the sick."

"Well, wouldn't it be nice if he were here to do that, but you and I don't have the power to heal the sick."

"Yes we do," said Mark.

"Oh, really. Enlighten me, Saint Mark."

"Nick and Lettie only call me Saint Mark when they want me to be ashamed of trying to be good."

"You and I don't have the power to heal the sick."

"You said it yourself, talking to Cole."

"*I* can call him that, buster, but he's General Coleman to you."

"You keep correcting me so you can avoid hearing what I'm saying."

She knew it was true, so again she sat back into the couch and looked out the window. "I'm listening."

"You said that the early Christians, when the plagues came to the Roman Empire, they nursed the sick, they fed them, they kept them warm, and that saved half or two-thirds of the ones who would have died."

"Yes, that's true. I guess that means you read the book."

"I did," said Mark. "It's like it was talking to *me*. Saying, This is what Christians do, and you're not doing it."

"It's not what thirteen-year-old Christians in America do when the sick people are all in Africa."

"It'll get here soon enough," said Mark. "But if I already went to Africa, and nursed the sick, and caught the virus myself, but had a ninety-percent chance of living through it because the people I helped now help me in return, then I'd come back here completely immune, so I could help take care of the family when the nictovirus finally does get here."

"I see you have it all planned out," said Cecily.

"Except the part about whether I live or die, but I figure that's in the hands of God."

"Yes, isn't it, though. Except it's also in *my* hands, because you're not going."

"I could die right here—a terrorist sniper, food poisoning, meningitis, a traffic accident, a bolt of lightning. Think you can prevent any of those?"

"Food poisoning for sure. Traffic accident probably."

"You know you can't," said Mark. "It's like the lady on TV said, the one from CGA. Which is better, to save my life by *not* helping and just letting the government kill the sick people who try to get away, or to risk my life doing what Jesus did?"

"He didn't risk his life healing the sick, he could just *heal* them."

"Excuse me?" said Mark. "Jesus didn't *risk* his *life*?"

"Who's being sarcastic now?" asked Cecily triumphantly.

"*I* don't get sarcastic when I'm wrong," said Mark. "I get sarcastic when you're just being silly."

Cecily laughed. "Oh, my, you're way too good at this. I'm not sure you should get married without letting the girl take serious fighting lessons."

"And once again you're dodging the point."

"Mark, you can't go. This CGA—if they actually get permission to enter Africa, it's going to be hard enough for them to get anything done without having to worry about a thirteen-year-old. You'd have to have a guardian with you."

"I know," said Mark. "That's why I asked Aunt Margaret."

"You actually talked to her before you talked to me?"

"I talked to you weeks ago," said Mark. "Just because you ignored me doesn't mean I didn't try."

"I never ignore you," said Cecily. "I just hoped that you'd get past this phase."

"And I'm hoping you'll get past yours," said Mark, rising to his feet angrily.

"My decision is not a phase, young man."

"Neither is mine," said Mark. "Adults talk about 'phases' whenever they don't want to take kids seriously. But I'm thirteen. If I were a Jew, I'd be a man."

"I'm sorry I said 'phase.'"

"Aunt Margaret won't take me," said Mark.

"I'm not surprised."

"She says she's too old, she'd just catch it and die before she emptied a single bedpan."

"She's probably right," said Cecily.

"But she said she'd live in our house and take care of Nick and Lettie and Annie and John Paul if you decided to take me."

"I can't take you!" said Cecily. "My children have only one parent left. I'm not putting the other one at risk!"

"How odd. You *drive* in District traffic all the time."

"The odds of catching the nictovirus in Africa and dying of it are way higher than the odds of dying in a traffic accident."

"You risk dying to go talk to the President and make money and help him block Christians from going to care for the sick in Africa," said Mark. "People risk death all the time to do whatever they *want* to do. You like being somebody who the President talks to all the time, so it's worth the risk."

"You are so far over the line, young man, that you can't even see it anymore," said Cecily.

"I'm speaking truth to power," said Mark. "That's what you raised me to do."

"I'm not 'power,' I'm your mother."

"The only person in my life with more power over me is God," said Mark. "Dad liked being a good soldier and serving his country. He died doing that, but it didn't mean he didn't love us. And the way he died set an example for us. For *me*. I learned that my life is only as important as the things I'm willing to die for. Well, I'm not brave or strong, I'll never be a soldier. But I can be a Christian because *anybody* can. All they have to do is be willing, and I'm willing. How dare—" Then he stopped himself.

"Go ahead," said Cecily, challenging him.

"Did you *mean* any of the things you taught me about being a Christian?"

"Go upstairs," said Cecily, turning away from him. It hurt too much to look at him. Because she was never going to let him go, and he was going to hate her for it. He was going to believe all his life that she had deprived him of something vital, a chance to do something that mattered. That's what young boys hungered for more than anything—a chance to be men, to do something real, to know in their hearts that they *deserved* the respect of good men and women. And she was taking it away from him.

But she had attended all the funerals of family members that she intended to. God could not possibly want her to bury one of her sons. Or worse, have him die on some far-off continent and never even know where he was buried.

When she turned back to look at him again, he was gone.

The television was talking now about the new hurricane that was going to pass across Cuba and head for Florida or, possibly, any point on the Gulf Coast. She closed her eyes and tried to breathe without crying for her brokenhearted, too-good-for-his-own-good son.

All the people living in those places were steeling themselves for the possibility of evacuation, devastation, rebuilding.

Cecily saw herself in a hurricane. Rushing with her minivan full of children, trying to get out of town as the storm surge battered against the coast. In the passenger seat, Nick was shouting. Something about a little girl out in the water. Drowning. In her dream, she stopped the car and commanded the children to stay inside. She ran out to the water, but the waves were so high. She was a good swimmer, but was she that good? What was the point of her adding her own death to that of the little girl?

But how could she drive on and leave her to die? So she plunged into the water, walking when she could. The girl was clinging to a piling of an old wharf, mostly gone, just a few poles sticking up above the water. Cecily swam from pole to pole, trying to reach her. And finally she did, and the girl clung to her, and Cecily turned to go back, terrified now of making the swim with this extra weight around her neck.

And there were her children, every one of them, in the water behind her, a human chain from the last pole to her. She was able to swim alongside them; they bolstered her, helped her stay afloat with the added burden, to get her to the next pole. And once she was there, Mark swam out boldly ahead of her to the next pole, the other children clinging to him one after another, remaking the chain. Once again she swam alongside them. In the way of dreams, she kept going and going, and always there were her children beside her, and without them she could not make it, but with them she could.

They got to the shore, to high ground, and she looked over to the road where she had left their van, just as a storm swell reached it, raised it, floated it up, and then sucked it out into the ocean, where it rolled and sank under the waves. And she knew that if the children had obeyed her and stayed with the van, she would have lost them—them *and* the little girl she was trying to save.

She woke up gasping, surprised to find her clothing dry, the television on, and the day outside the front window sunny and hot-looking. There were tears down her cheeks, and she realized that her fingers had been ticking through an imaginary rosary during her fretful nap. But she had not been saying any Our-Fathers or Hail-Marys. She had been saying, Thank you for my children.

She pressed her hands to her face. What did this mean? It was just a dream, brought on by her argument with Mark combined with the hurricane story on the news. She imagined death, rescue, it all fit together. It was just a dream.

But it felt like so much more than a dream. It felt like an answer. It felt to her as if she had been *given* this dream to make things clear to her. But what was clearer now? What was she supposed to see? That she should take the whole family to Africa? Absurd. They didn't even *want* to go. Leave them, then, and take Mark, and trust in God and Aunt Margaret to take care of the younger kids if she died there?

Or maybe she was supposed to learn from it that

the hurricane strikes where it will, and when it will, and to spend your life trying to keep your kids away from the hurricane won't work. The hurricane will find them. They'll plunge right into it. All you can do is prepare them to be brave and good and make the best of whatever comes to them.

No! she silently shouted at herself, or whatever voice it was making her think these things. I am not taking Mark to Africa.

THREE DAYS later, the Christians Going to Africa were still on the news, but now they were dominating it, because the demonstrations were bigger each day. And it wasn't just the Baptists and Pentecostals of Christians Going to Africa now. There was a Catholic group calling itself Mother Teresa Alive, and there were black churches and white churches, Methodists and Presbyterians and Mormons and Jews and Muslims of every stripe, with their own signs, their own quotes from scripture.

The polls still said that most Americans thought of these people as lunatics, but approval of the demonstrators was rising—up to thirty percent now and rising. She was not surprised when President Torrent called her in to take part in an emergency meeting of his kitchen cabinet.

"It's beginning to look bad," said the President's favorite poll reader. "Even people who *hate* do-gooders and/or Christians are saying that you should let them go. So their approval is at thirty-two but support for letting them go is at fifty-five. Even when the question is phrased as negatively as possible, they still think that a quarantine is meant to keep the disease away from America, not keep Americans from going to where the disease is."

Others at the meeting talked on and on, as always, with Torrent listening politely to everybody but shutting down anyone who tried to turn it into an argument.

It's like helmet laws for motorcycles, someone said. People with a death wish need to be protected from themselves.

It's just political, they're trying to make you look bad, they can't attack the quarantine itself but they can make you look like you hate black people or Africans or Christians.

You can't be seen to give in to demonstrators.

You have to talk to them, to show you're sensitive.

Let's get the former presidents to rally around you on this, go talk to these people together.

Ignore them and they'll give up, it's insane and you can't be seen to bow to such madness.

Torrent allowed his advisers to say almost anything. He listened not only to what they said, but also to who was saying it.

Which is why Cecily was unsurprised when he stopped an ongoing discussion and looked at her across the large table. "Cecily," he said, "what's the view from the Christian Right?"

"Is that what I am?" she said. "I always thought of myself as the Catholic Left."

That got her a few chuckles around the table, but not from Torrent. "You actually *talk* to these people, I need to hear from you."

"'These people,'" murmured Cecily.

"Unfortunate choice of words," said Torrent impatiently.

"No, no, it's a very good choice of words. It's very us-and-them. Only I'm in the wrong meeting."

"What do you mean?"

"I have a thirteen-year-old son who is demanding that if I really believe any of the things I taught him about religion as he was growing up, I'll take him to Nigeria myself so we can help nurse the sick."

There was dead silence around the table. Most of them were probably imagining what it would be like if one of *their* children got such an absurd notion. Some of them were no doubt thankful to the God they didn't believe in that they hadn't polluted their children's minds with any religious nonsense.

But Torrent was focusing on her, his face expressionless but relentless.

"I told him no," said Cecily. "I told him no so many times in the past few days that he's stopped asking me, though I know he's making plans to do it anyway. He feels it like a calling. The way some people feel the call to be a minister, or to be a scientist, or an artist, or a soldier, or President of the United States."

Still silence, still the President watching her, waiting.

"So I think of all those people out there demonstrating as my children. They're not afraid of death for themselves. They don't want to die, but they've found a cause worth dying for." She looked around the table. "Those people aren't crazy and they aren't grandstanding and they aren't secretly hoping you don't let them go. They actually think they could do some good in Africa, especially if you let them take supplies and get *re*supplied the way you're doing with our troops over there."

Torrent's gaze turned cold. "It's not the same thing."

"The landings and offloadings are. Charity groups could send food and medicine."

"We're already shipping plenty of medicine and food," an adviser pointed out.

"And letting the corrupt remnants of the government turn them into black market fortunes," said Cecily. "These groups would send supplies to their own absolutely trustworthy people there on the ground in Nigeria and the other countries where the epidemic is spreading. Far more of it would get where it was needed. So my question is, Why not? They want to go, let them go. Donate the use of the planes to take them there."

"It's a one-way ticket," said another adviser angrily. "Don't they get that?"

"They get that," said Cecily. "My son said he figures that you'll only let back into the States people who caught the virus and lived through it. Immune people. He says that Africa will produce a group of American nicto survivors who can come home and treat the victims of the epidemic when it gets to our shores."

"It will never get to our shores!" roared the adviser who thought he was closest to the President.

"Calmly," murmured Torrent.

"Never," the man repeated, but more softly.

"That is a foolish thing to say," said Cecily. "We all know that this virus is going to become endemic, like measles and smallpox and the common cold and cholera and malaria and sleeping sickness, killing steadily at a low level. Even if you can prevent it from seeping out of Africa now, or for ten years, or twenty, someday this antiseptic curtain will fail, and it will reach us. President Torrent is a historian. He knows this."

"I know what I know," said Torrent softly. "This meeting is about what *you* know."

"*I* know that the map of Africa is going to be redrawn at the end of this crisis," said Cecily. "The language groups, the nations, the *tribes,* to use the old politically incorrect but perfectly accurate term, they'll reassert themselves and it will be a new continent. They'll come out of this stronger than ever. If you don't let these charitable groups go to Africa and help, then what will Africa believe about America, about the whole world outside their continent? 'You were content to let us die,' that's what they'll believe. These people demonstrating out on the Mall are offering us a chance to redeem America in their eyes."

"All very nice," said another adviser, about to begin a refutation, but Torrent raised a hand.

"There are millions of people in Africa," said Torrent. "What are the odds that any of them will actually be nursed by these few do-gooders?"

"The odds are very good that those who are cared for by the 'do-gooders' will survive at a markedly higher rate than those who are left without help. However few or many they are, there will be more of them in relation to the general population than the raw numbers would indicate."

"You've really thought this through," said Torrent quietly.

"Yes," said Cecily.

"You never liked my quarantine policy."

"I kept looking for a better national policy, and I couldn't find one. Then I realized that I'm not the President, and what I should be looking for is a personal policy. That one I've found."

"Demonstrating?" asked Torrent.

"No, I'm not going to picket. Or call a press conference. I'm just going to take my oldest boy with me and go to Italy, where Catholic Charities is on the verge of reaching an agreement with the Italian government to fly them into Nigeria, with permission from Libya and Niger to cross their airspace."

Torrent looked angry now for the first time. "The Italians haven't told me that."

"I'm not working through government channels now," said Cecily, rising to her feet. "I'm submitting my resignation, effective immediately. Mr. President, I'm going to Africa."

Torrent also rose. "No you're not. I'll revoke your passport."

Cecily shook her head. "Don't make idle threats," she said. "The moment you oppose me, I *will* go on the air. Former adviser to President Torrent and all that. Much better if you make it look like this was your idea. Your own adviser, the widow of Reuben Malich, is leading the way to Africa. The administration is fully behind the effort to provide relief for Africa, and all those Americans who catch the nictovirus there but recover fully from it will be welcomed home as heroes."

Cecily looked around the table. Most of them weren't even looking at her—she had embarrassed them. The few who did meet her gaze seemed more amused than anything.

"You know that's the only way to play it," she said to them all. "It's the only way that turns this into a plus." She looked Torrent in the eye again. "Use me or oppose me, that's your choice. But my son Mark and I are going, one way or another."

"What about your other children?" asked Torrent.

"Yes, will you look in on them from time to time?" she said. Then she smiled. "I'm their mother. Don't imagine for a second that I haven't arranged for them to be well taken care of, no matter what happens to me."

Then she walked out of the nearest door, feeling Torrent's eyes burning into her back as she left.

ELEVEN

VACCINATION

You have to have a plan. You also have to know when to throw it out and improvise. Even then you can only improvise on the basis of what you're prepared to do. Pianists can improvise on the piano, jockeys on horseback, but don't expect them to swap instruments and make anything happen.

Unfortunately, many a politician, because raw chance makes something come out well for him, supposes that he must be good at improvising, when his only skill is pretending that this is how he wanted it to turn out from the start.

SOME GOVERNMENTS don't need to have an actual crisis in order to fall apart. They just have to believe there *might* be a crisis, and presto! The top government officials take off for other countries, where they have their money stashed; mid-level bureaucrats call in favors from friends and contacts in neighboring countries and get the hell out; and low-level government functionaries, fearing retribution from people who have had to bribe them in order to get a train ride, a ration book, or married, lie low and hope people won't notice them during the ensuing bloodbath.

So it was that even before the first reported case of sneezing flu in Bangui, the capital of the Central African Republic, the government was, to all intents and purposes, gone.

The rebels and bandits who had been making life hellish, mostly in the north but also everywhere, suddenly found themselves, in a word, victorious. They all rushed to the capital in order to assert their claim to be the rightful rulers of one of the most miserable places on earth—a place whose economy had been wrecked by the actions of both government and bandits. Upon arrival, they started shooting one another and, of course, anyone within a half-mile of the shooting, since the bullets easily passed through the flimsy walls of the houses of the poor.

The bandits and rebels from the north and west also brought with them the first cases of nictovirus. Just one more service of the new "government."

Cole had been tracking all this from his headquarters in Calabar, Nigeria, where he had co-opted several abandoned university buildings as the base of operations for U.S. special ops in the region. Calabar was near the border with Cameroon, making it possible to hop from one country to the next if that became necessary; Calabar was also near the coast and nearly surrounded by rivers, for easy evacuation.

"What is the State Department thinking?" he asked

his few aides. "Our embassy staff should have been out of Bangui last week. Now there's no safe way to get them out of there."

"Looks like a job for Iron Man," said Sergeant Jeep Wills, who was handling communications for Cole. When Cole was out on an operation, Wills was the one who decided which urgent information could wait till Cole got back, and which needed to be dealt with immediately through the Noodle. He had done a very good job and Cole was impressed, especially considering that Wills looked to be about fifteen, though his records indicated that he was twenty-one and had graduated from high school in three years and then did the same with college. Smart kid.

"Iron Man has a suit that can deflect bullets," Cole pointed out. "We just have Kevlar. And we actually exist."

"But I mean it," said Wills. "Just got this from State." He handed Cole a printout of an email and sure enough, one group of rebels had decided that the most useful point in Bangui to capture was the U.S. embassy.

"Unfortunately," said Wills, "there were only four people staffing the embassy, so there was no realistic possibility of holding out against a serious opponent. Actually, no possibility of holding out against a troop of Boy Scouts going for their hostage-taking merit badge."

"And what's the good news?" asked Cole.

"There are only four embassy personnel to rescue and get out of the CAR and they don't have families in-country, so at least the State Department kept the number of hostages low."

"That's it?"

"Minor stuff. There are only about two hundred bandits holed up at the embassy, declaring themselves the legitimate government of the CAR, or Sangoland as they want to call the country. Naturally, this has drawn all the other bandit groups that don't already have their own captive embassy or government office building, and there's a lot of gunfire. Fortunately, they're so badly trained that nobody hits anything except windows."

"You got all this from the State Department dispatch?" asked Cole.

"Well, that and emails from Sergeant John Seibt, the token soldier and lowest on the four-man totem pole in the embassy."

"He's a hostage, and they let him send out emails?"

"He told them that he was the only one who could contact the U.S. government, and since none of them reads English he can pretty much write what he wants to whomever he wants."

"Did you just use 'whomever' correctly?"

"Yes, sir," said Wills. "That's why it sounded so wrong to you."

"I guess the State Department wants us, at great risk to life and limb, to extract people they could have brought out peacefully last week."

"That is the gist of their communications. Seibt, however, says that it's going to be complicated because these clowns are so undisciplined they might be anywhere at any time doing anything. But whatever they do, they do it with weapons in hand, which are always going off, sometimes to their surprise and sometimes not."

"The embassy staff is kept where?"

"Wherever his royal highness, King Idi Amin Muhammad Jesus Buddha de Gaulle, happens to be at the moment."

"Oh, please," said Cole. "That's really his name?"

"He wanted to honor all his heroes. This is really funny stuff, General Coleman, sir, as long as you don't actually have to go in there and get them out."

"Which I have to do."

"You could send one of the other teams."

"No," said Cole. "As somebody pointed out, this is a job for the Tin Man."

"I said 'Iron Man.' Can't be the Tin Man, cause you got such a big heart, General Coleman, sir."

"Thank you for setting an example of respect toward a brevet general who is probably going to get killed in this operation."

"So take a look at the embassy on the Google-maps satellite view," said Wills.

"Are you kidding?" asked Cole.

"The Army has access to much better pictures," said Wills, "but this isn't the Pentagon and we're not picking bombing targets, we just want to know where the streets and buildings are. Our software is based on Google-maps anyway, so it's pretty much the same thing."

Cole hunkered down next to the computer screen and looked at the layout. "Can we zoom this image any closer?" he asked.

"Close as it gets," said Wills. "State is emailing us PDFs of the floorplan and elevations of the embassy building. The Google satellite map lets you see how the town is laid out."

"Looks like it's a navigable river," said Cole. "I wonder if we should come in wet so we can make it, like, a surprise."

"Of course, sir. Having captured the U.S. embassy, they will certainly not be expecting a military foray by American troops."

"I'm not looking for strategic surprise, Wills, just tactical. The river?"

"The Ubangi. Or, since they spell in French there, the Oubangui." Wills gave the French version an Inspector Clouseau pronunciation. "But really, sir, if you just come in with a chopper up the river and set it down in any of these fields and parking lots along the river, it'll be surprise enough. The guys who have the embassy are surrounded now by everybody else, so anything that happens six blocks away, they don't know about it."

"This is such a Keystone Kops situation," said Cole. "Somebody's going to get killed."

"Yes, but probably not any of ours," said Wills. "If you're careful."

"How dangerous is this Idi de Gaulle guy?"

"Sort of medium dangerous, for Africa. Meaning he

kills anybody he feels like killing, as long as they're unarmed or he has the drop on them."

Cole took the mouse, backed the satellite map out to a wider view, and then pointed to a little "thumbtack" with the letter A on it. "Since the embassy has the letter B, what's this place with the letter A?"

Wills laughed. "That's a special feature of Google Maps, sir. The 'A' is the pushpin marker for the whole Central African Republic, because that was my first search."

"And they have it pointing to this dirt patch surrounded by warehouses or shops or whatever?"

"A place of absolutely no significance. Maybe on that spot there's a sign that says 'welcome to the CAR.'"

"I'll take it as a sign. The patron saint of directions, Google, has told us where point A is. We only have to fly low up the river, come to ground there, and then move as quickly as possible to point B."

"And then come back again?"

"No," said Cole. "We'll extract to the shoreline right here, in this jumble of barges at the end of Avenue Colonel Conus."

"Um, sir," said Wills, "these barges were here when the satellite picture was taken, but—"

"Wills, if there's one thing I've learned in my travels across Africa, it's that once a bunch of anything gets piled up somewhere, it's pretty much going to stay there until somebody steals it."

"Just my point, sir—barges are portable and can be

stolen. Therefore, until we can get a UAS in there to keep watch—"

"Or until somebody blows it up," said Cole.

"And that would be you," said Wills.

"A spectacular exit," said Cole.

"Go out with a bang."

"Or at least a puff of smoke. But only if we have to."

"I'll alert the chopper kids that their skills are going to be wanted . . . about when?"

"About fifteen minutes after we get those floor plans from State. And wake up the Navy and ask them to give us air cover on about one minute's notice, if we need it. It's okay if they're seen, but they should hang back till I call for them. They're basically the failure scenario—if we get taken, their job is to blow the hell out of the embassy."

"Very dramatic," said Wills. "But that isn't going to happen, right?"

"We just got our third software update on our Noodles and Bones," said Cole. "We're one step away from having the ability to think ourselves through walls."

"You can already leap small buildings in a single bound," said Wills.

"The embassy is a large building."

"With lots of flat roofs at lots of different levels," said Wills. "And you'll have the codes to open all the doors."

"So I shouldn't go crashing through walls?" asked Cole.

"Just on the off chance that someday we want to go back and re-embassize it, sir, it's probably better to blow up as little as possible."

"State asked you to say that, didn't they."

"Very respectfully, yes, General Coleman."

"A bunch of bunnies with spectacles, that's what the State Department is, Sergeant Wills."

"Well said, sir."

"Nearsighted bunny rabbits," Cole repeated, doing his best avuncular general imitation.

Wills chuckled. "It's such a pleasure sucking up to you, sir."

Cole nodded benignly. "Carry on, Sergeant."

"Ay-ay, sir." Of course Wills had to use old-fashioned Naval language, even though nobody would laugh. It all came from letting soldiers get away with nicknames like "Jeep."

It took about two hours to get all the information together and brief the jeesh. Then they put on their Bones, got into a chopper with a nice assortment of lethal missiles attached, and headed almost due east. Just before refueling in midair outside CAR airspace, their chopper would loose four Preds to take up their coverage zones over the target.

It was less than five hundred miles to Bangui, and they spent the time talking through their assignments. It was such a luxury to work with a team like this. Every one of them was capable of leading the mission, and if something went wrong, they'd all react intelligently.

"You're all aware of the software updates?" asked Cole.

"Did they erase my cookies?" asked Drew.

"You know they didn't, or your Bones wouldn't recognize you when you put them on," said Cole.

"Then I'm fine. You know all these updates are for is to fix bugs that might get us killed, and then replace them with new code which is full of new bugs that can get us killed."

"But differently," added Mingo.

"So you didn't read the read-me file?" asked Cole.

"I never do," said Drew.

"Yes we did," said Load. "All of us, even Drew. We're not stupid, sir."

Sir, not Cole. That had been happening more and more. Not a big deal, and maybe it was just because they saw how Cole's major-general stars had everybody else groveling. But Cole thought it was because whatever these guys were into, Cole had failed their test and he was *not* one of them anymore. He could still trust them in combat, because they were great soldiers. But he wasn't in on their secrets anymore—if he ever had been. He was just another "sir" now.

Well, no, he was certainly more than *that,* after all their combat together, but still: He was outside the circle.

"Here on the map, sir," said Benny. "There really is a town named 'Bimbo'?"

"Looks like," said Cole.

"And a few miles south," said Benny, "a town named

'Yabimbo.' He put on a fake gruff voice. 'What're ya talkin' about, ya bimbo!'" Then a girly voice. "No, sir. Bimbo's about ten miles north of here."

Just precombat clowning. They all knew this was a stupid, stupid setup with almost nothing under control. But winging it was what they were good at, so of course they got the assignments where too little was known and the timetable was urgent.

They came in low up the river, but high enough they could see their landmark, the big stadium. When they were opposite the road that came straight south from that, the chopper swung in and moved up a little stream that fed into the Ubangi next to the road. It took about two seconds to realize that the "stream" wasn't exactly a babbling brook—it stank like raw sewage and lots of dead things in various stages of decay.

"At least we won't have any trouble finding this place again," said Arty.

"Yes we will," said Cat. "Because now we and everything we own smells just as bad."

They found a good spot to land the chopper, a grassy field with no buildings facing them. Not that they didn't have observers—quite a few workmen looking over fences in the middle distance. But no kids—it wasn't a residential area. And in a way, it was nice to see people who weren't hiding in terror from all human contact. Sure, there might be rebels shooting one another all over town, but out here they were beyond the range of bullets with enough force left in them to do much damage, and the nictovirus had not yet settled in to stay and kill.

So they were watching the Americans arrive and maybe some of them were thinking, Damn Yankees, and maybe some of them were thinking, Hurrah, the Yanks will save us now! Sorry, folks, Cole said silently. We're just going to pick up our package and run like hell. You'll have to live with your new government as best you can. And the sneezing death that's right behind them.

They hit the ground, offloaded a couple of generous-sized supply packs just in case—they included collapsible stretchers because you never knew what condition the embassy staffers would be in—and the moment the last pack cleared the deck, the chopper was up in the air and moving off, back down the river. When Cole called, the chopper would come back, but this time farther upstream at the rendezvous point—whether there were any barges there or not.

They were all experienced with their Bones now, and they kept good time, running parallel about fifty yards apart from one another. Leaps and bounds, that's how they traveled, but popping up and down at random intervals like the moles in a whack-a-mole game. Sometimes one guy would be going over a building, or hopping up onto it and then off the other side, if he thought the roof would hold his weight, while the rest were only having to leap fences or hop over parked cars. Then it would be another guy's turn to be most exposed to enemy observation and fire.

Over the intercom in the Noodle, Cole heard Arty say, "Donnie Darko Street is getting closer to the river and I'm running out of room."

"It's 'Avenue David Dacko,'" Cole said, with all the patience of an older cousin. "And it's time for the back-door team to head up the Rue de l'Industrie and cut over on Victoire. Seeya, guys."

Cole led the three who stayed with him—Cat, Babe, and Arty—along both sides of some big warehouses. Cole was on the riverside of the buildings, and sure enough, all the barges seemed to be there, just like the satellite picture. Then they got to the place where Avenue Colonel Conus came down to the river and followed it away from the river for about thirty yards before turning left to go into a weedy vacant lot that led straight toward the American embassy, which they could see towering over the street.

This is where they stopped to drop off their supply packages in the lee of a high wall surrounding an even more depressed-looking weedy lot.

"You in place?" asked Cole, and the other team said yes, and that was it. Except that Cole thought to check the drones and saw something he didn't like.

He saw nothing.

Not five minutes ago, as they were coming in on the chopper, the press had shown Avenue David Dacko crowded with bandits. Now there wasn't a soul there.

Cole gave the command to share the image with the others. "You getting that?" he said.

"Looks like everybody went home to get ready for the birthday party," said Mingo.

"Has our plan been compromised?" asked Cole.

"I'd say yes, if we *had* a plan," said Arty.

"I think we were spotted coming in and the other bandits took off," said Mingo. "We weren't trying to be invisible."

"You'd think they'd stay to take a few shots at the evil Americans," said Cole.

"Maybe they have friends in Nigeria and they've heard about us," said Drew.

"Whatever it is," said Cole, "we still have to do it. The backdoor team had better hold off and let us see if it's a trap coming in the front."

He heard assent from both teams and then he said to his guys, "Gentlemen, start your engines."

They bounded over a couple of fences and then leapt Avenue David Dacko. A very empty avenue, except for a couple of thoroughly shot-up cars. No time even to tell the other guys that it gave him the same kind of uneasy feeling that Butch and Sundance had before going out to get shot to pieces in the plaza. It was just another bound and Cole and Cat were up in the air soaring over the embassy wall, looking down at the embassy grounds, with Arty and Babe right behind.

There wasn't a soul waiting for them out in the open, and they had jumped high enough to see that there was no ambush on the lower roofs, anyway.

But somebody was there with a nice welcome for

them, because after Cole and Cat landed, and while Arty and Babe were in the air, there was a savage popping sound from the Noodle and suddenly Cole's Bones became a dead weight, still flexible but dragging him down instead of giving him a boost.

Then there were yells from both Arty and Babe as they landed without benefit of their Bones. Only Cole didn't hear them over the Noodle, he just heard them with his ears, kind of muffled because of the helmet covering them.

Cole flashed on the two jets that he had seen brought down by the electromagnetic-pulse death ray during the assault on New York. This had to be something similar, an EMP that jolted their electronics.

That was the problem with high-tech equipment. If you got dependent on it, and somebody figured out a way to shut it down, you were in deep poo.

But there was a chance that their equipment had only been stunned, not killed. Cole clicked twice and said, "Reboot," and to his relief, the boot sequence initiated. His electronics weren't permanently fried, they'd just been given the old blue screen of death.

The boot sequence was only about thirty seconds, but that was long enough to die.

"Reboot!" Cole yelled. "And get close to the building! Crawl!"

It was the hardest five yards Cole had ever crawled, dragging the Bones along with him. They were heavy and awkward, and it didn't help that almost at once there were bullets flying. But because they had moved immediately, they were in the shelter of the embassy, and the gunmen weren't in a position to see them.

They were in a perfect position, however, for the bad guys to drop grenades on them, so they couldn't stay there long.

"What good does rebooting do?" asked Arty. "They'll just zap us again."

"They can't," said Cole. "It takes them a lot longer to recharge than it does for us to reboot."

"What if they've got a dozen spares already fully charged?" asked Cat.

"So they get to knock us down three more times," said Cole, "and *then* they're done. But I think we just saw all they've got."

He was back online and gave the backdoor team a quick account of what happened to them in the front yard. "They might have an EMP for you, too," said Cole, "or they might have something different. One thing's for sure—they absolutely knew we were coming."

"Gotcha," said Mingo, who was leading the other team. "We'll come in soft and low."

"We're bouncing onto the roof," said Cole to his own team. "On 'go.' Ready . . . set . . ."

Cole didn't actually *say* go, because he didn't have to. They were all in the air at the exact moment he would have said it, and with their Bones working again, they were at roof level in a split second. They grabbed the parapet and flipped themselves over onto the roof, then came up ready to shoot.

Apparently somebody had promised the bad guys that their little EMP weapon would completely disable the Americans, because Cole had never seen such horrified surprise as was on the faces of the bandits on the roof. On his end of the embassy building, where he and Cat were pointing their weapons at the bad guys, there wasn't even a fight. They just threw down their weapons, ran for the edge of the roof, and jumped down onto the low security building that guarded the gate.

There was shooting on the other side, though, so Arty and Babe must have run into some guys with more fight in them. It took only a few moments, though, and there was stillness again. Cole checked only to see that both Babe and Arty were still moving, then flipped to his view of Mingo's team. They were at the back door, having met no resistance.

"Ground floor is yours, Mingo," said Cole. "Remember that only one of the Americans is white, so they might have dressed our other guys up to look like bandits. Be careful who you shoot."

"Yes mom," said Load.

But they all knew that reminders were a good idea in combat, to make sure something didn't slip out of memory in the heat of the moment.

It was quick progress through the building. Cole fired his weapon only three times before he and Cat came through the door of the big conference room and found the hostages tied to chairs, with four men holding automatic weapons to their heads. Cole clicked the code to send the picture to the other guys, which would bring them straight here as fast as they could come. Meanwhile, though, he had no time to wait.

A tall, grinning man in a business suit was holding a pistol. "Just put your weapons down, Americans," he said in French- and African-accented English. "Or we kill your friends. I am Idi Amin Muham—"

He didn't have a chance to finish because Cole put a bullet through his head, then turned and took out two of the guys pointing guns at the embassy staffers. Cat took out the other two.

The other bandits in the room were already throwing their weapons on the floor. With their genius leader dead, what was the point of fighting now?

Cat kept vigil while Cole cut through the duct tape holding the embassy staffers to their chairs.

The first person he cut loose was not the ambassador or the white CIA station chief—it was the sergeant-at-arms. When the duct tape came off the young man's mouth, Cole asked him, "Sergeant Seibt?"

"Yes, sir."

"Good work."

"I had no idea they knew you were coming, sir," said Seibt.

"I know," said Cole. "And we used every speck of info you gave us."

With Seibt helping, it took only a few more moments to get the others unbound, so that everybody was standing up and ready to go when the backdoor team came in. Mingo looked around at the five dead bodies and the cringing not-dead bandits against the walls, and said, "Nifty."

Cole said into his Noodle, "Got all four, safe so far, come pick us up."

Getting out was going to be tricky—anybody set to ambush them out here wouldn't know that Idi de Gaulle had bought the farm. For that matter, it might not be de Gaulle's boys waiting for them. Somebody had given them small EMP devices. That was very, very high tech, which means it definitely was not invented here. So whoever supplied them might be waiting with another set to take them down on the way out. Or even nastier surprises.

"Let's go through the west wall," said Cole. "On the ground floor."

Mingo, Drew, Load, and Benny each picked up one of the embassy guys in their arms like babies. The ambassador protested but Cole just said, "Shut up and do what you're told or we'll leave you here." The ambassador was furious, but he shut up and did what he was told.

The Bones gave them the strength to carry these full-grown men as if they were light as a feather, and with Cole's team leading and following them, they raced down the stairs to the main floor.

Cat found the spot they wanted on the west wall, set four charges, then went back out of the room to where the rest were waiting. He detonated the explosives with a sharp short whistle into his Noodle, and when they went back into the room there wasn't a west wall.

With four of them still carrying the embassy staff, they ran through the gap and into the alley between the embassy and the shops next door. They heard gunfire but didn't stop to fight—none of it was coming close. They bounded into the air to cross Avenue David Dacko and in five seconds they were behind the wall where Cole's team had stashed their supplies.

Using a drone, Cole saw that the chopper was in place beyond the barges, hovering only a foot or so above the river. "We need any of this stuff?" he asked the others.

But instead of waiting for an answer, he picked up his package. The other guys in his jeesh did the same. So everybody had their arms full as they bounded down Avenue Colonel Conus. They leapt over a wall just as the chopper came over the barges and set down on the dirt road that fronted the river inside the boatyard. They got the embassy staffers on board first, then tossed in the parcels and the chopper was already rising as Cole's team clambered on behind them.

There were more shots as they flew down the river, just above the water, but nothing dangerous, and now it was time to debrief.

"Anybody see anything that looked like the EMP device they used on us?" asked Cole.

Mingo might have, but he couldn't be sure. "I mean, what would it look like? A sci-fi raygun or what?"

"What did you see?"

"Like an old-fashioned tommy gun, with the round clip, only it was way deeper, like this." He held up his hands to draw it in midair. "And the barrel came out of the middle of it. No sights, tripod mounted."

"Sounds likely," said Cole. "The cylinder would be the array of batteries."

Mingo took over. "That's why it only made us reboot and didn't kill our electronics. Even if they've got batteries as good as ours, and even if they've got some brilliant way to discharge all the power at once, there's just not enough electricity in Bangui to do a real EMP. The ones that brought down those jets in New York caused a citywide brownout. A really portable aimable EMP device is just not possible."

"But they came close," said Cole. "What if we hadn't read the manual? What if we'd just shed the Bones and gone in without them?"

"Almost did," said Arty. "I was about to push the escape bar when I heard you shout to reboot."

"So what do we know?" asked Cole.

"Best guess," said Cat, "is this was a setup from the start. This Idi Amin de Gaulle clown was the front. Somebody wanted to try out his little EMP device on our electronics, so they got de Gaulle to take over the embassy. They probably promised him that their device would make us sitting ducks so he couldn't lose."

"Whoever it was," said Mingo, "they were able to clear the streets of the rival bandit gangs."

"They probably paid them to come and pretend to be besieging the place," said Babe. "Then told them when to go home."

"The thing is," said Benny, "it worked. They brought

down the suits. If you weren't all such amazingly strong, agile, and intelligent human beings, you really *would* have been sitting ducks. And if they'd had the brains to deploy properly, they could have killed you all as you crawled across open ground to the embassy, or else during the reboot."

"Couldn't deploy like that," said Drew. "They had to stay out of sight of the Preds. Everybody knows we've got eyes in the sky wherever we go. No place to set up a killing ground without us spotting them in advance."

"But the manual EMP-shooters, where did they have those?" asked Arty.

"Inside the building," said Mingo. "It can shoot its pulse through a window without damaging it. Nothing we could have seen."

"Wish we could have taken one home with us," said Cole.

"Not our mission," said Mingo. "Want to go back for it?"

"By now the EMP-shooters are long gone," said Cole. "The real owners of them had to be waiting in hiding somewhere to grab their toys and take them back to wherever they're from in order to report on how they worked."

"It's no secret that we were electronically enhanced," said Babe. "We were demonstrating our Bones all over Nigeria. But am I right in thinking that this handheld EMP thing is designed specifically to counter our Bones and Noodles? I mean, soldiers use a lot of electronics in the field, but nothing they couldn't work around and keep going if it got trashed."

"How many weeks we been showing our stuff?" asked Benny. "You can't tell me they invented that peashooter in three or four weeks."

"They knew what was being developed," said Drew. "And when we demonstrated the goods in Nigeria, they set up the ambush."

"Were they trying to capture the Bones?" asked Arty. "Maybe they were deliberately trying *not* to destroy our stuff, because they wanted to study and copy it."

"Maybe," said Cole. "Makes sense."

"So the EMP might really be stronger," said Arty. "Might really be able to kill our Bones."

"I don't think so," said Mingo. "Unless they've got a way better battery than we have, and can drain it all in a microsecond, what we saw was already at the cutting edge of what's possible in something that size."

"But they might have that better battery," said Cole. "I can't help thinking. Whoever made the big device the rebels had in New York City, it's got to be the same people who came up with the handheld version. And it's worth remembering that up till the moment the nictovirus emerged, the Chinese were all over Africa."

Everybody nodded.

"We Asians are naturally good with electronic toys," said Arty. "And all those machines the Progressive Restoration had must have been built somewhere, too."

"Time to go have a talk with Aldo Verus," said Cole.

"Why? He won't tell us the truth," said Cat.

"But we might force him to tell a better grade of lie," said Cole. "And he might tell the truth. When he was using the big EMP weapon in New York, he was trying to take over the U.S. Doesn't mean he's not patriotic, he just hated the previous president. Why should he hate this one?"

The guys looked around at one another, faces showing nothing—but the fact that they looked at one another meant something.

"Absolutely right," said Cat. "Aldo Verus would have no reason to hate this president."

Again, there was an ugly implication: That Torrent was exactly the president Aldo Verus wanted to install.

But this was not the time to go into a discussion like this—not with four embassy personnel on the chopper, even if they were huddled miserably at the back. And the jeesh were talking through the Noodles, so there was no way they could be overheard, and they had their breathing masks on, there was no way a lip-reader could make sense of anything they said. But for all they knew, the Army kept a recording of everything they said over the Noodles. So when this discussion came, it needed to be under better circumstances than this.

They refueled in midair just inside the Cameroon border, and then returned to Calabar and set down on the university grounds just south of the medical school. They all got out of the chopper, but the rescued embassy staffers transferred directly to a Marine chopper and headed out to sea. The Marines were wearing complete hazmat suits, and the message was clear:

Nobody knew whether the hostages had been exposed to the nictovirus during their close association with Idi de Gaulle's bandits, so they were going to be quarantined for a while.

A month? Or was there a blood test that would give results sooner?

Just how good *are* our breathing masks? Cole wondered. We were in awfully close proximity to these guys, or at least the men who carried them were.

After the Marine chopper lifted off and swung out toward the ocean, Cole took off his breathing mask. So did the rest of the jeesh, one by one.

"Wouldn't it be just our luck," said Benny, "to take all this trouble saving them, only they already caught the nicto and so they all die anyway."

"I don't know," said Mingo. "I think it would be *their* shitty luck, not ours."

"Ah, General Coleman, to smell fresh air again!"

Cole turned to Cat, who was taking a deep breath and stretching.

Then, suddenly, Cat made an almost convulsive movement forward, bending at the waist. It brought his face within inches of Cole's, and at that exact moment, he sneezed.

Cole felt the spray all over his face. Instinctively he recoiled, but part of recoiling is also a quick inhalation. A gasp. Drawing whatever was still in the air from the sneeze deep into Cole's lungs.

"Cat," said Cole. "What the *hell*?"

"It was kind of a surprise for me, too," said Cat.

"Don't worry, not every sneeze is the nictovirus. I always sneezed coming out of scuba gear. Change of air, you know."

Cole leaned close and whispered in Cat's ear. "Bullshit."

Cat just laughed and turned away. "Suit yourself," he said.

"No," said Cole. "You guys have all been 'suiting yourselves,' and I want to know what this is about."

They were far from any of the university buildings, the Noodles were off, and the chopper crew certainly couldn't hear them as they worked on refueling and checking out their bird. This was as good a place as any.

"Aw, guys, the general saw through our little show," said Mingo. "Don't worry, Cat, you did a good job, he's just smart, that's all."

"What little show?" asked Cole.

"There's no way to get home from this assignment," said Mingo, "as long as we haven't caught the nictovirus. Because we *might* have it. So they're going to leave us here for a long, long time."

"And we don't want to," said Arty. "Don't get me wrong, we love our job, it's been great. We've just got a few things to do in the States. So if we get the nictovirus, and then live through it, we're immune, right? So we can go home and come back, go home and come back."

Babe added, "I got the idea from Chinma. There he was, straight from Nigeria, right from the heart of the epidemic, and yet he walks into a conference room in the White House and the President puts his arm around his shoulders and nobody bats an eye. Because he's immune, see? The safest houseguest in the world."

"Great plan," said Cole, "except for the thirty percent kill-off. Or more."

"We thought of that," said Benny, "and we decided that we'd just have to chance it. We'll never get home till we've had the nicto. Right? So better at a time of our choosing. Whoever dies, dies."

"Did it ever occur to you I might not feel that way?" asked Cole.

"Yes," said Drew. "That's why we didn't discuss it with you."

"Just went ahead and infected me," said Cole.

"You're our commander," said Mingo. "We're a jeesh. All for one, one for all."

Cole turned to Cat. "How did *you* catch it?"

"Not the way those clowns from Muslim Nigeria caught it, if that's what you're thinking," said Cat. "I just caught it."

"But not by accident."

Cat raised his eyebrows. "Can't say," he said.

"Well hey, thanks for maybe killing me, Cat."

"No sweat," said Cat. "We saved one another's lives often enough before, at the mountain, you know, and here in Africa, that I figured your life was mine and mine was yours."

"Well great," said Cole. "Now we've got to be quarantined and—"

"No sir," said Drew. "No need for a quarantine. Not when the whole base has already been exposed."

"It's kind of like a vaccine," said Arty. "Except that you get the real disease."

"What gave you the *right*!" Cole demanded.

"It's going to happen," said Drew. "Catching the nictovirus. No matter how President Torrent does with his attempted quarantine. The nicto won't respect his little boundaries, it's coming *eventually,* and so we're going to go through it right here on this base, where we can look out for one another."

"Everybody's going to be too sick to—"

"Don't be such a pessimist, Cole," said Mingo, walking back toward the three-story College of Medical Sciences building that served as barracks and headquarters.

"You going to include this in your report to Torrent?" asked Arty cheerily.

"Not likely," said Cole. "I need you bastards too much to court-martial you. If any of you live, that is."

"That's what we're counting on," said Cat, with a wink. Followed by another sneeze. "Oh my," he said. "I'm really starting to feel under the weather."

TWELVE

SICK LIST

Praying for rain is such a bad idea. Even in the midst of a terrible drought, someone will say, Of course I want it to rain, but not today.

Politics is the art of simultaneously satisfying groups with conflicting goals. The traditional way of accomplishing this is to speak to the groups separately, lie, and then, if you are caught, deny it. You count on the voters to forget or lose interest or change their minds, and they almost always come through for you.

In our time, between national television and the internet, contradictions are more easily caught, so now the best method of pleasing everyone is to promise nothing while seeming to promise everything. New Deal, New Frontier, Change, Progress, Morning in America—there is no limit to the willingness of voters to ascribe to the vague slogan whatever goal is dear to their hearts.

In times of crisis, however, where something is at stake beyond the next election, real decisions must be made. Some voters will discover that their most precious goals are not as important to you as someone else's. Even if you solve the crisis and avert certain disaster, they will never forgive you for having treated their aspirations with contempt. Govern long enough, resolve enough crises, and a large majority will wish to be rid of you.

This natural depletion of popularity only happens to statesmen. Political hacks never have to face the problem, because they never actually make a decision.

The temptation is to eliminate politics entirely and retain power without regard for the next election. This is always done with the intention of governing well; you can take the long view, act for the future, see things through to completion. The newly fledged dictator-for-life will always make wise decisions, he is sure.

But the praying-for-rain problem doesn't go away, it simply takes a different form. Now, instead of uniting to throw you out at the next election, your opponents and rivals conspire to have you killed. In order to forestall them and continue with your most excellent governing, you must find them and kill them first. The bloodbath begins.

People do not have enough appreciation for lying and vague politicians. In their avoidance of commitment, they rarely do much harm. It is the honest statesman who becomes a tyrant, not the hack.

CECILY DID not have to go to Italy and travel with Catholic Charities there. Instead, she was included in the military flights that President Torrent arranged as part of his "wholehearted national support for people who volunteered to go to Africa to help victims of the nictovirus."

One thing about Averell Torrent—when he changed his mind, he changed it all the way. In his press conference the morning after she walked out of the White House strategy meeting, he already had much of his plan worked out. Military flights, military prefab housing where needed, including decent sanitation, and regular supply flights bringing food and medicine, both for the volunteers and for the people they would care for.

He didn't even claim that it was his own idea. "My goal was to keep everybody safe, even the people who didn't want to be protected. But some of my advisers told me in no uncertain terms that you don't tell Americans *not* to do what faith and compassion tell them they *must* do.

"So if these health-worker volunteers are going, let them go with the full support of the people of the United States. Donate whatever you wish—either through your own religious organization or through the fund that we're setting up for that purpose. Not a dime will go for overhead—it will all translate into food and medicines for the sick, and housing, food, and transportation for the volunteers."

He was as good as his word. Aunt Margaret barely had time to get back down to northern Virginia from her home in New Jersey so she could stay with the kids.

Aunt Margaret had words for Cecily, of course. Harsh ones. "If you planned to orphan them, why did you have them?"

"I'm coming back," said Cecily calmly. "So is Mark. But if we don't, they have you. And they'll know that both their parents died standing for what they believe in. Even if it took Mark goading me to make me do it."

"The parent is supposed to lead the child, not the other way around."

"'Whosoever therefore shall humble himself as this little child, he is the greater in the kingdom of heaven,'" said Cecily.

"What is that, the Bible? Catholics don't read the Bible."

"I've been reading a lot of scripture lately."

"So you decide to be a martyr, *then* you read the Bible?"

"I love you too, Aunt Margaret," said Cecily.

For the next hour or so, Aunt Margaret huffed and grumbled through the house, putting her things away in the guest bedroom and checking the cupboards and fridge to make sure that Cecily had some "food that was worth eating instead of all that organic crap without any of my favorite chemicals."

But by the time Mark and Cecily had loaded their luggage into Stevie Popadopolos's car—as per the regulations: "one suitcase, one carry-on, and don't bother with warm clothing or electrical appliances because you'll never have a chance to use them"—and they were saying their good-byes to the other children, Margaret was crying, and when she hugged Mark she whispered into his ear, "I'm so proud of you."

"I'm not," said Nick gracelessly. "I think he's lost his mind."

"He'll miss you, too," said Cecily.

"No I won't," said Mark, but he hugged his brother and they held on to each other for a long time. They were only a year apart, and this would be the first time they were apart for longer than a school day. Or a new videogame, since Nick played like an addict and Mark rarely touched them.

When Nick pulled away he said, "I couldn't do it, anyway. No electronics, no games. It sounds like—"

"Hell," offered Aunt Margaret.

"I was going to say 'school,'" said Nick, "but hell is almost as bad."

For once Lettie seemed to understand that this wasn't about her—though she *was* losing her mother for several months, at least—and both she and Annie hugged Mark and Cecily and then backed off to watch. John Paul was only six, but he got it that this was something serious, and though he was trying not to cry, a little bit of emotion leaked out every few minutes.

Cecily saw Chinma standing in the doorway of the house, looking at them somberly. She beckoned to him. He immediately ducked back into the house, so Cecily left the others and went inside.

"Where you going, forget something?" asked Stevie loudly.

"I'll be back in just a moment."

She found Chinma curled up on the living room sofa. The television was not on, though he was looking at it. "I should go," he said.

"I know it's your country," said Cecily, "but the fact is, you *can't* go. Your asylum status in the U.S. absolutely forbids you to return to Nigeria. If you do, you'll lose your right to be here."

"I should go," he said again. "I already *caught* the monkey sickness. I can't catch it again. I'm the safe one."

"We're going to be very careful," said Cecily.

"Why are you going?" he demanded, and for a moment he looked almost angry. "They're my people, not your people!"

"In one sense, they're not your people," said Cecily. "*Your* family, your whole language, they're gone. But in the only way that matters, there are no people who are not my people."

"Father said Christians never mean what they say."

"Well, he never met us, did he? Chinma, be at peace. You've already faced your share of death and loss and suffering. This is a time for you to heal. Be good to Nick and Lettie and Annie and J.P., and obey Aunt Margaret, and get to learn to speak English even better so you can go to school in the fall. That's your job. What Mark and I are going to Nigeria to do, that's *our* job. Okay?"

He hesitated, then nodded.

Cecily went back to the car. Mark was already inside and so were their bags. Cecily kissed everybody again and whispered to Aunt Margaret, "Chinma is feeling bad because he blames himself for this epidemic. He was the first victim. He didn't cause it, but if he's morose, that's why."

"Got it," said Aunt Margaret. "No blaming Chinma for the deaths of thousands. I'll try to avoid that."

"For an old lady, you're such a brat," said Cecily.

"I was a brat when I was young, too, you know," said Aunt Margaret.

"I don't doubt it." Then Cecily was in the car and Stevie pulled away from the curb.

Mark was silent the whole way to Andrews, and Cecily wasn't inclined to chat, either. The silence was probably killing Stevie, because to her, talk was like oxygen, but she was a good friend and let the silence reign.

Until they were stopped at the drop-off curb and Mark started to get out of the car.

"Wait," Cecily told him.

Dutifully he sat back down, but did not fully close the door.

"This isn't the last chance, but it's a chance."

"For what?" asked Mark.

"To change your mind. No shame in it. You're only thirteen, it's okay to tell your kids, I wanted to go to Africa but I was too young."

"I have kids? When did this happen?"

"You know what I'm saying."

"If you've changed *your* mind, Mom, don't lay it on *me*."

She ignored his defiance. Male bravado. Definitely *not* a phase—a lifetime commitment, or at least until the testosterone ran down. "When the door closes on the airplane, Mark, that's when there's no turning back."

"Then let's get inside so they can close it."

On the plane, she had halfway expected Mark would read the Bible, or maybe he had loaded his Kindle with medical information. How to care for dying people. But instead he had a paperback of the long-awaited final volume of some massive fantasy series, and the few times she tried to talk to him, he looked up as if he were in another world, and she was a hallucination interrupting his preferred reality.

Books about heroes, warriors with swords and bows, powerful wizards, ruthless and beautiful women. The same kind of thing Nick cared about, only Nick wanted to see it on the screen and play through it and win, while Mark wanted to be carried away in a story that had more to it than fighting. Reuben and Cecily had seen these tendencies in both boys from the start.

Nick had to be active all the time—though neither of them had guessed that his main "activity" would turn out to be sitting in front of a TV screen, twitching in response to some game designer's plan.

Mark, on the other hand, would sit still for minutes, sometimes hours, listening to adult conversation. As soon as he learned to read, that took the place of listening—though Cecily and Reuben had both learned very early that when the boys seemed least to be listening, that was when they were most likely to hear and remember everything that was said.

And Mark was a crier. That really flustered Reuben. "I wasn't even yelling at him," he'd tell Cecily. And she'd say, "He's not crying because you yelled, he's crying because he disappointed you."

Crying because somebody else was in pain, because he had inadvertently hurt somebody, because the movie was sad, and sometimes because it was happy. Hyperdeveloped empathy, Cecily called it once, and Reuben said, "Empathy's the thing you have to switch off if you're going into the soldiering business."

"Well, I guess that's not where Mark's going to go," said Cecily.

But they both knew it wasn't true. Reuben was consumed with empathy for others. That was part of what made him a good soldier—his ability to sense what the other guys on his team needed to hear him say. And his ability to guess what the enemy would do. Not to a level that would qualify as magic in one of Mark's books, but often enough to make a difference, to make Reuben a superb leader of men.

They hadn't got parts and pieces of Reuben. Mark and Nick were their own men, their own mixture of genes and upbringing and whatever God put into them and maybe whatever was really *them*, independent of everything and everybody.

Mark is the one who cries at the drop of a hat, so I'm taking him to a place filled with suffering and death.

But he won't just watch. He'll have something real to do, something that isn't in a book, isn't on a screen, isn't imaginary, and wasn't prescribed for him by some homework-manic teacher.

Oh, God, please let this boy learn from what he goes through. Don't let it hurt him, don't let it break his spirit, don't let him become hardened to suffering.

And while you're at it, keep us both alive, will you?

She wanted so badly to grab him and hug him and yell at him for getting them both into such a nightmare and then rock him to sleep in her arms. Always she could feel him in her arms, her firstborn, the one who taught her how to nurse a baby, the one who taught her how little she needed to teach, he just learned any-thing, everything, kept coming up with new achieve-ments every day, and all she could do was hold out a hand when he needed one, comfort him when he needed comfort, feed him, clothe him, and then stand back and watch what he was becoming.

What am I doing, taking you to Africa, to Nigeria, to a land of plague and war? The Book of Revelation is all coming true in this place we're going to, and we have no weapon at all, nothing to protect us.

And then she thought: Cole is there. Cole and all of Reuben's boys. The finest soldiers in the world. They're there, too. She thanked God for them. And then, fi-nally, as night rushed toward them across the Atlantic, she slept.

When she awoke, Mark was curled up against the window. Not so tall-looking now, his body so young and thin, his sweaty hair clinging to his forehead and cheek, his fist up under his cheek the way he always slept on car trips with the family.

Whatever sleep they had wasn't enough, but when the plane landed, there was nothing to do but get up and gather their belongings and shuffle toward the door and out into the bright sun of a Nigerian morning.

Theirs was the first plane of the relief mission to arrive—one of the perks of being a presidential adviser—but it was clear that the people awaiting them, Nigerian and American, weren't quite sure what this influx of untrained people would be good for.

By her nature, Cecily couldn't stand back and wait

to be told what to do. She was obedient enough when they were shuffled from the plane to a trio of city buses and driven from the deserted airport to the abandoned university campus that was now a makeshift American military base. But when the whole planeload of volunteers were left sitting in a large lobby of the College of Medical Sciences building with only about half enough chairs and absolutely nothing to see or read or do, Cecily got up and began to make a pest of herself. She knew how to talk to military people, how to explain things without raising the stress level too high.

"If you don't have any place ready for us to sleep or eat, that's fine. But maybe if someone could brief us on what we should and shouldn't do for patients of the sneezing—the nictovirus—what their symptoms are, what might help them keep a fever down, what they can eat—"

"Ma'am," the lieutenant assigned to them finally said, "you don't get it. We don't do *anything* for them. They aren't *here*. Mostly we just try to keep sick people off the base, keep our contact with the locals to a minimum."

Cecily was stunned. "Well, didn't anyone tell you we were coming?"

"Did anybody ask us if we wanted you?" asked the lieutenant. "No, sorry, ma'am, I didn't mean that the way it sounded. We've kept ourselves separated from the local population because our soldiers have to stay healthy to do their work. The few health workers who actually interface with the patients aren't allowed on the base. For fear of contagion."

"Then we need to get off the base as quickly as possible," said Cecily, "because we're here to interface with the patients."

"I know," said the lieutenant, "and if it was up to me I'd let you all march through the gates and go to it, whatever you think you're here to do. But our base commander has the crazy idea that he doesn't want you all to be sent home in body bags. Or buried here so that the virus doesn't enter American breathing space even in corpses. To put it bluntly, ma'am."

"Who is your commander?"

"General Coleman, ma'am."

Of course. She knew he was the head of American military operations on the ground in Africa, she just hadn't put it together that they would be brought straight to his base of operations. For all she knew he was out on a mission right now. Hadn't he just gotten through rescuing the U.S. embassy staff in Bangui? Cole wasn't the type to sit around and wait for a bunch of civilians to arrive.

Then again, Cole was also not the type to leave them with no support, no instructions, nobody to greet them.

Most of the people found some miserable spot on the floor to lie down and sleep, using wadded-up clothing from their suitcases as pillows. The second plane arrived only a couple of hours after theirs, and those people made it even hotter and more crowded.

But then food came, big serving bowls pushed in on carts, and metal dishes in stacks and utensils in bins. Some of the food was familiar—peanut butter sandwiches, ham and cheese sandwiches, turkey and cheese, roast beef—but there was also a gloppy mess of white-colored mashed yams that had little flavor, but whatever there was, she hated it and so did most of them.

"Get used to it," said one of the soldiers serving them. "Yams are the staple of the Nigerian diet. When in Calabar, do as the Nigerians do. Except for their spices. These people think jalapeño peppers are boring."

Cecily thought of how Chinma had said American food was bad. But as far as she could tell, these yams were as bland as plain macaroni. "These yams don't taste all that spicy," said Cecily.

"Yeah, well, that's because this is food for Americans. If we served you what the Nigerian cooking staff eat out in the kitchen, you'd cry like a baby."

It took more than an hour, and two loads of food, before everyone was fed. Then there was the bathroom problem. The base supposedly had all the comforts of home, and the military kept everything absolutely clean—no slacker when it came to discipline, was General Cole—but there were suddenly more than a hundred new people on pretty much the same toilet schedule, and there just weren't enough holes in the latrines for everybody, without leaving a lot of people to dance around or hold very still outside the doors, waiting their turn.

Finally a doctor—judging from the lab coat—came into the room and talked for a few minutes with the lieutenant in charge, a different one from the one she had talked to before. The lieutenant called out in a loud voice, "Please quiet down and pay attention, folks! This is Doctor Miller and he's about to give you your training."

"Such as it is," said Miller. And then he was off and running.

It was badly organized and sometimes incoherent. He talked about the course of the disease, but then kept interrupting himself with meaningless or depressing anecdotes that always seemed to end with him saying, "Of course, he died." Cecily wanted to say, Does anybody live through it?

But when he started to repeat anecdotes, it dawned on her that he had not personally seen any cases of the disease. He was going on rumors.

Get us out of here to a place where we can be trained by somebody who actually knows what he's talking about!

Then he got onto the topic of safety. "Gloves! Masks! Wash everything! Touch no one!" The same message over and over. The third time he said, "Staying safe is your absolute highest priority!" someone raised his hand and Doctor Miller called on him.

Oh, it was Mark.

"If staying safe was our *highest* priority, sir, I don't think we'd be here."

The doctor was about to erupt with anger at this insult to his dignity, but many of the adults in the room laughed and some of them even clapped, and he got the message. His lecture was not going over very well.

"We came to help people," said a man. "I'm a doctor back in the States, I'm prepared to train people on antiseptic procedures. What we need are the masks, the gloves, the equipment we're going to be using."

"There is no equipment," said Dr. Miller. Angry now, he had decided on brutal candor. "There is no treatment. Don't you understand that? You get this disease. You sneeze. You cough. It feels like nothing. And then the fever creeps up on you and you feel like you're going to explode out of your skin and you start to bleed in random places and then you either die or you get better—very, very slowly. The whole thing takes about two and a half weeks if you die, two months to get back to full health if you happen not to die. There's no medicine except ibuprofen. What do you think you're going to do for these people?"

There was enough hostility in the room that Cecily decided to speak up, using her we're-all-friends-here voice. "We can wash them. Bring them food and water. Try to keep the fever down. Help them understand that they're not alone, that someone cares whether they live or die. We can pray with them and for them. We can read to them, tell them stories, take their minds off what they're going through. We can give them human company. And we'd like to get started, please. Where are the masks and gloves? Where do we wash? Where are the sick people?"

Her little speech was punctuated by a fair number of amens—something Catholics would never do, but it was actually kind of fun to be part of a vociferously Christian group.

But as the evening wore on, several things became clear. Nobody knew where the patients were, because the hospitals were all closed. There weren't enough beds in Nigerian hospitals to hold even a tiny fraction of the sick—they were told to stay home, keep off the streets, try to stop the disease from spreading. The result was that markets didn't open. Food was running short. Desperate people were breaking into the houses of the sick and stealing what food they had—then getting sick themselves. There was no place to take them.

"This is a university," said Cecily. "There are dormitories? The students aren't here?"

"Correct, ma'am, but Americans would not like Nigerian accommodations."

"What we don't like," said Cecily, "is this very hot and way-too-small room. We'll get used to Nigerian student dorms, and if there aren't enough of them, then find us some empty houses or classrooms and we'll make do. And tomorrow we'll go out and find patients to feed and take care of. We didn't come here for you to entertain us, Doctor Miller. We came to help sick Nigerians."

She got so much applause from the others that Miller apparently felt the need to take her down a peg.

"And what about when you get sick? Do you think we're going to let you back in here with our healthy soldiers?"

"No, we don't!" shouted a man.

Cecily came forward and put a gentle hand on Dr. Miller's shoulder. "It's okay, Doctor Miller," she said. "It's okay. We don't work for you. We're not your responsibility. Almost all of us are adults who are used to running things in our regular jobs. We'll organize ourselves, we'll look after one another. Some of us will probably get sick. Some of us may die. But it won't be your fault. Nobody will blame you. You aren't responsible for us. All we ask is that you get us the basic equipment—the masks, the gloves, sponges, basins, bedpans, ibuprofen, clean water. All of those things were supposed to come on the planes with us, so we aren't even using your supplies. Just point us to the city and let us get started. What we do after that is up to us."

And that speech was how Cecily got herself elected manager of the Calabar Relief Operation. She didn't want the job, but somebody had to be in charge enough to say, Yes, do that, or No, try this instead, so that things could move forward.

What Cecily couldn't understand was why Cole hadn't already arranged for this before they arrived. For that matter, where was he? Surely as the major general in charge of the whole African campaign, he should have put in an appearance. Surely as her friend—even if their last parting had been a little testy—he could show up and . . .

Something was wrong. If not Cole, then one of Reuben's jeesh, somebody should have been there.

They must be out on an operation.

But why wouldn't somebody just say that? "General Cole would like to be here, but he's out doing his job and he won't be back for a day or two." How hard was that to explain?

All this incompetence, all this disorganization, this is *not* how the army works. Something is seriously wrong.

Never mind that by the time she thought of this, it was dark and she was lying on top of the most uncomfortable mattress she had ever lain on in her life. Gravel would be more comfortable—smaller lumps.

She got up and put her clothes back on. They were still damp with her sweat from traveling. She had a tiny LED flashlight in her purse and used that to find her way. The three other women in the room didn't even stir as she left.

Cecily thought of looking for Mark in the men's dorm, but that would be disruptive. It was soldiers she wanted right now, and since this was an Army base in a foreign country, there'd be plenty of them awake already.

Sure enough, it took no searching at all—the duty officer found *her*.

"Excuse me ma'am," he said apologetically. "This city isn't safe at night. Stray bullets, all kinds of things."

"You're just the man I'm looking for," she said, which was true, since any soldier would do. "I'm a good friend of General Coleman. My husband and he served together. I'd really like to see him."

He said nothing. He tried to hold his face still. But his reaction was as clear as day.

"No, don't tell me the lie you were trying to think of," she said. "My husband was Reuben Malich. When I say he and General Coleman served together, I'm talking about the day of the assassination. Do you understand?"

She could see from his expression that he knew now who her husband was, and he was suitably impressed. It worked much better with soldiers than saying she was an adviser to President Torrent. Dozens of people could say that. But Reuben Malich had only one widow.

"Whatever's wrong here," she went on, "I'm going to find out about it. Above all, I'm going to see General Coleman, and I'm going to see him tonight. If you help me, it'll cause a minimum of bother and then I can get to sleep and you can go on about your business."

Ten minutes later, she found herself in a room with a very sleepy and irritated Dr. Miller, the duty officer, and two very tough-looking captains. It was obvious that their plan was to stonewall her. The fact that they thought there was a need to stonewall told her almost everything she needed to know.

"General Coleman is here on this base," she said, "or you'd simply tell me he was not. If he knew I was here, he'd let me come see him. So he doesn't know I'm here, and that suggests some kind of mutiny or that he is badly injured. Which is it?"

"Neither," said one of the captains.

"Very well," she said. "I may have resigned my position as an adviser to President Torrent, but I still have a private cellphone connection to him. It's still early evening in Washington, D.C., so I will certainly reach him and he will certainly want to know what's going on here. And if you try to prevent me from making that call—"

Dr. Miller sighed. "Oh, Lord, she's one of those. '*Do* you *know* who I *am?*'"

"Who I am," said Cecily, "is a friend of Cole's, and I'm going to find out what's going on with him, come hell or high water."

"Well, he's sick," said Dr. Miller. "Isn't that obvious?"

It was clear that one of the captains wanted to do something nonlethal but memorable to Dr. Miller, while the other captain was relieved. Cecily turned to the relieved one. "He has the nictovirus?" she asked.

"He's been exposed," said the captain. "No symptoms yet, but he's quarantined himself. And the rest of his team. They were all exposed. Captain Camacho and Captain Black *are* symptomatic."

"Well, that sounds like a championship-level screwup," said Cecily. "Nevertheless, I'm here to deal with sick people. I'll wear a mask and gloves and I won't kiss him on both cheeks as we Washington policy wonks are apt to do. But I'll see the general now, please. And I promise I won't say much about how badly you're all handling this situation."

"This is none of your business," said the hostile captain.

"As the President's personal representative in the Christian relief effort, Captain, it is most definitely my business, and you in particular are my business. If I see you again tonight, or hear your voice, or see any evidence of your existence, then you will be my business for a long, long time. Have I made myself clear?"

The captain was eager to put her in her place, but he wasn't quite sure what her place was, and apparently he began to think that she might have as much clout as she claimed. While he stood there in an agony of indecision, Cecily helped him. "You aren't actually needed in this room right now, Captain. Perhaps there are other duties you could attend to while Doctor Miller helps me find a mask and gloves." Then she turned her back on him and led the doctor and the cooperative captain out of the room.

Of course she knew perfectly well that the hostile captain was actually the more competent of the two— the other one caved in far too easily—but only one of them was useful to her right now, and it wasn't the competent one.

A few minutes later, she was in Cole's quarters. Apparently it was the office of the head of the medical school, converted to military use, and the bed looked comfortable. Cole was not in it, however. He was stiffly sitting in a chair behind the desk, in full uniform.

"Cecily," he said. "How dreadful to see you here tonight."

THIRTEEN

SYMPTOMS

"Everything" is too long a list to work with.

No one knows everything about anything.

No one knows something about everything.

Everyone knows something about some things.

Anyone could be the world's foremost expert on something.

Anyone who thinks that just because they didn't already know a thing, it must not be true or important, is an idiot.

CHINMA STUDIED hard, trying to make sense of Lettie's math textbook. She was only ten years old, and yet she was far ahead of any knowledge Chinma had acquired at the village school.

There were people in Nigeria who got very good schooling. Ire had been given an accountant's education. He would have known everything in this book. But Ire was firstborn son of the second wife. He was expected to amount to something.

Or maybe it was Chinma's own fault. The little marks on the pages seemed to run away from him, and the more closely he looked, the harder it was to see them. He could always see the ones he wasn't looking at, but as soon as he thought about one he could see, he'd look at it and it would run away. So he always had to look at a place that was different from the letter or number he was supposed to be looking at, and so he was very slow at reading and calculating.

No wonder the teacher had told Father there was no reason to keep Chinma in school. Only Mother's stubborn insistence had kept him there. And what had Chinma done with her hardwon victory? Spent every moment he could up in trees. *That* had worked out so very well.

He still had his money from monkey-catching, but when he exchanged it, his 27,000 naira had turned out to be only 180 dollars. Nick and Lettie had been impressed that he had so much, but Mark had told him just what his money would and wouldn't buy. Forty-eight Big Macs, or one iPod Nano and forty-five tracks from iTunes, or a round-trip train ticket to New York plus a couple of cab rides.

Why would he want any of those things? But he could see Mark's point—that his 180 dollars would disappear very quickly if he spent any of it. He could see how useful it was to know how to do the numbers and figure things out, but Lettie's math book didn't talk about the things he wanted to calculate. And yet when

Mark told him what his money would buy, he had understood instantly how Mark figured it out. He just couldn't *do* it.

Chinma didn't like being stupid in Oyi, and he didn't like being stupid in America. He *wasn't* stupid, he was sure of it. But everything came so much more easily to other people than to him.

The army doctor had given him glasses, but they were no good, they made everything blurry. Maybe that was because when the doctor had him look through the machine at the eye chart, none of the settings worked to solve his problem of letters that ran away. So Chinma finally told the doctor that the setting he had right at that moment was perfect. It wasn't, but what could he do? The doctor was so eager to help him.

I see everything, Chinma wanted to say. I see things that other people miss. I see *perfectly*. But when I look at something very small and close to me, it disappears. Do you have a lens for that? But that would have been rude and presumptuous of him. The doctor never *asked* him anything to which that information would have been the right answer.

I should have said it anyway, Chinma thought. Americans say what they want to, instead of politely waiting to be asked the right question. Americans are rude. But they get their point across quickly and easily and then things work out right.

"There you are," said Aunt Margaret.

Chinma looked up from the book.

"Why don't you wear your glasses?" asked Aunt Margaret. "You look all bleary-eyed."

"I forgot," said Chinma.

"I need to tape them to your head," said Aunt Margaret. "You always forget."

Chinma had no answer to this, so he continued to look off into space—not challenging her by looking her in the eye, but not turning back to what he had been doing before, as if she were unimportant.

"Oh, yes," said Aunt Margaret. "I received the oddest email from Cecily—Mother—"

"Mrs. Malich," Chinma prompted.

"She wanted to know if you could write to her. She has some questions. Did you have an email address in Nigeria?"

"I don't think so," he said, truly distressed to disappoint her, for he had no idea what she was talking about.

"Don't they have the internet in Nigeria? They must, or Cecily could *not* have emailed me!"

If I knew what it was, perhaps I could tell you. But she seemed to take it for granted that he knew what she was talking about, so if he admitted that he didn't, he would look stupid.

"Well, you can write her a letter using my account."

That was how Chinma ended up in front of a computer screen, staring at a bunch of letters, all of which fled when he looked at them. Plus the screen was too bright.

"Just type what you want to say, I'll take care of addressing it."

But I don't have anything to say, thought Chinma. It was Mrs. Malich who wanted to write to *me*. "All right," he said.

He looked down at the keyboard. He could see that all the keys had letters and numbers on them, and sometimes tiny words, but whichever one he looked at became invisible. This was not going to work.

He bent closer to the keyboard and now he could see the letters.

"What in the world," said Aunt Margaret. "Where are your glasses?"

They won't help. "I don't know," said Chinma.

"Did you lose them?"

He could see her wasting time searching for the glasses, and if she did, he'd have to wear them, and then there was no hope of his seeing the keys. "What should I write?" he said.

"Just say hello," said Aunt Margaret, "so she'll know she can write to you at my address."

Just in time he realized she didn't mean "say hello," she meant "write hello." Chinma looked for the *H*. He found it. It disappeared. He looked again, and this time kept his face very close to the keyboard. It stayed visible. He pressed it.

"No, no, just press the key once and let it go," said Aunt Margaret.

On the screen were the letters *"hhhhhhhhhhhhhh."*

"You seriously don't know how to type an email, do you," said Aunt Margaret.

Now he had shamed himself. He shrugged, keeping

his head down and trying not to let tears come into his eyes.

"I have an idea," said Aunt Margaret. "Why don't I type the letter for you, and you just tell me what to say?"

Chinma gratefully got out of the chair and stood aside so she could sit down.

She immediately put her hands over the keyboard and began to move them so fast Chinma couldn't even see what she was doing. But words appeared on the screen, lots of words, and then she took the mouse, moved it on the table, and made the whole letter disappear.

"There, I've told her she can write to you at my address."

"Thank you," said Chinma. He started to leave.

"No, she's there right now, she's going to answer, I think it was rather urgent."

So Chinma waited.

So did Aunt Margaret.

Finally Aunt Margaret laughed. "Well, we're not doing any good sitting here staring at the computer, are we?" She started to get up. He started to leave the room.

There was a click from the computer. "Wouldn't you know it? I get up, and her letter comes. I think the computer was just waiting for me to stand up."

"Why would it do that?" asked Chinma, marveling that she would keep a machine so perverse.

"It doesn't, really, that's just how it seems sometimes. Yes, it's her letter, and it isn't long, she just wants to know from you . . . oh, she can't mean this." Margaret swiveled in the chair. "Chinma, it seems that nobody in the place she's at has any idea of the course of this disease, this nictovirus. She knows it might be very painful for you to talk about it, but she has to know what actually happens in the disease. How it progresses. Since you've actually had it."

These were questions the scientists had asked him over and over. He knew he could answer them. He immediately started talking. "It starts with a tickling in your nose, and you sneeze. More and more. But then you have to keep swallowing . . ." Chinma struggled for the English word. "In your throat, nose stuff."

"Mucus. Snot. I get it."

Chinma registered the words and moved on. "While that's happening, you get . . . stopped up."

"Stuffed up, I think we say here."

Chinma knew what "stuffed up" was, and that wasn't what he was talking about. "No, I mean—stools don't come."

"Oh, constipation. That's interesting, I've never read anything about that."

"Very bad constipation," said Chinma, trying out the word. "Days and days, and your stomach gets full and heavy and you don't want to eat."

She was typing furiously. "You're fine, I'm keeping up."

"You just want to lie there and your stomach hurts, but you can't sleep because it's so hot."

"The weather? Or your temperature?"

Chinma touched his head, his chest. "Everything."

"Fever then."

"And I got a headache. And you start to cough and sneeze all the time until your chest hurts. People cry from the headache and the stomachache and the coughing, but nothing helps. And then all of a sudden everything comes loose and you shit and shit and shit."

"Okay," said Aunt Margaret, "I can see that the language barrier is quite selective."

"Shit and shit," said Chinma, "and you can't get away from it and nobody will clean you up. Most of them die in their shit."

"I must ask—are the stools solid or loose?"

"Solid at first," said Chinma, "but then piles and finally watery and then nothing but you still try to push out the nothing because it hurts so bad."

"Severe dysentery," said Aunt Margaret as she typed.

"So blood comes out instead," said Chinma. "It comes out everywhere, and if you didn't shit to death you bleed to death. The ones that die, they bleed a lot."

"But not everybody does?" asked Aunt Margaret.

"I didn't bleed," said Chinma. "The people who don't die of it don't bleed as much." She was typing, and he realized that she might have misunderstood. "But a lot of people die without bleeding at all."

"Very important distinction, thank you," she said. She typed more. "Does it help to stop the bleeding?"

"I don't know. It wouldn't stop."

"No clotting?" she asked.

"What?"

"Didn't the blood dry and form a scab?"

"No," said Chinma.

"Does it gush out or seep out or drip out—"

He had no idea what she was asking. So he waited.

"Does it come out fast? The blood? Lots of it, or just a little at a time."

"Little at a time." He remembered his little sister, the baby. She was covered with blood but nobody could even see where it was coming from. It just came out of her skin in very fine drops.

"When the bleeding starts, you only have a few hours left," said Chinma. He had held the baby and when she died he was covered with her blood.

"But if you aren't going to die, there's no bleeding."

"Sometimes a little bleeding but then it stops," said Chinma. "And a lot of people who don't bleed die anyway."

"Is there anything else?"

"If you don't die, you're very weak. You just lie there. You don't have the strength to get up and go for water. You get really thirsty."

"Can you drink? When someone brings you water?"

"Nobody brought me water."

"What did you do? You must have been horribly dehydrated." Then she corrected herself. "Very thirsty."

Chinma nodded. "I made myself crawl to the river. We aren't supposed to drink from the river because it's dirty and makes you sick, but it's the only water I could reach."

"Why didn't someone bring you water?"

"Everybody was sick," said Chinma. "But after I got water I felt a little better and I brought some back for Mother and the others. They were just getting the fever then, coughing and starting to shit. I went back for water again and again, but then the baby died and Mother screamed at me to go away because I killed her."

And suddenly Chinma was overwhelmed by the memory and sank to the floor.

"Oh my Lord," said Aunt Margaret, getting up from her chair.

Chinma lay back on the floor and breathed deeply. He could feel his head trying to make him faint, and so he lay very still and breathed slowly and deeply to make the fainting go away.

"Are you all right?"

"Yes," said Chinma. Please stop trying to make me talk until I can breathe again.

"Are you sick? Is this something left over from the sneezing flu?"

He shook his head a little. Why was she asking? Didn't Americans get light-headed and faint when they were overcome with grief?

"What can I do?" she insisted.

"Wait," he said.

She didn't understand him, or didn't believe that he had said "wait."

"Wait," he said again, and then closed his eyes and spread out his arms and breathed and finally the light-as-air feeling went away from his head. Carefully he rolled over and stood up.

"Are you prone to fainting fits?" asked Aunt Margaret. "I mean, does this happen often?"

Chinma shook his head. "What else does Mrs. Malich want to know?"

"Just—I think . . . how long till you get your strength back?"

He thought about it. "I don't know how long it was. After you're getting better, you sleep a lot. I remember when I first got hungry again. That's when I knew I wasn't going to die. Then it was only a couple of days before I could climb trees again. That's why the soldiers didn't kill me. I climbed a tree to get away from the stink. But I climbed it very slowly and I didn't go as high as usual because I wasn't sure I could hold on."

Aunt Margaret kept typing for a while, and then, once again, the words of the email disappeared.

"There, I hope that helps her. You were very good to be willing to talk about this all again."

"I told the doctors."

"Did you almost faint when you told them?" asked Aunt Margaret.

"No," he said. That was because he hadn't thought about his baby sister covered with blood and dying in his arms and then Mother screaming at him when he crawled into her room dragging the baby on a mat behind him.

"If you already told the scientists this, I can't understand why in the world this information hasn't been released and these volunteer health workers weren't briefed."

Chinma wanted to get back to the math book. Well, no, he didn't, but the math book was what he had been working on, and he wanted to get out of Mrs. Malich's office. It was a room that the children were never supposed to go into. Mark had impressed that on him very firmly.

But instead of leaving the room, he said, "If I give all my money to the police, will that be enough for them to let me go?"

Aunt Margaret turned slowly and looked at him with an odd expression. "You're not under arrest, you know."

"But Mrs. Malich said I can't go back to Nigeria because of the officials." Or had she actually said that? "Because there's a law against it."

"You're here under political asylum laws," said Aunt Margaret. "If you return to your home country, it means you must not be in danger after all and so your visa is revoked."

"So if I give the man my hundred and eighty dollars, will he let me go?"

"Why do you want to go there? Are you unhappy here?"

"I should go there to help," said Chinma. "I can't catch the monkey sickness anymore, and I know what happens. I can tell them. I've seen many people live and die. I know which ones. And I speak Yoruba and a little Hausa and I understand some Ibo."

Aunt Margaret's eyes narrowed. "Actually, you really might be helpful. It's just a stupid *rule* that keeps you from going. There can be exceptions to the rule. Or at least there *should* be." She turned around and started lifting papers on the desk. "Oh, what am I thinking, she won't leave it lying around." She started using the mouse to bring up different things on the computer screen. "Well, she won't put it on the computer, either. Probably memorized it and *ate* the note on which it was written down."

She got up from the desk and went to the door of the office. "Nicky! Nick! I'm an old woman, don't make me climb the stairs!"

In a few minutes Nick and Lettie and Annie and John Paul were all crowded into the office, looking around at things they had long been forbidden to see.

"I don't recall asking for anyone but Nicky," said Aunt Margaret.

"Nobody calls him Nicky," said Annie. "He hates it, he's *Nick*."

"He's Nicky to me," said Aunt Margaret, "and he likes it fine or I'll smack him."

"What did you need?" asked Nick.

"Your mother has a special phone number she uses to call the President," said Aunt Margaret. "Do you know if she has it written down anywhere?"

"She wouldn't tell *us*," said Lettie.

"I didn't imagine she would," said Aunt Margaret. "But Nicky is an observant boy, and I thought he might have noticed where she went if she was going to call the President on that line."

"He always calls *her*," said Lettie. "I mean Nate Ogzewalla does."

"I keep asking Nicky, and I keep hearing answers coming from you, my dear, and yet your answer is always that *you* don't know the answer, so would you kindly allow me to find out if Nicky *does*?"

"I told you he doesn't answer to Nicky."

"Lettie," said Nick, "just shut up."

"Thank you, Nicholas J. Malich," said Aunt Margaret.

"His middle name doesn't start with *J*," said Lettie.

Aunt Margaret raised a hand in order to slap her. But to Chinma's surprise, instead of cowering Lettie laughed and dodged out of the room.

If he had ever tried that when Father or one of the mothers raised a hand to smack him, he would have been beaten hard with a stick. But Lettie clearly wasn't afraid for a moment. Had anyone *ever* beaten her? Certainly Chinma had never seen it since he'd been here, and yet Lettie often needed to be beaten, because she was always provoking people. Chinma didn't understand American families yet, that was clear.

"She never searched for it," said Nick. "It was just in her cellphone."

"So much for being security conscious," said Aunt Margaret. "If she ever lost her cellphone, the President's private phone number would be there for anyone to take."

"I don't think it matters," said Nick. "It's just a cellphone and if somebody else got the number, he'd throw it out and get another."

"Oh," said Aunt Margaret. "Well, that makes sense. The problem is that it doesn't get me any closer to calling the President."

"Just call the switchboard and say that you're taking care of Cecily Malich's children and you need to speak to Nate Ogzewalla," said Lettie from outside the office door.

Nick nodded. "That'll do it."

"But I don't want to talk to Mr. Ogzewalla," said Aunt Margaret. "He'll just tell me I can't talk to the President, and he'll promise to deliver my message, but then he won't do it because, as everyone knows, gatekeepers exist to keep the gate closed, not to open it."

They all stood or sat in silence, contemplating this conundrum.

"Why not just use her cellphone and find the number that the President answers?" said Lettie.

"Her cellphone? It's here?"

"Well it wouldn't do her any good in Nigeria, would it?" said Lettie.

Aunt Margaret looked at Nick in consternation.

Nick grinned. "Lettie sees everything. I never see anything."

"A good reason to make you stay outside your computer games for at least fifteen minutes a day."

It took about one minute to find Cecily's cellphone.

It was off, and when Aunt Margaret turned it on, it demanded a password.

"Well, there you are. It needs a password and I don't know it."

"Rube," said Nick.

"What?"

"The password. It's Dad's nickname, what the guys on his team called him. Rube. R-U-B-E."

"Oh, so you *do* notice things," said Aunt Margaret. Sure enough, the password got the phone working. "Speed dial," she said. But the first number got her nowhere. "Can you believe it?" Aunt Margaret asked them, pressing END. "The President is *not* the first number on her speed dial!"

"Who is?" asked Lettie.

"Your school," said Aunt Margaret.

It wasn't until the seventh speed dial number that Aunt Margaret finally smiled and nodded.

Chinma looked at her in awe. She was a woman. She was telephoning the President of the United States without permission. And instead of looking frightened or even respectful, she was triumphant.

"Mr. President, I am Margaret Diklich, Cecily's aunt, and I am tending her children, and you can arrest me later for using this telephone number but there's something Cecily desperately needs, though she doesn't know she needs it, and you're the only one who can get it for her."

Chinma watched in awe. This woman talked to the President as if he were a slightly naughty little boy.

"What she needs is a certain political refugee that is living in this house with her children. Apparently the law says if he returns to Nigeria he loses his asylum here, but I suspect that if anyone can get an exception to that rule, it's you."

Again she listened.

"Isn't it obvious? Chinma is the world's most qualified expert on the course of the nictoviral disease and what treatments are effective. And he's completely immune to the infection. Those meddling Christians haven't been decently briefed on anything, it is the most completely screwed-up operation in history, and I'm including Gallipoli, Fredericksburg, and the occupation of Iraq when I say that."

Now they could all hear laughter from the cellphone. The President was actually *enjoying* this conversation.

"I believe Chinma should be sent straight to Cecily, yes, and furthermore, from what he's told me I believe they will need hundreds of thousands of doses of stool softener and just as many doses of loperamide—that's the generic name of Imodium—and ibuprofen, plus a million bottles of clean water."

The President's question was audible to them all. "Why?"

"Because from what Chinma told me, it seems that the people who die without getting to the bleeding stage of the disease are actually dying of dehydration caused by constipation, which causes them to resist eating and drinking, followed by devastating dysentery, which drains them of whatever fluids they *do* have."

The President said something, but rather softly.

Aunt Margaret laughed. "Yes, those are very much like Chinma's own words. They shit themselves to death, Mr. President, and not one person seems to have bothered to tell anyone in this expedition that the main treatment for these poor victims is to keep them hydrated."

More from the President.

"Thank you very much, Mr. President. I will have Chinma's bag packed in fifteen minutes." Then she flipped the phone closed.

"Chinma is *going*?" said Lettie.

"Chinma is needed and he volunteered and so, yes, he's going."

"Then so am I!" shouted Lettie.

"Chinma is immune to the disease and he knows something," said Aunt Margaret. "You are not immune to anything except good manners, and you know nothing. So no, you are not going."

"I know a lot of things!" shouted Lettie.

"You didn't know the password," said Nick.

"I knew everything else!" screamed Lettie.

Aunt Margaret turned to Chinma. "What in the world would *your* parents do about a child like this?"

It was about time someone asked him that. "They would beat her until she fainted."

Lettie turned to him in scorn. "Oh, they would not."

Nick, who had seen Chinma without his shirt, asked, "Shall we show her, Chinma?"

"Show me what?" Lettie demanded.

Chinma stood up, turned his back, and raised up his shirt. He knew what they would see, because other nonfavorite children in his family bore similar scars, though perhaps he had the most.

Lettie said nothing at all.

Chinma lowered his shirt and turned back to face her.

"I didn't know," said Lettie quietly. "I'm sorry."

"Good heavens," said Aunt Margaret. "The child has a spark of empathy after all. Come, Chinma. Let's get you packed."

FOURTEEN

CALABAR

War will exist as long as any community desires to impose its will on another community more than it desires peace.

Coercive men see only slaves and rivals in the world.

If the meek refuse war to defend themselves against coercion, then they deserve to be slaves.

Peace-lovers can only have what they love by being better at what they hate than those who love war.

There is no road to peace that does not pass through war.

CECILY HAD made the rule that the American caregivers could only move through the city of Calabar two by two. To do otherwise was to invite attack by the opportunistic brigands who still lurked on the fringes of the city.

But the presence of the caregivers had brought a calm to the city, born of hope, for word soon spread that the Americans had medicines that would help.

Cecily warned everyone never to promise a cure.

"The most you can ever say is, 'This *might* help improve the chance of survival.' Anything else, and you will create bitterness and anger wherever death comes despite our help." Everyone agreed, but still the rumors spread that the Americans had brought a cure.

Rumors also spread that the Americans had a cure because they had created the disease and infected Africa with it because the Americans hated black people and always would. There was nothing Cecily could do about this, and she warned the others that arguing would accomplish nothing. "If you are met in a household by angry accusations, walk away and go on to the next house."

But there were those who could not keep their tongues still. "If we created the disease, and if we have a cure, why are so many of our soldiers sick with the nictovirus?"

For the disease was actually worse inside the American base on the university grounds than it was out in the city. The monkey sickness, as it was called in Nigeria, was still fairly new to Calabar; Lagos and the western part of the country had been ravaged already, but the majority of the households in Calabar did not yet have the disease. The American soldiers, though, had been so confident that their barriers against infection from outside the base would work that they were careless about their safeguards inside it, and so once their wall was breached by the disease, it spread quickly and there was no soldier who was not at one stage of the disease or another.

Fortunately, the number of soldiers was not large—Cole's command was special ops, and so they worked in small units. There were only about three hundred soldiers in Calabar, and since one caregiver could provide for the basic needs of ten patients, only sixty of them remained on the university grounds to care for the soldiers in two twelve-hour shifts.

The rest of them went out into the city, at first the neighborhoods near the university—Akim Qua, Big Qua, Uwanse, Atimbo, Satellite Town—but then ranging farther and farther into Calabar. They brought with them bags of medicine—ibuprofen, stool softeners, and antidiarrhea medicine. The instructions were simple: Take the stool softeners as soon as the sneezing turns into coughing; then, when the fever starts, switch to the antidiarrhea medication and begin taking ibuprofen.

Using an ancient offset printer at the university, one of the soldiers who was not yet desperately ill had printed out instruction sheets in English, but that only went so far—the poor and uneducated could not read it in English, and there were many, especially among the elderly, who could not have read it in any language. So the caregivers had become adept, by necessity, in acting out a pantomime.

Within a few days, however, students and faculty members began showing up, offering their services as interpreters. They were all fairly fluent in English, though few of them had much experience with medical terminology; all of them spoke Efik, the dominant local language. Cecily had never heard of Efik, and a

Nigerian interpreter explained why. "Efik is a language of the delta, where all the oil is. Therefore everybody treats our language and our people as if we did not exist. Hausa, Yoruba, Ibo, English—they are all languages of strangers who rule over us in order to take our oil and give us nothing."

"They gave you the nictovirus," said Cecily.

The woman grinned at her.

"Teach me how to greet people in Efik," said Cecily, "so we can get into their houses."

Soon Cecily had all the Americans practicing the phrases. "Ndi owo ku ufok?" Is anybody home? And then: "Mme ono usobo edi-oh!" Medical workers are here!

Soon the university people—who were quickly christened "the varsity team"—were masked and gloved and taking full part among the caregivers out in the city.

Naturally, many sick people came to the university, but interpreters just outside the campus entrances explained to them that if they had any family to help, they should stay home and administer the medicine and plenty of water. If they truly had no one to help take care of them, then they were taken in to the university teaching hospital, whose staff had come back to duty now that there was actually something useful for them to do. The danger was that they would be overloaded, but most people understood how enormous the epidemic would be, and believed readily that the hospital offered no advantages over their own homes.

So Cecily spent her days out in the city, like any of

the other caregivers. She refused to be turned into an administrator. She left the clerical and sorting tasks to those who seemed reluctant to deal with the sick and poor—and she refused to let anyone criticize them as slackers, at least in her presence. "We came here to do what we *can*. Everyone's a volunteer, and every job needs to be done." And if that didn't silence the complaints, she'd quote: "And the eye cannot say to the hand: I need not thy help; nor again the head to the feet: I have no need of you." Let them argue with Saint Paul if they wanted to find fault.

At night, she would return to the university and look for Mark and Chinma. She had expected that Mark would go out into the city with her, but that changed on that first night when she realized that Cole was sick and the whole base had been exposed. "You'll stay here and take care of the soldiers," she told Mark. At first he protested that he had come to help Nigerians, but she replied that he had come to help the sick, and the American soldiers would need him as much as the Nigerians. He spoke their language, he even knew some of them personally. They would be happier with him helping take care of them.

She did not say, though she knew he understood: It's safer here, surrounded by America's finest soldiers. Nobody will try to hurt you because they happen to hate Americans.

Soon she learned that there was no particular anti-Americanism among the people. Even those who believed that the disease was part of an American plot tended to blame the government—some of the very same people would announce their intention to get a visa and move to America someday. It was as if they held the wicked rumors in one part of their minds, and the image of America as a place of freedom and safety and prosperity in another. As she wrote in an email to Aunt Margaret: "The rumor mind and the television mind, and never the twain shall meet."

What she could not get the local people to stop doing was calling her "Obufa Mma Slessor." She would introduce herself but they would nod and instead of trying to say "Cecily Malich," they would say "Obufa Slessor" or "Mma Slessor."

"What does this mean, this 'Slessor'?" Cecily asked her interpreter of the day.

In reply, the young man—a medical student when the university was running—took her to a large statue near the entrance of the university. It was of a European woman hugging a pair of African twins. "Mary Slessor," the interpreter explained. "A hundred years ago she came here and made everybody stop killing twins."

"Killing twins?" The concept baffled her.

"They believed it was a bad witch mother who had two babies at once," said the interpreter. "Or a curse on the family. They killed the babies and the mother. Very bad thing, and Mary Slessor made them stop. So: This statue is her with the twins she saved."

"Why do they call *me* that?"

"Be happy for it, Mrs. Malich," said the interpreter. "They see you as a white woman coming to save them, so they call you 'Obufa Mma Slessor,' the New Mrs. Slessor. Because of that name, everyone treats you and your people with respect and you are safe in the city."

That was reason enough to let them keep using the name—though she made it a point to introduce herself as Mma Malich once she actually got in the door.

As for Chinma, Cecily quickly learned he was little help as an interpreter. He spoke only a little English, but he spoke Efik not at all—he had lived in a part of Nigeria where Yoruba was the dominant language, Hausa and Ibo were often spoken, and no one ever used Efik. So Chinma was more useful—and safer—working side by side with Mark in the soldiers' quarters. It would help Chinma improve his English, and since he was immune to the disease, he didn't need to wear the mask, though Cecily still insisted on gloves when handling the patients, because there were other diseases that could be spread by the constant exposure to fecal matter.

For when it came to actual care of patients, rather than passing out meds and instructional leaflets, there was no escaping the feces. As they moved through the city, everyone knew that it was the door where no one answered their knock that they were most urgently needed. Families tended to catch the disease in quick succession, since infected people would come home and live normally for several highly contagious days before the first symptoms appeared.

So it happened often—more and more, as time passed—that when they went into the house where no one answered their knock at the door, or hand-claps outside it, or their calls in English and in their memo-rized Efik phrases, that inside they would find the entire family desperately ill. The healthiest would be groan-ing in the agony of acute constipation and painful coughing and sneezing; the weakest would have little energy left to groan, for they were covered in the filth of their own dysentery and coping with high fever, dehydration, and agonizing headache.

Into these houses Cecily and her companion—a dif-ferent person every day—would go, and instead of just handing out meds, they would first take water to every-one and help them drink. Then would come the medi-cations, usually capsules and tablets, but liquids for the children and those too weak to swallow a pill.

And then, finally, would come the cleanup. Bottled water was too precious to use for this, so they would have to use whatever water was available in the house or could be borrowed from still-healthy neighbors. Every caregiver had quickly gotten used to the stench and no longer recoiled from touching what had to be touched and washing what had to be washed. It was impossible to make everything hospital-clean, but they left every house in better condition than they found it in.

They marked with orange tape the lintels of the houses where no one was able to get out of bed. The food crews would then know which houses to visit on their daily rounds. For the first few days, gas-masked American soldiers went with the food crews, but as the soldiers took sick, they were replaced by Nigerian stu-dents, armed only with sticks; but they, along with

Cecily's reputation as the New Mrs. Slessor, were enough to deter brigands and pilferers.

As word of what the caregivers were doing spread through the city, order began to return. People with white breathing masks went back to their jobs; farmers from the hinterland began to bring food into the city again, so they could return with medications and knowledge of methods of treatment. Extended families formed a widespread network throughout the region—most people in the city still had many relatives in the hinterland, and that network began to keep the city alive.

All of this was gratifying—it was clear that the coming of the American caregivers was making a great difference. The city would not starve; people were far less likely to be robbed, raped, or murdered as they lay sick or tried to flee the city.

What Cecily was watching most closely, though, was the mortality rate. She could not measure any control group—they were not going to leave some portion of the city within their reach untended—but she could try to gather statistics on the recovery rate among those who were treated.

The best indicator would be the soldiers—they were all known by name, they were gathered in one place, and they could not move in and out of the countryside without anyone missing them. The reports from Lagos and other areas of early infection were of death rates as high as fifty percent in some areas, and never lower than thirty percent. If the soldiers died at the same rate, then all their effort was making no difference at all.

So part of Mark's work, Cecily decided, was to gather the stats as they came in—the number of soldiers who were sick, the number reaching each stage of the disease, and then, eventually, the number who died or who were still alive when the fever broke.

"I'm supposed to care about numbers?" he asked impatiently.

"Yes," she said. "This plague will probably reach the United States someday. We need to know if our treatment regime works, and if it does, how much difference it makes."

After his twelve-hour shift every day, Mark went to Sergeant Wills's workstation and emailed the day's stats to the health authorities in Atlanta. It was tedious at first; it didn't get hard until men started dying. They weren't numbers to Mark, or even mere names in a list. Especially because the first to die was one of his father's jeesh—Cole's jeesh.

Mark had cared for Cat Black personally; Cole's team were all in one room, except for General Coleman himself, who stayed in the headquarters office and continued to hear reports, communicate with the Pentagon and the ships offshore, and give occasional orders from his bed, as long as he was in condition to do so.

Cat was a bad patient from the start, grousing about everything, but as Mark told Cecily, "He's mostly just embarrassed, I think, because he hates having somebody else give him a bedpan and a urine jar, and wipe him up afterward."

"Maybe it's harder because of who you are," said Cecily. "I didn't really think of that."

"I asked him already," said Mark. "If he'd rather have a stranger do this, or Reuben Malich's son."

"What did he say?"

"That he'd rather be wiped up by several imams and ayatollahs of his acquaintance, because he thought *they* deserved to be up to their elbows in his . . . stuff."

"In other words, he was okay with having you continue."

"I don't think he cares very much anymore," said Mark. "The fever started today, and I switched him over from glycerin suppositories to loperamide and ibuprofen."

Cat was not the first patient to need the switch, or even the first of the soldiers—but he *was* the first of Reuben's jeesh to start down that precipitous slope. Within three days the jeesh were all fevered, trying to deal with dysentery, and still wracked with pain from coughing and the headache.

Cat became delirious, and sometimes flung himself around brutally, as if he were hallucinating some enemy, or maybe just a bothersome insect. More than once he hit Mark, not deliberately, but hard enough to knock him down. Cecily had to hear about this from Cole himself, when she reported to him; one of the still-walking soldiers had reported it.

"I think if the fever hadn't weakened Cat so much," said Cole, "he might have seriously injured Mark. Even as it is, I suspect Mark is hiding some bad bruises."

But as long as Mark didn't tell Cecily about it himself, she pretended not to know. She figured that Mark was determined to bear whatever pain it took to care for his father's friends. The fact that he didn't mention it did not surprise her, but it did please her. He was not a complainer.

As Cat sank further into his fever, he began to be harder to dose with his medications. He spat out pills, or let them lie in his slack mouth without swallowing. That was something Mark had to talk about, because Cat's dysentery was worse than anyone else's, and yet he was least likely to get his meds. And as for dehydration, he wasn't drinking enough, and even though the university hospital had the equipment for intravenous feeding, the Pentagon absolutely forbade using any of their equipment, for fear of injecting their soldiers with HIV from insufficiently sanitized needles.

As soon as Mark told her about the problem, Cecily went with him to see Cat, and was shocked at how weak and emaciated he looked. But then, all the men in the ward looked devastated by the disease. The others, though, were conscious enough to greet her, and Benny and Arty were still not in the fever stage, so they could make a few wan jokes and then call her aside and whisper about how well Mark was doing, even though he had another roomful of patients to take care of along with them.

"He's a good man," they both told her. There seemed to be no sense of irony or condescension in their use of the word *man* for a thirteen-year-old; they said it as they might have said it of any soldier.

Cat did not recognize her, though, and as she watched Mark struggle to get water into him, Cecily realized for the first time that Cat was probably going to die of this. She had already seen enough Nigerians die—she had come upon patients who were already as bad as this on her first day working in the city—that she knew the signs of those who could not stay above the hydration line. As Cat got weaker, it would only get harder to put water into his system; as he got less and less of his medication, the diarrhea and fever would only get worse, dehydrating him faster.

But he was also a strong man, and so he did not die as quickly as most patients who fell below the line and couldn't rise above it. So it wasn't until the next night that Mark told her, "Cat's bleeding."

She knew what it meant and what it looked like, but she let Mark tell her what he had seen, because he needed to say it to somebody. "It was seeping out of his eyes like tears," he said, and shuddered. "And his nose. And rectally—it was the only thing coming out, and it looked like pure blood to me, bright red."

Cecily held Mark's hand.

After a while, Mark got up. "I'm going back to him," he said.

"You have to get your sleep," said Cecily. "There are living patients who need you tomorrow."

Mark shook his head. "He's not going to die alone."

"He's got the rest of the jeesh in the room with him."

But Mark shook his head. By "alone" he meant "without somebody holding his hand," though he couldn't say so. And none of the others was in any shape to do it.

Cecily could probably have made him go to his room, but she couldn't have made him sleep, and he would never forgive her for it. But she could go with him.

That's why she was in the room when Cole came in. He was shuffling along weakly, leaning against the wall. He was the last of the jeesh to get the fever, and it had only come on him today. But Cecily knew that he had been wracked with coughing—some of the men had even broken their own ribs with coughing, especially the more muscular among them—and that now his headache was fierce. He must have been told what condition Cat was in—perhaps Mark himself informed him earlier in the day—and as soon as Mark saw him come through the door, he got up from his chair and helped Cole to come and sit beside Cat.

Cole was wearing his breathing mask—it was a regulation he insisted on, because even if all the soldiers were infected, their caregivers were not, and men in the sneezing and coughing stage should keep their sputum to themselves. He said nothing to Cat, but he held his hand and bowed his head and closed his eyes for a while, so Cecily assumed he was praying, though perhaps he was only remembering. It had been Cat who went with Cole into Aldo Verus's cavern fortress in Washington State. Cecily knew what it meant to Reuben when he had been in combat with a man who truly had his back—a man to be relied on in a fight. She could only assume that Cole felt the same way about Cat.

Cecily brought a chair for Mark to sit on the other side of Cat's bed—a cot, really, everything Army issue and flown in when the university was first converted to military use. Then she went over and sat on the floor between Arty and Babe, because they were the only ones awake and watching the scene. She held *their* hands, which they seemed to appreciate. That was when they whispered to her about Mark being a good man.

It was about ten at night when Cat stopped breathing. It didn't bring a silence to the room—Drew and Mingo were both snoring and rasping too loudly for Cat's lack of breath to make much difference, and Benny and Arty were still in the savage coughing phase, and that noise, too, continued at frequent intervals.

But Cat's chest stopped moving.

Mark leaned closer—he had never seen death before, could not be sure, would still cling to hope. Cecily reached across Cat's body and cupped her hand behind his neck. "Oh, Mark," she said, "I'm so sorry."

Mark buried his face in his hands. Cole held out a shaky hand and rested it on Mark's head for a while. Then he started to get up from the chair. And failed.

"I'm so weak," he whispered to her. "I'm sorry, can you help me?"

Mark needed her and she didn't want to leave him. But every soldier on this base needed Cole. So she helped him get up and walk to the door. He was so weak that she knew she would have to help him all the way back to his quarters.

Mark stayed with Cat's body. Behind them, she could hear Arty say, softly, "Good-bye, Cat." Benny added, "God bless," and then went into a coughing fit.

Out in the corridor, Cecily talked softly as she helped support Cole's weight. "From what Mark tells me, the others are all staying hydrated and I think Cat may be the only one we lose. I hope so."

Cole only nodded.

"What about you?" she asked. "Are you being too macho to take your meds and drink? Getting up to come down here was crazy enough."

"Mark and Chinma boss me around," he said.

She knew that he understood that keeping himself alive was his primary duty right now. The Pentagon had asked him if he needed to be relieved, but he told them that there was no reason to bring in anybody else to be infected, he had good support from the caregivers group and enough soldiers were still functioning to keep the base going.

This last had been a lie, which he candidly admitted to Cecily after sending the message. Only a quarter of the soldiers were still in the coughing, prefever stage—they were able to perform some of their duties, but not all, and not well. He discussed it with Cecily because he needed to know how long it would take for the survivors to be back on duty.

"Limited clerical duty? Maybe three or four days after the fever breaks, if they've stayed fed and hydrated. Combat? Probably two months or longer."

Cole had chuckled at that.

"What's so funny?" she asked.

"These guys are special ops, every one of them," said Cole. "Bet you they report themselves fit for combat as soon as they can stand up without falling over."

"But you won't send them on missions," Cecily said.

"We'll assess our ability to carry out our mission when the time comes," said Cole.

Now, walking down the corridor with him, Cecily knew that having the disease himself must be changing his view of combat readiness. The nictovirus had brought down Cat Black, and Cole himself must be able to feel how weak and unsteady he was at the beginning of the fever stage. At the end of it, if he lived, he'd be far weaker. There'd be no jaunts down the hall for quite a while after that.

Cecily got him to his room. "I just want you to know," she said, "that Reuben would have been proud of the way you've led his jeesh."

Cole coughed, long and hard, wincing with every spasm.

She waited for the coughing to end. "Did I imagine it, or in the midst of your coughing did you actually say 'Bullshit'?"

He lay down on his cot. "I'm not their leader."

"After all your missions together, with you in command—"

"I'm their commander in combat and that's it," said Cole.

Even in his weakness, the anger was palpable. "What is it?" she said. "I thought you loved these guys."

"I did," said Cole. "I do."

"Then what's wrong?"

"They're crazy now," said Cole. "They won't say it outright, but they have some insane belief that anything that goes wrong in the world is Torrent's fault."

"The President?"

"Yes," said Cole.

She knew there was more to it than that, but she wasn't going to push. He'd tell her what he thought she should know.

Besides, though she had long suppressed them in order to work with the man, she had suspicions along those same lines herself. So had Cole, once.

"Cat did this to me," said Cole.

"Did what?" she asked.

"Infected me."

She didn't want to argue with him, but how could he know?

As if he heard her skepticism, he said, "He sneezed in my face."

"But it must have been an accident," she said.

"He leaned into my face to sneeze," said Cole. "And he admitted it. They all admitted it. They got themselves infected on purpose, and since nobody wears masks around here, inside the base, they probably infected everyone else."

"They were the breach of the quarantine? On purpose?"

"They think Torrent's quarantine will fail. They think he expects it to fail, *wants* it to fail. So they exposed themselves and all of us to the nictovirus so that whoever lived would be immune. There'd be a team of soldiers who had already had the disease and wouldn't get it again."

Cecily thought about it. "It makes a perverse kind of sense. Except for the ones who die."

"They're soldiers. They thought of it as an acceptable attrition rate. Especially since they think every other army in the world will go through the same thing."

"So your group here will be the first company of immune soldiers in the army."

"That's the plan. If you can call it a plan. Russian roulette with half the chambers full."

Cecily thought about it some more. "You think they were wrong."

"They were damn well wrong to infect everybody, especially me, without asking me first."

"Come on, Cole," said Cecily. "You know you could never have given that order."

He glumly conceded the point by not responding.

"Are you still angry at Cat?" she asked.

He shook his head and then winced at the pain the movement caused him. "He's the best off," he said.

"What do you mean?" she said. "If the others live—"

"Whether they live or die, that's in the hands of God. And Mark. And all you Christians," said Cole.

"So what did you mean by that? Cat being the best off?"

He almost answered. But then he gave a weak little wave of his hand. "Go back to your son. He needs you more than I do. I'm sorry I dragged you away from him."

And as she left his quarters, he said, "You were crazy to come here, crazy to bring Mark."

She stopped in the doorway. "I know," she said.

"God bless you for it," said Cole.

TWO DAYS later, Mingo's fever broke, and it seemed likely that Babe and Drew were also about to make it over the hump and start the slow recovery. They were still as weak as babies.

Meanwhile, Arty and Benny were now in the full crisis of fever, and so was Cole. So were most of the soldiers on the base, since they had been infected at nearly the same time.

Cecily couldn't believe that some of the caregivers complained about how many resources the soldiers were using up. "We came here for the Nigerians, not to take care of soldiers," one man said. "We're not camp followers."

Cecily didn't answer him as she wanted to. She merely waited for a few beats of silence, in which everyone else seemed a little embarrassed for him; or perhaps they were all expecting her response to be harsh.

Instead she merely said, "They're sick, they're children of God, and they're here," she said. "You aren't on the base rotation, are you?"

The man admitted he was not.

"Then it doesn't affect you," she said.

"There are thousands of people out there that we haven't gotten to yet," insisted the man, perhaps not realizing how every word stabbed her to the heart. "And they'll die without our reaching them because this base is taking up so many of our people."

"Those people out in the city," said Cecily, managing to keep her voice calm, "have families, most of them, and they're taking care of one another. We're all these men and women in uniform have. I hope you don't think that because they volunteered to serve their country in uniform, they are somehow undeserving of God's love and our help."

That was as close as she came to rebuking him, but he wasn't a complete fool—he understood what she was saying and he kept his thoughts to himself from then on, at least around her.

In the city, by necessity the dead were being taken to mass graves, and though the burial squads made some effort to keep a record of the names, many bodies were picked up from the street with no way of finding out the names. On the base, however, the soldiers were all known, all placed in body bags and carried to a tent at the edge of campus. The Navy sent choppers and soldiers in hazmat suits to carry them back to the ships for blood samples, then flew them back to the States to be sealed in coffins and returned to their families.

That was where Cat's body went, along with the other American soldiers who died in the first wave.

By now they had enough soldiers who had passed the fever stage to have some idea of what kind of difference the care they were getting would make. Four were dead, and twenty-nine had passed through the fever and seemed likely to recover. If they did in fact get well, then it looked like there might be a twelve percent mortality rate. That was a vast improvement over the death rate when people didn't get this treatment. Even though it was only preliminary, Cecily wrote to the President that he could safely call the caregiving operation a success, and every effort should be made to get the word out, worldwide, about the treatments they were using. It could save lives in African countries where the nictovirus was just entering. And everywhere else, if the quarantine failed.

If this epidemic did spread beyond Africa, and most people were able to get decent care from their families and medications from their governments or health care systems, the treatment they had devised—based on Aunt Margaret's interpretation of Chinma's account of the disease—might well save a billion and a half lives, or more.

It was two days after Cat died that the talk radio host showed up in the military plane. Cecily had been warned that he was coming, but she assumed he would watch the offloading of supplies and the loading up of bodies, maybe talk to a couple of caregivers—the ones who had the time to talk to him, which meant the least effective or experienced ones—and then he'd go home.

But he didn't. Instead, he showed up with a microphone in his hand and a recorder in a shoulder bag and accosted her as she was leaving a house where she had helped a family deal with a child who had just started bleeding.

He started to introduce himself. "Hi, I'm Rusty Humphries from Talk Radio Network, and—"

His smile, his glibness, they made her angry, and she walked past him, saying, "I know who you are."

Doggedly he pursued her along the street.

"Everyone back at the University of Calabar said that you were in charge."

"They were wrong," she said.

He kept following. She walked faster. So did he. She couldn't go any faster without running, so apparently she was going to have to be rude. She stopped and faced him. "Look, Mr. Humphries."

He held the mike up to her mouth.

She pulled it out of his hand and dropped it on the ground.

"Hey," he said. "That's a fifteen-hundred-dollar microphone."

"What *we're* doing here isn't about ratings or selling airtime or whipping people up into a frenzy," she said.

"I know what you're *really* here for," said Humphries.

Oh, he was going to go speculating about her motive, was he? "And what is that?"

"You're here because you believe these are children of God and you have a responsibility to help them."

She was not really prepared for him to take them seriously. "That's right," she said. "And talking to you doesn't further that cause."

"I think it does," said Humphries. "And here's why. I have millions of listeners to my radio show every day. You need meds and water bottles and food and that takes money. You also need more volunteers. So we need to show people all over America that you're not a bunch of Christian kooks who went off to Africa to die, like those wacko liberals who went to Baghdad to try to stop us from bombing there. I want to let them hear your voice, hear you talk about what you're doing, let them feel what it's like to experience this disease. Because you know and I know that sooner or later, everybody in the world is going to have to deal with this."

Cecily bent over and picked up the microphone and dropped it into his shoulder bag. "I'm not in charge, Mr. Humphries. I'm just a caregiver who had to tell a family that their eight-year-old firstborn son is going to die, in spite of the best care they and we could give him. I have more houses to visit and more work to do, but I wish you well with your radio show, which is more than I would have said five minutes ago, so I guess you made your point."

"Thank you," said Humphries. "That was great. It will really help me get the message across."

"What, your fifteen-hundred-dollar microphone picked it up, even though it's in your bag?"

"No," said Humphries smiling, "but the five-thousand-dollar microphone did." He pointed to a tiny mike clipped to the front of his shirt. "I know who you are, and who your husband was, and even though I'm not a Catholic and I don't have a vote on who is and isn't made a saint, I sure think you're the kind of American citizen I hope my daughters grow up to be. God bless you, Cecily Malich."

And with that he walked away.

Persistent devil, she thought. The last thing she wanted was publicity for herself personally, and maybe she could make a big stink about it and make him not put it on the air. But then, here he was on the street in Calabar, with a terrifying disease all around him, wearing no face mask, and he didn't seem to be doing anything more than trying to get word back to America about just what this disease was and how to treat it and how important it was to fight it here in Africa. So Humphries was doing exactly what she had asked President Torrent to do—let the world know how to save as many lives as possible.

Later that same day, she was heading for a poor neighborhood not far from the Big Qua River northeast of the university, when a dilapidated flatbed truck came barreling into town along the I.B.B. Road, which became the Ikang highway just beyond the airport. When the driver saw Cecily and her companion, Alice, a young housewife from Lynchburg, he brought the truck to a shuddering stop and leapt out of the cab. He was old enough to have mostly-white hair, but he was still big and strong and both women stepped back a little as he rushed toward them.

"Mma Slessor?" he shouted. "American Christians help monkey sickness?"

"Yes," said Cecily. "That's why we're here. We have medications if your family has the nictovirus—"

"No, no, we have plenty, very good, now you listen: In Aking, I make a delivery, and trucks come in. Army trucks."

"The Nigerian army?" she asked.

He shook his head. "No no no, Arab-looking, Sudan men, Egypt men? They speak language I don't know, they come and scream at people and shoot in the air and take food and fill up gas. They say, Calabar, Calabar, so I know they come here."

"Soldiers coming here?"

"Six trucks," he said. "I go to my truck, I drive slow out of town so they don't care about me, and then come here as fast as I can."

"Do you have room for us in your truck? Can you take us to the university, so I can warn the American soldiers there?"

"American soldiers have monkey sickness, don't let anybody in. But they let *you* in."

"Yes," said Cecily. "They will indeed."

As they started up the road, Cecily asked him about himself. The language barrier was too great to learn more than the fact that he was a short-haul trucker, his family lived mostly in the countryside but also in Calabar, and the Calabar portion of the family had come through the monkey sickness with only two deaths. Out of fifteen people, Cecily figured that was a merciful total, and certainly so did he. "Other families kaput kpata kpata," he said, pidgin for *wiped out*. "Others half die. Only two quench in our family because of the Americans. I don't let them kill you!"

Apparently the Americans hadn't taught his family enough, because he hadn't had the disease yet—and wasn't wearing a mask. But she could hardly complain, since his gratitude for their caregiving had prompted him to bring an early warning so the soldiers would not be taken by surprise.

Not that there was much the soldiers could do. Only thirty of them had gotten past the fever and they were still too weak to stand. Only a few others hadn't yet gotten to the fever stage. Most of these special ops soldiers would be lucky if they could hold a pistol and shoot at someone as they entered their rooms. The rest would never even know what they died of.

All Cecily could hope for was to get word to AFRICOM to send in a Marine helicopter strike force. But how long would it take them to scramble the choppers and get to Calabar? How close behind this driver were the Arab troops? Every American soldier in Calabar could be dead before the first Marines arrived.

They were nearing the turnoff to the university when she saw an elderly caregiver couple talking with what's-his-name from the radio. She couldn't leave them behind—they would be the first fatalities if they were still out here when the enemy soldiers arrived.

FIFTEEN

WAR CORRESPONDENT

A string of unbroken success leads people to expect their leader to be infallible, and when he falls short, they hate him. Complete failures are even worse, for then the leader is seen as weak. He is no longer treated as a factor by his rivals, who immediately move to fill the vacuum.

The successful leader is one who is able to convince his people that they are in desperate straits, and only he has the strength and wisdom to keep them safe. Then the trick is never to put this reputation for strength and wisdom to the test. Glorious but untested reputations last forever.

RUSTY HUMPHRIES was not offended by Cecily Malich's initial hostility. He knew that conservative radio journalists like him had to deal with public attitudes toward reporters that had built up over two generations of arrogance combined with smug know-it-all political correctness. The kind of newspeople who pretended to be for the common man but disdained and despised everything the "great unwashed" believed in and cared about. And to Mrs. Malich, he would seem to be a jackal, coming to profit from the worst epidemic since the great influenza of 1918.

The fact was he *did* have to put on an entertaining show every night. He had to chase ratings like anybody else, because without listeners there'd be no advertisers, and without advertisers there'd be no show. Unless you worked for NPR. Ever since he started sending comic songs and bits to Rush Limbaugh, he'd known that a solemn that's-not-funny attitude toward the news would never work for him.

Yet even with his teasing attitude, Rusty took his job seriously. Terrorism wasn't funny. Neither was fundamentalist Islam. Neither was famine, neither was genocide. Yet Rusty went to Palestine and interviewed members of terrorist groups, and went to London to talk to Muslims from a radical mosque, and went to Darfur where refugees were starving when they weren't being machine-gunned or bombed, and then played the tapes on the air.

He said to dangerous fanatics some of the things that Americans were dying to say. His listeners cheered. Of course, he ran the risk of literally dying for having said it. These were often pretty humorless people. But Rusty knew that his grin was better than Davy Crockett's—he had a talent for looking merry and happy no matter what he was actually *saying,* so bad people couldn't really believe they were being ridiculed to their faces. He walked out of some pretty dire places alive.

So Rusty's listeners were used to the idea that when something truly wasn't funny, Rusty would still find what was funny about it—while speaking truth to violent men. If there was a trouble spot, and he could get a visa and transportation, Rusty went there.

The trouble was that epidemics couldn't be jollied along. As Rusty's producer said to him, "You can't interview the virus. And all the people are dying."

So he hadn't tried to get into Africa until President Torrent made an exception to his quarantine. With the departure of hundreds of Christians to try to minister to the sick and dying, Rusty saw his chance. If these people could go there, he could get there, too. The problem was going to be getting back. He talked with his contacts in the Pentagon and they promised him that if he would consent to spend three weeks in quarantine before coming home, they could get him at least to the ships off the Nigerian coast.

That was his ticket in. He knew that once he was on a ship, he'd get to shore, and once on shore, he'd get his interviews and let his listeners know something about what it was like to be in the middle of a plague zone. Afterward he'd sit out the quarantine. Wherever the quarantine was, maybe he could do his show. If he had to, he'd do three weeks of radio over the phone.

As with his trip to Darfur back in 2008, he'd find humor in his own woes, while taking the victims of the sneezing flu—and the Christians who had risked everything to come and care for them—seriously.

And without his ever saying so, his listeners would know that he, too, had risked his life.

It would be great radio.

That was his plan, and so far it was working. Mrs. Malich had inadvertently given him a terrific interview—he didn't mind a bit when he got treated like in-your-face condescending journalists, because he knew his listeners loved hearing journalists get slapped around a little, even when it was a journalistic good guy like Rusty. You put a microphone in the face of a smart, honest American woman while she was busy trying to heal the sick, and you darn well *should* be given what for.

The danger was that he couldn't really make his recordings with a breathing mask muffling his voice. So he had to make sure he talked only to people who didn't have the nicto, because he really did want to return home to his half-orphan daughters. They didn't deserve to lose yet another parent.

Yet if he had to die, better to do it drumming up support for a good cause, while trying to tell people how to cope with an epidemic that was bound to hit American shores sooner or later, despite President Torrent's apparent belief that he could hold back the tide and move mountains to improve the view.

Was he the only person in America who wasn't shiveringly thrilled every time Torrent opened his mouth? Come on, kids, the man's been president for three years, he's revealed himself to have the instincts of your standard liberal-bordering-on-socialist politician. Doesn't it bother anybody that this guy has tight control over the nominating and funding process in *both* parties? That you can't get a major party's nomination to either house of Congress without sucking up to him first?

And now this quarantine—part of Rusty's pleasure in being here was the fact that these Christian demonstrators had practically forced Torrent to change his policy. He had it on good authority—a friend who was at the meeting—that Mrs. Malich had really helped change his mind. Rusty wished someone like her would run for president, but he knew she had too much sense. Isn't that the main problem with American politics? We keep having to choose among candidates who are so stupid they want the job, and so egocentric they think they can do it.

So he was standing on the side of a main road talking to a couple of African Methodist Episcopalians, a married couple who were retired. When they heard about the epidemic, they knew they had to spend their last years—or, if things went badly, their last weeks—ministering to the sick. "It's how we walk in the footsteps of Jesus," said the wife. "He said, 'Come follow me,' and then where did he go? To the sick and afflicted."

She had a great way of talking, and the husband interjected wry comments now and then, which she slapped down in a half-playful way that Rusty knew would get great laughs from both men and women in the audience.

Then he heard a truck coming up the road. That was fairly rare in Calabar, even now that things were getting back to normal. He was sure it was a truck coming from outlying farms, and so he asked the Haywards to wait a moment till the noise from the truck had passed.

But it didn't pass. The truck came to a rattling stop and Cecily Malich opened the passenger door. "Get on this truck, right now!"

What was this about? Rusty's natural instinct was to say, Uh, I don't think so. But she looked urgent enough that he sensed a story.

That sense became even stronger when he started toward the truck and she kept waving. "You too! Mr. and Mrs. Hayward! We've got to get back to the university!"

When they got to the truck Mrs. Malich seemed to assess the Haywards' ability to get up onto the back of the flatbed truck and decided it wasn't likely to happen. "Please direct this driver straight to the College of Medical Sciences building," she said as she helped them into the cab. "I have to get to General Coleman."

Rusty was happy as a clam that after all his working out and dieting, he looked so fit that she took it for granted that *he* could climb up; and so he did, then gave a hand to Mrs. Malich and her companion.

The truck was moving before they were completely on, and yet Mrs. Malich made no complaint. As they rode, she filled him in on what she knew about the army unit that was coming.

"Doesn't sound like we'll be glad to see them," Rusty agreed.

"I've got to get a call in to the Pentagon or the ships just off the coast here or to the President, if I have to, because if we don't get help here, and fast, it's going to be a massacre."

"It might just be a hostage thing," said Rusty.

"For us caregivers, yes, it might," she answered. "But remember that hijacked plane that had a Navy SEAL on board? They kicked him to death—and then treated the *civilians* as hostages."

"So our boys lying in their beds trying not to die from dysentery and fever and dehydration," said Rusty, "you think they'll come in and shoot them all?"

"The driver thought the soldiers looked Arab. Definitely not African. Coming out of the northeast—Chad is up that way, if you go far enough, and then Sudan."

"That's a long drive," said Rusty. "Like crossing the whole United States."

Mrs. Malich was almost talking to herself. "Which means that if they decided on this raid because they heard that our boys were all infected, they had to put this together and hit the road—what, four? Five days ago? Five days ago, most of our boys were still in the coughing stage. Weakening, but still able to fight."

"How did they hear about it?" asked Rusty. "I don't think even MSNBC would have reported that we had a whole base full of soldiers who were too weak to lift a weapon."

"It wasn't the press," she said. "Word got out from

the cooking staff, I think. With the best of intentions, I assume—the people here know that the reason the Hausas of the north aren't still coming down and slaughtering whole villages is because of what General Coleman and his men have been doing for them. But once the word gets into the rumor mill in Nigeria, it spreads across country faster than you'd believe— everybody's related to people all over the place and they don't have much public entertainment here, what with electricity being so intermittent."

"So rumors are their soap operas," said Rusty.

"And their NBA," said Mrs. Malich.

"I think this doesn't look very good for our soldiers. Can you fire a gun?"

She shook her head. "Have you seen the kind of kick those things deliver? I could fire it once, and then be hospitalized."

"Not as bad as that!" Rusty wondered if he could shoot at the enemy. He had fired guns many times, but never had to aim one at someone with intent to kill. He knew that once you fired your weapon, you had announced to the enemy where you were—so you really needed to make your shots count for something.

"Remember we came here as Christians and health workers," said Mrs. Malich. "If we take up weapons and shoot at the bad guys, then we're combatants— and combatants out of uniform."

Rusty got the point. "I have a feeling that *their* version of Guantanamo, if we live to get there, won't be as nice as ours. Tearing up Bibles and flushing them down the toilet would probably be the nicest thing they did. If they have toilets."

They slowed to a stop at the checkpoint, which was manned by four university students with clubs. Mrs. Malich stood up on the back of the truck and the students recognized her as Obufa Mma Slessor and let them through.

Once they were at the headquarters building, Mrs. Malich asked the Haywards and her companion to tell everyone to prepare to evacuate immediately. "We want to be out in the city when they come here."

"Hard to hide the white folks," said Mr. Hayward.

"You aren't as black as anybody from around here, either," said Mrs. Malich.

The Haywards laughed, but they got the point. There would be shooting at the university. The caregivers needed to be somewhere else—nursing the sick, just as they were supposed to.

Mrs. Malich walked briskly to the stairs and up to General Coleman's quarters. Rusty trotted along behind, glad that she hadn't tried to ditch him at the door. Then it occurred to him that he might actually be helpful. If they didn't get the right answers from the Pentagon, he had friends there at the highest levels. He might be able to light some fires.

Oh, wait. Mrs. Malich was a close adviser to President Torrent. That trumped any connection *he* had.

Mrs. Malich knocked a couple of quick ones but then opened the door without waiting for an answer.

General Coleman lay on his bed looking like a

famine victim. He was white as a ghost, his skin hung off him like a Biggest Loser winner, and this was a man who didn't have an ounce of fat on him before he got sick. His body must have been eating away his muscle tissue during his illness. There was a white boy there, and when he greeted Mrs. Malich as "Mom," Rusty was able to make a wild guess as to who he was.

Mrs. Malich made her report crisply, leaving out everything nonessential in the first go-round. Rusty wasn't sure Coleman was even awake, but when she was finished, he feebly said, "Good job. Help me up."

"You're still burning up with fever," said Mrs. Malich. "Just tell me what to do and I'll do it."

"Both," he said. "You do it, and I'll do what I have to do. Mark, can you bring me my bones?"

Rusty had a horrible image of a man with all his bones removed, before he remembered that "Bones" was the unofficial nickname soldiers were giving the exoskeletons that were being prototyped. He had vaguely understood that they were being tested in Africa, but he had some idea of them being experimental. Now he realized that since the exoskeletons augmented a soldier's own strength, they might be able to get somebody in Coleman's shape up to something approaching normal walking ability.

Did the exoskeletons help with balance? Because the way Coleman wobbled just sitting up on the edge of his bed with Mrs. Malich helping support him, Rusty worried that he'd fall over the first time a bullet passed near enough to cause a breeze.

"Send a message to Admiral Sowell. Sign on as me. We need choppers and Marines in hazmat." Just that much seemed to wear him out. But now Mark was helping put on the exoskeleton while his mother went to the desk and started typing a message into the computer.

Fortunately, the artificial intelligence routines in the Bones made them practically assemble themselves—Mark didn't have to do much more than bring the semi-attached pieces close to the right position, and they seemed almost to grab each other and lock in place without anyone's help.

Mrs. Malich got up from the desk. "They acknowledge and will comply."

"Any ETA?"

"Less than fifteen minutes after they get into the air. And they're monitoring your Noodles and drones so they'll know where they're needed."

"Evacuate the Christians," said Coleman. It was only a whisper now.

"Already started," said Mrs. Malich. "They've been asked to head out into the city—to the areas we've been working in. But I'm not counting on loyalty from the population. Not if these enemy soldiers are ruthless and you can't fight them off here. The people will play up to whoever seems to be winning. That's how you survive in Nigeria. The people who didn't play that way are dead or in exile."

Rusty could hear how this would work on the air. Not very well, actually. Watching Coleman, he could see how absolutely weary and feverish he was. But on tape, all you'd hear was a kind of brusqueness. Coleman sounded almost bored. And rude to Mrs. Malich. Meanwhile, Mrs. Malich didn't sound like a Christian health volunteer. She sounded like senior management or a soldier's wife.

Sound alone could be deceiving. But then, sound with pictures could be deceptive, too.

He was already taping, of course—voice-activated, *sound*-activated. He never wanted to miss something because he didn't know it was going to get said, or because he got caught up in the moment and he forgot to start the recorder until the best bits were over. *This* tape, though, would never be played over the air. But it might just help him remember everything that happened so he could tell the story to his listeners, if he ever made it home.

"Mark," said Coleman. "Get the jeesh into their Bones, whoever can."

Mark took off at a run.

Coleman's Bones were fully engaged. Now he seemed to have a newfound strength. He stood up, he walked. But Rusty could see that the energy was all in the equipment. Almost as if the exoskeleton were animating a corpse.

With his arms working now, Coleman reached for the helmet that went with the outfit. What did they call it, the Bean? No, the Noodle. As soon as it was engaged with the Bones, Coleman started clicking and smacking his lips—commands to the helmet and exoskeleton,

Rusty knew from what he'd seen and read before. Then he was talking.

"Drones up. Hostile force. Trucks, from east of Calabar, over the river, Ekang road." Coleman clicked a couple more times. "Reapers or Preds? I need to know how much armament we have." He listened. "It'll have to do." And then, after a moment. "Got the flu, nothing much."

Meanwhile Mrs. Malich was looking at the small LCD readout on the outside of the Noodle. Rusty leaned in and could see that it was cycling through Coleman's vital statistics—heartbeat, blood pressure, that sort of thing—and Rusty realized it was so that if the wearer was unconscious, medics could still assess his condition. He was at 105 degrees. This was not good at all. Whatever Coleman was planning to do, his fever was reaching its crisis. Also, his judgment wouldn't be at its best with that kind of temperature.

"Water," said Coleman. Mrs. Malich gave him a bottle with a straw built into the lid and Rusty realized it was an attachment to the exoskeleton—it stayed in place and the straw actually extended to reach Cole's lips when he made a quick slurping sound. That is so cool! I want that suit, thought Rusty. I want clothes that do what I tell them.

Coleman started moving. Out the door, down the corridor. He started talking, and Rusty gathered that he was now talking to his men. Doing a roll call? They were coming out of the door. Four of them. Apparently two others were in bad enough shape that they couldn't even make the Bones work. All four of these looked much better than Coleman. And when the others saw him, they started telling him to go back to bed.

"I'm not dying in bed," said Coleman. "Come on."

To Rusty's astonishment, they then began to run down the corridor—a shambling step, more machine than man—and Rusty was starting to follow when his ear was caught by Mrs. Malich talking to someone.

"They won't go," said an old man, one of the caregivers.

"They can't get caught here," said Mrs. Malich.

"These kids are the job we took on," said the man. "We're not leaving them now."

"You can't protect them if this enemy force gets into the university. This place is indefensible against a strongly armed enemy."

"You sound like one of them," said the man, chuckling.

"My husband *was* one of them," she answered. "I've been hearing this for fifteen years."

"Then you know why we're staying."

"Yes," she said. "You love these men."

"They'll need water and meds and food, those that can eat. They need us to try to keep them cool."

"I won't try to make you do what you don't want," she said. "If it were my husband in one of these rooms, I'd hope for someone like you looking out for him."

Rusty didn't know whether he'd ever play *this*.

Maybe it depended on the outcome. If everybody died, then this scene would play on every news show. If they lived, it might just sound mawkish, as if they knew they were being recorded and they were playing to the tape. He would tell his listeners that they didn't know, but if, after all that, you said, "Everything turned out okay and none of them died," it would feel like anticlimax. They're looking into the face of death, but if death turns away, it stops being tragedy and just becomes melodrama.

What am I thinking. *I'm* here. If everybody is killed, this tape won't play anywhere except maybe in some Sudanese assassin's tent.

If they even *were* Sudanese. But Rusty kind of assumed they were. He'd seen the aftermath of what they did in Darfur. Heartless murderers, that's what they were, in Rusty's honest, politically incorrect opinion. Had nothing to do with their being Muslims and everything to do with their being cruel, murdering scum.

And now Mark and another boy, an African, were talking to Mrs. Malich. "Mark, this isn't optional. You're leaving now. With me, out into the city."

"Go ahead, Mom. I'm not leaving them."

"I'm not leaving *you*."

"You've been working with the people out there," said Mark. "Chinma and I have been working in here. It's our job. It's what we came for."

Mrs. Malich was crying now. Tough as nails, she was. But for her son, she cried. "Don't do this to me, Mark. We came here to heal the sick, not get shot at."

"We could have been killed by the D.C. sniper back home," said Mark.

"You were four years old back then, and we weren't in Virginia yet," said Mrs. Malich. "Please come. I beg you."

"Go," said Mark. "The other kids need you to get home safe."

"I need you to get home with me!" said Mrs. Malich.

"And you have responsibilities," said Mark. "People out there depend on you. Go."

To Rusty's surprise, the African boy, Chinma, stepped between them. "Nobody will change minds. Do your jobs."

And that was that. The young African was right, and they both saw that he was. Still weeping, Mrs. Malich touched Mark's face. He kissed her hand. Then she took off at a trot.

With that, Rusty made up his mind. He wasn't going into the city. He was casting his lot here, with the sick and dying soldiers and the brave people who were staying with them so they wouldn't die of the nictovirus during the attack. If they lived, he'd live, and he'd leave with the best story. Out there, the combat might quickly move away from him. He might miss it all. But here, the story was inside the four walls of every room that held soldiers and their caregivers.

Rusty left Mark and Chinma in the room with the two remaining men from Coleman's team—Benito Sandolini and Aristotle Wu, Mark told him—and went from room to room, talking to the soldiers, the care-givers, whoever was conscious and willing to chat. Rusty told a few jokes on himself, got them laughing here and there. Some of them had been listeners back in the States on local stations, or satellite radio, or Armed Forces Radio, and so they talked to him like an old friend. "I knew you'd show up here, Rusty. Just the kind of insane place you'd go."

He finally worked his way down to the supply room, where a handful of caregivers were arguing. "I'm not taking up arms," one man insisted.

"The enemy doesn't care—if you're here, they'll kill you," said a woman.

"I'm not here to kill, I'm here to heal."

"Then go out into the city and be safe!"

"Don't do this. If any of us picks up a gun, we're all fair game."

"We're fair game anyway, don't you know what these guys have done in Darfur?"

"You don't even know who they are."

Rusty remembered what the African kid had done, and he bustled in, all cheerful business. "Well, I've got that on tape, and it's really dramatic. But nobody's go-ing to change anybody's mind, so why don't you get back to the soldiers, and if the bad guys break in here, well, *then* you do whatever *you* think is right at the time."

"Who are you?" asked a woman.

"I'm Rusty Humphries. Who are you?"

"You were taping us?" asked a man.

"Automatically comes on. Don't worry, it'll never play on the air. Go. Your patients need you."

"We're the night shift," said the woman. "And you aren't in charge here."

Now Rusty was getting a little irritated. Apparently talking sense only worked when you were talking to sensible people. "Let me put it to you another way. You're standing down here doing nothing. If that's all you're good for, get out of here. Me, I'm staying with these American soldiers and I'm going to do whatever I can to keep them safe. Like moving them up to the top floor."

"How will that help?"

Rusty wasn't sure it would—he'd just made it up right then. But, as always, he came up with a pretty good reason *after* he'd made up his mind. "We've got to buy time. We've called on the fleet to send choppers and Marines, but it'll take time to cover the distance. We just have to keep these boys alive long enough for the Marines to take over. You can do that, can't you? It's not picking up a gun, it's moving the victims. Okay?"

All they needed, apparently, was a plan and somebody to tell them what to do, as cheerfully as Rusty knew how, yet with all the steel in his voice, too.

It didn't take long. Under the circumstances, the sick men had no choice but to try to walk, and they managed pretty well if there was someone to help them. Mark and Chinma helped the last two of Cole's team. Rusty was helping them to a room well along the corridor when he heard a distant explosion. It was starting.

Some soldiers just couldn't get up and walk, even with help, and the cots had no wheels and there were no elevators and none of the caregivers were strong enough to carry them up one or two flights of stairs. So they had to remain on the lower floors. In every case, a caregiver stayed with them. No speeches, they just stayed. Nobody in this place was going to die alone.

Up on the top floor, the soldiers were lying on rows of pallets, far too many for each room—but a little crowding was bearable if it kept them alive long enough. Rusty watched the ballet of caregivers moving among the soldiers, talking to them, touching them, giving them water.

This is how you fight an epidemic.

Then somebody sneezed, and everyone turned to look. It was Mark.

He looked around at the others. "I always wear the mask," he said quietly.

Chinma touched Mark's shoulder and said nothing.

Rusty could imagine what the other caregivers were thinking. Mark had caught the nictovirus; so could they.

Then again, if the enemy soldiers had their way, they'd all be dead before sunset. Rusty chose not to make this observation aloud, however.

In the silence of the room, the sound of gunfire could be heard outside. "Maybe that's the Marines," said somebody.

One of the soldiers spoke up. "It's the bad guys," he said.

"How do you know?" asked a woman.

"The sound of the weapons," he said. "None of ours are firing."

Another soldier said, "Didn't hear any choppers, either."

Silence again. More gunfire. Distant. But not so *very* distant.

"Dang it," said Rusty, "I always planned to die in a place where I was the best person there. Now I've got to die with all of *you*. The angels are going to line up to take you to heaven, and I'll have to find my own way, on foot."

Mark seemed to know what Rusty was trying to do, and laughed. "Heck, Mr. Humphries, where you're going it's just downhill all the way."

Everybody laughed, and Rusty gathered Mark close to his body and ruffled his hair. "You're way too old to have somebody muss your hair like this, aren't you?"

"Yes sir," said Mark.

"Well, suck it up, boy," said Rusty.

SIXTEEN

BONES

Making plans for the future of nations is foolish. The system is too complex. The rules do not change, but the gameboard shifts continually, and your opponents and you are not the only players. Every speck of nature is arrayed against the progress of civilization and must be tussled with every step of the way. Storms, droughts, famines, earthquakes, plagues—all have toppled rulers, crushed civilizations, or at least dashed the hopes of a potentially great player of the game.

The best a ruler can hope to do is make incremental changes to open up options in the future. A suggestion here, a word there, a bit of information to a trusted ally or a predictable enemy. The use of force where required, diplomacy where no victory is possible or necessary.

It isn't a matter of throwing the dice over and over. In truth, you will do better if you avoid ever throwing the dice. In the game of nations, a bad throw can end your game.

Instead, what you need is to get lots and lots and lots of dice. It greatly improves your odds of finding what you need when history requires that you finally commit yourself to a throw. Against an opponent with the normal pair of dice, you want to roll a dozen pairs. Against nature, you want to roll a hundred.

COLE WAS not sure he was even in control of his Bones. He knew he was walking forward, but he could hardly feel his own muscles moving. Just the faintest twitch moved him forward. Of course, there was no leaping and bounding—the Bones responded to the movements of the body inside them. But the designers had done it right. They had taken into account the needs of an injured, feeble soldier. When you used great force, the Bones magnified you into a superman. When your movements were weak, the Bones did not push beyond a sedate pace.

Cole's real problem was his own brain. The fever had him, and he knew it, but he didn't know how to compensate for it. He could see, but in the bright sunlight he could not see well; he knew he was hallucinating here and there, seeing figures in motion on the periphery of his vision who did not exist, but it was hard to tell the hallucinations from the Noodle's informational displays. Was that what a drone was seeing, or a movement on the street, or an impish bit of fever playing with his mind?

It wouldn't be helpful if he turned and fired at something that didn't exist. Or at a civilian. But his judgment was so slow, he could probably be shot himself in the time it took to make up his mind.

And how was his aim?

It didn't matter. There was no removing himself from this mission. He and the jeesh could move because they had the Bones, and the other guys couldn't, and so it was up to them to hold off the attackers as long as they could. At this point their lives became expendable.

Mingo, Load, Drew, and Babe were all in better shape than Cole was. Better if they did the shooting, and Cole stayed back to pass information to them from the displays. It would be no help to them if Cole died meaninglessly because he couldn't think straight. But if he was needed—*when* he was needed—he'd shoot as best he could.

Worst of all, strange ideas kept running through his head. He knew it was just the paranoia of the jeesh infecting his feverish mind, but he couldn't shake the feeling that it was President Torrent who had sent this squad of soldiers to attack them. That somehow it was part of his plan to make martyrs out of the American soldiers and Christian caregivers in Nigeria.

He thought of the Indian Mutiny of 1857, when native Indian soldiers rebelled against the British East India Company. In the aftermath, it gave the imperialists in Britain a pretext to end Company rule in India and add Empress of India to Queen Victoria's titles. Or the sinking of the *Lusitania,* or the taking of the Alamo, the sinking of the *Maine*—outrages that galvanized the public and made jingoists and imperialists out of them all.

He remembered a class session on the Crimean

War, and the popular song that gave rise to the term *jingoism.*

> *We don't want to fight, yet by jingo, if we do,*
> *We've got the ships, we've got the men,*
> *And got the money, too!*

They're coming here because Torrent needs them to wipe us out in order to stir up the fever of imperialism in American hearts, and to justify his actions to the world.

Torrent would never do something fake, like the Gulf of Tonkin or the ridiculous pretense Hitler staged of Polish troops attacking Germans in 1939. Torrent would have something real, and completely untraceable back to him. Yet somehow he made it happen, because it would serve his purposes so well.

How else would the Sudanese know that the entire American base in Calabar had the nicto at the same time?

This is insane, a part of his mind kept saying, but the thoughts raced through his head again and again, around and around, accompanied by the same stupid song. This is just what Torrent wants, just what he wants.

"Cole," said one of the men. "What are you talking about?"

He realized he was singing the song—whispering it, really—but one of the features of the Noodle was that it would amplify the slightest sound from the leader's helmet and transmit it at a fully audible volume level to his men.

"Sorry," said Cole.

"Don't go south on us, Captain," said Babe.

I'm not the captain, thought Cole. Reuben's the captain. His jeesh, not mine.

Torrent's sending enemy troops to kill us, just like the trap in Bangui. Just like in New York City, which made him think of the technology they were going to face.

"They've got the EMP thing," said Cole. "They've got it. They're going to immobilize us."

"Damn," said Mingo. "You're probably right."

It had taken a fever to put himself on the same paranoid level his men were already on. Torrent couldn't be behind this. But somebody was.

What to do to do to do. Can't fight without Bones, but if we use the Bones they can shut us down.

"They can only shut us down for thirty seconds at a time. Long enough to reboot," said Drew.

That's right, thought Cole.

"Okay, here's the plan," said Mingo. "We go as two pairs. Only one man shoots and moves forward at a time, and nothing big, no huge jumps that put us up in the air and expose us."

"Like any of us can do that right now," said Babe.

"Other guy hangs back," Mingo continued. "When they zap the first guy, second guy stays under cover but keeps the enemy from hurting his partner till he can reboot. Got it? Never expose all four of us at a time."

They're counting to four, but I make five. They're doing this without me. They can do this without me. They never needed me. I shouldn't even be here. I should be back at the university lying in bed waiting for them to come and kill me.

"Is that all right, Captain Cole?" asked Mingo.

"Captain Cole?" echoed Drew.

They were calling him "captain," like in the days when Averell Torrent was National Security Adviser and sent them out on missions to intercept or destroy Progressive Restoration weapons. For some reason this touched Cole very deeply and he got tears in his eyes.

"Call him General Cole and he might answer," said Load.

And just like that, Cole snapped out of it. Not completely, but he was rational again. Able to respond.

"I'm here," said Cole. "Good plan. I'll tell you what I see. If I see anything real. Follow Mingo."

They made their way to the north and east of the university, toward the Ikang Road. The drones showed Cole that the old man had been right, there were six trucks, already at the outskirts of the city, heading along the main road that passed between the airport and the university. They didn't look like troop trucks— the Pred operators would have interpreted them as a convoy of panel trucks, probably bringing in food, if the old man hadn't reported that there were uniformed soldiers inside.

"They know where we are," said Cole. "Not us specifically, but our base at the university. Still in the trucks. Reaching where the Ikang Road turns into the I.B.B. They'll come south down the road along the west side of the university. No attempt to hide."

"Marines get here in five minutes, right?" said Drew.

Cole checked the display showing him the ETA of the choppers and Marines from the fleet. "More like eight," he said.

"Trucks'll be empty by then," said Drew.

They took up positions that covered the road, but they knew if the enemy weren't idiots they'd get out of the trucks long before this point and come in from a dozen different directions. At the same time, they knew the clock would be ticking. The old man's heroic ride had bought Cole's men about ten minutes of prep time, a ten-minute head start for the Marine choppers.

Meanwhile, the Predators circling overhead were armed.

Cole clicked himself over to talk to the drone's sensor operator. "I need Hellfires, starting with the lead truck."

"I've got it," said the operator, and three seconds later Cole's display showed the lead truck blowing up. The second truck bumped into it, but everybody poured out of all the trucks except the first one so only a few men were caught in the explosions as Hellfire missiles took out all the other trucks. "Thanks," said Cole, and switched back to his men.

"Heard some explosions," said Mingo. "Preds?"

"Hellfire. Reduction of enemy force by at least one-sixth," said Cole. "And they're on foot now. The computer counts 105 of them. Must have had about twenty-five per truck, plus drivers."

"Can you see what they're carrying?"

"No," said Cole. "The UAS operators can, but I can't focus that well." He switched back to the DGS in Langley. "Can you guys see how the targets are armed?"

The sensor operator's voice came into his ears. "Looks like automatics but we don't see anything with exploding shells."

They want the killing to be up close and personal, thought Cole.

The sensor operator started enumerating weapons. "Ten of them have something I've never seen before, bulky back end, narrow front. Flamethrower? Why make one with an inflexible nozzle?" A view of a man carrying one popped up on his display.

Cole knew what it was. "They're EMP devices."

"We need to get those on the recognition drills," said the sensor operator.

"Haven't captured any yet. You're the first to spot them from the air."

"Then how did you know what it was?"

"Because you didn't recognize it," said Cole, "and whoever set up the trap for us in Bangui sent these guys after us."

"Stands to reason."

Cole's Noodle was still open to his men, so they heard all this.

"Sounds to me," said Babe, "that when Cole is sick, he thinks like us."

"You got it," said Cole. He checked his vitals display. "I'm at 105 degrees."

"Same number of degrees as enemy soldiers," said Drew. "Coincidence? You decide."

They all laughed softly.

"About two hundred yards out. Mingo and Babe, you're too far out front, pull back. You'll get cut off by the group coming from your right." Cole knew they were seeing the same drone display he was, now, and knew what he was talking about.

"Got 'em," said Mingo, and in a moment the locate display showed Mingo and Babe moving back, getting ready to spring a little surprise on one squad of five.

Meanwhile, the bad guys started shooting. For a moment Cole was disoriented, trying to figure out which of his men was the target. Then he realized there was no target. These clowns were just shooting. The modern equivalent of the rebel yell, apparently. Bullets as emotional display. No discipline. They were no damn good, these Sudanese goons, except against helpless civilians and desperately ill soldiers.

He realized that he had made an ID without reporting it. "Sudanese army, right?" he asked the drone pilot.

"Computer just matched them up," the pilot reported.

So I still have some mental function, thought Cole. That's encouraging.

Then Mingo and Babe sprang their little ambush. Five shots, five-man squad wiped out. "Good shooting for sick men," said Cole.

"Got their cousins next," said Mingo.

Now the enemy knew they were under fire and they got a tiny bit more cautious. As in: frozen in place. But Mingo and Babe couldn't wait to pick them off one by one. There were other squads still moving forward—eighteen of them—and Cole heard Mingo tell Babe to fall back.

Now it was Drew's and Load's turn. It took them eight shots, but the bad guys were ready, so it was just a little harder.

They'd killed ten enemy soldiers so far. There were still ninety-five of them, moving toward the university. The ones close to where Cole's men had taken out their targets were moving more slowly—but the ones that had fanned out farther were still going at a quick pace. One squad was already closer to the university than any of the jeesh except himself.

"All of you, shoot and fall back," said Cole. "We aren't the objective, the base is. We got no victory if we kill half of them and the other half get inside the base while we're busy."

It was the classic problem of an undermanned defense. You could beat the enemy at any point where you concentrated your forces, but they could always get around you. So you had to keep falling back, falling back, so they couldn't surround you, and finally you had fallen back as far as you could go and now they had you pinned, they could bring *their* force to bear, and numbers would win.

Well, so be it, thought Cole. We have to make them all slow down. Slow down, buy time.

He was saying it out loud, like the song a few minutes before. "Slow them down, buy some time."

"Got it, Cole," said Drew. "Now shut up please."

Cole shut up. And started moving. Hallucinations or not, he was the rear echelon, and his men were coming back toward his position. He needed to stay ahead of them, heading back toward the university. He also had to keep his eye on the enemy, make sure where they were.

Ordinarily Cole would have gotten into place and taken out an enemy squad by himself. But he couldn't trust himself to shoot that well, or move that fast, or stay concealed. He'd do more good for his men closer to the university, keeping track of all the enemy squads, calling their attention to the most urgent problems.

More shooting. Now the enemy's bursts of gunfire were meant to kill. "Stay out of sight, guys," said Cole.

"Hard to shoot through concrete," said Mingo.

"Most of this stuff isn't concrete, it's just plaster on wood," said Cole. "Shoot through it."

"Ouch," said Mingo. "That means they can, too."

"Can they pulse through it?" asked Drew.

The answer came almost before he asked. "Babe's down," said Mingo. "Pulse, he's not hit, but I've got to stay and cover him."

"Three squads heading right for Babe's position," Cole said as he showed Mingo the relevant view.

"Maybe I should lose the Bones," said Mingo. "I'm in better shape than anybody."

"You're weak as a puppy," said Cole. "Don't get

delusions of grandeur because the Bones make you feel like you can move. Keep the exoskeleton, make them take it away from you. I can't get there, can you, Load?"

"Already on my way."

Cole could see that the others would deal with the fifteen enemy soldiers heading for Babe. But that still left seventy of them on their way to the university. Which became Cole's assignment to himself. Hurry up, buy time.

He moved as quickly as he could, but all this movement wasn't making his fever any better. His bowels were grinding with pain, though he knew there was nothing in them. Unless they were filling up with blood.

Okay, God, I know I'm going to die, but let me help my men first, just let me stop the enemy long enough.

The ETA of the choppers was still four minutes off. A lot of things can happen in four minutes. Like the fact that two squads were converging on the north entrance of the university grounds and Cole had no hope of getting there in time.

There was gunfire from the gate. Who was there? Cole's Noodle didn't show him anything except other guys with Noodles. Had some of the soldiers come out of the hospital after all and made some kind of stand? He prepared himself for the sight of a bloody massacre of his men.

But when he finally staggered to where he could see the entranceway, there were a lot of bodies, but none of them were Americans. Most of the bodies were Nigerian students. The only weapons they seemed to have had were clubs.

Guarding the sick American soldiers with big heavy sticks, against automatic weapons. And yet they had brought down eight of the bad guys. Where were the other two?

No time to look for them. Five other groups were converging on the university from other directions.

"The two you're looking for went inside your headquarters building," said the DGS operator. "In case you missed that."

"I can't . . . can't chase them. Got too many others out here."

"Anybody inside got weapons?"

"Lots of weapons. Strength to lift them? No."

The sound of automatic weapons fire inside the building made Cole want to scream, but he didn't have either the strength or the time. He got to a spot where he could watch the entrance that the rest of the enemy soldiers were heading for and waited.

If they'd had any kind of training, they would have split up and covered every entrance. Instead, they all just headed for the nearest one, bunching up as they neared the door.

Then again, training wasn't what was driving them. For them, this wasn't a job *or* an adventure. It was one or both of the two things that would get Arab soldiers to keep fighting when victory was in doubt and there was a strong possibility that they'd get killed—religious fervor and vengeance. It didn't matter much to Cole what was driving them. What did matter to him was that when these guys met resistance, they kept right on coming. That made them crack troops, by the standards of your normal Arab army.

Another burst of gunfire from inside the building.

I'll kill this crowd and then get inside over their dead bodies and find those two bastards who are shooting at my men.

Cole opened fire. To him it felt like he was putting his last ounce of adrenaline and strength into his movements—he should be leaping about like a cricket, but instead he was staggering like a drunk.

Except for one thing. He knew how to use his weapon, and his Bones were designed to help him do it. Once he aimed, and his Noodle was looking at the target, if his arms and hands wobbled the Bones would compensate. And it didn't matter that his trigger finger was so weak and trembly—the Bones were designed for that wounded soldier fighting to defend himself to the last. Normally it took serious pressure on the trigger to make it work, but now the Bones were converting it into a hair trigger, so that the slightest intent to fire caused a bullet to come out of the muzzle of his weapon; if he sustained it at all, then it was a burst.

And there was another feature Cole had never thought that he would need—assisted targeting. With his weak and trembling hands, he had no hope of precise aim. So he activated what Mingo called "girly mode," in which the Noodle took over the targeting and aimed the weapon, learning from the first shots exactly how to hold the weapon to hit the targets, one after another. Cole still had to pull the trigger—barely—and he could override the aim if he wanted to, but it was mostly going to be machine work.

The bad guys saw him, but his bullets were already hitting them before they could bring weapons to bear. It was so fast Cole could hardly believe it had happened. Twenty-five men converging on the door, and now every one of them down. And all Cole had suffered was the sharp hard blows of a scattering of bullets against his Kevlar. The assisted targeting had worked, his Kevlar had worked, and the Bones had kept him from falling over with the recoil of the weapon.

He would have gone into the building then, but bullets started spattering around him from another direction, hitting him, which was tolerable until there was a sharp burst of loud static. When his Bones and Noodle went down, so did Cole. Another group of enemy soldiers must have come up while he was killing the first crowd, and they had hit him with the handheld EMP, and even though he said "reboot," they'd have a crucial thirty seconds in which to kill him.

His Kevlar was still holding. They kept firing as they approached. He struggled to curl himself into something like fetal position, and felt the impact of bullets on his back. Only now the Bones weren't working and so the bullets were skidding him across the pavement and it was only a matter of time before a bullet hit him somewhere that the Kevlar didn't cover. Or they came close enough that the velocity of the bullets would punch on through.

He was halfway through the reboot when another EMP hit him.

That's it, he thought. I'll never get inside the building to stop the two who made it in. I hope some of the shooting in there was my soldiers taking out the bastards.

The enemy fire continued but nothing was hitting him. Shouldn't they be on top of him by now?

Then he realized he was hearing choppers. The cavalry had arrived.

It was their job now. It was okay for Cole to go sleep or die or whatever it was his body was doing. Shutting down, anyway, and there was no reboot command for his brain.

SEVENTEEN

BOYS WITH GUNS

Civilization is about creating children, protecting them till they re-produce, and making sure that each generation retains the behav-ior patterns that led to that civilization's being successful in the first place. Fail at any of these tasks, and your civilization is fodder for the dissertations of archaeologists.

CHINMA LOOKED around at the people in the room—the helpless soldiers, the scarcely less helpless caregivers—and he could only think of his village, watching from above as the soldiers came in their trucks and shot ev-eryone down. At least there were no babies for them to toss in the air for target practice. That would probably come later, in the city, as the victorious Sudanese death squad searched for the rest of the Americans.

These soldiers would not speak the same language as those who massacred the Ayere people. Nor would they be of the same race, nor wear the same uniform.

But their faces would be the same, the rage of blood-lust, the delight in evil.

This time, though, there was no tree for Chinma to climb.

He wouldn't climb it even if there were. This is why he had come back to Nigeria, he understood it now. It was a mistake for him not to die with his village. A mistake for the Ayere people to still have one survivor. And now the mistake would be rectified. It was only a shame that these others had to die with him.

The firing outside was growing closer.

He looked around at the soldiers—especially the ones that he and Mark had tended in overlapping shifts. Benny and Arty, Mark called them, not Captain Sandolini and Captain Wu. Walking up the stairs to this room had about done them in—they had no strength at all right now. Mark was pressing a damp cloth against Benny's face, trying to keep him a little cooler than the fever wanted him to be.

Chinma saw that Arty was moving his hand. It was at his side, and he was making faint squeezing motions and flapping his hand just a little as he did.

Chinma knelt beside him. "What do you want, Arty?"

Arty could not even open his eyes, but he could whisper one word: "Pistol."

"You are not strong enough to shoot," said Chinma.

"Pistol," repeated Arty.

"And I will not let you kill yourself with it," said Chinma, assuming that Arty merely wanted to avoid falling into enemy hands. But suicide was wrong—that was one thing that the ancestral gods and the Christian minister both agreed on. Pain was terrible, but not as bad as going to hell for having killed yourself, Chinma understood that.

"Pissssstol," Arty said more fiercely, then fell back slack, exhausted.

"What is he saying?" asked Mark, now interested.

"Pistol," said Chinma.

At that word, Benny's eyes opened. "Me too," he whispered.

Mark asked Benny, "Is your pistol in your room downstairs?"

"Locker," said Benny.

Chinma had no idea what that meant.

"Come with me, Chinma," said Mark. "Run."

Chinma followed Mark down the corridor to the stairs at the end. Mark practically flew down, but Chinma had not known many stairs in his life until he lived at the Malich house, and he didn't have the confidence Mark did in his ability to hit every third step and then hold on to the banister to make a fast turn around the landing and start down the next flight.

So when he got to the room where they had tended Cole's jeesh for the past two weeks, Mark already had Benny's locker open and was rummaging through it. "Got it," said Mark, holding up a pistol.

Chinma headed for Arty's footlocker as Mark ran to the window to look out.

"Here they come," he said.

Chinma found the pistol. "I have it."

Mark was already running for the door. Then he stopped so abruptly that Chinma ran into him. "Stupid stupid stupid," he said.

Chinma thought for a moment that Mark was calling Chinma stupid because he ran into him, and he was going to apologize but then Mark rushed back to Benny's footlocker, flung it open again, and this time came up with a small box. "Ammunition," he said.

Chinma did the same, while again Mark ran to the window. "Oh God, those poor students."

Chinma ran up beside him and saw what was happening at the entrance to the campus. University students with clubs were running into a hail of bullets and swinging clubs at men with automatics. But they must have surprised the soldiers, because there were half a dozen of them on the ground, dead or unconscious, and even more before the last student died. Only two of the soldiers remained, the only ones standing.

Those two began jogging toward the building where Chinma stood beside Mark.

"Let's go," said Mark. "Better not let them catch us down here."

The room they were at was on the first floor above ground level, and the stairs that they and the enemy soldiers would have to share were closer to the soldiers than to Chinma and Mark. They ran full-out and reached the stairs at about the same time as they heard the enemy soldiers start clattering up.

Chinma, being barefoot, was much quieter running

up the stairs than Mark, whose shoes made a noise. Fortunately, the enemies' own footfalls were so noisy that they didn't hear, and instead of following them on up to the top floor, they started down the corridor. They would find no one in the room where Chinma had helped tend to Cole's jeesh, and no one in Cole's quarters, but there were a few weak soldiers and their stubborn caregivers in other rooms on that floor. They were about to die.

But Chinma understood that he and Mark were no match for those soldiers, neither boys against men nor pistols against automatics. The people downstairs would die, but they would get these guns to Arty and Benny.

The gunfire downstairs started before they got back to the room, short savage bursts, and when they flung open the door a couple of women shrieked. Mark sharply hissed at them to be quiet.

Chinma held out Arty's pistol, but saw that Arty could not take it.

Arty was shaking his head slightly.

"You have to load it," said Mark.

"How?" asked Chinma.

"Watch me."

Mark took a loaded clip out of the box and slid it up into the hilt of the pistol. But there was already a clip in Arty's weapon. Was it already loaded? Chinma looked up helplessly, but then a lean middle-aged man, one of the caregivers, stepped to him, took the pistol, and quickly ejected the empty clip that was in it. Then he handed back the pistol.

Chinma was vaguely aware that the man was now explaining to someone—his wife?—that he didn't *load* the gun, he merely *un*loaded it.

Meanwhile, Chinma got the clip facing the right way, slid it in, and then watched Mark do something that made a cha-chink noise—it looked like he pulled the pistol apart very quickly, then put it back together. All he could do was stand there, looking at his own pistol.

Someone took the pistol out of his hand, pulled back hard on the top of it, and got the same noise.

"The safety," said Mark.

Chinma looked up at the man. He was the radio man, the one who recorded what people said. The man pushed a lever, then handed the pistol to Chinma, stepped back to his position against the wall, and nodded once.

Both boys put their pistols into the slack hands of the soldiers lying on the cots.

The firing downstairs had stopped, and they could all hear the footfalls of the enemy soldiers rushing up to their floor.

We're three rooms from the stairs, thought Chinma. "They kill the others before us," he said aloud.

Mark looked at him, nodded grimly. "You're right, you're right." He took the pistol back from Benny's hand. "We have to bring them straight to us." Mark ran to the door, flung it open, and fired the pistol out the door, up into the ceiling.

Then he ran back to Benny and put the pistol into his hand once more.

"There are only two of them," Mark said to Benny and Arty.

"Hold up . . . my hand," whispered Benny. Mark knelt beside him and propped Benny's hand so he could point the pistol at the door.

The enemy soldiers were quiet now; having heard a gunshot coming from this floor, they were wary now. But in the silence of the room, with the door open, everyone could hear the soft footsteps coming closer.

Chinma tried to prop up Arty's hand, but the man was trembling and the point of the gun wasn't just shaking, it wavered many centimeters at a time. Chinma propped up Arty's head so he could see to aim, which left Chinma's arms widely spread. Both Arty's head and the pistol were heavier by the moment, and neither one was steady.

One of the enemy soldiers dodged past the door, firing a burst of automatic fire into the room, but high, so no one was hit.

"Get down!" Mark hissed at the caregivers, but he hardly needed to say it—the ones who had been standing hit the floor the moment that burst came into the room.

Then Mark stood up, took the pistol out of Benny's hand, put his feet in a wide stance, and held out the pistol, pointing toward the door. "God help me," he said softly.

The pistol trembled, but it was a lot steadier than Arty's hand.

Chinma knew that this was the only way. Arty and

Benny would defend them all if they could, but their arms didn't have the strength.

Chinma had the strength. He had never held a gun until this day. His family owned guns, but he had never been allowed to touch one. But he could copy what Mark was doing.

He took the pistol out of Arty's hand. He wished that the radio man would come and take it from him once again. The man must know how to shoot, and Chinma did not.

At that moment of hesitation, his peripheral vision showed a movement at the door, and before Chinma could look, Mark's gun went off. Chinma only saw the enemy soldier falling backward, out into the corridor, and Mark also staggered backward from the gunshot.

Off balance, Mark shot again as the other enemy soldier stepped through the door, already firing his automatic weapon. Mark's shot missed completely. The enemy's bullets, though, flung Mark backward onto the sick soldiers lying helpless on the floor.

Chinma didn't stop to look. He had seen bodies hit by automatic weapons before. He had known every person he had watched them kill. This time, however, instead of a camera he had a gun, and instead of being up in a tree he was in the same room with the killers. Mark had knocked down one of them. The other one was already firing again, starting to swing his weapon to put bullets into the men on the floor.

Chinma didn't have time to take the stance Mark had taken. Then again, he was only three meters away from the gunman. He pulled the trigger and the recoil threw his hand up and back.

The gunman twisted around, but he was not knocked down. He saw Chinma now, and was bringing his weapon to bear when Chinma fired again.

This time he controlled the recoil better, and saw where the bullet hit the man, high in his shoulder. The man cried out and staggered but he didn't drop his weapon. Chinma fired again, aiming much lower, and now the man crumpled and fell to the floor, dropping his weapon.

Chinma walked over to him, just as the gunmen in his village had walked over to the wounded and dying.

The man jammered at him in a language Chinma didn't know. Then in English he said, "Satan!"

Without thinking or aiming, Chinma shot him in the face, because that's what he was looking at, the hate in the man's face. The bullet went into the man's mouth and he was dead.

Then Chinma turned to the door and saw that the man Mark had shot was trying to crawl toward his weapon. Chinma shot him, too, and then walked out and stood over his body and aimed straight down at his head and shot him again. The body jerked and was still.

Behind him, he could hear a man saying something about cold blood.

"He just saved your butt," said the radio man.

The first man said, "We didn't come here to kill."

"You forget what people were saying a few minutes

ago? That boy had to watch everybody in his village, everybody in his family, get murdered by men like these. Did you ever think that maybe he just didn't want to watch *you* die?"

Chinma heard them, and the words registered. There were no more enemy soldiers. Mark and he had shot them both. There was still firing going on outside, and it sounded close. More soldiers might come in. The work wasn't done.

Chinma walked back into the room, still holding the pistol. He saw the man with the booming voice—the "radio man," Mrs. Malich had called him—and he handed him the pistol. "Can you load it? Can you shoot?"

"Yes sir I can," said the man.

Chinma walked to where Mark lay on the floor. The caregivers had pulled his body off the men he had fallen on. There were only two wounds on his body, but one of them was right into the center of his chest. Chinma reached down and took the pistol out of his hand. Mark hadn't dropped the pistol, even as he died.

Chinma went back to where the box of ammo was and took out a couple of clips and put them in the pockets of his pants. Then he walked to the door. "Stop them at the stairs," he said to the radio man.

"Good idea." And the man followed him out into the corridor. The radio man paused at the body of the enemy soldier. "What about using his automatic?"

"I don't know how," said Chinma. "How many bullets are left?"

"I don't know," said the radio man, and he walked on, leaving the automatic where it lay.

They came to the top of the stairs as the shooting became a wild flurry outside—but farther away, or maybe it was just that Chinma's blood was pounding in his ears. He was more frightened now than he had been before. Maybe because now he knew he was going to be doing the shooting, and before, he had only realized it at the last second.

If I had been as smart as Mark, I would already have had my pistol ready, I could have shot the second man the moment he appeared. Mark had just shot a man, and yet *he* fired in time, and only missed because he was off balance. If I had shot at the same time, my friend would not be dead.

They waited at the head of the stairs, but the radio man said, "I think I heard choppers a minute ago. I think the Marines are here."

The door downstairs banged open, and there was the sound of many feet, some running, some walking. Too many for them to fight off on the stairs.

"They're our boys," said the radio man. "They're talking English."

From the next floor down, there were voices, and now Chinma tried to understand them. He had been expecting foreign babble before, and English was not his native language. But he knew the words now.

"We're too late, they got this floor."

"Only a few," said another. "They must have taken them up, everyone who could go."

Then silence, but a lot more boots coming up the stairs to the floor just below.

Suddenly the radio man started shouting. "Nobody but Americans up here, men!"

A voice came from below. "Who are you! State your name!"

"Rusty Humphries, dammit, don't you know my voice? What, is your radio broken? 'If I didn't say it, it's prob'ly a lie! Rusty! Heck yeah!'"

And a couple of men from below began to sing along. "'Rusty! Heck yeah!'"

Humphries stopped their singing. "Okay, rock stars, that's enough. Two of 'em got up here, but they're dead now. Got a lot of sick soldiers up here, guys. Do you have masks? You really don't want to catch this thing."

"Doesn't sound like you're wearing a mask, Rusty!" shouted a man from below.

"Yeah, but I'm stupid," said Rusty. "So I probably caught it and I'm as contagious as anybody else. So when you come up, make sure you're wearing protection, just like they taught you in high school."

That got another laugh.

A couple of men appeared on the landing below. They were wearing face masks—not the white surgical masks that the caregivers used, but the larger green masks that Chinma had seen in the footlockers.

"Who's the boy?" asked a soldier. "You said nobody but Americans."

"His whole village was wiped out and President Torrent gave him asylum. I got his story from the folks back in the room where we were holed up, and I got to tell you, if he wasn't American before, when he dropped that enemy soldier he became an American as far as I'm concerned."

Chinma dropped his pistol. He didn't need it now. He ran back to the room. He wasn't sure why. Mark was dead. There was no more danger. But he needed to be there.

He came into the room and saw how frightened everyone still looked. Hadn't they heard the shouting and talking? "American soldiers here now," he said. "All safe."

Everyone began talking softly to one another and to Chinma.

"Do you think they could help us carry these men back down to their rooms?"

"What about the people we had to leave on the floor below?"

"Are you all right?"

But Chinma didn't know the answer to any of their questions. He walked toward Arty. The man's eyes were closed, so Chinma started past him, toward Mark's body.

Arty caught feebly at his leg, at his hand. Chinma stopped, knelt. Arty couldn't talk loudly enough for Chinma to make out what he was saying, above the noise of other people's talking. He leaned closer still, so his ear was just above Arty's mouth.

But instead of saying anything, Arty leaned up his head and twisted it so he could kiss Chinma on the cheek. Then Arty dropped his head back onto the pillow that Chinma himself had brought up the stairs with them when they fled up here only ten minutes before. Arty's eyes were open and filled with tears. "You did right," he whispered. Chinma didn't really hear him so much as read his lips.

"Mark is dead," Chinma said softly.

"I know," said Arty. Chinma leaned close to hear. "Very brave," added Arty.

"Very smart, too," said Chinma. "He knew what to do. I didn't know what to do, but he did."

"Son of a soldier," said Arty. Then he closed his eyes, worn out.

I am not the son of a soldier. That's why I didn't know what to do.

Chinma walked back to Mark's body. This time there was no pistol to retrieve, just the body of his friend. Someone will have to tell Mrs. Malich that he is dead. And the story of how he died. His story will have to be told, and I will have to tell it. But I don't know his story. I only know how it ended. Still, I can tell the part I know. I can tell his mother that he died as well as his father did, because he brought down the enemy and saved the lives of everyone in that room, everyone on that floor, everyone in that building who survived.

What I can't tell Mrs. Malich or anyone is my story. Because I did not kill to save anyone. I'm glad they were saved, but I killed that man because he was like the men who killed my family. He was the kind of man who would put bullets into old men and women and children, who would kill helpless sick people as they lay on their beds or on the floor. I killed him because if I could, I would kill every such man in the world. I am not a good Christian like Mark, who didn't want to kill anybody. I wanted that soldier dead. I wanted him dead by my hand. I wanted to put bullets in every one of them.

A bullet for every member of my family. Even the ones who didn't love me. Even the ones who left me to die when I was sick. Because they were my family and they had lived through the monkey sickness and there was no reason for them to be murdered and burned like that. No reason.

And then, also for no reason, as Chinma knelt beside Mark's body and held his still-warm hand, all his rage fled away, and all his fear. What was left was the body of a friend. And what he had not let himself feel about his family, his village, his people, he could feel about this boy who had chosen to come to a country filled with disease in order to try to save the lives of strangers.

"You should be alive," said Chinma. "I should be dead."

A couple of nearby people heard him talking and stopped their own conversations to hear. Nearer the door, the Marines were helping bring out the sick, so the room was loud. But Chinma was not talking so that the living could hear him. He knew that Mark could hear him, however loud or soft his voice might be.

"God kept me alive *again*," said Chinma. "Now I

have to be as good as you, so I deserve to live." He knew he could never be as good as Mark—as brave, as kind, as smart—and he began to weep. He could not do it. It was too hard. Why couldn't he have died instead of Mark? The world would be a better place if he had.

Chinma knelt up and leaned back his head and began to cry out the names of the dead in his village. His father, his mother, his brothers and sisters, the other wives, the other children, everyone whose name he could think of.

He was still wailing their names, crying out so that everybody could hear the names of the dead, when a Marine touched him on the shoulder. Chinma glanced at him but did not stop.

The radio man, Humphries, pulled the Marine away. "This is his country, son, and this was his friend, and between them they saved us all. He gets to show his grief however he wants."

EIGHTEEN

RECOVERY

The former colonial nation of Nigeria has ceased to exist, unless the new Hausa nation chooses to retain that name. No matter what they call themselves, that government is in a state of war with the United States, as Congress has just affirmed.

The southeastern, Ibo-speaking portion of Nigeria has declared itself the Independent nation of Biafra, and the United States extends provisional recognition to the new government. Provisional recognition is also extended to the new Yoruba-speaking nation in the west of Nigeria and the newly independent Ijaw- and Efik-speaking delta lands.

These new borders are rationally based on the distribution of the speakers of the dominant languages, taking into account the history of the various ethnic groups in the area.

With more than three hundred languages in Nigeria, it was impossible to consider giving every language national status. The full recognition of the United States will be extended when each of the new nations adopts a constitution permanently affirming the rights of the speakers of minority languages.

Most of the oil in the former Nigeria was and is within the new boundaries of Ijaw-land and Efik-land in the delta. Nevertheless, the delta government has promised the new Yoruba and Ibo governments a share of oil revenue for ten years, in recognition of the fact that they were equally deprived by the previous government of any significant benefit from oil revenues in the past decades.

Peace with the Hausa government of the north will only be possible upon the following terms: the renunciation of any claim on any other portion of the former Nigeria, a commitment to make restitution to Biafra, Yoruba-land, and the delta for revenues unlawfully withheld from them during the period of Hausa rule over the south. They must also extradite to an international tribunal those members of the former government whom the Departments of State and Defense have identified as being most responsible for atrocities, genocide, and the theft of public moneys, both before and after the nictovirus outbreak.

Now we come to the serious business of the Sudanese attack on the American establishment in Calabar four days ago. Our NATO allies have *all* responded vigorously, and have joined us in declaring Sudan to be a rogue nation and an aggressor against us, against Nigeria, and against their own citizens. What is now to be decided is whether the state and government of Sudan shall be permitted to continue to exist.

We gave the Sudanese ambassador pictures of the dead soldiers in Sudanese uniform and copies of the identification papers found with or on their bodies, but the official Sudanese response is that these are forgeries. Since we know that they are not, we regard the Sudanese denials as defiance and as an attempt to escape the consequences of their own illegal actions.

These forces were chosen from, under the orders of, and supplied by, the armed forces of Sudan, with the full knowledge and approval of the highest echelons of the Sudanese government. Therefore we hold Sudan fully accountable.

We demand the extradition, within twenty-four hours, of all Sudanese officials responsible for the decision to attack American soldiers and civilians on a mission of mercy in Nigeria.

We also demand the immediate withdrawal of Sudanese forces and government officials behind the line of Malakal, Kaduqli, and Al Ubayyid, opening the way for NATO forces to provide security and provisional government for the long-oppressed African people of that region.

Whether that area will become one or more separate nations is a matter for the people who live there to decide for themselves, after order has been restored and basic human needs are met. NATO promises that this occupation is temporary and that local government will begin to function as soon as it can be established.

If the Sudanese government does not declare its intention to abide by these conditions within the next twenty-four hours, and does not turn over the officials and officers named in our list nor begin withdrawing forces behind the designated line within forty-eight hours, I will ask Congress for a declaration of war against Sudan.

If such a war begins, then when it ends there will be no nation called Sudan in the world. Instead, the northern, Arabic-speaking portion of Sudan will become a permanent part of the nation of Egypt, which has accepted that responsibility and the rest of Sudan will become a free and sovereign nation or nations with the right of self-determination that has long been denied these citizens by the criminal government in Khartoum.

I also ask Congress to declare that August tenth of this year, and July tenth of all subsequent years, be commemorated as a day of national mourning for those American soldiers and charitable workers who were slain on July tenth of this year; and as a day of national gratitude to those Americans, soldiers and civilians, who nobly defended the many who survived the attack; and also to the Nigerian students of the University of Calabar who gave their lives defending, with clubs against automatic weapons, the entrance of the university grounds where our soldiers lay sick and nearly defenseless. Their sacrifice will never be forgotten by the American people.

Finally, I affirm that the American quarantine of Africa continues in full force. It is encouraging that the treatment techniques developed by American charitable workers in Nigeria have proven effective in reducing by more than half the mortality rate of those infected with the nictovirus. But these techniques are currently being employed only in small portions of the areas affected by the epidemic.

Even where they are being used, a reduction of mortality from an estimated forty percent to an estimated fifteen percent still leaves us with that staggering mortality rate of fifteen percent. This disease cannot be allowed to leave its continent of origin if we can possibly help it. We will not relax our vigilance.

This means that despite the anxious wishes and pleas of their friends and family here in the United States, neither the surviving soldiers nor the charitable workers now in Nigeria can be allowed to return to the United States at this time. Only when it is known that someone has had the nictovirus and fully recovered from it can he or she be allowed to leave the epidemic zone and return directly home. Others must wait out a three-week quarantine.

This is all the information I have for you right now. Be assured that I will brief you again about the responses of the governments of the Arab portion of Sudan and the Hausa portion of Nigeria as the deadlines approach.

I will not take questions at this time. Thank you very much.

CECILY HAD thought that Reuben's death would destroy her. She had been so close to him, so dependent on him, but to her surprise, she had not been destroyed at all. Grief-stricken, yes. She missed him every day, not just the times she needed him, but also the times she knew he would have loved. She couldn't tell him things, she couldn't show him things. Yet she could go on. His death wasn't debilitating. She finally realized it was because their marriage had been an enterprise; they were entrepreneurs in this little business called a family, and by continuing to provide for and raise the children they had made together, she was keeping the marriage going. She was still doing her part, and in her heart, she could say to him, See what we've done? See how our work is turning out?

She had thought she understood grief and loss.

Then she came back onto the campus of the University of Calabar, returned to the headquarters building, saw the hazmat-suited Marines clearing away the bodies of the dead university students and the dead enemy soldiers and thought, the enemy got this far before the Marines came. But they were stopped at the door. Look at all these bodies, stopped at the door.

But she knew, already, even then, before anyone spoke to her, before the face-masked Marine captain matched her to a photograph and said, "Mrs. Malich?"—she

knew that something terrible had happened. The worst
had happened. She knew it but held it at bay, because
there were so many things it might be. After all, she
had been very close to Reuben's jeesh. If one of them
had died—or more than one—or all of them—they
would treat her like this, wouldn't they? Gently take
her arm and lead her into the building. Take her into
Cole's office, where Cole most definitely was not, his
bed made, no sign of the mess in which he had left his
quarters when he got up to go out and face the enemy.
They must be preparing to tell me that General Coleman was killed.

She even asked: How is General Coleman?

Grave condition, his body badly bruised from repeated bullet strikes on his Kevlar, but his most serious
condition is the fever and dysentery from the nictovirus, we have him at the university hospital now with an
IV from the fleet and two doctors working with him,
he'll probably recover, he's not bleeding at the eyes and
nose, we think he'll live. Mrs. Malich, please sit down.

She knew now.

"Mark is dead," she whispered.

Contradict me. Tell me, No, no, of course not, I'm
sorry if we gave you that impression, no, Mark is fine,
he's upstairs, let's call him down to you right away.

"Yes, Mrs. Malich," said the Marine captain. "If it is
any consolation to you, he died as a hero." He told her
a brief account of what Mark had done—calling the
enemy soldiers to his room with a single shot, then killing the first man through the door, then dying instantly

from two bullets from the second intruder's automatic weapon, one of which passed directly through his heart.

"The Nigerian boy Chinma then shot the man who killed your son."

Cecily nodded. She had heard.

"Is there anything I can do for you?"

Are you God? Can you bring him back? Then what can you possibly imagine I would want you to do for me?

Instead of saying any such thing, she shook her head. And then she thought of something she might need. "Where is he?" she said. She was surprised at the calmness of her own voice. But then, she had known Mark was dead for some time. Ever since she arrived at the entrance of the building, she had known it since then. This was not a shock. She could handle this for a moment, for this moment she could stay calm, and then for this next moment, and again, to her surprise, for the moment after.

"We can't take you to his body, ma'am. Many witnesses report that he exhibited symptoms of the nictovirus before he died. We cannot allow you to risk infection. His body has been sequestered with the other victims."

"We are all infected," said Cecily. "Sooner or later. And I will see my son, and I will see him now. Will you help me or not?"

So he helped her. He had Mark's body brought into what had once been a small conference room for the university. He left her there and closed the door.

She had handled it for long enough. The door closed just as her control burst.

She cried out his name. She kissed his face. She tore open his shirt and touched the bullet wounds, the one that killed him and the other one through his abdomen about four inches down. She stroked his chest, felt the ribs under the skin, ran her fingers through his hair, all the time calling his name, apologizing to him for letting him come, for not being a better mother, for not forbidding him to put his life at risk.

Then, after a while, she sat beside his cold body, holding his hand and talking to him. Telling him how proud she was of him, of the way he had lived, the way he had risked his life to help others, and how, at the end, he had been as good a soldier as his father could have hoped he'd be.

"I'm sorry I wasn't there with you, at the end. But I'm glad you didn't need me to be there in order to know what the right thing was and to do it. You never needed anyone to tell you that."

And then, stroking his face again, touching every part of his face, the way she had played with him and teased him as an infant, this is your eye, this is your ear, what is this? yes, it's your mouth, and this is your nose. You were such a sweet baby, but you couldn't sleep, it was so hard with you because you wouldn't sleep and I was exhausted all the time and I thought, being a mother is so much harder than I thought, but I didn't regret it, because you also were such a smiler, you always had a big toothless grin for me when I changed you or fed you. You'd stop nursing, break away, just to smile at me, and then start sucking again, you were such a happy baby, you just didn't sleep for very long at a time, and it was so hard to get you to fall asleep in the first place. I carried you inside me, the first time my body went through all the baby changes, all the surprises and mysteries, the woes and pains of it, were all for you, that first time, I was no more experienced at this birthing thing than you were, but we made it through. I thought it would lead to your growing tall as your father, taking a wife, giving me grandbabies, making it all happen again, the cycle repeating. But instead it was all for *this*, for this place, to save the lives of these people. That was your choice. I let you have your choice. Even though it terrified me, and now all my worst fears have come true, but it was your choice, it was your life, and even though you didn't use it the way I wanted you to, you used it well.

She wept until there were no more tears to weep, until she sat beside the table where they had laid his body, her head lying on her arms, her hand still holding his hand. She was exhausted and, perhaps, asleep, though she was not aware of waking up. Only that someone's hand was on her shoulder.

It was the masked Marine captain. "Ma'am," he said. "May we take his body now? We would like to take your son back to the ship to prepare him for transfer back to the United States."

"Yes," she said.

She kissed her son's cold hand for the last time,

knowing that once they sealed it into the coffin it would not be opened for any reason.

"Back to you, Reuben," she murmured. It was what she had said when he got up and brought the baby to her for nursing in the middle of the night, because she got so little rest. Reuben would be asleep again, because he had that ability to fall asleep in an instant, when he decided to. So she'd wake him when the baby was through nursing and say, Back to you, Reuben, and he'd get up and take the baby.

Now she faced the wall, leaning her forehead on it, sobbing again with all her heart, there were more tears in her after all, as they took her son's sweet hurt body out of the room. She could not watch them put him into a body bag and hoist him into a helicopter. It would be unbearable.

But even more unbearable was to stay in that room now that he was gone. So she got control of herself again, and ran after them, caught up with them. She watched every bit of it. Putting him into the bag, zipping it closed over his body, over his face. Attaching the documentation, which she checked, making sure that everything was right, that there would be no mistaking who this was and where his body should be sent.

She followed them to the helicopter, and she knew they took extra care to be gentle because she was watching. These sailors and Marines knew that these bodies all deserved respect and they gave it, but they were even more careful so that they didn't do anything that would cause her any more hurt than she already had. She loved them for their carefulness, she hated them for the terrible thing they were doing, taking her little boy away in a bag that was much too big for him, a man-sized bag.

She watched them close up the helicopter, watched it rise into the air, continued watching until it was out of sight, and then looked around, surprised that there was still air, still ground, still sunlight beating through the haze of this land where it was always summer. It would rain this afternoon. It was the rainy season. It would rain almost every day. They were all used to it. It was just a fact of Nigerian life in the spring and summer. It would rain this afternoon.

Again the hand on her shoulder. "Will you come inside with me, Mrs. Malich?"

But why should I? she wondered. What's the point? What is there for me to do?

"There are some soldiers who want to see you," he said. "If you'd rather be alone, then of course they'll respect that."

"I would rather be alone," she said.

"I'll tell them. But would you come inside? It's going to rain."

She let him lead her inside. And as they went, she sneezed.

She stopped when she sneezed. Not one sneeze, but two, three, four in rapid succession.

She wanted to explain to him that it wasn't the nictovirus, it was just the crying, it got mucus moving in her head, and now she was sneezing because of that,

that plus the hot, muggy air outside, and the dust churned up by the wind the helicopter made. It's not the nictovirus, but I wish it were.

She was wrong, however. It *was* the nictovirus. They had made one miscalculation in all their attempts at keeping the caregivers from getting infected. They wore masks and gloves and never breathed unfiltered air in the presence of the sick. But the nictovirus was hardy, and clung to their clothing, and when they took off their clothes and shook them out or folded them, it stirred the virus back into the air. It was only in small concentrations, and it took time before any particular person might get the virus that happened to thrive inside the lungs, but it would happen to them all. It had happened to her among the first, though she was not the least careful. It had happened to her only a few hours later than it happened to her son.

She went back into the building, back to Cole's quarters, and without asking permission of anyone, she placed the most terrible telephone call of her life. She called Aunt Margaret and had her bring the children to the telephone and put it on speakerphone so they would all hear it at once, and she told them how Mark died. She got through it with her voice reasonably clear, though she could not hide her grief. Then she told them that she had to stay in Africa for now, because of the quarantine, and they shouldn't worry about her. When they were notified that Mark's body was ready for burial, they should go ahead. "I don't want him waiting for me, Aunt Margaret," she said.

"Find a good place for him, please, and hold a service so his brothers and sisters and his friends and my friends can all say good-bye to him."

Margaret said, "I understand, honey, I do. I'll keep things going here."

And there was something in the way she said it that let Cecily know that Margaret understood the thing she hadn't said: that she had the nictovirus herself, and she didn't know if she would ever come home.

The children were all crying and Cecily listened to all of their questions and whatever any of them wanted to say, and when there was no more talking, she said, "Please write to me, even if my own letters to you get held up. Write to me on paper, and send it through the military mail. I won't have much computer time for the next while."

Then the phone call ended, and Cecily knew that the children would be all right, the ones who were left alive, they would be safe for now, as safe as children could be in this world. She was here and could not go to them, but they would be all right.

She could not go out and care for the sick anymore. Not because she was sick herself, because for the first days, before the fever came, she was physically capable of doing the work. No, she simply couldn't talk to a mother whose child was dying or might die or had just died, she couldn't offer her any comfort, could say no words of Christian solace. It wasn't in her. Not because she had lost her faith—she hadn't, she knew that Mark was with Reuben now, she felt that with fierce intensity.

She simply couldn't talk to them or see them with their grieving faces, because now she had such a face of her own. There was nothing in her to give to them.

So she stayed in a room in the university hospital, among Nigerian women patients, middle-aged and elderly, and helped them as long as she could. Then the fever came, and she took to her bed the way they had, and someone else came and mopped her brow and gave her water and made her drink and take medications. It was all so familiar, yet all so strange.

She knew she was going to die, and it was fine with her. She was finished with being a mother, she had been released from that responsibility with Mark's death, and so it was all right to go ahead and die from this virus, she would be only a week or two behind Mark. The other children would be orphans but she knew that they would grow up surrounded by love. God would take care of them, because she had let go. When the helicopter rose into the air, she had let go in her heart.

Not my purpose in life anymore. And therefore I have no purpose, and therefore no life, and the nictovirus comes to me now as a gift.

Deep into her week with the fever, her head constantly throbbing with pain despite the ibuprofen, her bowels tormented with dysentery trying to void food she hadn't eaten, water she had barely sipped, someone started shouting at her. Wake up and start fighting this thing! he shouted, and he sounded angry. Nobody told you you could quit this job, you signed on for the duration and it's not over. Start cooperating with your treatment! Start caring whether you live or die!

Go away, she thought. Whoever you are, stop yelling at me.

But he didn't stop. He came back and talked to her again, sternly, like a father talking to his daughter. He talked about the children who remained, reminded her of little stories about them, what they looked like, how they argued, things they had done and said. They're waiting for you. When you come out of this you'll be immune. No quarantine. You can go home.

It's not my job anymore, she thought.

Then she realized that he was talking to her like a soldier. He was an officer, commanding a soldier who had lost her courage. He was Reuben. He was telling her that their partnership had not been dissolved. Just because one of their children was gone didn't mean she had any right to abandon the others. They had five children together, and there were still four. And even if another died, and another—for it was possible, when the nictovirus made it to America, as it surely would—she was still the mother of however many children were left.

She answered him in her mind, for her lips could not speak. It's easy for *you* to say that I need to go back to work, *you're* safely dead, nobody can tell *you* that your work isn't finished. Why is it always me? My chores are never done. I'm so tired. My head hurts. My mouth is so dry. It's so hot. So cold. So hot. Let me be finished with this.

"Cecily," said the soldier's voice. "Your fever is falling. You're going to make it."

She opened her eyes. Her head still hurt. The light in the room was dim. It was night. The soldier was sitting beside her. It wasn't Reuben after all. It was Cole. And behind him stood Mingo.

"Cole," she said. "Mingo."

"Thank God," said Cole.

"She knows us again," said Mingo. "That's a good sign."

"She's going to be fine," said Cole.

I'm never going to be *fine* again, she wanted to say. I'm just going to be alive, going through the motions, doing my duty. But I will never, never, never be fine.

"Which of you was yelling at me?" she asked.

They looked at each other. "When?" asked Cole.

"While I was sick," she said. "I thought one of you must have—it was a soldier—I thought it was Reuben but it must have been one of you."

"I don't know," said Cole. "We were watching over you in shifts. Well, I came to it late because I had troubles of my own. We're all still walking around like old men, shuffling. It's a slow recovery. But we took turns watching you because—it was our assignment."

"Assignment?" she asked.

"From Rube," said Mingo. "Long before he died. A pact."

"Plus we all care about you for your own sake," said Cole. "And for the children back home."

"Mark's dead, isn't he?" she asked through parched lips.

"He is, Cecily," said Cole. "I'm so sorry."

"I knew he was. But I had such strange dreams. I thought maybe."

"It wasn't a dream. He was really your son, and he finished the job the rest of us tried to do—keeping everybody safe. I'm sorry we couldn't save him. It's hardest on Benny and Arty, because they were there, so weak and feverish they couldn't do anything to help him. But nothing like what you've lost. Nothing. I'm sorry. I'm talking too much. But you had us so scared."

"Why," she murmured.

"Well, besides the matter of your dying? You bled, Cecily. Out of your eyes and nose. It was a death sentence, and we couldn't bear it. When you started bleeding, all the caregivers who weren't too sick to join us prayed for you. It was all we could do."

"And someone yelled at me," said Cecily.

Then she fell back to sleep.

Each time she woke the headache was a little less. She began to eat again. They took her off the IV. They removed her from her room in the hospital and put her in the Mirage hotel, where the rooms were full of recovering caregivers. The government was paying the bill for them, she was told, and all the employees in the hotel were nictovirus survivors, so everyone was immune. The recovering caregivers were treated like royalty by the Nigerian staff.

No, the *Deltaland* staff, she was told. Nigeria was now a country to the north, a drier place, a Muslim country that spoke another language and had nothing to do with them.

Gradually she began to take notice of the world again. Someone brought her a summary of all that had happened while she was sick. The relatively peaceful division of Nigeria into lands with borders that finally made sense. The short, savage war with Sudan which ended with the dissolution of that country, though how the country would be divided was still being negotiated.

The nictovirus had now spread throughout sub-Saharan Africa. It was like a fire that burned slowly where the population was more sparse, so it seemed to slow, perhaps to stop, then flare up when it reached dense population again. Wherever it went, there were massive efforts to educate people in how to cope with it, what treatments worked. Medicines were made available free of charge and in such quantities that there was no incentive to blackmarket them.

And still President Torrent's quarantine held. And still thousands of American volunteers took their life into their hands and came to Africa, to every country that would allow them in. What Cecily had helped start in Nigeria was now happening in Rwanda and Kenya and Liberia and Senegal and, last of all, in South Africa, though there the volunteers were English and Dutch, and in other countries they were French, Portuguese, Brazilian.

For wherever there was a reasonable hope that their

language could be understood, people from outside the quarantine zone volunteered. Most of them were Christians, and many of them were new-fledged, people who had once been cynical, Catholic or Protestant in name only. But the nictovirus and the dangerous work of nursing those sick with it had, oddly enough, rekindled faith that had long been reported as dead. Christianity was a credible religion again in countries that had once stopped caring.

Cecily talked about that with Drew, when he came to visit her. "Is it possible that God sent this terrible disease so that Christianity would matter again?" she asked.

"Anything's possible," he answered, "but personally I don't think so."

"Why not?"

"Because God doesn't need to send plagues. They just come, naturally, like earthquakes and lightning and drought and asteroids that fall onto the Earth and blow it to smithereens and wipe out most of life. God doesn't have to make up disasters, they're part of life. What he cares about is how we respond. Sometimes we're pretty bad. Sometimes we're the disaster ourselves. But sometimes we do okay. Like this time. Like the way some people heard the call and came."

"I didn't hear any call," said Cecily.

"Oh, Cecily, you did hear a call, and don't you forget it. What difference does it make if it was Mark's voice you heard, or God? But your boy brought you here and you did a mighty work because of him."

She cried again then. She cried most days. Sometimes many times a day. But it was different now. She cried for Mark, but she wasn't crying in despair, she was crying out of love and grief. This was familiar territory now. It was like her tears for Reuben. It didn't mean her life was over. She no longer wished to die.

Then one day Babe and Arty came to her with the news that the first person had been cleared to go back to the United States. "That radio dude," said Arty. "Bastard ran around without a mask and he never caught it. He just cleared his three-week quarantine and he's going home. But that opens the door for those of us who are now immune."

"You're going home?" asked Cecily.

"We have formally requested to be assigned to train soldiers in the use of the Noodle and Bones," said Babe. "Since we've had real combat experience with them, and nobody else in the military has, it's not like we've got a lot of competition for the job. And since the equipment has proven itself to be worth the cost, they're going to need a lot of training."

"Well, that's good."

"You sound a little disappointed," said Arty.

"Well, I've been spoiled, and so have the children. Having you all in the D.C. area, you know."

"Oh, well, not to worry, Cecily," said Drew. "Old King Cole talked to his buddy, His Imperial Majesty the President, and we're going to do all our training out of bases in the D.C. area. Specifically because, as he put it to old Averell, if he tried to do it anywhere outside of easy visiting distance to you and your family, we'd all resign our commissions then and nobody'd get the benefit of our experience."

"I bet he didn't say it quite that way."

"We were all in the room listening to the conversation," said Arty. "On speakerphone, so the dude would know we all meant it."

"Well, you're very kind. The children will be glad." And then, once again, she burst into tears. "I'm so tired of crying. I'm emotional all the time."

The paperwork started. She was strong enough now to walk around, to talk to other caregivers. The first wave of them were pretty evenly divided between those who were going to stay and continue nursing the sick, now that they were immune, and those who were going to go back to America, having done their service.

And, of course, there were the thirteen percent who wouldn't be doing either, because the nictovirus had killed them. As it had killed fifteen percent of the soldiers.

It was Cole who brought her the news that her travel orders and permits had come through. "The President wants to see you, he says, but only when you feel up to it, and he doesn't expect you to resume your duties until you feel strong enough. And Cecily, he says—and I think he means it—that if you choose not to return to work, he'll not only understand, he'll make sure that your income will continue regardless."

"That's not right, not with taxpayer dollars," said Cecily. "I was overpaid as it was."

"It won't be taxpayer dollars. He knows you well enough for that. He talked to some businessman friends. Told them your story. What you used to do for him. How you got things working here. He says about a dozen of them are fighting to have you on permanent retainer, as a consultant, whether you come in and actually consult with them or not."

"Charity money," said Cecily with a little bitterness.

"Right," said Cole. "And if the families of sick people here had refused to let you nurse them because it was 'charity nursing,' would that have been stupid?"

"We'll see," said Cecily.

"I'm going back, too," said Cole. "I'm back to being Colonel Coleman again. The stars disappeared with the job."

"Who's doing it now?"

"Nobody. Torrent got what he wanted, he's had his war, he now has control over African borders."

"What do you mean by that?" asked Cecily.

"I've been around the other guys too much," said Cole. "Talking like they do. I mean, Torrent needed us to help deal with the first, ugly, panicked responses to the nictovirus and the quarantine. Like the attempted genocide by the Hausa, the anarchy in the CAR, taking down a few brutal regimes. By the time we got sick, our job was done and some others were stepping up to the plate. South Africa got rid of the sick government in Zimbabwe. Actually, quite a few presidents-for-life were arrested. Or tried to flee their countries and live on stolen billions in Swiss bank accounts, only to find that all the money in the world couldn't get you out of Africa. It's been a good change. It's not democracy everywhere, but responsible government is actually on the rise, and graft is way down."

"That's good news, but what do you mean about talking like the other guys do? It sounded like you were saying President Torrent engineered all this."

"Look, it's the things he's written over the years. While we've been cooling our heels here we've had good internet access, and they've been showing me all kinds of speeches he made back when he was a professor, but also stuff he's said here and there since he was NSA and even as President. He's actually kind of obsessive about the need for America to become an empire. A benign one, but an empire all the same. To create a worldwide Pax Americana."

"I know about that. It's never been a secret," said Cecily. "Reuben talked to me about that back when he was getting his doctorate and Averell was one of his professors."

"Yes, but it's one thing for him to theorize, and another thing for him to put the whole thing into play."

"He didn't cause the plague."

"Of course not," said Cole. "But he's *used* the plague. What he's doing in Africa? It's like everybody's been working from his script. Did you know that in 1997 he wrote a paper on boundaries in Africa? How they needed to be redrawn to fit with languages and tribes?"

"A lot of people have been saying that for years."

"But he actually *drew* the lines. And then he ended

it by saying that it couldn't happen until some kind of crisis broke down the old colonial system. Broke the back of the crime lords running all these countries and profiting from them as they were. He specifically said that an epidemic in Africa might be the broom that would sweep clean. Because it would hit *every* country instead of just a few, the way other disasters and crises do."

Cecily had to think about that for a moment. "All it means is that he was right. And it was a good thing that when the crisis came, a man who had already thought it through was President and happened to have the boldness to act."

"Exactly what I tell them. *Told* them. And it always comes back to the same thing. The handheld EMP device."

"What does that have to do with it?"

Cole sighed. "They had it in the CAR. And those Sudanese had the exact same model."

"Maybe it was Sudanese testing it in the CAR," said Cecily.

"Do you really think the deep scientific tradition in Sudan developed a handheld electronic interference device?"

Cecily chuckled. "Okay, so they got it from somewhere else."

"But where, where, where was that?" asked Cole. "I'll tell you. I think it was Aldo Verus."

"Well, then, it was *not* President Torrent."

"Not so fast," said Cole.

"Because Aldo Verus is in jail?"

"Partly. And because Aldo Verus did not get into the business of developing high-tech weapons on the sly until he attended a symposium for responsible leaders of industry—which in that context meant politically-correct billionaires—at which Torrent gave a really interesting presentation in which he said that as long as national governments had a monopoly on weapons development, the best weapons would always be in the hands of the kind of people who chose the military as a career."

"Ah," said Cecily. "I wonder what he meant by that."

"I'm sure you're wondering. But Aldo Verus knew exactly what it meant. I'm betting that's when he started hiring people to develop his little toys. And because he's a wacko, it all looked like it came out of the CGI department of sci-fi movies. But the point is, Torrent went to the people who could make it happen, and he said the words that needed to be said, and then it happened."

"But that was years ago," said Cecily. "You say it like it's a conspiracy, when it's really just a very smart man full of ideas, who has always talked a lot."

"Or planted seeds, depending on how you look at it," said Cole. "But it's not me talking. Pretend you're hearing this from Drew, which is in fact where most of the talk comes from, because he's the one actually doing the research."

"You and I had our suspicions, too," said Cecily. "Remember? Right after the civil war. We thought it looked awfully convenient that everything had somehow worked so that Torrent went from Princeton to NSA to vice president to president in, what, five months?"

"Yes, and whatever happened to our suspicions?"

"I translated all of Reuben's papers and I never found—or, rather, *he* never found a smoking gun."

"That's what Mingo says. No smoking gun, because Torrent is too smart for there to ever be a gun that was held in his hand. But he is always prepared to step in and take advantage of the situations that come up. And they always come up. And when they *do* come up, he seems always to have a connection, deep in the background, with the source of the problem."

"Torrent always says that only fools make plans, and really complicated, longterm plans come from madmen."

"He doesn't *plan*," said Cole. "Any more than a spider *plans*. He just lays a web out there and waits for something to hit it, and then he pounces and makes it his own."

"Nothing you're saying sounds evil to me," said Cecily. "I know this man. So do you. And he's been a good president. Not conservative enough for Rusty Humphries, of course, but then, neither am I."

"And there you are," said Cole. "You come to the same place where I am. The *evidence* shows a really smart, bold, ambitious, opportunistic guy who is president now and deserves to be. But my jeesh—Reuben's jeesh—they go beyond the evidence. They aren't lawyers, they're soldiers. They make battlefield judgments.

On the battlefield you never have enough information, not even with drones and satellites watching over you, because you can never know the enemy's intentions. And yet you still have to make decisions. So you learn to make guesses. Flying leaps. Reuben was brilliant at it. If he'd lived long enough, he would have been a four-star for real, not a temp like me, and he would have been brilliant at it, because he had good instincts, he could leap to a decision based on fragments of information, and he'd be right."

"Not always at home."

"Because at home it wasn't a battlefield, and you were the five-star there. He was outranked and outclassed."

"Never," said Cecily.

"A joke," said Cole. "But that's how these guys talk about you. That's why they want you on their side. You'll see. When we're all back in the States, they'll come to you."

"What *side* are we talking about?"

"Call it 'Torrent skeptics,' maybe. Here's the way they lay it out. We get the Noodles and Bones and the first time we deploy it, there's the handheld EMP waiting for us. What was that developed to counter, if not the Noodles and Bones?"

"It hits *all* electronics, doesn't it?"

"Noodles and Bones are like those jets that can't fly without computers constantly controlling the trim of the aircraft. Without the software, they're nothing. There's no manual override except to take off the Bones entirely. No, they're right, the handheld EMP is too weak to use against anything heavily armored or far away. It's a close-combat defensive weapon, and the only thing it hurts is a weapons system that did not exist, at least in this form, until now."

Cecily thought about that. "Are you saying that you think Torrent tipped somebody off? Because the exoskeleton concept has been around for a while."

"And so has the EMP device. It could all be coincidence. That's Torrent's cover—remember, this is the guys talking, not me. Here's another. Those six trucks from Sudan had to have been equipped and trained especially for this mission. They came into Calabar knowing exactly where they were going. Right down to which building to head for."

"So they were competent."

"So they were tipped off—the guys say. Because the training for that mission had to have begun *before* anybody outside the highest circles of the military knew that the nictovirus had penetrated our base."

"Which, as I recall, was the guys' clever idea."

"Torrent is in the loop. He finds out that some of us are sick, and he gets my estimate that the whole base will be sick, and at the same time. He has your schedule of the progress of the disease. He knows that there is going to be a window of about a week when we will be useless as a military force. He also knows that there are these Christian do-gooders all over the place."

"There were rumors flying all over Nigeria about

how the American soldiers had the monkey sickness," said Cecily.

"Right, and Sudan has always had close, close relations with snitches in Nigeria."

"They certainly had friends in the Hausa government."

"There's always an alternate path," said Cole. "I say this to them, and they nod, and then they go right on believing that it's Torrent. He sets things up, he knocks them down. This attack on our base—what vital interest of Sudan's did it serve?"

"When has Sudan's government ever done anything that served any interest? They're motivated by hate and the lust for power."

"And faith!" said Cole.

"Faith as a mask for thuggery and evil," said Cecily.

"Agreed," said Cole. "But what if they were *given* the handheld EMP specifically so they would carry out that mission?"

"You think President Torrent has some loose cannon selling EMPs to rogue nations?"

"The *guys* think that wasn't it amazing the Sudanese had exactly the right information to carry out this mission so fast the Marines *didn't* get here in time, and happened to have been given the only weapon that could prevent us from using our Noodles and Bones as effectively as we otherwise could have?"

"Nothing in that points to Torrent."

"Except that because of this event, Torrent got the

political clout, internationally, to begin redrawing the map of Africa. First in Nigeria, where the new lines are actually pretty clear because this place has been civilized for a long, long time. Then in Sudan. And now working west and south through all of black Africa, getting rid of the old colonial lines and replacing them with . . . new ones."

"New colonial lines?"

"Not the old kind of colony," said Cole. "But these new nations, they're going to be limping along at first. Huge cities whose only industry is spending government money suddenly aren't the center of government. Everything's going to be discombobulated for many years. And there's Averell Torrent, extending a hand, making them dependent on the United States, their good friend, their big brother in the West."

"He's being a good president!" said Cecily. "What should he do, *snub* them? It's a chance to bring peace and order to a place that has desperately needed it . . ."

He was grinning at her.

"What's so funny?"

"Torrent knows how to fix the world, Cecily. He *knows* how to fix it. All he needs is the power to do it. And that power requires public support in America and international cooperation outside it. And to achieve *those*, he needs a few little things here and there—a Sudanese incursion to destroy an American base right when they're sick with the sneezing flu. An itsy little civil war in the United States."

Cecily raised a hand. "Be careful now. You're coming perilously close to saying that President Torrent had Reuben killed."

"I'm saying that Torrent sets things in motion and then takes advantage of however they play out. I'm betting that if the other side had won that civil war, Torrent was all set to become, in short order, the consensus president in the new Progressive Restoration."

"He can't possibly be that cynical."

"Look at him! He's a Democrat *and* a Republican. Why not a Progressive? Or a Green? Just so it gets him into position to save the world."

"He did not kill my husband," said Cecily. "He could not have sat with me, week after week, talking to me, listening to me, *befriending* me, if he had killed my husband. I would have seen it in him."

"Would you?" said Cole. "What if the reason he's consulting with you, seeing you constantly, is because he knows that he's ultimately responsible for Reuben's death. He didn't give the order, but he set things in motion that eventually put DeeDee in Reuben's office when your husband became the key figure in the assassination of a president?"

Cecily's head hurt already. She didn't need this argument. "I'm done," she said. "I can't go through any more of this. Whatever I say, you have yet another conspiracy to throw at me."

"Here's the last one, then. And for once it isn't one of Torrent's. I'm going to give you a quotation, and you tell me what it means. 'Torrent thinks he's Octavian, but if he is, who's Julius?'"

Octavian—the man who became Augustus Caesar, the one who united the empire under his leadership after the civil wars, when a grateful public accepted the de facto end of the republic even though he kept the forms of it alive.

But whoever said that was denying that Torrent was the great peacemaker who created empire out of the ashes of other men's broken ambition. Because there was Julius Caesar, the consummate politician from an old but poor family, who parlayed his way to power through borrowed money, sucking up to the public, and at the same time forging alliances and winning military victories that made him the greatest Roman of his age.

And then he was killed for it by people who feared that he would destroy the republic.

Of course, he already had. Killing him didn't bring it back, it just changed who would be at the head of the new empire.

"Do you really think they're planning to kill him?" asked Cecily.

"I don't know. They're coy about that. But they joked about using the Bones to get past the White House defenses—and that was the first night I ever saw the Bones and Noodle in use. From the *start* they've been thinking of that as a possible use of this equipment."

"God help us all if that's what they have in mind."

"Why do you say that?"

"Even if they're right. Even if Torrent is the death of democracy in America and the beginning of a new world empire, if he gets killed, what takes his place?"

"The old messy chaos?" asked Cole.

"We already *have* a Pax Americana. Not complete peace, but enough of it that we have this whole vast world economy that absolutely depends on safe transportation and communications from every place to every other place. But it requires us to keep putting out fires. So let's say Torrent really is trying to get the whole thing so well organized that there *are* no more fires to put out. A system that can last a thousand years, like the Roman Empire. So he's gathering all this power into the center, and then somebody kills him. Do we go right back to where we were before? Or do we break through the floor and go back to the way it was before the global economy? We're in the middle of a huge epidemic. Torrent is the only reason it hasn't already spread throughout the world. If he's suddenly gone, does the quarantine hold? Does American support for the changes in Africa continue? And what do the Chinese do? And the Koreans, and the Iranians, and the Russians?"

"So you're against assassinating him," said Cole.

"On practical as well as moral grounds, Cole," said Cecily.

"What if we had proof that he caused *both* sides of the civil war a few years ago? What if we had proof that he set in motion this Sudanese raid with the handheld EMPs? The first one killed your husband. The second one took your son. If he set those in motion, Cecily, would he deserve to die?"

Cecily turned away from him. "Don't play that card, Cole. It's wrong of you."

"I'm telling you what they're going to say when they talk to you in the States. You're the only person they'll still listen to. They think they *know* that Torrent set in motion the plans that killed Reuben, and now Mark. They think he has exploited their deaths in order to gather really incredible amounts of power to himself. They believe his empire is built on the bodies of people that they love—people *you* love. They hate him, Cecily. They want him dead. And they want your blessing."

"They won't have it."

"Good," said Cole. He stood up.

"You really came here for this? To drag me through this?"

"To prepare you so that when they come at you, you'll know exactly what's going on."

"So you're planting seeds. Making sure I do things your way."

"Making sure you do things *your* way. Decide what you want, Cecily, but don't do it because you were blindsided, played on. Do it with your eyes wide open."

Cecily turned away from him. "Well, you've done what you came to do."

"I'm sorry you're angry with me, Cecily."

"I'm not," said Cecily. "I'm just sad. I didn't think I could get any sadder than I already was, but I'm so sad I can't even cry. I lost my husband, I lost my beautiful boy, and now I find out that my husband's friends, these men who have been uncles to my children since Reuben died, I find out they're plotting to kill the President?"

"I don't know if they are," said Cole. "I just think they might."

"I'm going to go back to Virginia," said Cecily, "and I'm going to go into my home and I'm going to lock the doors and only come out to buy groceries."

"Won't work," said Cole.

"I know it won't work," said Cecily. "Any more than Torrent's quarantine of Africa. All I ask is to be safe *for a while*. That's all anybody ever gets, and I'm not greedy, I won't ask for more."

"God knows you deserve more," said Cole.

"I don't know what I deserve," said Cecily.

"*I* do," said Cole. "And I'm sorry you already can't have it."

"Oh? What is that?"

"Happiness," said Cole.

"And what is *that*?"

"A man and a woman together, watching their children grow up to have happy marriages and many children of their own."

"That's it? That's your whole definition of happiness?"

"It's the only one that nature gives us."

"No heaven? No eternal bliss?"

"I don't know about that," said Cole. "I believe in God and I believe that in the long run, good people will be happy with him. But here on Earth, where we have to make our life. That's the happiness that a person can find *here*, the only one that lasts. And I'm so, so sorry that yours has broken. What's left is still really, really good, Cecily. The other kids—they're great too. But it won't ever be complete again. Not in this life. That's what makes me sad."

"Well, Cole, by your standard, you're worse off than I am, since you don't have any part of that."

"I don't know about that," said Cole. "For a long time, I borrowed a little of yours. Being Uncle Cole to your kids—that was great. And all the cookies."

She laughed. She could do that? Laugh? Apparently so.

"And now I've got a son. Adopted. Not formally, yet. But he cared for me and my jeesh alongside Mark, when we were all sick at once. And then he stayed with me after the battle, watching out for me, keeping me hydrated and medicated. When everyone else thought I was probably going to die. He was there whenever I opened my eyes."

"Chinma," she said.

"I'm bringing him back with me. I cleared it with Torrent. Even though there's no reason for him to have asylum now, he's still an orphan and a hero in the service of America. The President made the State Department see it that way, and Chinma now is a legal immigrant, a permanent resident, whatever they call it. And I'm his legal guardian."

"I always thought he'd stay with us again."

"I hoped you'd feel that way. Because he'll be a lot better off living with you, with your kids. But that doesn't change the fact that he's mine. Your kids were not mine, I just borrowed them, had to give them back.

But there's nobody left that I have to give him back to. I can put my hopes on him. You see? I'm part of it all, with him."

"I'm not sure how this is going to work."

"It will," said Cole. "And if I ever actually find a woman to fall in love with, she's just going to have to deal with the fact that I already have one son, this African kid I didn't even meet till he was twelve years old, but he's my son."

"Good for him," said Cecily. "Good for you both. And yes, he can stay with us. And you can visit all you want. And I'll probably even make cookies again."

"Frankly," said Cole, "that's all I really care about right now. Torrent? He can take care of his own damn self."

He reached out, clasped her hand in both of his for a few moments, and then let go of her, stood up, and walked out.

Two days later, Cecily and Chinma got on a plane together. She thought she might find it hard, to take this return flight with a boy who wasn't Mark. But instead, it was a great comfort to her. Chinma's life had been so hard. Harder than hers. And now she would be part of making it better.

NINETEEN

SIC SEMPER

A ruler's friends judge him by his achievements, his enemies by the means he used to attain them.

COLE BROUGHT Chinma early to the ceremony at Arlington National Cemetery, and watched all the others arrive. He greeted them all, of course, but then engaged in little conversation. Not that anyone seemed all that chatty. Everyone had things on their mind. Remembering how close they all had come to death. Remembering those who had died.

There had been a very different feeling at the graveside memorial for Cat Black. Though he died of the nictovirus and not in combat, his service record earned him a place at Arlington. The official ceremonies with military honors were repeated for those whose bodies were sent home while their comrades were still in quarantine in Africa. The actual burial had belonged to the family. But the second ceremony belonged to Cat's comrades. Not all the family was even there—few had a taste for going through it all a second time. So before and after the salute was fired into the air, there was chatter. Old stories about Cat, comic and courageous. Tears were shed but there was laughter, too, and if someone had measured it the laughs would have outnumbered the tears. Cat's death was months behind them now. Before the assault by the Sudanese soldiers. In another time. He was missed and he was mourned, but the keen edge of grief had been dulled by time.

The second ceremony for Mark Malich was different. Cole felt it himself, between him and Chinma. The boy was often playful, and as his English got better, he turned out to have a sly wit, though he persisted in making puns between English and Ayere words that no one on earth except a few professors and some Ayere who had gone to live in cities before the massacre could have understood. Here, though, there was no playfulness.

Cole wondered what memories Chinma was reviewing in his mind. Memories of Mark? Their service together as they cared for Cole and the rest of Reuben's jeesh? Their time together in Mark's family's home, when they shared a bedroom but little else? Or were his thoughts on others—his family, whose burial had consisted of flames and earth piled on by bulldozers? Or his brother, who had died bleeding after a monkey bite?

Chinma said nothing and showed nothing, but Cole had learned by now that this blank, almost fierce expression was what he did when he was feeling strong emotions that he didn't want to show.

When Reuben's jeesh arrived, two by two, there was none of the joviality that had quickly surfaced at Cat's services. And Cole was left to wonder what these pairings meant. Simple carpooling? They were the same pairs that had formed in Calabar—Benny and Arty, who had remained behind and tried as best they could to protect the sick and the caregivers, then Mingo and Babe, Drew and Load, the pairs that had gone out in the city. Cole was the odd man out, of course. He always had been, since he had never really been part of the jeesh until after Reuben's death.

But they had come and saved him when he was pursued through D.C. by the Progressive Restoration's hit squads and then their deadly machines. They had followed him into battle dozens of times, with never a sign that they didn't trust him. He had thought of them as his best friends in the world, and perhaps they were. But there was still a solidarity among them that left him out. And never more so than now.

Rusty Humphries showed up. Cecily had told him she was inviting him, and Cole was pleased that he had not brought any recording equipment. He came straight to Chinma and shook his hand and talked to him with real interest for a few minutes. "I'd like you to come out to Oregon to visit me. My only combat duty was those three minutes at the stairs in Calabar, and you were the soldier standing beside me, so I want my girls and my boss and my producers to meet you."

Soon, though, Humphries retreated to a corner of the tent that had been set up for the ceremonies and was as quiet as anyone. The mood had taken him, as well.

Cecily arrived just before the ceremony was to start— not that it would have started without her. She had been to the grave before; Benny and Arty got back to the States a week later than the rest, and she had scheduled the ceremony to give them time to get back with their families before bringing them out to Arlington.

Aunt Margaret was with them—Cole had known her long enough now, both in her house in Jersey and in his frequent visits to the Malich home in the past couple of weeks, that he called her Aunt Margaret to her face. It wasn't as if the kids needed adult supervision. Even six-year-old John Paul behaved with perfect dignity, and Lettie didn't goad her little sister Annie or find any other way to become the center of attention. Nick waved to Chinma and Cole, but that was all the fraternizing before the ceremony. The family went to the front and sat down, and only then did the others find chairs and sit down.

But still the ceremony didn't start. The delay wasn't long, but it was inexplicable, until Cole looked out through the transparent plastic side panels of the tent and saw a lone figure in a dark suit walking toward them. It was Averell Torrent, without Secret Service, without entourage, without media tagalongs.

He came and did not take any place of honor. He sat among the others; took a chair, in fact, right beside Chinma. He shook the boy's hand and nodded, but said nothing to anyone. The only deference to him as President had been to hold off on starting until he could arrive. He had done it perfectly.

The Arlington chaplain said a few words, and then it was Cole's turn to read the citation that Congress, at Torrent's request, had voted for Mark. It was almost identical to Chinma's citation, except that Chinma's did not mention giving his life.

Though it was early October, it was a sunny day with only a light breeze, so they came outside to watch the rifle salute. Sixteen soldiers, an unusually large number, and the regulation three volleys, just as if Mark had been a soldier in the Army.

As President Torrent had said in the message he sent to Congress requesting medals and honors for those who had taken part in the defense of Calabar, Mark was too young to have served in the military, but he did a soldier's duty all the same, taking the place of a soldier who was too weak with illness to hold his weapon. So he was retroactively enlisted, with his enlistment beginning, as nearly as could be determined, at the exact time when he picked up Benny's weapon to fire it into the corridor to draw the enemy soldiers to their door.

And then the ceremony was over. It hadn't taken very long. There had been no sermons or speeches.

Everyone waited in place as long as Cecily and her children stood looking at the two markers, one with Reuben Malich's name and the other with Mark's. For Mark's rank, he was listed as a private, and his unit was Cole's jeesh.

Since his age would be obvious from the dates, Cecily had asked that there be a nonregulation addition: After his date of death were the words "by enemy fire in the line of duty." This would ensure that anyone who happened to see the marker would not think that Mark was buried there merely because he was a soldier's son, but rather because he had earned that marker himself.

Cecily would one day be laid to rest in that cemetery, but she would share her husband's marker and his grave. Mark got his own because he had earned his own.

When Cecily and the children turned away from the graves, then everyone else moved as well, and began to speak in low voices, if they spoke at all.

Cole watched what Torrent did. He did not rush forward to speak to Cecily first; he did not hurry away as if he had pressing business to take care of. He merely stood and watched Cecily and the children.

Cole almost flinched when he saw Mingo head toward Torrent, followed by the rest of the jeesh. Did they mean it when they hinted at wanting Torrent dead? This was certainly an opportunity. Every man on the jeesh was capable of killing with his bare hands in a sudden, unpreventable movement. Even though none of them was back to full strength, it was where and how you struck, not necessarily the force of the blow, and Cole had a mental image of Torrent suddenly falling over dead as the jeesh walked away, dusting off their hands after a job well done.

No one would believe Cole had nothing to do with it.

Cole walked a little nearer, to where he could see the men's faces as one by one they filed past the President and shook his hand. "Thank you for coming, sir." "Well done, sir." "It means a lot to her, sir."

There was nothing in their expressions to hint at irony, and as they walked away, there was no microexpression of scorn or anger. They seemed quite sincere as they thanked him for being there.

When they had shaken his hand, they left. They apparently felt no need to talk to Cecily or the kids. They would see one another often in the days and weeks to come, everyone knew that. It was enough that they had been there for the ceremony.

Cole did not leave, however. Nor did he speak to the President—he, too, would have a chance to speak to him over the next few days. Torrent was clearly waiting for Cecily, and soon she sent her children back to the car with Aunt Margaret. Cole saw Chinma walk over and stand in front of the headstones, now that no else was there.

Cecily walked up to President Torrent. Cole did not retreat from his position. If they didn't want him to hear and see, they could walk away from him.

"Thank you for coming, sir," said Cecily. "I didn't expect it."

Torrent took her hands in his and said, "If there were anything I could do to undo the circumstances that led to either of those deaths, I would do it." The words sounded heartfelt.

The cynic in Cole thought: He is admitting that there was something *he* did that led to their deaths.

The believer in him answered: He made recommendations and decisions that put them in place to be killed, but they were all legitimate decisions, and their deaths could not have been foreseen.

Their individual deaths could not have been foreseen, but the fact that somebody would die had been certain. If Torrent really got Aldo Verus to start funding the development of high-tech weapons, he knew that someday those weapons would be used. And was it possible that Torrent had, one way or another, triggered everything else?

After all, Torrent *could* have brought the four members of the U.S. embassy staff in Bangui home a week before they were taken hostage by people with the handheld EMP. Why did he wait? Was it because he didn't want any assault on the embassy until the EMP was in place, so its effectiveness could be tested?

Had Torrent had anything to do with Reuben being assigned to think of ways to assassinate the president? Did he cause those plans to be given to terrorists? Did he suggest Reuben as the logical fall guy for the assassination, since he had thought up the plans? If he did, there was no way to pretend that it was a coincidence Torrent couldn't help.

At once another part of his mind found the excuse Torrent needed. Maybe he suggested that they find "a good tactical thinker" to develop the plan for them, and somebody else thought of using Reuben Malich. They might even have heard Torrent recommend him for some other purpose, and thought they could use him for this instead. Maybe they were even sticking it to Torrent—not everyone who worked with him was bound to love him, though you'd never know that to listen to the media. Setting up his protégé for disgrace or death, just to show Torrent he wasn't as much in control as he thought.

All imaginary. I'm just making this up. Like people who speculate endlessly on the motivations of the aliens who abduct humans; they can speculate all they want, but they don't have any credible evidence that the aliens are abducting anybody, or that they even exist.

But once you start thinking this way it's hard to stop. The human brain, Cole knew, was wired to spin out stories, to assign causality. Whenever something happened, the brain kicked in and said, This is because . . . and then the brain itself would fill in the blanks with whatever was available.

It was this propensity for causal speculation that led us to the great achievements of science and technology . . . and to witch trials and pogroms.

Isn't it enough that Torrent has single-handedly united our deeply divided country, contained a virus that he had nothing to do with causing, broken down the barriers to redrawing the map of Africa, and maintained the general level of peace on Earth that is essential to maintaining a prosperous global economy?

Isn't it enough that he's the best president since Lincoln, maybe the best ever?

But the seeds of doubt had been planted. They had taken root. Because Torrent's own writings showed that he had thought of everything, including the methodology that a man would have to use in order to set himself up as ruler of a country and, eventually, of the world. He had laid it out, not in one place but in this or that essay or article or speech, and then had spectacularly become the President of the United States and head of both major parties in a shockingly short time. *If* he were following his own plan, and working to become ruler of a global empire, how could it possibly look any different from this?

If he were a great statesman of Churchillian or Disraelian or Lincolnian stature, and merely did the right thing whenever circumstances required him to act, wouldn't it also look exactly like this?

How, from the outside, could anyone know?

But there was a trail. If the guys on the jeesh were right about Torrent, then he had done more than plant a few seeds. If the seizing of the embassy in Bangui and the Sudanese raid on Calabar had been at Torrent's prompting or at least with his cooperation, someone would know it. Someone could put it together. Someone knew the truth—if Torrent was not what he seemed to be.

Torrent kissed Cecily on the cheek—one cheek, this wasn't France—and then walked back the way he had come. No doubt there was a squad of extremely nervous

Secret Service agents at the end of his walk, checking their watches and scanning the view from drones overhead.

What if, unbeknownst to any of them, the greatest threat to Torrent's life had been right here at the ceremony, from men that he had often used to carry out his most difficult, sensitive, or dangerous assignments? Torrent had said it himself, once. Treason only matters when it's committed by trusted men. No one was more trusted than Reuben's jeesh—Cole's now. But not really anybody's. They were their *own* jeesh now, highly skilled, with access to powerful weaponry and experienced in using it. No one foresaw the danger.

If there was any danger. Because even if Cole were ready to denounce them, what could he say? There was nothing but innuendo, nothing that would cause the Secret Service to do more than interview the men. And then they would know that Cole had accused them. It would be the end of their friendship.

Well, if they were really plotting to kill the President, there was no friendship. Even if Torrent was as guilty as they thought, the proper course was denunciation and impeachment, not murder. But how would he know if their plot was real until and unless they actually did it?

Cole joined Chinma at the graves and together they walked Cecily back to her car, where Aunt Margaret and the Malich children were waiting.

Meanwhile, Cole had his own observers in place. If the men took some kind of action, he had a decent chance of finding out about it in time to put a stop to it.

IT TOOK a week to get permission to go see Aldo Verus, though Cole knew if he had asked the President, he could have had permission in ten minutes. The trouble was, he would have to tell the President *why* he wanted to speak to him, and for that Cole had no good answer. "Because I want to know if you prompted him to develop the weapons he used in his assault on the United States"—that would not be a smart thing to say, whether Torrent had done it or not. It would be the end of Torrent's trust in Cole—and *if* Torrent was not the monster of ambition that Reuben's jeesh thought he was, Cole wanted his trust, wanted to be part of his brilliant governance.

The Pentagon was not a pleasant place for Cole these days. While nobody would disparage his achievements in the field, the bureaucratic officers actually hated a man more because of such things. And for Cole to fail to keep his command from becoming infected with the nictovirus had become a matter for a lot of vicious gossip. Coleman was careless, Coleman did not maintain good discipline, so it was his fault his men were incapacitated when danger came.

It was the kind of thing that would effectively put an end to his career in the military. Once Torrent was out of office in five years, Cole would be in his mid-thirties—and unemployable. Too young to retire—he hadn't even completed his twenty. And Cole didn't feel much like marking time till he could retire, accepting the kind of nothing assignments that the bureaucrats would take such delight in devising for him.

Cole toyed with the idea of resigning his commission now. But then he would lose his assignment with the President—he was really only useful to him as an Army officer—and Cole did not want to find himself shut out. Especially since without access to the President, Cole could do nothing to protect him.

So he stayed in and reported to his office in the Pentagon. There were plenty of junior officers—especially the kind who were real soldiers and not bureaucrats—who wanted to associate with him. It's not as if he were a pariah. Even his enemies made a great show of being his buddy. But now that he no longer had the clout of a major general, he was treated with a bit of condescension. Like somebody who flew first class one time, because someone else was footing the bill, but from then on was pointedly seated in coach, while the important guys kept sitting in front of that curtain.

After returning to duty, he had spent a couple of weeks making all his formal reports on everything that had happened under his command in Africa. He could have spun it out into a couple of years of work—but he wasn't interested in going over old ground. He made sure credit went where it was due. He used his few good connections to make sure that the men he had most relied on—like Sergeant Wills—got good, career-helping assignments.

He also made sure that there was a complete list of

every American, including the caregivers, who had survived a case of the nictovirus. They were, as of now, the
only Americans known to be immune, and that might
be important someday.

But then he was done with his clerical work and his
network-mending and his polite sucking up to officers
who hated him and were trying to destroy him because
he had done what they would neither dare nor be able
to do in the field.

He sent a note to the President telling him that he
was fully available for any duty the President had in
mind except physical combat. And then he had nothing
much to do except wait. In his position, he served at the
President's pleasure, and when the President had nothing for him to do, he might as well sharpen pencils.

He spent much of his time working out, training,
trying to restore his body to the level of fitness he had
enjoyed before the nicto. But training could only take
up so much of the day before his body rebelled.

During the rest of the time, he investigated what he
could, trying to find sources to verify or dismiss the
points his jeesh had raised in their secret indictment of
the President. How do you track down things that
might have happened any time in the past fifteen years,
ever since Torrent came out of graduate school with
two doctorates and a dozen offers from the top universities in the world?

He couldn't even Google Torrent's name—since he
was currently President, there were more than a hundred
million hits on his name. Googling him with someone

else's name, if they had any fame at all, would also turn up far too many links to use. It was better to track through certain meetings and speeches: Who was there? Whom did Torrent have opportunities to know?

The trouble was that Torrent had made it a point to know everybody. Long before he was appointed NSA, he had met more than once with every living politician in America, it seemed—it was one of the reasons his nomination sailed through Congress when others were blocked.

That was when he started trying to get in to see Aldo Verus. Verus had commanded a military force with the large, plane-zapping EMP device. He might be willing to tell—or at least hint—or maybe inadvertently reveal—who came up with the thing and therefore who might have developed the handheld EMP. Or he might be willing to say incriminating things about Torrent, which then could be checked out and expanded on if they turned out to have some basis in truth.

When he got permission to see Verus—which included getting Verus's own consent—he immediately invited Cecily to come with him.

"Aunt Margaret is still in residence, so I can certainly go, unless the President happens to call me in that day."

"Has he called you? Since you came back?" asked Cole.

"No," said Cecily.

"Me, neither. I even dropped him a whiny little note saying, 'You never write, you never call.'"

"I doubt it was whiny," said Cecily. "And I did the same. But . . . nothing."

"Well, it's nice to know the country can be governed without recourse to us," said Cole. "Meanwhile, let's go meet the man I captured. I never had a chance to talk to him without actually pointing a gun at him or chasing him up a ladder or tackling him."

Nothing had been said about their real purpose, of course. Cole and Cecily both assumed that someone was listening in on all their phone conversations, whether friend or foe. They might not be, but to assume they had privacy would be naive and dangerous.

They went to the prison together. They submitted to the normal prison rigmarole and finally got a chance to sit in a room with Aldo Verus, with a guard watching through a fairly large window.

Verus looked younger than he had when Cole caught him. Maybe being in a Club Med prison had given him a chance to relax.

"My condolences on your son," said Aldo Verus to Cecily, almost as soon as they had sat down.

"Thank you," said Cecily.

"And congratulations to you on yours," said Verus to Cole. "Chinma seems to be a remarkable young man."

"The adoption isn't final yet, but thank you, I'm grateful to have him in my life."

"I'm curious," said Verus, "about the arrangements, though. I understand he's living with Mrs. Malich, even though you're adopting him. What do you do, take him on weekends? It sounds like shared custody after a divorce, without your actually having been married."

Cecily laughed. "My, but you've been keeping tabs on us."

"Not at all," said Verus. "When your request to visit me came in, I had my staff research everything about you. No, Colonel Coleman, I have *not* been obsessively tracking you since you apprehended me. You were doing your job, I was doing mine."

Cole refrained from asking him what "job" it was that required Verus to order the deaths of American cops and soldiers and then try to dismantle the Constitution.

"So why are we having this meeting?" asked Verus. "If Averell wanted to talk to me, he'd come himself."

"The President?"

"He has before," said Verus. "Well, technically, he wasn't President yet. But I was already traitor-in-chief. Didn't he tell you? Oh, yes, Averell and I are great friends."

"Mr. Verus," said Cecily.

"Call me Aldo, please."

"That is not likely," said Cecily.

"Why, because your husband was killed by some nutcase? Whatever you might think, that had nothing to do with our attempt to set to rights the stolen election of 2000 and get the country back on track."

"We're not here because of my husband's murder," said Cecily. "We're here in pursuit of the makers of the EMP device."

"Oh, yes, of course," said Verus. "My people had a really big one that brought down airplanes bent on assaulting the sovereign city of New York, so if somebody has one the size of a submachine gun it must be from the same source."

"Well, was it?" asked Cecily.

"My people developed our EMP device, in-house. We invented it, we built it, we used the only one we ever shipped out of our factory, and no one else got anything from us. We didn't sell the plans, we didn't sell the EMPs. And do you know why? Because it would inevitably be used against soldiers of the United States, and contrary to the lies that have been told about me, I am a patriot and would never do anything to harm American soldiers going about their lawful business." He grinned at Cole. "What you and your boys were doing was not, of course, legal, which made you war criminals and therefore fair game. You see how these things work? It's always lawful to kill the people you want dead—but only if you win the war."

"Since leaving your employ, do you know where the engineers and scientists who worked on your EMP device went?" asked Cecily.

"What makes you think they've left my employ?"

"You're in here," said Cole.

"But they weren't my valet or my barber, thrown out of work because I'm 'inside,' as they say. They worked for one of my corporations—a dummy corporation *then,* but we undummied it when the need for concealment vanished."

"When was that?" asked Cecily.

"When I was arrested."

"Actually, secrecy was the hallmark of your trial, Mr. Verus," said Cecily. "You told nothing about your operations."

"Well, nobody likes a tattletale."

"So they still work for you?"

"I said they might," said Verus. "Who's asking?"

"Not President Torrent," said Cecily.

"Ah," said Verus. He closed his eyes for a few moments. Then, eyes still closed, he started talking. "You come to me for information. Yet you could ask Averell for all the information about all my interrogations. Why don't you ask him? Because you don't want him to know you're prying into my past actions. And why wouldn't you want him to know?"

"Of course he knows," said Cecily.

"So you told him you were coming to see me?"

"No," said Cecily.

"Exactly," said Verus. "If you had told him what you were doing, you could have gotten in to see me much more easily than the process you used. So you are here to ask me questions *without* your boss knowing you're talking to me."

"We assume he knows," said Cole. "He has a way of knowing everything."

"But you weren't going to make it easy for him, no. So you're not here as his representatives. In fact, you're probably representing another side. Another set of interests."

"Our own," said Cecily.

"Yes, yes, of course, everybody's always representing their own interests, ultimately. But you don't have any personal business with me. Unless you're looking for funding to start a cookie business, Mrs. Malich?"

That seemed to unnerve Cecily; she glanced quickly at Cole.

"Aha!" said Verus. "So you have *cookies* between you! An affair, not of the heart or of the bedroom, but of the palate!"

Cole raised his hand just a little, to signal to Cecily not to let him get under her skin.

"Yes, Mrs. Malich, don't get your dander up," said Verus. "Cole has serious business to conduct here." Then, in a fake deep babytalk voice, like Shirley Temple trying to imitate a grown man, Verus said, "What's your business, Mr. Coleman? Do you want to set up a company manufacturing nonmilitary Bones and Noodles to provide mobility for cripples?"

Cole shook his head. "I assume you're probably already doing it."

"Exactly," said Verus. "We had a prototype exoskeleton better than the Army's before we began our attempt to restore majority government. We proved our weapons-design capability, and now that branch of my operations—despite the unfortunate arrest and imprisonment of a significant portion of my staff—has more customers than it can handle. And one of the things we're working on is a civilian-friendly version of the exoskeleton to provide arthritics the ability to open a screw-off cap."

"Mr. Verus," said Cecily, using her stop-goofing-off-now-kids voice.

"We can end the interview right now," said Verus, "or we can conduct it in whatever way amuses me. Because it *does* amuse me, to see the two of you going off the reservation."

"We're not—" Cecily began, but Cole talked over her.

"Mr. Verus, our mission is personal in a way, but it has to do with Africa. Almost as soon as our exoskeletons were deployed, we were enticed into a trap at the American embassy in Bangui. We assume this was intended as the first real-world test of the effectiveness of the handheld EMP against our Bones."

"How did it do?"

"If you made them, you already know," said Cole. "Even if you didn't, you probably already know."

"Well, I do know a lot of things," said Verus. "I even know your fellow soldiers—the ones that were with you when you—what do we call it?—busted me."

That silenced Cole. But Cecily didn't realize the implications Cole saw. "Mr. Verus, we want to know how the Sudanese got word that our soldiers in Calabar were debilitated with sickness."

"Oh, come on, all of Africa knew by then. *I* even knew. I remember thinking, Oh my, those soldiers must be sitting ducks. I'm surprised their commander didn't bring in another force to protect them. What an oversight. Not very clever, for a modern major general." Verus leaned closer to Cecily. "If I were you, I'd have to wonder if Coleman somehow set up his own base to be targeted. You notice he *wasn't* in the building when the intruders got in, or any useful member of his 'jeesh.' And he *did* make sure that outside help was at least fifteen minutes away. They had the layout of the whole place and knew exactly where everything was. I think the fingers point at Coleman."

Cole rose from the table. "We're done here," he said.

"Struck a nerve, did I?"

"Come on, Cecily, we don't have a moment to spare."

"Oh, Colonel Coleman, have I hurt your feelings that badly? Don't you know a joke when you hear one? Though there *are* people in the Pentagon dining out on that particular rumor."

Cecily looked flummoxed, even a little angry, but she followed Cole out of the room. "What is this," she asked Cole as they went back through security. "He makes an absurd accusation against you, and you take offense?"

"What?" asked Cole. "No, no, it's what he said right before."

"I don't remember what he said right before."

"About the jeesh."

"It's not a secret that they call themselves that," said Cecily.

"He was toying with us, and he brought them up himself. 'I even know your fellow soldiers.' Now why would he say that?"

"Because he's a jerk and wanted to get under your skin. Or impress us both with the depth of his researchers' work."

"Cat and mouse," said Cole. "He thinks we're just mice, and he and Torrent are cats. So when he says he knows the jeesh, I believe him. What's the first thing they would have done, looking into Torrent's possible involvement on both sides in the civil war, years ago? Of course they put in a request to interview Verus. What if they made friends with him?"

"Oh, come on," said Cecily. "Those guys are not so dumb as all that."

"You saw how he was playing us, Cecily," said Cole. "On the spot, he spun out a scenario that makes me part of a conspiracy against my own men."

"And you said it didn't bother you."

"It didn't," said Cole. "It *informed* me. It tipped his hand."

"How? I don't see it?"

"It's how interrogation works, Cecily. You aren't looking for answers to your actual questions. You're looking to understand how his mind works. And Verus's mind works *exactly* like the conspiracy charges that our friends have laid against the President."

By now they were heading for the car. "Do you really think—they're getting this stuff from Aldo Verus?"

"Think about it, Cecily," said Cole. "They seem so absolutely certain, yet all they tell us is the same kind of ambiguous nonsense that Verus just used to attack *me*. It's pure crap—except for one thing. What if they heard it from Verus? Verus actually ran his side of the civil war. So he has enormous credibility if he starts implying that Torrent was in on things with him from the start, that everything that happened, happened by Torrent's design or with his consent or active help. He offers no proof, but they believe him because *he* is the proof. He would know!"

"Who would believe anything that man said?" asked Cecily.

"He didn't talk to them with that supercilious manner, Cecily. He talked to them in a way they *would* believe. 'I can't tell you anything, boys, or I'm afraid I'd be found to have succumbed to food poisoning or died of a preexisting heart condition in my cell. Certain people have a very long reach. But think it through for yourselves, boys? Who benefited most from everything that happened?' And thus he points the finger at Torrent, over and over, and they begin to think about it and brood about it. Heaven knows it worked exactly that way with me. The more they hinted about Torrent, the more I began to wonder if they were right. It just *gets* to you."

"But aren't you leaping to conclusions, from one simple thing Verus said?"

"He said he knows our friends. There's no reason for him to say that, except to taunt us."

"How does that taunt us?"

"Because of what he knows our friends are about to do right now. Or, if I'm really unlucky, are already doing. Pardon me while I make a call."

Cole pushed a speed-dial number and Sergeant Wills came on the line almost at once. "Everybody's accounted for," said Wills. "Mingo, Babe, Load, and Drew are with training groups, and Arty and Benny are leading a group of visiting congressmen through the facility."

"Are they really?" asked Cole. "Check again, right now, and call me back if *any* of them aren't where they're supposed to be." He flipped his phone closed.

"You're having Sergeant Wills watch them?"

"I'm having him monitor their activities when they're at the training facility," said Cole. "It's part of his duty anyway to know where they are. And they know he knows me, that he's a protégé of mine, not that I have the ability to protezh anybody these days. So I was expecting them to—"

The phone chirped. It was Wills. "The congressmen are being led around by somebody else. Benny got a call and made his excuses and he and Arty left."

"And the others?"

"You said to call if anybody was off the reservation."

"Check the others, but I'm assuming we have a situation. Thanks, Jeep." He hung up again.

"Jeep?" asked Cecily.

"Jeeps used to be made by a company called 'Willy's.' Wills, Willy's Jeep, Jeep."

"This nickname thing. Is 'sergeant' too hard to say?" said Cecily. "So what do you think is happening? The moment we happen to go see Verus, they choose that day to try to test the White House defenses?"

"What is the President doing right now?" asked Cole.

"This is too much of a coincidence," said Cecily.

"And I don't know what the President is doing, he doesn't check with me."

"But you can find out better than I can."

"You have a cellphone of your own in his pocket."

"Only when I'm on assignment. Yours he carries all the time."

"And what am I supposed to say to him?"

Wills called again, and now it was certain: All six of them were gone, off the base. "Get me some eyes in the sky keyed to my code only, and make sure they're cut off from any visuals or chatter," said Cole.

"Got it," said Wills.

Cole broke the connection and resumed with Cecily where he had left off.

"I think you could suggest to Torrent that he stop whatever public thing he's doing in the Rose Garden or the White House lawn and get into the most secure place in the White House, while alerting his staff."

"He won't do it, not just on my say-so."

"Tell him it's my say-so—and if he has one of those handheld EMP devices in the White House, he's going to need it. Preferably six of them."

"I can't—this is a terrible accusation to make against our friends, Cole! I can't accuse them like this!"

"I was watching them. They certainly knew I was watching them. Therefore they were also watching me."

"That's ridiculous. If they were, wouldn't *you* know it, just as they knew you were watching them?"

"I did know it," said Cole.

"Who? Who was watching you?"

"You were, Cecily," said Cole.

"I was not!"

"You didn't know you were, but think about it. Didn't you tell at least one of them that you and I were going to talk to Aldo Verus today?"

"I might have, but why wouldn't I?" asked Cecily.

"There you are."

"You didn't tell me not to!"

"And if I did, what would you have thought?"

"That you were crazy to suspect them."

"And what would you have done?"

Cecily thought for a long minute. "I probably would have talked about the situation with Drew. To see if he could get you and the boys to be friends again."

"And the result would have been the same," said Cole. "They would have known where I was going to be at a certain time today. Inside a highly secure facility, talking to Aldo Verus for hours and hours."

"So this is really Aldo Verus's conspiracy? Not theirs at all?"

"No," said Cole. "No, Aldo Verus has learned from Torrent, or Torrent has learned from him, or heck, maybe all rich and powerful and smart guys know how to work this way. There's no conspiracy, no *plan*, not with Torrent or with Verus, because plans can be discovered and conspiracies crack. They just set things in motion. Plant seeds. And then watch very closely to see when the time is ripe for them to turn the resulting turmoil to their own advantage. Torrent really means it when he says that he would have prevented certain deaths if he could have. Not because he ever *ordered* their deaths, but because he set in motion the events—all the events—that led there, without knowing for sure that that was where they'd lead."

"This is all too complicated to believe," said Cecily.

"No, it's not. Conspiracy theories, *they're* too complicated. This is really quite simple. Torrent is able to respond quickly to the terrible things happening because in many cases he already knows that they might happen, because he set them in motion himself, years ago. He knew Aldo Verus was a loose cannon because he set him loose. He knew that somebody might use Reuben to make up their plan to kill the previous President, because he had mentioned Reuben to them as a guy to watch. He knows all the players, he knows their motives, he knows their capabilities, he doesn't have to know their *plans,* he simply recognizes what they're doing. The way I just recognized what Verus was doing."

"Then if he's so smart, why did he tip his hand?"

"Because he's a hand-tipper!" said Cole. "And Torrent is not. Torrent never tips his hand, but Verus has so much fun being Mr. Bigshot that he can't *help* tipping his hand, and that's why I might just get there in time to save the President's life. But only if you buy me time, because the jeesh will be working fast. They know I might catch on, so they're not wasting a second. So will you *please* call the President and get him to *not* be wherever it is they expect him to be?"

She must finally have believed him, at least enough to make the call, because she dragged up her purse and pulled out a disposable cellphone she didn't usually use and entered the whole number manually. "Ever since Aunt Margaret got through to the President using my phone, I buy disposable phones and throw them away after each call," she said.

"Expensive," said Cole.

"Secure," said Cecily. And then the President answered. "Cole has reason to believe that a six-man team of assassins with the ability to leap the White House fence and blast through any and all your defenses is on its way. He suggests that wherever you are in the White House, you should be somewhere else, and you should alert your security forces."

Cole reached over and took the phone. "Do *not* leave the White House, sir, whatever you do. If you're in a vehicle they can take it apart or blow it up. Only by hiding somewhere in the building are you safe. And call in serious military help, sir. The Secret Service is well equipped but they haven't trained to meet these guys."

Torrent was skeptical, of course. "Cole, these men are your friends."

"Sir, they gave me reason to suspect them months ago, and today all six of them are missing from where they said they would be. They have been listening to Aldo Verus's conspiracy theories about you, sir. They blame you for everything in the world, including the death of Reuben Malich and Reuben's son Mark. Now get somewhere deep in the White House where they won't expect you to be, and do it now, sir. I'll be there as soon as I can. You might tell the Secret Service to let *me* through, however."

"Will you also be jumping the fence? Because it'll be hard to tell you apart from them, Cole."

"I'll come in through a defended position, and I'll show ID."

"I'm going to look very stupid if this turns out not to be real."

"It's conceivable, sir, that this is a hoax designed to turn me into the boy who cried wolf. If that happens, well, then I fell for it. But I couldn't *not* give warning, sir, or that would make me part of what they're doing, wouldn't it? Please go now, sir."

"I'm already going—do you think I was just standing there in the Rose Garden? The Secret Service is already rushing the Chinese ambassador out of the building, along with all the tour groups that happened to be here at the moment. And I'm heading—is this line bugged?"

"I doubt it sir, but I can't be certain—they all have access to Cecily's phone, if they want it."

"Then I will not tell you where I'm going to go. How will you find me?"

"I don't have to find *you*, sir. I have to find *them*. And they'll be making noise, if they're there at all. This will not be a stealth attack. It'll be brute force."

Cecily reached for the phone and Cole handed it to her. "Sir," she said, "is there any chance your security forces have any of those handheld EMP devices that were captured in Calabar?"

The answer must have been negative. "No reason, sir," she said. "It would have been convenient if they were there, that's all. But of course you had no reason to suspect you'd need them. See you in a few minutes. We're crossing the Key Bridge right now." She pressed the END button.

"I wish you hadn't said that," said Cole.

"Why?"

"Because if they're listening—and if they're tied in with Verus, someone almost certainly is—they know how much time they have. Because traffic's a bitch on M Street this time of day and my car doesn't have a siren."

"We could take K Street, the Whitehurst Freeway."

"It's so complicated to get on it from here, it wouldn't save us any time."

Traffic was backed up waiting for the Thirty-third Street light to change, and Cole pushed the trunk button and got out of the car. "Get into the driver's seat, Cecily, and get to the White House as soon as you can. But please wait until I close the trunk."

"What are you doing?"

"Riding my Bones to the White House, of course."

"You have Bones in the trunk?" she asked as she ran around the front of the car.

"I couldn't do anything against them if I didn't," he said.

He pulled all his gear out of the car and onto the

sidewalk, then slammed the trunk closed. The light had already changed, and some cars way back in the line were honking, but not the ones whose drivers could see what he was doing.

He put on a Kevlar vest, then pulled the Noodle onto his head and switched it on, hoping that he could tune in to their communications. But of course they had thought of that and he was shut out. Meanwhile, though, the Noodle had detected the components of the exoskeleton and the thing was already assembling itself on Cole's body. It must be highly entertaining to the drivers who were staring at him, to see the equipment essentially crawl up his body and lock in place, but he didn't much care who saw him put on the suit. He had the latest improvements—there had been quite a few since the models they used in Calabar had been made—but if there had been any tweaks since he got this one a week ago, the other guys would have them and he wouldn't. Couldn't be helped—they had better contacts within the design team than Cole had.

Once everything was on, he picked up his armament. With the Bones to help, he could have carried some heavy weaponry, as no doubt the jeesh was doing. But they might have to blast their way in and through many obstacles, while Cole was counting on being admitted legally. All he needed was antipersonnel weapons. It had to be able to punch through Kevlar, at least at close range. But no explosives, nothing that might hurt White House personnel. He had to worry about collateral damage. They couldn't worry about it—if they were cautious about that, they would probably fail in their mission.

So once again, he was going to be playing by a different set of rules from his enemy. But that was always the story for American soldiers.

He shouldn't let himself think through the emotional implications of having to regard Mingo and Drew, Benny and Arty, Babe and Load as "the enemy." Yet thinking was better than feeling, for every instinct told him that these were his comrades, his friends, and it would take thought to overcome those instincts. Opposing him in battle wasn't his choice, it was theirs. They had done their best to separate him from this, to make sure he wouldn't be blamed for it. They had no malice toward him. He also had none toward them. He would take no satisfaction from killing any of them. It would grieve him terribly, after the fact. But during this operation, they were renegade soldiers attempting to assassinate the President of the United States. He would be careful to try to avoid causing collateral damage, but he could *not* be careful and try to avoid killing his targets. On the contrary, he had no choice but to try for a kill every time, because they would not hold back. With soldiers like these, if you did not kill, you would die.

If he was lucky, the Secret Service at the White House would account for at least a few of the jeesh. The Secret Service had been beefed up with a lot of special ops soldiers and maybe, having been alerted, they'd even stop them all. Then Cole wouldn't have to shoot at his friends. But these six were the best of the best. They might still be weakened from the nicto, but, like Cole, they had been training hard to get back up to speed. And even at half-strength, because they had the Noodles and Bones there was nobody in the White House detail prepared to cope with what they brought to the field.

As he bounded over and between cars up M Street, Cole linked up with the drones that Wills had launched for him. He jumped on top of a bus that was crossing his route at Wisconsin, and when a District cop yelled at him to stop and started to go for his weapon, Cole bounded straight at him and slapped it out of his hand. If this guy started shooting at Cole, he might hurt somebody. "Sorry," Cole said. "No time."

He turned down Pennsylvania and then it was a straight shot to the White House. Of course, with the high alert they were on, he would look as suspicious as anybody, and he would need to stop his flying progress well before the White House. What worried him was the snipers that had been permanently stationed on the roofs of the buildings around the White House since the assassination a few years ago. Their job was to kill anybody behaving exactly the way Cole was behaving, no questions asked—and he wasn't in communication with them.

"Jeep, you there?" Cole asked his Noodle.

"Ay-ay," said Jeep. "White House knows you're coming. But no sign of your guys yet. You sure this isn't a false alarm?"

"Not sure of anything, but I still don't want the snipers to shoot me on the way in. I'm coming down Pennsylvania and I know there are guys on the other side of Washington Circle, on the IFC and down at H Street."

"I'll do what I can but they don't report to anybody I'm tied in to."

The drones had to stay out beyond the periphery of the White House no-fly zone, and all four of them reported the shooting and explosions at the same time. The guys seemed to be coming in south of the Eisenhower Building, at New York Avenue, but Cole assumed that it was a diversion—there was no reason for them to use explosives to get over the barriers, so they must have planted something that would fire a rocket at the security station there.

So Cole audibled the drones' pilots to watch the rest of the perimeter, especially Alexander Hamilton Place, but possibly coming over the top of the building on Fifteenth Street.

It was Hamilton Place. The drone pilot with the best angle counted all six, so the diversion had been triggered remotely—Cole doubted they would have brought anybody else into the plot, except himself if he'd been a true believer.

So they were on the White House grounds while he was still working his way down Pennsylvania. Even though Pennsylvania was the most direct route, since it pointed right at the White House, it was also the most formidably defended. Cole jinked south on Nineteenth to F Street and was able to bound his way along at top speed until the Eisenhower Building blocked him. The gate just south of there was where the diversion had been. And sure enough, there was a huge clot of security personnel running around looking for something.

And Cole was something.

He held up his ID and shouted his name. "I am Colonel Bartholomew Coleman, U.S. Army Special Forces! This was a diversion! The intruders are on the grounds on the east side, they came in over the fence at Alexander Hamilton Place!"

They heard him—the Noodle was augmenting his voice because he had told it to, another feature to help a man injured while wearing it.

"How do we know you're not one of them!" shouted a Secret Service agent who, like everybody else, was pointing a weapon at him.

"Because I'm showing you my damn ID and telling you where they really are! Now get your brains out of your shoulder holsters and go protect the President!"

He had wasted enough time on them now. Supposedly they had been forewarned that he was coming; certainly they knew he had ID. But that didn't mean one or more of them wouldn't shoot at him as soon as he took to the air. Couldn't be helped. He couldn't go the rest of the way at regular pedestrian speed and hope to accomplish anything. Thirty seconds' head start was enough for these guys to accomplish their mission, and they had at least a minute and a half on him.

He leapt up into the air, but followed a somewhat zigzagging route because, sure enough, somebody shot at him. It was only the one shot, however, and so maybe the rest of them had realized he was a good guy—the *only* good guy with armaments that could match what the bad guys had brought.

Cole was coming at the White House at the south end of the West Wing. If the guys had been able to achieve strategic surprise, they might have caught the President in the Oval Office or in the Rose Garden, but Torrent wouldn't have holed up anywhere that obvious.

Cole thought through the floorplan of the White House. Where would Torrent go? Nowhere in the West Wing, and certainly not the press area. The guys had come in on the East Wing side—did they know something? No, Torrent wouldn't be thinking geography and distance, he'd be thinking what was an unlikely place for him to be. A room that you wouldn't look for the President in.

Wouldn't be a bathroom—those were all designed as dead ends. And he wouldn't want a small space anyway. It would be too Saddamish to be dragged out of a hidey-hole.

"Jeep, are you in contact with Security?"

"What do you need to know?"

"Do they know where the President is?"

"They do not. Secret Service walkies are jammed."

So the guys had stolen a page from the bad-guy handbook and were screwing with the electronics. Not an EMP but they didn't need one.

What room would the President know well, yet had no regular business in it so that other people wouldn't think of him being there?

There was shooting from inside the White House, and then screaming. The Noodle indicated the shooting came from three different areas, and Cole realized that with three teams, the enemy did not have to know where the President was, they could search. Or simply shoot into every room. As he had told Cecily, he didn't have to know where the President was, he only had to know where the enemy was. But which team mattered most? The one that was closest to getting to the President. And that meant Cole *did* need to have some idea of where Torrent was.

He made his guess: the family kitchen. Second floor of the residence, northwest corner. The staff would have been evacuated. The President would know it as a place for snacking.

Cole leapt up onto the Truman balcony but did not crash his way into the Yellow Oval. He had been there before and if they anticipated his entry point it would be an excellent killing ground. Instead he crashed backward through the window of the living room. Somebody was in the room next door—the master bedroom—firing heavy-duty ordnance, and some of it started coming through the walls into the living room. Cole's first instinct was to hit the floor, but so was everyone's, and so the shooter would know that and aim low to cover the floor. Cole jumped up instead, effectively bounding over the bullets, and then kicked his way through the door connecting the living room and bedroom directly.

He caught Arty swinging back toward him and took him out with three bullets to the face. Cole was using the assisted aiming routine—he couldn't afford to make a single mistake and it had saved his life once. And the face was the only thing not covered with Kevlar.

No time for regret. No time to think about the fact that it was Arty's gun that Chinma had used to stop the intruders in Calabar. Except that he couldn't stop the thoughts from entering his head.

Jeep's voice. "Two down in the West Wing. The Marines are here, and the ones in the East Wing are pinned down. So it's just the two in the residence that you need to deal with."

"Arty down here," said Cole. "So only one?"

"Unless the East Wing pair break free."

Cole came out of the bedroom into the west sitting hall, and there was a bad sign—the door to the kitchen had been replaced by a good-sized hole. They had already come through here. If the President was in the kitchen, he was dead.

Where else? The Treaty Room? The Lincoln?

Then he whirled back around and rushed into the kitchen.

Mingo was there. Mingo with Arty? They hadn't kept the previous pairing after all.

Or else the two pinned down in the East Wing weren't there at all. Another diversion? Another illusion?

"This isn't your party, Cole," said Mingo. "We tried to keep you out of it."

Cole shot him in the face and he went down. If he stopped and talked, the President would die. And Cole couldn't leave any of them alive behind him.

"Mingo down," said Cole. "Who's in the East Wing?"

"No ID yet," said Jeep.

"Nobody's seen them?"

"Negative."

"Then they aren't there," said Cole. "Staying in one place?"

"Yes."

"Not there, not there, tell them to get over to the residence."

Where now? Maybe he'd been right about the kitchen, wrong about which one. The big kitchen downstairs was an even less likely place for the President to go. This wasn't where he'd head for late-night snacks, this was the kitchen that did the serious cooking for major events.

Cole sailed down the flights of stairs to the ground floor. Too bad the stairway was so far over to the east. He could hear shooting on the ground floor as he went. Then an explosion. He ran down the center hall and saw that the Secret Service headquarters had been grenaded. But Drew was dead on the floor, too—the Secret Service had some kind of serious firepower, because whatever killed him had taken a bite out of his side like a shark, blowing past the Kevlar like it wasn't there.

There was a blood trail heading to the pantry, which was the route into the kitchen. Cole followed it, only to find a dead Secret Service agent, who had apparently staggered in here. Or was he following an uninjured soldier? It had to be Benny. The one whose pistol Mark had used. What would Benny do?

Would he lie in wait to spring a trap on Cole?

Never. Benny would accomplish his mission.

Cole glanced into the kitchen but there was no one there. Through the refrigerator room and on out into the basement hall.

Chocolate shop? Flower shop? Carpenters' shop? The bowling alley? Nowhere to hide in there, the thing was only one lane wide.

Benny would already be searching. All Cole could do was follow in his footsteps, which could mean he got to the President first—or second. What he really needed was to find Benny. To draw him away from the President.

Calling out to Benny wouldn't work—he'd never be stupid enough to answer. But calling to the President would tell Benny where Cole was—and that might draw him to Cole, distract him from his mission.

"President Torrent!" Cole cried out.

"Cole!" came a shout from the carpenters' shop.

Cole couldn't believe it. The President *answered?* Telling the enemy exactly where he was! Was he insane? What if Benny was closer?

Well, he was, but not the way Cole expected. Benny

and the President were in the main room of the shop, but Benny was on the ground, his Bones nonfunctional, and four nails in his face.

Torrent stood near the bandsaw, holding a nailgun. That explained the nails, but not why the Bones had stopped working.

"Is he dead?" asked Torrent.

Of course he wasn't dead, Cole might have said. Four nails in the face wouldn't kill anybody.

But instead he had to respond to Benny's movement. He was bringing up a handgun to shoot Torrent, and Cole was on the wrong side of him, the backside, with nothing vital he could hit without having to go through Kevlar.

Except that Benny was on the ground, and Kevlar was designed to protect a man who was upright. Cole shot him between the legs, up into the body cavity from below. Benny didn't get the shot off after all.

Cole still stood near the entrance to the room, facing the President. Torrent was looking down at the body. Or perhaps at the handgun that had been a split second away from firing at him.

Cole started toward the President.

"No, no," said Torrent. "I'll come to you."

But Cole walked right past him. Straight to the black-plastic-lined garbage can across from the bandsaw.

Sure enough, inside it was one of the handheld EMP devices. Nothing else could have brought Benny down. Certainly not a nailgun.

"Thought you didn't have any of these," said Cole, lifting it out of the garbage and turning back to face the President.

Torrent was holding Benny's handgun, pointing it at Cole's face.

Cole instantly clicked off all communications between himself and Jeep.

"What did you just do?" asked Torrent. "I know that was a command!"

"I cut off all outgoing audio."

"Cut it off?"

If Torrent had been a soldier, Cole would already be dead. Soldiers didn't wait to have conversations, they killed the moment they had the opportunity.

"Video was already off, in case the enemy had jigged the system and could see me that way."

"Why wouldn't you want anyone to hear? You just made it easier for me to kill you."

"I know," said Cole.

"How can I leave you alive? None of the *captured* EMP devices is in the White House. This one proves that I know who makes these things."

"It's more important that you remain President than that I remain alive," said Cole.

Torrent lowered the weapon. "I haven't been doing what you think," said Torrent. "But everyone will think it."

"I know you didn't plan the details, sir," said Cole. "I know you never meant to betray anybody."

"Nevertheless, that was the effect," said Torrent. "I

hate it. I grieve for the pain I caused. It was like members of my own family dying. But it's the only way I know to do my job, which is more important than any one life or any dozen or hundred or thousand lives."

"Exactly," said Cole.

Torrent was taken aback. "I know you better than that, Coleman. It's impossible to believe you don't *care*."

"I've been wrestling with this from the start, Mr. President. Cecily and I suspected you had more to do with events than you were admitting—the civil war, even the assassinations. We couldn't prove it, but we decided to watch you. And you gave us every chance. We saw you make hard decisions quickly and intelligently. We saw you turn every circumstance to the advantage of America. I think that if anyone can take us there, you can."

"Where do you think I'm trying to take us?" asked Torrent.

"To peace on Earth, sir," said Cole.

"I don't understand," said Torrent. "You have the proof that I know the people who make these things. I got it into the White House, I had it here when the only conceivable purpose was to protect me against my own best soldiers. *They* didn't have proof, and they wanted to kill me. Why don't you?"

"They missed the point," said Cole. "A good ruler isn't always a good man. Or rather, he *is* a good man, but he uses a different standard of good."

"A higher standard!" Torrent said, agreeing with him.

"A larger one, let's say. You have to look past what's

good for any one person—even people you know well, people who trust you—and choose what's good for *everyone,* even if it hurts the people you trust."

"I needed an incident," said Torrent. "I needed a *Lusitania,* a provocation. But I didn't understand just how debilitated you all were from the nictovirus. I thought that at least a few of our soldiers would be up to fighting them off. I thought it would be bloody but we'd win."

"We did," said Cole.

"Too late to save Cecily's boy," said Torrent.

Cole wondered—is he a good enough liar to fake the tears coming down his cheeks?

"Cole, it bought me a chance to remake the most troubled continent."

"And you took that chance," said Cole, "and you're doing it."

Torrent dropped Benny's handgun. "You're not my enemy."

"Oh, I hate you, sir. I'm so angry I could cry. I could scream. I could hit something, even kill. But I'm a soldier, sir. I understand that there are casualties in war. Collateral damage. I understand that commanders give orders that sometimes have terrible consequences for many of their own, that they often lose their best, and yet they must give those orders."

"So knowing what you know, you'll still support me?"

"I think that's the gist of it, sir."

"No matter what you say, Cecily will never—"

"I will never tell Cecily, sir," said Cole. "It would destroy her and accomplish nothing."

Torrent turned to the side, leaning back against the table saw. He touched his hand to his forehead. "I'm glad," said Torrent. "I didn't want to kill you. You're one of the best I've got."

"But you would have done it, if it had been necessary," said Cole.

"You know that I can't do this without reducing democracy to a sham, at least for a while," said Torrent.

"It already is," said Cole. "Whatever we have, it hasn't been democracy for decades."

"I still have to take on Russia and China, not to mention the loonies," said Torrent. "I could still lose."

"Qin Shi Huangdi was overthrown and his dynasty terminated. But the empire he founded lasted two thousand years. He built well. He didn't have to have a long and happy life himself, did he?"

"So you're with me?"

"No sir," said Cole. "I will support your cause. I will work toward the same objectives as you. But I am not and never will be *with* a lying snake like you, sir."

Torrent nodded. "Just remember, Cole. Until the snake did his work, Adam and Eve were perpetual babies. The snake started the whole thing going."

"Where can I ditch this thing?" asked Cole, indicating the EMP device.

"I kept it down here," said Torrent. "It's why I ran here when you gave me warning. It goes up on that shelf. The carpenters know I keep it here. I told the head carpenter it was my last line of defense, and he accepted that without further questions."

"So do I, sir," said Cole.

"You could have died protecting me," said Torrent, "and you could have died at my hand."

"But I didn't," said Cole. "Aren't you glad?"

"You killed all your friends."

"I killed three of them," said Cole. "Your security forces took care of the others. And the moment they raised their hands to try to stop the work you're doing, they stopped being my friends."

"What do you hope to gain from this, Cole?"

"The same thing as you, sir. Peace on Earth." Cole stowed the EMP device up on the top shelf. Then he rebooted Benny's Bones manually. "You took him by surprise, sir, with the nail gun, just as he was coming through the door." Cole glanced to make sure the cord on the thing was long enough that it was even possible. It was. "And then I arrived and finished him off."

"That's how it happened," said Torrent.

"I'm calling everybody now."

"Yes, go ahead."

Cole clicked open the connection with Jeep.

"What happened, Colonel Coleman?" Jeep demanded.

"We weren't sure we had them all, Jeep. I had to patrol the floor before I wanted to announce where we were. I was afraid they were keying in on my communications somehow."

"Is the President all right?"

"The President actually saved his own life," said Cole. "He took down Benny with a nail gun in the carpenters' shop."

"You can actually kill with that?"

"I don't know. I said he took him down. *I* took him out."

Security forces came rushing in from everywhere. Cole sat down on the floor of the basement hall, leaning his back against the wall. Since he was dressed exactly like the would-be assassins, he got more than a few startled glances, until a Secret Service agent realized the problem and sat down beside him. So that it would be clear that he was either an okay dude, or in custody.

"I wish we could pretend these guys were a bunch of foreign assassins," said Cole glumly.

"I know," said the agent. "You knew them, right?"

"They were my team," said Cole. "But they got distracted from the mission."

"What mission?"

"Preserve and protect the Constitution of the United States," said Cole. "No matter what you think of the President, assassinating him does not preserve and protect anything."

"I think our president is a great man," said the agent. "I've seen them come and go, but he's the first I've ever said that about."

"Great men," said Cole. "They can be hard to take, sometimes, don't you think?"

"Not to me," said the agent.

They pushed the gurney carrying Benny's body out

of the carpenters' shop and past where Cole and the agent sat.

"Sic semper," said Cole to Benny as he passed.

"What was that? I thought that was Marine Corps."

"Marine Corps is Semper fi. Semper fidelis. 'Always faithful.'"

"So what's 'sic semper'?"

"What John Wilkes Booth shouted after he shot Lincoln and jumped down onto the stage. 'Sic semper tyrannis.' May this happen to all tyrants. Lincoln was a great president. But to some people, greatness in a president looks like tyranny."

"I'm sorry your friends went bad."

"I don't know," said Cole. "They didn't think they were bad. They thought they were doing the right thing for their country. That's why this stinks. They really thought they were good guys."

"So do terrorists," said the agent.

"Yeah," said Cole.

And so do presidents and the people who help them do their work. You place your bet and see how history plays it out.

What if I watch Torrent and find out that they were right after all, and I was wrong? That sometimes a ruler needs to be killed to save the people? That democracy is more important than peace after all?

Was this what Mark and Reuben died for? To bring this man into power and keep him there? Is that what I should live for? Or am I betraying my country right now, sitting here, knowing that I've killed the only guys who really had a chance of stopping this man?

I upheld the law. I fulfilled my oath. And even though I know he was perfectly willing to kill me if he thought he had to, I also know that when I gave him a reason not to, he took it, and I'm alive. That says something about him. He really does not want to kill. He really does want to have people around him that he can trust.

I guess I just put myself on that list. For now.

TWENTY

SITTING IN A TREE

We did our best to keep this virus from our shores. The quarantine bought the world a year in which to prepare. Some nations did, some didn't.

We have stockpiles of the medications that help.

We have thousands of volunteers who went to Africa, learned how to care for disease victims to enhance their chances of survival, and now they are home again, immune to the disease and ready to help.

We have used every means at our disposal to teach people all that we can about how to treat the nictovirus.

And even now, our scientists are racing to try to find a vaccine that will reliably prevent the disease without causing it.

Whether they succeed or not, we will weather this together. We will not panic, we will not shut down our economy, we will keep food flowing into our cities and we will buy and sell throughout the world. We will not lock our doors against our neighbors, but we will follow the example of those brave volunteers and help those who need our help.

In the long run, we cannot avoid this disease. But we don't have to let it destroy us. Many will die, and we will grieve for them. But most will live. America will live. And we will remain a beacon of hope and peace, democracy and charity, for the world.

IT WAS full summer again. Chinma finally understood what all those words meant—summer, fall, winter, spring. In Nigeria there had been only rainy and not-rainy.

Now when he climbed the massive oak in the back yard of the Malich house—of *his* house now, he finally believed—he knew what it had been like without its leaves, slick with snow, completely unclimbable when encased in ice. He shared the trees here with squirrels instead of monkeys, and all the birds were different. But he still liked to climb.

He had walked this whole neighborhood, though no one else did. They *ran,* dressed in jogging clothes, but they were going nowhere, accomplishing nothing. What a strange land, where people had to invent hard work for their bodies instead of trying to avoid it. But he could eat the food now, and he drank the tap water without distrust, and he was used to the idea that the electricity was on all the time, and not just a few hours a day.

Most important to Chinma, however, was his eyesight. Cole and Mrs. Malich had both noticed the trouble he had reading and, even more, writing. The way he would track back over letters he had already written, or write them twice. Here in America they didn't assume he was stupid or lazy, the way the teacher in the village had. They assumed he was dyslexic, that letters appeared in the wrong order for him. But the reading tutor they found for him said that she could find no such problem.

It was Lettie who saw what no one else had noticed. He was struggling to read one of his textbooks and, as usual, having a terrible time, when Lettie said, "Why do you move your eyes like that?"

He didn't know what she meant.

"You sweep back and forth across the page. Why don't you just look at it!"

"I *am* looking at it."

"No you're not. You're looking past it. Sweep, sweep, sweep. It's like trying to use a broom to drive in a screw. Sweep sweep."

He thought she was making fun of him, and so he held his tongue and kept his face from showing anything.

"No I'm not making fun of you, Chinma, I'm trying to understand what you're doing. Why don't you hold your eyes *still* when you read?"

"Nobody does," said Chinma. "Everybody reads the letters in a row, sweep sweep."

"Right, like this. Look at my eyes. I'm reading. See how my eyes barely move? But you read like *this*." She moved them back and forth far more quickly, and traveling farther each time.

"When I don't do that, the letters hide," said Chinma.

"Hide?"

"They disappear. I have to keep going past them to catch them before they disappear."

"They don't disappear. That's just crazy. Look, here's what you've been reading. All the letters are there. None missing!"

"I didn't say they disappear forever," said Chinma. "Just when I look at them." And then, because he was feeling like part of the family now, he went ahead and said what he might have said to an annoying little half-sister. "I wish I could look at *you* and make you disappear."

Lettie whooped with laughter. "Oh, you're a brat after all," she said. "I was wondering if you had *any* feelings."

But later, she must have talked to Mrs. Malich, because she took him to an ophthalmologist, who did a complete examination. They touched his eye with things, and shone too many bright lights in, but he did what they asked and in the end, the doctor said, "I can't tell with these instruments whether it was congenital or he burned his retina by staring into the sun as a baby, but there is a gap in the rods and cones exactly at the focal point of the lens. It doesn't affect his far vision, only near vision, and anything larger than a normal-size letter on a page would be visible at the fringes. But normal-size letters completely disappear when he focuses on them."

They found large-print editions of everything they could, and what they couldn't find readily available, the school district paid someone to scan into a computer and make it larger. The letters now had a hole in the middle of them, but they were *there* and he could read them. He was also allowed to write very large letters on the papers he turned in, or type them into the computer where his word processor had a very large font. His schoolwork improved dramatically.

Mrs. Malich was all for seeking a doctor who could do surgery to correct the problem, while Cole thought that it wouldn't be such a terrible burden for Chinma to work with large print his whole life.

Chinma didn't really care how the argument turned out. He had found out he wasn't stupid and that other people read better because the letters never disappeared for them.

Meanwhile, Lettie had spent the past few months becoming tolerable. She even climbed trees with him, though she was careless enough that when she was with him he wouldn't do any really hard climbs. She would follow him no matter what he said, so he simply didn't go as high as he might have. And they would talk about things. Or about nothing. Just talk. He found out that she really wasn't mean. She was just *direct*—her word— and said what was on her mind.

"There are worse things in the world," she said. "I could lie and pretend only to have nice thoughts and happy feelings, and then one day I'd start poisoning all my teachers and they'd say, She was a loner, she kept to herself, we always thought she was strange."

"You *are* strange," said Chinma.

"At least I don't have an accent."

"Yes you do," he said. "An American one."

"Can you teach me some Ayere words?"

So whenever they were in a tree together, he would teach her words in Ayere, and to his surprise, she remembered them all. She would add them to her English conversation, to the annoyance of Nick and Annie. But J.P. loved it and laughed when she did it. "That was Ayere, wasn't it?" he'd say, and then mutter the new word to himself over and over.

"Why are you learning Ayere?" Annie asked Lettie and J.P. one day. Lettie didn't have an answer—a rare thing for her. It was J.P. who said, "We're his tribe now, aren't we?"

The monkey sickness was coming here to America. Already there were cases reported in Miami and Los Angeles and along the Mexican border. There was no more attempt at quarantine. It was going to have its way with the world, this disease that a sick and frightened monkey had sneezed into Chinma's face more than a year ago. Something that had struck him first was going to strike everybody.

Cole and Mrs. Malich had gone over it with the children, what to expect, how it felt. "I won't kid you," said Cole, "it makes your head hurt like somebody was driving screws into it from inside your skull. But I promise you, it passes, it ends."

"And if we bleed, we die," said Annie. "That's what a teacher at school said."

"If you bleed," said Cole, "then you have a really bad case, so yes, you're more *likely* to die. But your mother bled. As badly as anyone I've ever seen. But they got an IV in her and something to thicken up her blood, and your mom is tough. She stopped bleeding after only a few hours, and she got better so she could come back, make cookies, and yell at you for leaving your bikes on the lawn."

"We don't do that anymore," said Nick.

"Chinma does," said Lettie.

Everyone knew that was a joke, since Chinma was compulsively tidy.

Chinma went with Cole when he took the train to New Jersey to bring Aunt Margaret back. "You might as well give up and come," said Cole. "If you don't, the whole family will just come up here to take care of you, and that'll disrupt the children's schooling."

"It's summer vacation, I am not sick yet, and when I do get sick I don't mind dying. I've been breathing for a very long time now, and this virus is as good an occasion to retire from the occupation as any."

"You're not even sixty yet."

"It's better to die before you have to start lying about your age."

Chinma didn't know of anyone ever winning an argument with Aunt Margaret, but Cole figured out just what bothered her. "It's the constipation and the diarrhea, isn't it?" he said. "You just don't want anybody to see your bony old butt."

"As a matter of fact I don't," said Aunt Margaret, "and nobody *wants* to see it, either. Especially not covered with doo-doo when I'm thrashing around with delirium tremens."

"Lay off the booze and you won't get the d.t.'s."

"I meant just delirium. You are so literal. Everybody hates you for that, Cole. I tell you this as a friend, in the nicest possible way."

Chinma tried to imagine anyone in his village talking like that to one of the old women, especially Father's mother, who thought she was queen of the universe and snapped at everyone who did anything for her because they didn't do it exactly as she wanted. She always got her way because she could complain to Father and he'd make people do what she wanted. He could imagine Cole talking to *her* about her butt, or booze. He'd never get out of the house alive.

But Aunt Margaret came with them. Chinma listened to them talking all the way back to Virginia. He sat on the seat ahead of them in the train, reading *Fablehaven* on the Kindle with the typeface at its largest setting. The book was good because it had all kinds of dangers that were enjoyable to read about because they couldn't happen in the real world, and yet the bravery and cleverness of the children were real, and Chinma liked them. But he also listened to the adults behind him. He learned a lot that way. He also had to keep waking the Kindle up because he'd go so long between turning pages.

Everybody on the train was wearing masks. Chinma didn't see the point, but maybe it made them feel better to believe they would be the one person who didn't catch it.

Cole and Aunt Margaret also kept talking about how smooth the new tracks were, and how comfortable the new electric train was, and how wonderful it was that

President Torrent was finally bringing the American rail system up to European standards. Chinma had no point of comparison. It was certainly better than the buses in Nigeria. And the trains arrived at the station and left again exactly at the time on the schedule.

Today, up in the tree, he watched as Lettie came out to call him in for dinner. He could have come down before she spoke to him, but he liked watching her come all the way across the back lawn and climb halfway up the tree before he admitted he had seen her. And he suspected that she liked it, too, which is why she didn't even try to yell at him from down below. Any excuse to get up in a tree with him. Well, that was fine with him.

So she got up about three meters into the tree and said, "Dinner, as if you didn't already know."

"I hope none of you die of the monkey sickness," said Chinma.

"Well I should hope you hope that!" said Lettie.

"I mean, I'm happy here. I didn't think I ever would be, but if one of you dies, this place will never be happy again."

"Dad died. Mark died."

"But they didn't die *here*," said Chinma. He was thinking of bodies burned and houses bulldozed, though he would never say so.

"So are you coming to dinner or not?" said Lettie.

He came down the tree. She let him pass her on the way down, because down was harder and scarier, and also because she liked it when he reached up and helped her make the last jump, or so Chinma thought.

He followed her into the house across the back lawn, which was still bright with sunlight, because in these northern latitudes the day was much longer in the summer than it had been in Nigeria. He looked at her hair swaying across her shoulders with every step. He watched how confident she was. Bad things had happened in her life. Death had come to people she loved. And yet she kept her eagerness for each day.

Don't die, he said to her silently as he followed her into the house. Please don't die. This disease the monkey god forced into my nose as a prank on the whole world of humans, let it take no one in this house. Or if it must take someone, let it be me. I know that I'm immune but I've had this year of a life in a larger world, one with oceans and airplanes and brave soldiers as well as cruel ones. I've had a year in which the things I did made a difference and people were glad that I was alive. Take me now, God, before you take any of them.

Father had never listened to him, or any of the brothers, really, and certainly none of the mothers or sisters. But God would listen. Mrs. Malich said so. God didn't always do what we wanted, but we were *heard*.

Keep this family alive, God, and I will believe in you forever.

Then they sat down to a dinner of colorful vegetable-and-mozzarella pasta salad, in which all the seasonings were namby-pamby spices like basil and oregano, nothing with any fire in it. But he had lived here long enough now. He appreciated the fact that he could taste all the flavors. It had become delicious to him.

ACKNOWLEDGMENTS

THE EMPIRE franchise does not belong to me. It began with Donald Mustard and the rest of the team at Chair Entertainment, who had the idea of a video game about a red-state vs. blue-state civil war in America today. They wanted to develop it into a real franchise—games, novels, movies, comic books, everything.

At that point, they had only a little of the story—but lots of cool graphics and a firm conviction that the hero we began with had to die in the middle. I knew what a challenge this would be for a novelist, and I took it on as a partnership. They gave me a free hand with every other aspect of the story (though their cool graphic of a lake that drains to reveal a secret entrance to an underground factory was irresistible), and the novel *Empire* was the result.

Since then Chair was acquired by Epic Games, the movie rights were optioned by a major studio, the Xbox game *Shadow Complex* inspired by the first novel was launched to great acclaim, and I found my road into the dark future of the Empire story.

It is the character of Averell Torrent who intrigues me most, and who drives the plot of every book. He is potentially the kind of philosopher-king Plato talked about, but he also has to solve the problem of getting enough power to accomplish the great things that he envisions for the world. In case you haven't noticed, this kind of ambition is usually the worst kind of disaster for the human race, because one man's utopian dreams rarely match with other people's desires, and even more because it is usually in the getting of power that the dreams become corrupted. Something about breaking eggs to make an omelet. I happen to be an egg, not an omelet-maker, so I think of Torrent as the kind of person who is fascinating to read about in history, but quite dreadful to have as a ruler, because his ambitions can kill an awful lot of people and make the rest quite miserable.

But I'm playing fair with him. It would be easy to have a crazy man like Hitler or Idi Amin, or a religious fanatic like the Kims of North Korea (Communism functioning as a religion, for it always does) and the ayatollahs of Iran. Instead, I'm making him the kind of man that, if you had to have a king, he'd be the one you hoped for.

If he really existed, and this were a history, every page would be about Torrent. But this is a novel, and so it is not about him. It is about the people who are close to him, in a position to judge what kind of man he is, and also in a position to do something about it if he doesn't measure up.

As I was writing this novel, Africa took me by surprise. It was supposed to be the source of a bit of adventure and then I'd move the action to other places on the world stage. But I ran into Chinma, a couple of

sick monkeys, and a plague to rival those that deci-
mated the Roman Empire twice, contributing greatly
to its fall. I was steered this way in part by my reading
of Rodney Stark's *The Rise of Christianity: How the
Obscure, Marginal Jesus Movement Became the Dominant Religious Force in the Western World in a Few
Centuries*. Stark makes excellent use of the sketchy
sources we have in order to gain a fairly reliable-
seeming picture of how Christian practices led directly
and indirectly to its overwhelming the civilization in
which it emerged (though philosophically the reverse
happened, as well; see *How Greek Philosophy Corrupted the Christian Concept of God* by Richard R.
Hopkins).

One of Stark's key points is that because Christians
had less fear of death (or more social pressure to appear not to fear it) and a stronger commitment to self-
less service to one's neighbor, Christians stayed put
and nursed one another—and strangers—during the
plagues when other people fled. The treatments they
gave cured nothing, but still gave plague victims a far
better chance of survival. The result was that not only
did Christians have a much lower mortality rate when
infected with the plague, but also the pagans they
nursed survived at a higher rate—with very favorable
impressions of Christianity. We know this happened
because of the extremely favorable statements about
Christians, even from people who hated them; and
when Julian tried to restore paganism, he tried to get
the pagans to behave more like the Christians in pro-

viding one another what we now think of as social services and health care!

As always happens when I'm writing fiction, what I'm reading in history and science pops up. Only with the Empire books, I have the rare opportunity to look at contemporary problems and issues square on. When I'm writing stories set in fantasy worlds or far futures, it's hard to say much about the problems of contemporary Africa, for instance. So when the story of Chinma, a boy who happens to be the first to be infected with a devastating new plague through his contact with monkeys, intrigued me, I decided not to have him die and then drop him from the book, as I had originally planned. Instead, I kept him, and with him kept the whole continent of Africa as the center of most of the action of the book. If you're going to have a potentially civilization-wrecking plague in your story, either you kill everybody off right from the start (Stephen King's *The Stand*) or the whole book becomes *about* the plague and the efforts to deal with it. Epidemics cause panic and distort nations, economies, and individuals. History always has to bend to make way for them. So, in this case, must fiction.

I also looked into the HULC exoskeleton from Lockheed-Martin and imagined what it might become with a bit more development over the next few years. And since my fictional President Torrent has even more of a monopoly on power and media attention than our current president, I couldn't resist having him use that power to do the things that I believe would help most in our transition to a post-oil world, a transition that *will* happen, but does not have to involve a long sojourn in the Stone Age along the way (though that is certainly the way we seem to be headed).

This is also a novel about soldiers. I have done my best, having never served in the military myself, to learn from others. I have been an avid reader of history—which includes military history—for almost my entire life. From reading Bruce Catton's *The Army of the Potomac* as a child I learned so much about how destructive both bad commanders and good ones can be, and how the soldiers respond to both kinds, that I have seen military affairs through that lens ever since. I also read William L. Shirer's *The Rise and Fall of the Third Reich* at a tender age, and the horrors caused by those who seek empires without regard to the cost have been indelibly stamped in my mind.

I have also learned from good friends like Tom Ruby and the many officers he has introduced me to, and from friends and family who have selflessly served our country in the military—including my brother, who joined the U.S. Army in the late 1960s and gave me a chance to hear about military life in rich detail.

In the writing of this book, I was greatly helped by the patience of Beth Meacham, my editor, to whom this book is dedicated. This is not the first time that I have surprised myself with new ideas that take a novel off in a strange direction, and she has, with heroic patience, dealt with the delays that come from this and other bothersome little problems in a writer's life. I sometimes think of myself as a toothpaste tube, and Beth as the person who squeezes the end of it. Unfortunately, she is *not* the person with the power to open the cap (that would be my recalcitrant unconscious), so she can sometimes be frustrated with the nothing that comes out for such long stretches of time. Yet all I ever receive from her is the encouragement of a collaborator who believes in me and my work, and for that I am grateful.

As I wrote this novel—most of it while on "vacation" in a rented house in Salvo, North Carolina—I was greatly helped by my crew of first readers. My wife, Kristine A. Card, is always the first to see each chapter, but she is not the only one to make suggestions that help me know what my readers care about, to make sure I don't neglect story threads that matter to them. Erin and Phillip Absher, who were with us at the beach (and in so much else in our lives), provided such guiding responses; and because my son Geoffrey Card joined us with his family for a week, he brought his keen eye to the novel as well, offering many excellent suggestions that kept me from lazily abandoning small but important issues. Kathryn H. Kidd was farther away, but no less faithful in her response to and encouragement of the project. And Donald and Geremy Mustard at Chair gave this novel careful readings that resulted in significant improvements.

My daughter Emily is indirectly responsible for the existence of two of the chapters of this novel. She drove the family for five hours each way, to and from

Salvo Beach, so that I could write chapters instead of doing the driving myself.

In fact, I was able to write this novel because I did not have to pay attention to *any* of my ordinary duties as other people filled in for me, most notably my assistant (and the publisher of my online fiction magazine, *Inter-Galactic Medicine Show*—http://www.oscIGMS.com), Kathleen Bellamy, and my webwright and, at times, factotum, Scott Allen, who kept my plants watered, my garden harvested, and my fish fed while I was holed up typing this book.

To Tom Doherty, my publisher, I always give thanks—he is tried and true, and knows how to make and sell a book. My agent, the late and much-missed Barbara Bova, stuck with me for thirty-two years. She was the founder of my career and the protector of my interests in the publishing world. She was also a dear friend, and no one can take her place.

My daughter Zina, the last one still at home, will have a father again, now that this book is done, and Kristine will have a husband, and many friends and associates may even get answers to their emails.